THE IMPOSSIBLE SHADES OF CRIMSON

THE IMPOSSIBLE SHADES OF CRIMSON

A HUES NOVEL
BOOK FOUR

J. L. JACKOLA

Tivshe Publishing

Library of Congress Control Number 2023904764

Paperback ISBN 978-1-960784-04-9
Hardback ISBN 978-1-960784-05-6
Electronic ISBN 978-1-960784-06-3

Distributed by Tivshe Publishing
Printed in the United States of America

Cover design by Dark Queen Designs
Map design by Worldwyrm

Visit www.tivshepublishing.com

ALSO BY J. L. JACKOLA

<u>*UNBOUND PROPHECY SERIES*</u>

Ascension

Descent

Surfacing

Submerged

Riven

Adrift

<u>*UNBOUND KINGDOM TRILOGY*</u>

Severed Kingdom

Cursed Kingdom

Prophesied Kingdom

<u>*HUES SERIES*</u>

The Forgotten Hues of Skye

The Coveted Hues of Skye

The Shattered Shades of Crimson

The Impossible Shades of Crimson

<u>WICKED AND FATED SERIES</u>

Trial of the Gods

Tournament of the Gods

To those who see the impossible as possible.

AUTHOR'S NOTE

Dear Reader,

Thank you for continuing to read the Hues series. Skye and Mark are back, and Crimson is here to stay. As with the first three books, book four consists of characters who are mature and sexually confident. Please be aware of possible triggers.

This series contains intense and explicit sexual scenes, language, non-consensual sex, abuse, reverse harem situations, mmf/mm/mf scenes, violence, and death.

A storm is brewing so hang on tight.

J. L.

KANTENDA
DRANTH MOUNTAINS
FETTERRED FOREST
CHENTHOM

ELTANDER
NENOCHIN
APENDIA
DUGREILLE

SKYE

Skye snuggled deeper into Mark's arms, which were currently wrapped tightly around her. He kissed her head as she traced the tension in his muscles. Her body was weary and she only wanted to stay in his arms and sleep the day away. They'd spent the night and the early morning hours making love, knowing what faced them when the sun's rays entered the room. The night before Derrant called for her was always like this.. Mark would take her so many times that she was a mess of quivering muscles. Not that she minded. She took her fair share as well—tasting him, savoring him, memorizing his moves, his sounds, the intensity of each climax. Eleven years had passed since that first time Derrant had summoned her. As he did each year, Mark renewed her claim on her through nights of passion, ensuring the Death God knew to whom she belonged.

With each passing year, leaving him had grown harder. Their bond was stronger, their need for each other too great to endure the time apart, especially for Mark. The tension within him would increase with each day that drew closer. His temper grew short, and an edge overwhelmed his voice—one he'd never had before their lives changed.

The separation was almost enough to break them, but they endured. Skye counted the hours when trapped with Derrant, watching the fading sun through Eliana's magical window, hating every second she was away from Mark. She'd grown accustomed to Derrant in that time, understanding what drove him, what hastened his orgasms, and with it, he'd learned what drove her over the edge. At times he seemed determined to make her climax as if he knew of the spell she'd weaved to tie herself magically to Mark all those years ago. The intensity had become so bad that following her last visit, Mark had demanded she remove the spell. The connection had been created so he could know she was thinking of him, but her pleasure only drove him mad. It didn't matter that she loved him, that there was no room for another. She was still climaxing to another man's touch.

She'd tried to resist Derrant, but he was too good at what he did, too powerful, too seductive. No matter that she would never be his; he acted as if she were.

Skye reached up and kissed Mark, savoring the feel of his lips against hers, the strength and security he offered. He was her rock, and she hated that this was crumbling him, year after year. She tried to rise, but he tightened his grip.

"Mark, I have to go," she said, leaning her forehead against his chin.

"I don't want you to go," he whispered.

The urge to cry pressed behind her eyes, but she ignored it, knowing it would do no good. Kissing him again, she replied, "I know."

He loosened his grip, and she slipped from his hold, walking to her wardrobe. "Find something exceptionally hard to take off."

"He'll just use magic," she retorted, pulling out a dress with multiple ties, one that required pants since it opened in several slits along her legs.

"That works," he said, sitting up and watching her dress.

The sheets fell just across his hips, revealing the trail of thin hair that led down past his belly button, the trail she loved to follow with her mouth.

"I hope that thought was about me," he said as she used her magic to tie the back of the dress, crisscrossing the thick ribbons.

"Definitely was. Just thinking of what I plan to do to you when I return."

"Good, you know I'll be ready."

She knew. He'd remained faithful through each year of separation, even with the opportunity, even with her in another man's arms. He'd never once wavered from her, claiming that there was no other, saying that no one would come close, so why not wait for her? It wasn't worth the risk of losing her.

He wouldn't have lost her. She would have understood the need to lash out and take another like he'd done when they were younger, the years he'd spent watching her with Sam. He never had, and she loved him that much more for not doing so.

She walked back over and sat next to him, draping her finger down his trail.

"Don't tease, Skye. It will only make the days longer."

She hated the bitterness, the sadness that lie in his voice. Closing her eyes as his hand brushed her hair back, she savored the soft intimacy of the moment.

"I love you, Mark. Never doubt that."

The magic of the Shadow Realm brushed her skin, the portal forming. She'd delayed too long. Derrant had grown impatient and not waited for her own portal. She kissed Mark once more, his hand coming around and pressing her harder against his mouth. The desperation of the move was not lost on her as she clung to him one last time.

"No need for goodbyes this time," Derrant's voice came from behind them.

Mark let out something that sounded like a growl as the Death God stepped through the portal. It always amazed Skye how such a beautiful man could be so cruel. He was the Death God, but he looked like he'd stepped from the heavens.

"Did you come to gloat, Derrant?" Mark said through gritted teeth, his hand firmly on her waist.

"I could, but I won't. I'm expecting a visitor soon. Your debt has been...well, let's just say, it's been redirected."

He walked closer to Skye, his finger grazing her cheek, as she held Mark's hand firmly to keep him from reacting.

"What do you mean, my debt has been redirected?"

"It matters not, although I will miss you in my bed, Skye."

Mark growled again and freed his hand, grabbing the god's wrist. "If the debt has been paid, then remove your hand from my wife."

Derrant laughed, jerking his wrist from Mark's hold.

"Oh, but I do admire your protectiveness, Mark." He narrowed his eyes. "Keep it ready and on guard. It will be needed." He turned to walk away. "There is a storm approaching. One neither Eliana nor I can prevent."

"Storm?" Skye asked, not sure why his words had sent fear through her.

"Be sure to ask Crimson and my sons, but give her five days. She'll be occupied until then. Goodbye, Skye, Mark. I do hope I don't see either of you anytime soon. Eliana is too delicate to handle that loss."

With the last words, the portal closed with a *swoosh* that sent a blast of warm air over her skin. They sat there, too stunned to move, staring at the space where Derrant had been.

After a few minutes of silence, Mark asked, "It's over?"

"Yes, but how?"

Mark turned her around to face him and pulled her back down, kissing her passionately. The overwhelming relief that sat in her chest led her to return the kiss with a fervor. There would never be a time when she would be torn from him again. Never be a moment when she had to leave his arms. The thrill of it threatened to tear her from the concern that was flooding her mind. With the kiss, his tension fled. She could feel it as he relaxed into her, his love for her overtaking her senses.

"Mark," she said against his lips.

"Mmm."

"How did this happen?"

He pulled her closer, his hand reaching through the slit of her dress to touch her skin, pushing away the material of the pants. She could feel his need growing against her.

"It doesn't matter."

She pushed back. "Aren't you satisfied enough already?"

"No, I'm suddenly ravenous again," he replied, nibbling her neck.

"Mark, I'm serious. Stop for a second."

He rolled over so that he hovered above her. His hazel eyes were fierce with desire. "I get to spend the five days I dreaded with you now, Skye, and I promise you will not be leaving this room."

She laughed before giving him a small kiss. Her hand skimmed his body, and she suddenly wished she hadn't donned the restrictive pants.

"You can have me all five days and every day after, but something is going on. You heard him."

"I try not to listen to the man who's enjoyed stealing you from me for the last decade."

"But you heard him. There's a storm coming. That's what he said, and we need to be ready. So do Crimson, Pete, and Bormick."

He snorted. "Crimson and her harem."

"It's two men. I don't think that counts as a harem."

"No matter what it is, you're killing my hard on, Skye."

She cocked her brow. "I suppose I should be glad that thinking of Crimson is killing the mood for you. It's better than the alternative."

"Thanks," he grumbled.

"Wait, Derrant said we should ask Crimson but that she'd be occupied for—"

"Five days," he finished for her with a startled expression.

"You don't think—"

"No, she'd never do something like that."

"The debt has been redirected, paid by someone else, Mark. She took my place."

"You think Pete would allow that?"

"I don't know that Pete or even that brute Bormick has much say in what she decides. She got them to share her."

"True." He sat up and she could see him thinking it through. "There's only one way to know. Can you portal us there?"

"Oh, no, not doing that again."

She and Mark had paid an unannounced visit about two months after Crimson had taken back her kingdom. An innocent trip to await Crimson in her throne room had given them quite a show and the glimpse gave Skye good insight into why the two men had agreed to stay by her side. Skye had to tilt her head up to see that Bormick had her from behind while Pete had her from the front. She'd dragged Mark back out when Bormick had asked if they wanted to join. Needless to say, after the excessively long wait, Mark had been too turned on to wait any longer and they'd left.

"Then I'll send an enchanted raven. If that's truly what's happened, I'm sure Pete can confirm for us."

"Maybe. I want a meeting. Ask them to come here, give a date soon after the five days. We need to know what Derrant meant."

He raked his fingers through his hair, bringing himself to the edge of the bed.

"Going already?" she asked.

"You're a bit of a buzzkill when you talk realm business, Skye."

He pointed down to his softness, and she licked her lips in

response, pulling her dress over her head and ignoring the tight-laced ribbons.

"Are you offering me an incentive to stay longer?"

Sliding to his lap, feeling his reaction to her body, she said, "I thought you would have been worn out by now. Isn't that the point of these mornings?"

"It was, but it's not anymore and I'm never too worn out for you, Skye."

He touched her breasts, cupping them before bringing one to his mouth, taking extra care to run his tongue around her nipple until warmth spread through her again. The move sent shivers of pleasure rippling through her belly.

"I think we'll spend the day in here," he said against her flesh before gently biting her. She dipped her head back, her breast sinking further into his mouth as his hand slid below her waistband to find her growing arousal.

They'd taken each other enough to be satisfied for days, yet she still melted to his touch. She knew this time wouldn't be about laying claim like the others had. This would be a victory lap, a statement of ownership, and she was going to enjoy every minute of it.

"Get rid of the pants, Skye. I'm hungry again," he muttered, bringing his lips back to hers and greedily kissing her, their tongues fighting for dominance. His one hand skimmed her back as the other found its way to the spot that made her mew. "You're mine, Skye."

"Always."

She drew the hue from her pants, letting it swirl around them, then called to the muted tone left in its place. The pants disintegrated from her in a sweep of snow-like ash that joined the hue in its dance around them. Her abilities had transcended over the years so that her control of the hues was second nature.

She positioned herself over him before slowly descending until she'd fully enveloped him. His resulting moan called to the desire in her that never seemed to fade. The need for him never satisfied.

"God, I love you," he murmured.

She leaned back as he grasped her hips, bracing himself against her movements. The angle sent him further into her until he pulled her forward, reaching his hand through her hair and demanding her mouth meet his.

They moved as one, their bodies attuned to each other's needs, their souls intertwined. She was lost to his touches, the kissing that stoked the fire within her, the strength of his hands as they tightened, his muscles tensing. Her own climax grew, rising with his. The emotion, the electrical currents he caused within her were pulsing for an outlet, rising until she could take no more. His hands moved her pelvis to a rhythm he needed, one that pushed the electrical storm so that it exploded in a thousand charges through her. All she could do was cling to him with its force. His own release coursed through his muscles which tensed below her. He dropped his hands to her hips, bringing his head to rest against hers. There he remained as he caught his breath, her own ragged breaths slowing with his.

"I'm going to ravage you the rest of the day, you know that, right?" he said after a few moments.

"I would expect nothing less, but I think we might need a nap first."

He let his tongue drift down her neck, picking her up and switching places with her.

"After I have a taste of something sweet," he mumbled, kissing her stomach and lowering to his knees. She closed her eyes, her fingers nesting into his hair, and released herself to the onslaught of pleasure she knew was awaiting her.

MARK

Mark strode through the halls heading to the meeting room. He'd summoned Trent, Camin, and Noah, while Skye headed to the mage academy to speak with Elspeth separately. For the first time in years, he felt free. The tension he'd carried from the first moment he'd lost Skye to Derrant's hold was no longer present.

The years of torment were over. He was having a hard time believing it, yet she was still here, not trapped in the Shadow Realm with Derrant's body taking advantage of her, doing things to her that only Mark should do. And Mark had gorged himself on doing those things to her earlier in the day. He always took her desperately before she left for the Shadow Realm, ensuring she was well satisfied before Derrant took her. But after the news, he'd felt renewed, taking her repeatedly, tasting her as her body crumbled against his mouth. She'd returned the favor, greedily swallowing him down as he came, her tongue taking even the final drops of him.

He rolled his neck, trying to clear his head, feeling the swelling in his pants, something Noah raised a brow to, his eyes falling, then rising, his lips curving to a smirk.

"Skye left hours ago, and you still have a hard-on?" he teased, walking in stride with him to the room.

"Skye didn't leave and stop looking at my dick, you perve."

"Can't help it, it's very prominent and what do you mean she didn't leave?"

"I'll explain in a minute. Is everyone here?"

"Yes, just waiting on you, your highness."

Mark shoved him. He hated that title, and Noah knew it.

"Take a seat after you've closed the doors."

"I've got to close the doors?"

"Your king has directed you to do so," he taunted back.

Noah grumbled, but sealed the room off.

There were only a few in their inner circle who knew where Skye went each year, let alone knew the details of what had happened all those years ago, and the arrangement Derrant had forced him and Skye into. The rest were told she spent those days with the goddess, Eliana, honing her magic. The latter story inspired awe, their queen gifted to spend time with the goddess Mark had freed—the only part of the story that had been shared. If people knew the truth that not only Eliana favored Skye but the Death God with whom she shared a bed during those five days, the awe might shift to fear and even denouncement. They chose not to take the risk.

Mark took a seat at the table. When they'd built the meeting room, Skye had insisted the table be round, her love of Arthurian legend inspiring the decision.

"We have a situation. Trent, I need you to enchant a raven and send it to Pete. I believe he's spending time in Crimson's kingdom."

Camin leaned forward. "What's happened?"

"We don't know for certain. We had a visit from Derrant this morning."

"A visit? The Death God does not visit."

"That must have gone over well when he left with Skye," Trent added, empathy in his eyes.

"That's part of the reason we need to reach Pete. Derrant didn't take her."

Trent's mouth fell and Camin leaned in further, dropping his hands to the table. Camin's eyes were wide in disbelief. "He didn't take her?"

"No. He told us the debt had been paid. Redirected was his exact word."

"Redirected? What does that mean?" Trent asked.

"Skye and I think someone took her place."

"Who would be insane enough to volunteer for that job?" Noah asked.

"Crimson," Camin answered. "What is she up to?"

"We don't know, and it's only a guess. That's why we need to confirm with Pete."

Noah snorted. "Not with Bormick?"

Mark shot him a look. While he trusted Pete, albeit questioning his choice of indulging Crimson and keeping Bormick alive, he didn't trust Bormick. Nor did he think he ever would.

"There's more."

"More than that?" Trent asked, still looking baffled.

"Yes, he gave us a cryptic warning. Something about an approaching storm, one that he and Eliana cannot prevent."

"That's it?" Camin asked.

Mark shrugged. "Yes, other than that we were to ask Crimson about it."

"So, Crimson knows?"

"Perhaps, or she will if she's really switched places with Skye. That's why I need the raven sent with this note, no other."

Mark handed Trent the note; the man reading it, then nodding. The mages enchanted the ravens with special protection, but they weren't impervious to interception, so the note had been cryptic.

"Should we alert the other kingdoms?" Noah asked.

"Not yet, not until we talk to Crimson. Revina won't budge from her fortress, and Theodore is always a wild card. Derrant was specific, mentioning Crimson and his sons, which I interpret to mean Pete and Bormick. I don't think this will be Theodore's fight."

"Is he the threat?"

Mark had contemplated it but ruled against it. Theodore had curbed his ways, realizing a few years after their defeat of Crimson and Skye's freedom from the Shadow Realm that he and Skye were a force to be reckoned with. It had been a long road to reconciliation. Only after discovering their role in saving his kingdom from war and returning Crimson to her throne, had he settled peacefully with them. Skye had overlooked his hand in the last debacle and in the mage wars. She was more forgiving, but Mark still held a grudge.

The man seemed to have turned a corner, finally marrying, his wife having recently given birth. Mark had agreed to Theodore's request for mages, but only on Skye's terms. No more were they seen as servants of his kingdom but ambassadors from Skye's kingdom, with pay supplied by Theodore. Novice mages and a few full mages had agreed to the assignment, and so far, things had been peaceful.

They had made the same agreement with Crimson's kingdom, but only with the novice mages whose skills lie in healing. Pete had his own magic, so Mark had argued that full mages were not needed, and Skye had agreed. He still didn't trust Crimson. He'd sooner trust Bormick. And yet, Skye had developed some warped bond with the woman, one he'd witnessed firsthand while Crimson had been their guest. He still hated the thought of having Crimson anywhere near them, but Skye was headstrong, so he had relented.

"No, I don't think he is. What would he gain if he turned against us? Skye is too powerful, the Elite unstoppable with her in power, and if Crimson and Pete truly are aligned with us, then there's no way he could win."

"I agree," Camin said. "Pete is powerful as well, and his magic is only increasing as he accepts it. I have no indication that he's turned against us, and Crimson will follow his lead. They are too bonded, the three of them now on the same course. Their decisions will remain as one, with Pete leading."

"Not Crimson? I find that hard to believe," Mark said.

"She may think she leads, but it's Pete who holds the power. Her power was in her sexuality, which has now been caged between the two of them," Camin continued.

"Even stranger hearing that out loud," Noah muttered.

"You forget that Crimson has abilities as well," Mark said.

"Ones we don't fully understand," Camin defended.

"True, but as Skye tells it, she can steal magic temporarily. She was able to deplete Skye of her magic. She could do the same to Pete."

"No." Camin shook his head. "She won't hurt him. She can't without hurting herself. The bond between blood is too strong, that's why Pete allowed Bormick to be his equal with her. It would have left her wounded to separate them."

Mark stared at him. "How do you know this?"

"I've spent enough time with the man, enough to talk, enough to observe the three of them."

Camin's words made sense. Skye had sent Camin to help Pete with his powers. Crimson had come to them, asking for help, saying he needed training, and Camin was the best choice. Pete's magic was Shadow Magic, the opposite of Skye's and only Camin had ever been gifted with Shadow Magic, his time in the Shadow Realm lending need to it. Most of his tie to it had faded after the long return to the living realm, but he understood how it worked.

Mark thought about the urgency of Crimson's request, the quickness with which she'd released the Digremile kingdom to Pete, insisting he needed to build the kingdom as his.

"I think Crimson knew before this," he said.

"What makes you think that?"

"She's hellbent on Pete's ability to master his magic, to claim his kingdom, to win the loyalty of his people—a people and a kingdom she's ruled since the mage wars."

"She loves him," Trent mused.

"It's more than that. What if Derrant told her something? A warning like he gave me and Skye? If she did take Skye's place, she would have seen him—"

Trent looked baffled and interrupted, asking, "How does one summon the Death God?"

"I don't know, but he came to collect Skye that time Crimson betrayed us. She called him and he answered. I think there are a lot of unanswered questions. Ones Crimson has or will have answers to."

"Then we wait."

"Yes. We send the raven and await Pete's reply."

Waiting. He hated waiting, and it seemed the one thing Mark constantly faced in this life.

PETE

Shadows played along the ceiling as Pete blankly stared upward. It had been three days since Crimson had left, but it felt like an eternity. He didn't like this arrangement with Derrant, and he hated being apart from her. Sharing her with Bormick had been hard enough, but at least she was still with him. Now she was no longer in reach. Five long days without seeing her enticing green eyes, the long red waves of her hair, the curves of her body.

"Damn," he muttered.

Bormick stirred briefly before rolling to his back, his erection prominent through the sheets. The damned thing never went down. Even in his sleep, it stayed firm. Pete wiped his hand over his face, cursing Bormick for insisting on sleeping in the same bed. Pete had argued that with Crimson gone, it made sense to sleep apart, for Pete to head back to Digremile, but the brute had declined, stripping down and hopping on his favorite side. Tonight, Pete had tried again with no luck, just like the prior two nights.

Bormick had even suggested they give each other hand jobs to ease the frustration. Pete had cussed him out, only to receive a shrug.

They had developed a strange relationship that revolved around their blood link and Crimson. Having Bormick there had been awkward but only for the first few minutes, the two quickly falling into a coordinated rhythm that had stuck. They were like brothers, reading the situation, Crimson's moods, her needs. For some weird reason, it worked. Bormick was still a brute, uncouth and ill-mannered, but he treated Crimson like a goddess and Pete knew he would die to protect her.

The three of them became inseparable in the bedroom or anywhere any of them had the urge. Crimson liked sex, so it was frequent, unrelenting, and amazing. In all honesty, it took two of them to satisfy her. It was intense, too, having Bormick involved. Pete had seen more dick and ass than he'd cared for from another man.

He peeked over at Bormick, who was smiling in his sleep, grunting as his hand clasped his hard-on.

If he has a wet dream, he's cleaning it up, Pete thought.

He knew Bormick was horny. They both were. Crimson wouldn't have minded if either indulged in another woman's flesh while she was gone, but neither wanted to. Pete would have bet Bormick would have taken a woman the first night, but he didn't. When Pete asked, he'd given a shrug, saying there was no replacing Crimson, no one worth his dick, so he'd wait. Again, offering to let Pete jerk him off if it got bad.

"Ass," he'd muttered.

The shadows darkened and Pete sensed the Shadow Magic before the dark portal appeared across from him. He sat up as a cheerful Ash burst from the portal, which closed as she jumped on him, kissing him and whispering his name.

"Ash, what are you doing here?" he asked, pushing her very naked body back.

"Crimson sent me. She said you would need some release and that I could provide it."

"Crimson? She sent you?"

"Oh, yes. I shared her with the Death God last night. I'd forgotten how tasty she was."

He stared at her, a spark of jealousy slithering through him.

"Don't worry, she loves you, and told me to tell you that. She also told me that there were two to please." She looked over at Bormick, leaning toward him. "He looks scrumptious, just like you." She looked between them. "So alike, so much of both of you. How did Crimson get so lucky?"

"She really sent you?'

"Yes. She said to give you this." Ash slipped her small body down, her blonde hair trailing as her mouth found his firmness.

He tried to suppress the moan, not wanting to wake Bormick. He shared enough. Ash was his for now. Her tongue caressed the underside of his shaft, then circled over his tip, licking the trickle of pre-cum that escaped as he throbbed in her hand. Three days had passed. In his old life, that would have been fine, but now when he was used to multiple times a day. Three days was like a year.

She dipped her mouth, enveloping him, and he dug his fingers into her hair.

"You have a visitor," Bormick said. "I thought we weren't having visitors. My hand not enough, Pete?"

"Fuck you, Bormick," he grunted.

Ash's mouth left him, and Pete's dick ached in response.

"Crimson sent me."

"Oh, she did, did she? And what did she send you to do?" Bormick asked, pulling her body over, the sheet shifting so that he lined up with her. She lowered her body, moving sensually up and down on him.

"Fuck Bormick, she was busy."

"Well, she's busier now. That pretty little mouth can still satisfy you. My balls are so full it won't take long…the first time."

"You're an ass."

"He's a sexy ass," Ash said as Bormick fondled her perky breasts, then pulled her down with a kiss.

Watching them was causing Pete's dick to throb more and his irritation to rise.

"Good gods, Pete. Why do you get all the sexy ones first?"

"Because I'm better than you. Stop stealing my women."

Nipping at Ash's breast, Bormick tugged her nipple with his teeth and replied, "Crimson gave her to us."

Ash squealed, and Pete knew that look. She was cresting and damn if he was going to let Bormick have all the fun. She was his, and he preferred to think that she only came for him, even though he knew she was in her true form and the rule that kept her from letting men pleasure her didn't stand when she was in her unguarded form.

"Where did you find her, and how did Crimson know we'd like her?"

"I'm a—"

"Tree nymph," Pete said, enjoying the fact that Bormick had no idea a demon was currently riding him.

Bormick looked over at him, glancing quickly to catch sight of Pete's hand that was currently stroking his engorged erection.

"This is the tree nymph? You've been holding out on me."

"Clearly not."

Ash laughed before twisting herself from Bormick's grasp. "You two are funny. Do you ever stop talking?"

She crawled back to Pete as Bormick complained, moving Pete's hand and going down on him again. His head went back with the sensation.

Bormick moved behind Ash and plunged his fingers inside of her. "Damned if I'm going to let that go to waste."

Her mouth lifted with a cry. Pete glared at Bormick while

Bormick leaned down and licked her. She dropped her mouth back down on Pete, taking his full length and he grunted a loud, "Fuck," just as Bormick penetrated her. With each thrust, Bormick pushed her head down further on Pete. Having gone too long without sex, Pete was entirely too turned on. His body was a rage of sensations that threatened to send him over the edge much too quickly.

"You're going to blow first, Pete," Bormick taunted, but Pete could see him struggling.

Ash climaxed, her scream of pleasure taking her warmth from him just as he broke and spilled into her mouth. Bormick crashed right after, the muscles in his arms exaggerated with the force of his release as he squeezed her waist.

"Christ," Pete muttered, coming down from his high.

Ash slid her body up as Bormick collapsed. Her mouth met Pete's, her tongue pushing the taste of him into his mouth with her kisses.

"I missed that taste," she said, grabbing his still pounding length in her hand and returning it to its previous size.

He entangled his hands in her hair and brought her lips to his again, saying, "And I missed that mouth of yours."

She moved him to her entrance, where he slid right in, the dampness from her orgasm and Bormick's leaving her sopping and slick. He took her again, Bormick joining, their movements and positions coordinated just as they always were with Crimson.

They took turns with her until, when they were finally satisfied, Ash rose from the bed, crawling over Pete and kissing him before leaving the bed completely. She'd exhausted him so that his body felt like a limp rag. He could do more than touch her hand when she walked away. Bormick protested but with minimal effort.

"The Death God agreed to one night. It's been...satisfying, as it always is with you, Pete. And you," she said to Bormick, "were just as Crimson described. Yummy. The Death God calls. Good-bye, my pets, until next year."

She leaned over and kissed Pete once more. The magic of the Shadow Realm tingled against his skin, the portal opening and pulling her away in its black haze.

Bormick's soft snores filled the room, but Pete took longer to drift off, his mind on Crimson's gift, knowing it was unlike most women, knowingly sending another woman to her lover's bed. But Crimson was different, understanding they would be craving her and pleasing them the only way she could. They'd make it up to her when she returned. He smiled at the thought, his mind picturing all the ways they'd played with Ash and all the ways they'd pleasure Crimson when she returned.

MORNING CAME QUICKLY, Bormick's loud stretch waking him.

"Do you have to be so damn loud?" Pete complained.

"So, that was the tree nymph," Bormick replied, ignoring his question. "You were holding out on me, Pete. She's not Crimson, but she's close, closer than I've ever had. And what she does with that body, it's captivating. Don't tell Crimson I said that."

Pete smiled, pulling some clothes on and wondering what Bormick's reaction would be if he knew he'd spent the night fucking a sex demon. He bit back his laugh upon imagining it.

Bormick grabbed his morning erection. "Keep that smirk up and it'll be surrounding my dick."

"Fat chance, ass."

"I could put it there, too."

Pete huffed and left the room, determined to find something to eat. His extracurricular activities had left him famished. As he rounded the great hall, Hentrom came running to him.

"Your highness, a raven arrived this morning."

He handed the message to Pete, who felt the remains of the enchantment on it. He could tell the message had come from Skye and Mark by the seal on it. He opened it, reading the brief statement quickly, his brow creasing.

Crimson, not Skye?

Storm?

Meet.

The message was cryptic, and Pete knew immediately that it was from Mark. He also understood exactly what Mark meant. He would confirm Crimson's deal with the Death God but as for information, he had no more than what Crimson had given him, which had been very little.

Using his magic, he removed the ink from the note, then responded.

Yes.

In time.

Eight days from the summons. Midday arrival.

Then he handed the note back to Hentrom.

"Did you keep the raven separated?"

"Yes, my liege."

"Good, use it to send my response."

Hentrom bowed before hurrying off.

He could have replied that they'd come immediately upon Crimson's return, but instinct told him to wait. He would need to hear any information the Death God gave her. The day of her return would likely be awash, unless the news was serious. As much as Ash had satisfied them, Crimson was who they craved and with two days left before her return, they would need time with her, as selfish as it sounded. They needed her like a replenishment to their soul.

Passing through the great hall, he decided to forgo his breakfast a bit longer, heading outside instead. He looked to the sky as he walked, letting his hold on his magic go, sending it out, sensing, searching for any sign that something was amiss. He'd been doing this daily, something not sitting right with Crimson's words the day she'd gone to see the Death God. As the months had passed, he'd set it aside. None of them really knowing what to do with the information. Over the past few weeks, he'd grown more concerned, his senses heightened. Whether it was an effect of his growing powers or something more, he wasn't certain, but it was the nagging feeling that something was on the horizon, waiting to strike.

A storm.

Mark's note had said the same, that they were aware. Had the Death God visited them? Warned them? If so, this did not bode well.

A storm was coming. He felt the tingle in the air, a brush to his senses, but nothing more. Whatever it was, it was enough to cause him concern. If the Death God was worried enough to warn them, then they were in trouble. He prayed it wasn't more trouble than their combined forces could handle, for if it were, they were all doomed.

CRIMSON

The stone floor was cold on Crimson's feet after the warmth of the Shadow Realm. The portal *whooshed* closed behind her, the empty room she shared with Pete and Bormick greeting her. A sense of peace settled over her at being home again. She'd never cared in the past, but now she had something to care for, something to miss.

She moved her legs gingerly, each movement giving her discomfort. It had been a very long time since she'd indulged Derrant other than the one time when she'd pleaded Skye's case and offered to take her place. She'd forgotten how large he was, how intense. It made her crave her two lovers, their gentle touches, even Bormick's rougher ones. Derrant had taken her multiple times the prior night, the last one rough and demanding. She liked it that way, but with a god, it tended to leave more marks.

She leaned against the bed. Her body was tired, and she wanted nothing more than to sleep. But her mind was awake, running through what Derrant had told her, which still wasn't much. It was, however, enough to cause her to worry.

"You look exhausted." Pete's voice came from the doorway.

Her heart fluttered in response, and when her eyes met his, her body came alive, rejuvenated with just his presence. He came to her, lifting her chin and kissing her sensually.

Resting her hands on his chest, she murmured, "I missed you."

"Feeling's mutual." He ran his tongue over his lips, his brows furrowing. "You taste like smoke and shadows."

"Shadows?" she asked.

"Shadows from the Death God. I'm not sure how I feel about that."

"The rest of me likely tastes like him, too. A nice warm bath would cleanse his touch from me and a few hours with you would erase it completely."

"I can oblige to that," he responded coyly.

Rubbing her arms gently, his expression changed. He picked up her arm, seeing the bruises from Derrant's last turn at her. His thumb gently skimmed over them.

"I think I have even more reason to understand Mark's objection to this situation now."

"It's nothing more than a rough night, the same as Bormick gives me at times."

"But Bormick doesn't leave marks like that."

She brought her fingers to his lips.

"Shh. Make me a bath and wash him away."

He kissed her forehead, and she watched as he created a black claw-foot tub, water filling it and steaming after just moments. Her eyes grew wide. His magic still astounded her, even after all this time. His power seemed to have no limits, its touch against her skin a stimulating tingle as she walked through the trail of it, closer to the tub.

He removed her dress, kissing each of the handprints, the finger impressions Derrant had left, then the bruises that lined her inner thighs, before helping her into the tub. The warmth was decadent against her skin, assuaging the dull ache that remained from Derrant's touch. She sank her head under. She didn't know how Skye had done this for so long. Before she'd found love, it had never bothered her but now...to be torn from them for so many days ached.

Derrant was a good lover, and he'd indulged her this time, something he'd never done in the past, always taking and never giving. Skye must have trained him, or perhaps having Eliana back had done it. Whatever it was, it had been unexpected and welcomed.

Pete let his fingers drift through her hair before rising and bringing her a scented bar of soap from her nightstand. She was glad he'd found her first. His gentle touch was the one she needed, then she would be ready for Bormick.

She grabbed his hand as he passed her the soap. "Join me and help me wash."

Desire flared in his eyes, but she knew he'd restrain for as long as she needed. As she watched him remove his shirt, then his pants, she didn't think it would be long. She needed him, had hungered for him as Derrant had filled her.

He climbed in behind her, and she could feel his hardness against her back. Handing him the soap, she leaned against him, her hand tracing the muscles in his leg as he washed her. Her body responded instantly to his touch, her nipples rising, the warmth flowing through the bottom half of her.

"Did you like my gift?" she asked as his lips brushed her neck. His hands washed between her legs, lingering to stroke her.

She sighed as he responded, "Very much."

"Good. She told me you were her favorite pet, and to hold favor with a sex demon is saying quite a bit."

"So, I've heard."

"Did you share her?"

"Unfortunately." She let out a small cry as he rubbed her clit with his thumb, his other hand caressing her breast. His finger manipulated her nipple until it was erect. "I left out what she truly is."

A giggle escaped her until his other finger slid further to sink into her. Her body was on fire with the need to have him, to feel him inside of her. She wanted him alone. He was what she needed right now. She'd pleasure Bormick later. She'd missed him just as greatly, but her connection to Pete was different. Their connection was gentle and more spiritual. He held most of her heart, Bormick taking more of it over the months until she'd finally admitted her love for him. He'd broken one night during an intense love making session and admitted the same. Pete knew and had accepted it, the two men having some mutual understanding about it.

Pete pushed another finger into her, his lips tracing her neck as he brought her closer to climax.

Although she thoroughly enjoyed it when both men took her at once, there were times when she'd separate them, needing their undivided and individual attention to renew their bond with her in their own unique way.

She grasped Pete's legs as the need for release intensified, feeling his length behind her, patiently waiting for her own pleasure. The warmth spread, his thumb brushing her clit once more, until she could take it no longer. The overwhelming fire within claimed her, and she threw her head back against him, crying out his name. He turned her head, his mouth covering her cry as his fingers continued their stimulating movement. The fire built again, flaming higher with each stroke of his thumb and thrust of his fingers until a second inferno raged through her, crumbling her defenses a second time.

He drew his fingers out, her body collapsing against his as the currents of her orgasm continued to drift through her.

"I love it when you come," he said, nibbling her ear.

"Then make me come again," she demanded, lifting her body and shifting her position so that she sat upon him, the tub wide enough to let her straddle him. She positioned over him and enveloped him. His moan coursed through her like a tense nerve, calling the rest to stay on guard.

"Are you sure?" he asked.

She leaned her head against his. Her Pete, always sensitive to her; the one she turned to when she needed a gentle touch.

"Yes, I want you to take me." It had been all she'd thought of when she'd been with Derrant—when she wasn't in the throes of passion with him, and it was hard to concentrate on anything but him.

He brought his hand to her neck and pulled her in for a kiss, one that was laced with his feelings for her. As she began the rise and fall of her body on him, he blanketed them with his power, the soft warmth of it like a gentle touch on her body. They climaxed together; the water flowing with their movements until it stilled with their bodies, her chest leaning into his embrace, where they stayed until he picked her up and took her to the bed. They made love again, ending with his mouth kissing away the remnants of Derrant's touch again, bringing her to a final climax before she fell asleep in his arms.

CRIMSON DIDN'T KNOW how long she'd slept, but Bormick gave her the time, respecting her need to be alone with Pete. Both men were respectful of private time, allowing it, even though she knew they were holding their own needs back when those times came.

Pete was gone when she woke, likely having talked to Bormick.

She did a long cat stretch, then stared at the ceiling, wondering how she'd gotten so lucky. It was something she frequently did.

Pete had changed her, Bormick and she had changed each

other. With her ten years of imprisonment in the Forest of Lost Souls and now the endless months she'd had with Pete and Bormick, she no longer knew the woman she had been. That woman—spiteful, spoiled, obsessed with hurting men, with stealing the ones she'd wanted—no longer existed.

She was still powerful, demanding, not someone to be challenged, but the parts of her that had turned others away from her had faded, her heart opened by Pete and stretched further by Bormick. She'd never thought it possible, yet here she was, loved intensely by not one but two men who would die for her. One almost had. She knew she would do the same for them.

"Crazy," she muttered.

"Crazy? That you're talking to yourself or that you look like a sexy cat when you stretch?" Bormick asked, drawing her attention to the balcony where he stood watching her.

"Are cats sexy?" They didn't have such things in her kingdom, but Bormick had told her about the ones that roamed other parts of their world.

He gave her a coy smile. "Depends on the pussy."

She rolled her eyes, then asked, "How long have you been standing there?"

"Long enough to get hard from watching your tits."

"Is that all you think about?"

"It's all you think about, so what's wrong with me thinking about it?"

She laughed as he joined her on the bed. "Fair enough."

He drew her in, kissing her the way only Bormick could, her body folding into his arms. He pushed her back gently, brushing a strand of her hair from her face.

"Pete and I have been taking shifts to check on you."

"Check on me?"

He kissed her nose. "You've been asleep for an entire day."

"I have?"

"Yeah and I must say I'm irritated that he got to fuck you first and I had to wait." The tone he used gave her the impression he'd heeded Pete's request to let her sleep because he'd agreed she needed to rest.

"Sorry, he was here first."

"Eh, I'll more than make up for it," he said with a grin. His eyes fell to her arm, his fingers lingering on the bruises the same way Pete had. "Did the bastard hurt you?"

"No, he just likes it rough, like you."

"I do like it rough," he said, grabbing her ass and pulling her against him. "But I don't leave marks... Well, not on you anyway."

She gave him a sharp look of scolding, knowing he'd read it immediately. He put his hands up. "I haven't touched another woman since your amazing body came into my life."

Raising a brow, she asked, "Even when we first met?"

"Damn, my secret's out. So much for my bad boy image. I tried, but after your mouth on my dick, there was no replacement. I gave the wench to a soldier, then threatened to slit both their throats if they breathed a word about it."

"You couldn't get it up with another woman after you had me?" she teased.

"Oh, trust me, it was hard and ready, but that body was not yours, nor was it willing and you were very willing."

"So, your days of taking women forcefully ended with me?"

"Yes, they did," he said, nipping at her neck, his fingers brushing her breast.

"Good, I guess I have done something right. You know, I had a vendetta against you before all this. That bad boy reputation made you next on my list to die."

He narrowed his eyes at her. "You couldn't have captured me."

"I could have," she said, reaching down and grabbing his erection. "I had a comfy cell waiting for you. No one abuses the women in my kingdom, and you had some serious torture ahead of you."

"No one touches the women, but you could take the men?"

"Yes. Men want me. They can't resist me; no matter how they try, they always succumb and once they do, I get a little pleasure. In the meantime, they weaken to me, and I kill them."

"You are a cunning bitch, aren't you?"

"I have my own reputation."

He flipped her, pinning her arms. "And what do you suppose would have happened if you had captured me?"

"I did capture you," she purred.

He pressed himself against her, and she raised her leg so that he pressed against her dampness.

"What if you'd taken me as a prison? Would you have killed me?"

She felt the breath pushed from her at the thought.

"No, I would have been enamored by you, too intrigued, too drawn to you to let you go. And then I would have fallen for you and made you my king."

He curved his lip. "Capturing me for eternity like you did."

"Yes..." He loosened his grip on her wrists. "I still would have made you change your ways."

"Yes, you would have, just like you did. Have your ways changed, Crimson? Or do Pete and I need to worry about what you're doing in those dungeons?"

His finger traced the curve of her breast before he grasped it, bringing his mouth to it.

"Yes," she said with a moan. "I'm satisfied now. No other men can come close to either of you."

He sucked on her nipple, then lifted himself to look at her again, his blue eyes heavy with desire.

"Good, because sharing you is hard enough with Pete and the Death God, and you know how I hate to share."

"As much as I hate it."

He gave a laugh before saying, "Now, I'm going to take you because I've craved you for days."

"Even with the tree nymph?" she asked, using Pete's term. She'd have to tell Bormick the truth about the demon, but since her body was aching for him, she didn't want to deter his intent.

"She was quite a tasty snack. No wonder Pete couldn't resist her. Shit, she even gives you a run for your money."

"Does she now?"

He licked her nipple, teasing it and pulling it with his teeth so that her nails dug into his back in response. "Don't worry, you're still the best."

"Good answer. Now why don't you do everything you did to her to me, and show me how you made her come?" There was a glint in his eyes before he worked the sheets from her body and buried himself between her thighs, reminding her once again why he was hers.

BORMICK

Bormick watched as Crimson dressed, disappointment coming over him as the material of her gown hid her perfect full breasts. He rolled his neck as Pete grabbed her and stole a kiss.

Pulling a shirt over his head, Bormick growled, "Hey, this was my time, remember?"

"You're finished, and I wanted a kiss."

"I know where your kisses lead," he said. "And it's not to my dick."

"One of these days, I'm going to punch you for those comments, Bormick."

Crimson placed a hand on Pete's chest. "Come on, you two. We need to get to business."

"I thought that's what we just did," Bormick teased, trying not to laugh at Pete's weak threat.

Ignoring him, Pete asked her, "Time to tell us what the Death God said?"

"Yes, although it's not much more than we already knew."

Bormick moved closer to them and ran a hand through his

hair. Her tone had him worried, and he didn't care much for the tension that worry carried with it. "Then tell us."

"We need to practice," she said, walking past Pete and out the door.

Bormick turned back to Pete, who seemed just as confused, but shrugged and followed.

Bormick followed, wishing he'd gotten a few hours of rest after the morning spent on Crimson's body. She was wicked and the things she did to him left him craving her regularly. Thankfully, she craved sex as much if not more than he did. He'd never met a woman as insatiable.

He felt the reaction and adjusted his pants. She'd just gone down on him before Pete had said it was time to talk, her greedy little mouth licking him clean, then riding him until he'd come again. Pete had watched as he'd finished. Bormick had expected him to join in and had glanced at him in surprise when he didn't. The lump in Pete's pants made it clear he wanted to, but they'd had an unspoken agreement that they would both have alone time with her, and Pete had kept his word.

Bormick still didn't understand the strange relationship he and Pete had developed. With Stavin, it had been years of getting used to each other. They'd been friends a long time before Pete had killed him. Stavin had been a tool to use; a figurehead for Bormick to rule behind. Sharing their women had been fun. Stavin hadn't been up to Bormick's par, but it had still been a turn on.

Pete, however, was up to the same standard as Bormick. He was good at what he did, and he was well endowed. Watching him bring Crimson to climax was enough to make Bormick come and watching her take Pete to the hilt made Bormick's balls ache because he knew what that mouth felt like wrapped that deep.

They'd developed a rapport, not quite a friendship. Pete was constantly suspicious, overly protective of her, but that didn't bother Bormick. He wanted Crimson safe, and he knew if he couldn't do it, Pete would. He'd already saved her from Stavin's greedy ass. Bormick had cut Stavin off, telling him Crimson was off limits, yet he'd still taken her. He didn't mind sharing with Pete for some reason, but Stavin and the thought of any other man, even the Death God bothered him.

He watched Pete as Crimson led them to the throne room. He could see the tension in his shoulders. The tension told Bormick that Pete was concerned as well. When a man with the power Pete carried was worried, Bormick grew nervous.

Pete looked back at him, and Bormick grabbed his dick, gesturing to it with his eyes. Pete grimaced and turned away, which only made him laugh. Teasing the guy was enjoyable. Bormick had been serious with the offer he'd made Pete while Crimson was gone. Although men weren't particularly his taste, when no women were to be found and his hand couldn't do the job, Stavin had done it with his hand. It was better when someone else did the work. Pete would come around. After a few years of the three of them, as inseparable as they were, Pete might just let him experiment, especially when Crimson wasn't there to satisfy them.

There was something between himself and Pete that Bormick couldn't put his finger on. Pete called it a blood bond, having something to do with some ancient blood ritual. Whatever it was, it tied him to Pete as much as it did to Crimson. They were one mind when it came to her, anticipating her needs, switching off at just the right time, anticipating their own needs. If he wanted to fuck her first, Pete didn't even have to ask; he'd let Bormick lead the way, same way with him. They simply knew what the other needed.

He often wondered why Pete had kept him alive that first day, before he'd discovered their connection. He'd been dying; killing him would have been easy. Bormick remembered meeting Pete's eyes, knowing in that instant that he was the one who'd already claimed her, seeing the recognition in Pete's eyes of what had happened. He could have taken her away and left Bormick to bleed to death. The Mage Warrior and her husband wouldn't have cared.

But he hadn't. He'd saved the man he'd instinctively known had also claimed Crimson, changing their lives forever, changing Bormick's life. Crimson had already started to change him. He'd become obsessed with her. He couldn't keep her out of his head, let alone look at another woman without thinking of her. She'd owned him, owned his heart from the moment she'd walked into that room, proud and dominating with no ounce of fear. She was the perfect match for him, no matter what he'd told himself then.

Pete crossed his arms and waited for Crimson to talk as Bormick settled himself against the wall.

"Why are we here, Crimson?" he asked.

"Because we need space and it's storming out in case you didn't notice."

"I didn't have time to notice anything but your body."

Pete smirked, but Bormick could tell he was trying not to laugh.

"What do we need space for?" Pete asked.

"To continue training me with your power."

"No." Pete's answer was terse and unwavering, and both Bormick and Crimson turned sharply to him. .

"No?" she asked with a raise of her brow.

"No. You're not bleeding my magic. We're heading to see Skye and Mark tomorrow, and I need to have my power. The last time you drained it, it took two days to return."

"Why are we going to Kantenda?" she asked.

Pete had told Bormick about the raven, but neither had had time to tell Crimson.

"Because the Death God paid them a visit and gave them a similar cryptic warning. They want to know what's going on."

Pete had interpreted more from the short note he'd described than Bormick would have.

She looked over at Bormick, and he nodded in affirmation.

"Now tell us what the Death God told you," Bormick said, crossing his arms.

"Not a lot, other than we need to prepare, and he showed me something I didn't know I could do."

"What?" Pete asked the question in Bormick's mind.

She pulled her hair back to reveal the creamy skin below.

"How to rile Bormick up by flashing him some skin?"

Bormick glared at him, but Pete didn't bother acknowledging it.

Holding her hand out, Crimson said, "Give me your dagger."

Pete squinted, as if trying to determine what she was up to. Bormick pushed himself from the column and walked closer as Pete pulled the dagger out and handed it to her.

She held her finger out and pushed the tip against it.

"What are you doing?" Pete asked, grabbing it from her as she squeezed the blood forward.

She brought her finger to her neck. The blood seeped into her skin with a glimmer, a shape forming. A crescent moon set in dark crimson.

Bormick moved closer to inspect it, saying, "That's the mark of a Mage Warrior." He traced his finger over it, feeling the magic. He'd noticed the faint outline of a birthmark on her neck before but had never given it much thought.

"What's the mark of a Mage Warrior?" Pete asked, drawing closer.

"This. Every Mage Warrior is born with it. The mark glows when they use their magic. Each class has their own mark and I've heard the Elite do as well."

Pete's look grew concerned as he studied it. "It looks like Skye's birthmark, but hers has this black web-like marking to it."

Bormick's mouth dropped. "The Mage Queen's birthmark bears the mark of the Death God?"

"The mark of the Death God?"

Crimson even looked shocked as she answered him. "The gods have signs. Derrant's is a web of night, and no one has ever borne his sign."

"Skye does."

Bormick wondered when Pete had been close enough to her to notice her birthmark. "So it would seem the Death God has claim on more than just our girl. I wonder how her Elite feels about that."

"I can assure you he dislikes any talk of Skye in the Death God's clutches. I've been in the room when that discussion comes up, so I'm certain that marking makes him just as unhappy. Why is that so unique?"

"The birthmarks of the mages and Elite are distinct, Pete. All of them are the same, always. If Skye's holds Derrant's touch, then her magic is something greater than any Mage Warrior," Crimson answered.

"Christ, she's intimidating to begin with."

"Turn you on Pete? All that power in that tight body of hers."

"Shut up, Bormick." Pete was touchy about any mention of Skye in a sexual way, something that always gave Bormick pause. The woman was otherworldly; it was impossible not to imagine fucking her. "Let's move on from Skye. Tell us what you've been hiding, Crimson?"

"Hard to move on from that beauty," Bormick mumbled, as Crimson shot him a look.

"Nothing. The mark has always been there, but it lies dormant, empty, unlike Skye's. I was born without magic, as was everyone in my line but my line dissects from Skye's at one point, so the capacity is there. That's why I can borrow power, because I have the capacity to hold it and control it." She licked the blood from her finger. "This is how I've always called Derrant. He showed me when I was little—the blood sends him my where-abouts and the portal is created. The only other time I've felt it active was the time I took Skye's magic. But that time he had me call him differently, and her magic must have been the conduit instead of my birthmark. It stayed lit a vibrant violet until the magic faded."

"Gods, you're hot," he muttered. The sight of the birthmark sparkling on her skin was enough to drive him mad. It was sexy enough when she took Pete's magic.

"Really, Bormick? That's where your brain goes?"

"Of course. She's hot, Pete, and when she takes your magic, she's even hotter."

Crimson gave him a coy smile, then pursed her lips. "Skye's birthmark has Derrant's webs?"

"We already established that."

Bormick had to agree with Pete, but Crimson had her mind on something. "Where are they in relation to her birthmark?"

"Are we really going back to Skye again?" Pete asked.

Her eyes creased. "Humor me. Where do they sit?"

"Fine, they tangle over the moon shape. I noticed it one day when she had her hair up."

"Checking out the Mage Queen, Pete?" Bormick couldn't help but tease him again.

"I was not checking her out. We were training and Crimson was off with you at that time, your hands all over her, so what would have been the harm if I had?"

Bormick raised a brow, giving him a knowing look. Skye was sexy, like a forbidden fruit, one her Elite hovered over each time they'd met with them. She was the only one who rivaled Crimson's beauty, and he could see why Pete's eyes had wandered. His own perused her body each time, wondering what it would be like to have that tiny waist gripped in his hands while he pounded into her ass.

"Get your mind off Skye, Bormick," Pete scolded.

"That's a hard feat, Pete. That woman is like candy waiting to be licked."

Crimson elbowed him, but he saw the look in Pete's eyes, the quick scowl that was hiding the desire below.

Heeding Crimson's hint, Bormick continued with the subject of the birthmark. "If Derrant marked her, maybe it's about more than her power. Maybe there's more to her than we thought. I'd venture our sweet Skye is very comfortable in the Shadow Realm."

Crimson pursed her lips. "So Derrant claimed her and gifted her."

"And claimed you, and now he's gifted you?"

"So it seems."

She still looked lost in thought when Pete asked, "Why are you showing us this now?"

"Because Derrant showed me something I didn't know I could do. As long as I've activated it with the blood, I am a conduit. My tie to the Shadow Realm makes it possible. Now let me take your power."

"No, I'm not—"

"Let her, Pete. The Death God showed her this for a reason. Let her try it."

He knew Pete's way of thinking now. He wanted to protect her because that's who he thought he was, her protector. But Bormick saw the truth of it, had known of her reputation long before he'd dared take her throne. She was fierce and more than capable of defending herself. The two of them were her last defense.

He saw the resignation in Pete.

"Fine, but—"

"Shut up, Pete. Crimson, show us what you can do."

He was pushing it with Pete, but he didn't care. They toed the edge of enemies at times. He had a feeling it was that so-called warrior blood that ran through their veins. If warranted, they would brawl. It had happened before, followed by an extremely intense fuck session with Crimson, as they had both asserted their dominance.

Crimson reached up and kissed Pete, saying, "Trust me."

Pete acquiesced, and she moved back. Her power charged the air. Bormick didn't know if others were aware of it, but he was attuned to it, like an electrical charge that skipped across his skin. The Shadow Magic began to form, the gray mist that fled from Pete to her, the stream fading quickly as it fed her.

Pete looked down at his hands, then at her.

A sly grin formed on her face. "It's done."

As she said the words, a ball of black mist escaped her hand and landed hard against Pete's chest, throwing him backward. He returned to his feet quickly, power swirling around him, his blue eyes dark with it.

"Why do I still have my powers? And that hurt," he complained, rubbing his chest.

"I don't have to take it now. I've never had to. I can copy it, then leave the other person with their magic. It lasts a few days, longer than before, and"—she moved her hand, a stream of gray magic following it, flowing back to Pete—"I can return it anytime I want."

Pete scrunched his eyes, then looked at Bormick, who was certain Pete had the same question as he did.

"Why did the Death God show you this and why would you need a power like that?"

"There's something coming. He won't tell me what, will only tell me that he and Eliana cannot interfere, that it will upset the balance. We're on our own."

"Who's we?" Bormick asked.

"Me, his two sons, Skye, and her Elite."

"Shit," Bormick grumbled. "That doesn't tell us much."

"No, it doesn't."

"What does he mean, upset the balance?" Pete asked.

"No idea. He wouldn't elaborate."

Bormick didn't like the lack of answers, and he could see Pete felt the same way. No one liked going into an unknown battle, especially if they didn't know what they were facing.

"Well, then, you need to work on understanding Pete's magic and copying it faster."

"And you," she started, grabbing Pete's dagger again, "can familiarize yourself with your new weapon."

She handed it to Bormick, who stared at it in confusion.

"His new weapon?" Pete asked.

"This piddly thing is not a weapon," Bormick said, turning Pete's small dagger in his hand.

"It is a weapon, but why is he using it? It's been in my family for ages."

"Correct, after your ancestor took it from his dead brother's body. Derrant gave me that much insight."

"This tiny thing?" Bormick said again.

Pete grabbed it from him, then threw it into the wall.

"What the—"

The wall exploded around it, a long, spiked sword falling with the debris, the handle the same as that of the dagger.

Bormick looked over at them both.

"Trust me, I thought it was just a dagger until your friend's guts were splattered all over Crimson."

Crimson shuddered at the memory and part of him was thankful he'd been delirious when it had happened. Bormick walked over and picked the sword up, watching as it shrank back to dagger size. The stone in it shone brightly as he balanced it between his hands.

"You see, Pete had it only partially right. Your family were warriors, the second and third born, but they weren't all the same. You are a warrior, Bormick. You are bound to protect my line with your brute force. Pete, you are a Shadow Warrior, bound to protect my line with your link to the Death God himself—Shadow Magic. The brothers failed because they turned from their duty and the princess, my ancestor, was attacked, her magic stripped, leaving the rest of our line with empty birthmarks. They broke the blood pact that had been sworn in the Death God's name via the Shadow Magic the third brother wielded. My link to Derrant brought a fragment of my family's magic back. And the two of you are the redemption of your lines."

Pete looked taken aback while Bormick was left speechless.

"Two protectors, two lovers, one mage conduit."

"Damn, I thought you were hot before—"

Pete elbowed him.

"All right, all right. So, we protect you, which is what both of us would do, anyway. Pete already has done that."

"I think whatever is coming will make Stavin seem like child's play."

He'd never seen her so serious and as he looked down at the dagger, contemplating her words, he wasn't certain he wanted whatever was coming to get anywhere close to her.

MARK

The tension rolling from Mark's body drove him to pace the room. Waiting. It seemed all he did in life was wait.

"Mark." Skye stopped him, inserting her body in his path. She was trying to be the calm one, but he knew her well enough to note the tightness in her jaw, the stormier blue in her eyes, the tiny trembles in her fingers. She was just as nervous as he was.

"Mark, stop pacing," she said, her hand reaching to his chest.

"I can't, Skye. I'm on edge and—"

She kissed him, stopping his words, the action calming him instantly.

"You two need a few minutes?" Noah joked, as Mark drew her body closer.

A few hours was what he needed with her, although he wasn't sure that would even work.

Drawing back from his lips, she whispered, "Calm yourself."

"Hard to do when you tease me like that."

She laughed, but the *whoosh* of air from the room and the feel of Shadow Magic stayed her smile. She turned to where his attention had been drawn, her body still against his. He tightened his arm protectively as the black-rimmed portal appeared.

Pete stepped through first, followed by Crimson, then Bormick, the portal closing behind them. The two men flanked her, crossing their arms, muscles accentuated in a protective fashion. Mark observed them quickly, taking in their guarded stances. They knew something more. The question was, how much would they share?

The three had been inseparable since Crimson had taken her kingdom back. Mark had argued for Bormick's death, but Pete had argued that it was Crimson's decision, later siding with her to keep the man alive.

Whatever bond they shared was unbreakable. It confounded him. It was clear Pete loved her, yet he'd agreed to bring the other man into their relationship, sharing the woman he loved. Even if that wasn't quite the same as the way he'd been forced to share Skye, the thought still gutted him. It was hard enough imagining Derrant touching her, but having to watch it? The situation was one he would never tolerate. But with the three of them, it seemed to work.

"Crimson," Skye greeted her guardedly, then nodded to both Pete and Bormick.

He caught the more discreet flicker of Pete's eyes across Skye's body and Bormick's obvious one. The action happened each time the five of them were together. Pete's gaze didn't bother him. It was always more one of surprise each time he saw her, although there were times Mark wondered at the surprise. Pete had been in their world six months, had magic of his own that he'd grown into. There should have been no surprise left about Skye other than how breathtaking she was. And maybe that's all it was.

Bormick, however, bothered him. His looks were never subtle. Rather, they were similar to that of a hungry animal eyeing its prey. Mark moved a step closer to Skye, meeting Bormick's eyes, a glint of humor lighting them in reaction to Mark's protective stance.

"Skye. Clinging to your Elite? Afraid I might want another taste?" Crimson quipped.

Mark clenched his teeth, but Skye was quick to retort. "Aren't you satisfied enough with those two, Crimson?"

"More than enough, but they wouldn't mind if I played a little."

Both Pete and Bormick looked over her at each other, their brows narrowing.

Skye drifted from his arms. Everything about her movement spoke of her power, her confidence, her sexuality. The sway of her hips was alluring. The eyes of the other men fell on her again, but he stayed still—this was Skye's game with Crimson. He'd realized it the first time they'd been together. The game was a playful, taunting one that left him puzzled and uncomfortably stimulated.

Crimson stepped forward, her body flattered a little too well in the green dress she wore, its color bringing out the sage in her eyes. He drew his eyes from the ample breasts that spilled over her dress. He noticed Pete tense as she moved further from his side, the tattoos on his arms seeming to pop, his muscles were so tight.

Bormick shifted his stance. They didn't like this any more than Mark did. The women stood close, the game changing, a dangerous glare to Skye's eyes, an equally lethal one forming in Crimson's.

"Still dreaming of my husband, Crimson?"

It was hard not to say something, but he remained quiet.

"Always, Skye."

"Then let's try something fun. I'm game if you are. You can have him for a night, and I'll take your two."

Holy shit, he couldn't believe she'd just said that and had no idea what she could be thinking.

The room went silent. Mark's heart tumbled for a split second, his eyes meeting Pete's, who looked just as stunned. Even

Bormick seemed taken aback. Crimson's lips formed a tight line, then the corner of her lip rose. "You're a bitch, Skye," she said in a playful tone.

"And you're a whore, Crimson," Skye shot back.

Crimson's eyes twinkled with humor.

"Is it time we moved past my husband?" Skye asked.

"He's hard to move on from, Skye."

Skye pushed past her toward Pete and Bormick. Bormick's eyes skimmed her body even more overtly, and Mark wanted to punch him. Pete must have sensed the reaction, giving Mark a head shake.

This wasn't their game; this was a game of dominance between Skye and Crimson. And they'd been playing it since Skye had pissed Mark off to no end by befriending Crimson, but she'd insisted. It had been some form of a healing process for her and so he'd put up with it.

Now it had come to a head.

Crimson grabbed Skye's wrist, and he heard Noah draw his weapon at the same time he did, Pete drawing his power and Bormick the dagger that had been Pete's.

"Look, they're all ready to fight for us," Crimson said.

Skye looked down at her wrist. "Not willing to share any more, Crimson? Wasn't that what you asked me to do every time I saw you?"

"I do believe I offered to just have it be you and me a few times, Skye."

"Now that would be something," Bormick mumbled.

"Get my wife's body out of your mind, Bormick," Mark said through gritted teeth.

"You had me once, remember? I believe that was your head between my thighs while Derrant was fucking you from behind," Skye replied to Crimson, ignoring them.

Mark's mouth dropped at the same time as everyone else's in the room. They hadn't talked about what she'd done when she'd been taken by Derrant that first time. His jealousy had made him avoid it, and the indiscretion with Crimson while under her influence had made them put it all behind them, except for the one time a year when it resurfaced.

"You are quite tasty."

"And you're quite good with your tongue." She leaned closer to Crimson and whispered, "But Mark's better."

If it hadn't been so tense in the room, the scene would have had Mark incredibly turned on. Judging from Bormick's stare, he was.

"Now, are you ready to put this behind us?"

"But it's so fun to play with you, Skye, and Mark gets so worked up."

"Crimson."

She let go of Skye's arm. "Fine. Don't touch either of my men, and I won't touch Mark."

"Good."

"But that doesn't mean—"

Skye brought her finger to Crimson's lips. "Don't even."

Crimson's tongue licked her finger seductively. God, he didn't know why this was arousing him so much. He looked away, his eyes landing on the bulge in Bormick's pants. Great, every man in the room was worked up. He glanced around to see Trent and Camin lingering quietly in the corner, a grin filling Camin's face.

"Gross," Skye said, pulling her finger away.

Crimson let out a laugh. "Oh, Skye, I do love these banters we have. I promise I won't torment Mark. But you are free to watch or join later," she said with a wink.

"Do you ever think about anything but sex?"

"No, it's too enjoyable not to think about all the time. Mark's thinking about it right now, as is every man in this room because, secretly, they all want to see the two of us go down on each other. They're men, Skye. Even your precious husband would watch that and let you finish him off once you come."

Skye brought her hands to her hips while Mark scowled, trying to cover the fact that the image had been there.

"She's not wrong," Bormick said. "It would be quite the turn on. Now that would be something I'd willingly share her for."

"Shut up, Bormick," Pete grumbled. "You already share her."

"I'm not sharing with him," he said, gesturing to Mark.

"Not asking to share," Mark said, putting his hands in the air and realizing how tightly he was clutching his weapon.

"We'll borrow for the night, though. Or maybe the three of us can just watch," Bormick said with a laugh.

Pete turned to Bormick as Mark felt Noah's hand on his shoulder. "Don't," he whispered.

Mark had been about to storm over and deck him, but Pete grabbed Bormick's shirt, getting in his face.

"That's enough," he growled.

Bormick seemed to grow about a foot, the two staring each other down, testosterone and adrenaline filling the room.

"Are we done, Crimson?" Skye asked.

"Damn, I guess so. Pete, Bormick, stop fighting. Mark, you're sexy and amazing to fuck, but I have plenty to keep me occupied. I guess no more fun banter like the old days."

"Seriously, Crimson?" Skye said, the anger showing in the darker shade of her eyes. "Your fun banter has every weapon drawn."

"And every dick hard," Crimson teased.

"You two are disturbed," Noah muttered. "That is not a normal relationship."

"Do we have a relationship, Skye?" Crimson asked.

"Eh, I'd say it's similar to the one those two have," she replied, gesturing to Pete and Bormick, who were still staring each other down.

"You can't imagine how good the sex is when they're angry at each other."

They both looked sharply at Crimson.

"Later, boys. We have serious business to address." Then, before any of them could react, Crimson grabbed Skye's neck and kissed her. "One of these days, love."

Skye looked shocked as Crimson let her go, but recovered quicker than Mark did. He had to lower his hands to cover the firmness that had re-emerged.

"Really, Crimson? We get to a point where we're okay and then..." Skye threw her hands up.

"You love me, cousin," she replied, with an impish grin.

"As stimulating as all this has been, and I mean that in every sense of the word, can we please talk about whatever storm is coming?" Trent said.

"He's right, Crimson. Enough teasing Skye," Pete affirmed. "We need to tell them what you know."

"I'll kick your ass later," Bormick said to Pete.

"I look forward to it."

"Fine," Crimson said. "Mark, you're not going to like this."

"As long as it doesn't involve you touching me, I'm fine with it."

Crimson's laugh filled the room. "You enjoyed every minute of it, Mark. But I can guarantee this you won't like."

Skye shot Crimson a look. "What is it, Crimson?"

"There's something coming. Derrant won't say what it is, only that he and Eliana are unable to interfere and that their children must fight."

"Children?" Skye repeated.

"You and me as Eliana's kin, and Pete and Bormick as his. Mark as your Elite warrior, touched by Eliana's magic. The five of us will face whatever is coming."

"Only the five?" Trent asked. "What about the mages or the other Elite?"

Crimson shook her head. "He was very specific. The Mage Warrior, the Shadow Mage, the Conduit Mage, the Elite, and the warrior."

"Conduit Mage?" Mark asked.

"Yes, me." Crimson lifted her hair from her neck, then reached a hand toward Pete and Bormick. Bormick walked over, drew his dagger and punctured her finger.

"What the hell?" Mark muttered.

She squeezed the blood forward before pressing her finger to her neck. When she removed her finger, a birthmark took shape, sparkling a crimson hue.

Mark's hackles raised and every nerve in his body tensed. "A Mage Warrior mark? What the hell is going on?"

"It's my link to Derrant. My way to call him. He imbued me with the ability when I was born, and my soul was marked as his. Daddy liked power, you see."

Her nonchalance took Mark aback. He remembered her mentioning it in the same way when she'd held him captive. The reminder of what her father had traded his own daughter's soul for had given Mark a new perspective of her.

"Don't give me that pity look, Mark," she said, catching his eyes, hers a deep shade of green. "I've come to accept it. Having the Death God as a lover on the cusp of womanhood taught me everything I know. I don't fear being his when I die. I've always belonged to him."

Skye appeared taken aback but didn't comment. Instead she asked, "Why are you showing us this?"

"I thought it was only my way to call him or he to call me. He showed me that it's much more."

"When you took my place?"

"Yes."

"Thank you for that," Mark said, feeling obliged to be the first one to say it. He still didn't like Crimson, but what she'd sacrificed for Skye and him was something he couldn't pay back.

"It's nothing. Derrant enjoys my touch and the fact that I'm more willing than Skye."

Mark looked to Pete and Bormick for a reaction. "That doesn't bother you two?"

"I wouldn't say that," Pete replied, pressing his lips together in a grim frown.

"Crimson sent us a plaything to break up the days and relieve my swollen balls," Bormick added.

Skye scrunched her face in disgust and Pete gave them an apologetic look.

"I can see why you and Crimson get along so well now," Mark observed.

"Don't pretend your dick wasn't aching after five days, Elite," Bormick retorted.

"My dick is none of your business and it's commander, not Elite." Bormick tried to stare him down, but Mark only glared back at him.

"Can you boys behave while I finish here?" Crimson said.

"Yes, please," Pete gruffly agreed.

Mark ignored Crimson's request, asking Pete, "How do you put up with him?"

"With a great deal of patience."

Bormick let out a bellowing laugh. "Pete loves me. One of these days, he's going to suck my cock while Crimson fucks him."

Pete's fist broke the awkwardly uncomfortable moment as it met Bormick's jaw.

Bormick kept laughing.

"I swear to you I will hide her from you if you don't shut the fuck up, Bormick."

"Crimson, can you control your entourage long enough for us to get to the point? As amusing as all this is to watch, and I'm always open to watching what happens behind closed doors, unlike Mark, I doubt the storm Derrant is speaking of will wait for them to settle their rivalry. Or perhaps unadmitted lust for each other," Camin said.

Mark bit his lip to hold back the laugh as he heard Noah snicker.

"That's exactly what it is, Pete," Bormick said, rubbing his jaw. "Your punch is weak, ass."

"I was holding back. Next time, I won't."

"See? He loves me."

"Do you not see the look Crimson is giving you right now, Bormick?"

"That's the hot sex later look."

Pete looked ready to kill the brute. "Jesus Christ, Crimson, just explain it to them, or I swear he's sleeping alone tonight," he griped.

"That's intense," Skye said to her. "Is that a daily thing?"

There was something in the way she said it. Mark knew that voice, she was aroused, and he wasn't certain what to make of it. He couldn't judge her, not after the tent he'd had in his pants when she'd been bantering with Crimson.

Crimson's lips curved in a mischievous grin. "Oh, yes, it is. Sometimes they fight right before they take me. Now that's intense."

"I'm about to throw the whole lot of you out if you don't tell us what the hell that Mage Warrior mark means to us!" Mark yelled, tired of the antics, even if they were entertaining. He'd pay money to see Pete beat the shit out of Bormick. "And what the hell is a Conduit Mage?"

"I am," Crimson said. "Watch." She looked back at Skye. "Do you trust me?"

The hairs stood on Mark's neck, and he put his hand on his weapon.

"Yes."

"Skye," he said cautiously. Pete and Bormick looked at each other, then flanked the women so that Bormick was standing behind Crimson and Pete behind Skye.

Mark rolled his neck, his discomfort with the situation

bringing tension to his muscles. But it was Pete, and he trusted Pete over Bormick. The feel of Skye's magic touched the air, and he drew his weapon in response to her stunned expression. Noah did the same. Mark raised his but Pete and Bormick drew their swords, Bormick holding the dagger in his other hand.

"Don't do anything stupid, Mark. Trust her," Pete said.

"I don't trust her. That's the issue."

"Then trust me. I won't let anything happen to either of them."

The touch of magic faded, and Skye glanced back at him before looking at her hands. Mark tensed, but she seemed calm.

Skye brought her finger to Crimson's birthmark which Mark saw now matched the color of Skye's. She dropped her hands, looking curiously at Crimson and asked, "What did you do?"

"She bled your power again. Dammit!" Mark brought his weapon down, meeting Pete's and Bormick's, the sound clinging through the silence. Bormick growled and the feel of Pete's Shadow Magic touched Mark's skin.

"She's fine," Pete gritted.

"He's right, Mark. I'm fine." She lifted her hair to reveal that her birthmark was sparkling like Crimson's.

"I didn't bleed her power. I copied it."

He relaxed, Pete and Bormick doing the same, all three lowering their weapons. He gestured to Noah to lower his weapon, Trent and Camin pulling back their magic.

"That's what Derrant showed me. I am a conduit for other magic. I always have been. I just never understood how to use it, thinking I had to steal it."

"It's tied to your birthmark?"

"Yes. My line once had magic. Derrant tasked the two brothers whose lines Pete and Bormick hail from to guard my ancestor and protect her magic. They didn't and the Upper God stole it, draining the potential from my line. That's why Derrant punished them. When her magic was stolen, it left a shell, an empty trace of the birthmark. My connection to Derrant gives me the ability to fill it with any mage magic."

The idea of Crimson running around with Skye's magic horrified Mark. "How long does it last? And does it give you equal ability?"

"I don't know. I think a few days, and yes, what Skye has, I have for however long."

"Shit," Mark said.

"That's not reassuring to any of us," Noah commented.

"But I can also do this." She made a movement, magic pouring from her in a strand that landed against Skye's skin, then faded.

"You returned the connection," Skye stated.

"Exactly."

Pete's eyes grew larger. "You're right, Skye. It is some sort of connection. I couldn't place the feeling. I could sense something, but there was no difference to my magic."

"She's done that to you?" Mark asked.

"Yes."

Skye fingered Crimson's neck, which was now bare, the birthmark gone.

"It fades. It becomes black when I copy Pete's power and—"

"Violet when you have mine."

"And crimson with Derrant's tie."

"I don't like this," Mark complained. His senses were tingling, the hairs still high on his neck. "If Derrant showed you this ability, it can't bode well."

"That's exactly what I said," Pete added.

"And I agree. What are we facing that needs a Mage Warrior, whatever Pete is, and Crimson's new ability?"

Mark gaped at Bormick. It was the first intelligent thing he'd heard the man say.

"Just because I look like a brute and talk about sex non-stop doesn't mean I'm dumb, Elite."

Mark scowled at the name.

"He's right, Mark. He's surprisingly smart, and he's sharp when it comes to strategy. Even if he does resemble a neanderthal at times."

Mark laughed at the comment. Bormick asked what a neanderthal was and when he received no answer, he said, "I wasn't the most renowned thief in the kingdoms through luck."

"What do you need from us?" Mark said, moving on.

"I need Skye to train me to use her magic."

The suggestion sent Mark's instincts tingling in a way he didn't like. "No," he said before Skye threw him a look. He bit his tongue, gripping his fists.

"Derrant was clear. It's imperative that I learn to use Pete's Shadow Magic and hers. He was particularly adamant about Skye's."

"And there's that feeling that I don't want to know what's coming again."

"She needs to learn, Mark," Pete said.

"If the Death God is concerned enough to teach her, you should be concerned enough," Bormick said, and Mark looked at him in surprise.

"Skye?" Crimson said.

Skye looked at Mark, then back at Crimson.

"I don't know. I need...I need to talk to Mark and my council. I need some time."

Crinkling her brow, Crimson said, "We may not have time."

Mark's heart dropped, his nerves heightening with the tone in which she'd said it. Whatever was coming, he didn't want Skye anywhere near it. A sense of foreboding drifted through him as he realized he likely wouldn't have a choice.

SKYE

Skye didn't know what to say about any of what had been revealed. From the bickering between Pete and Bormick to the birthmark, all of it was making her head spin.

"I need a few..."

Crimson shot her a look that said it was now or never. She glanced over at Mark.

"Minutes," he said, stepping in. "Give us a few minutes at least. You just wasted thirty minutes bantering with Skye about me and them. I think you can spare a few minutes."

"We can," Pete answered for Crimson.

Skye gave him a thankful look, which he returned with a warm smile. Pete had a beautiful smile that would have had her swooning if she didn't have Mark. It did, however, stir something deep in her belly that she pushed aside, not certain she wanted to know what it was.

Bormick pulled a seat from the meeting table and sat, propping his feet on the table. "We'll wait in here."

"So, I guess that means we'll go out...in the hall...to discuss the fate of the world," she grumbled. "You just make yourselves at home."

Pete slapped Bormick's feet down as she and Mark followed the others out. Their relationship was an odd one, and it still amazed her that it seemed to work and that neither of them had killed the other yet.

"Can I carve that one up?" Mark said, his hand on hers.

"Shh," she said, kissing him.

"They're an eccentric crew, aren't they?" said Trent.

A wicked smile formed on Camin's face as he added, "I have a feeling their bedroom is quite entertaining."

"Can we focus on the issue? You're not seriously considering this, are you, Skye?" Mark asked.

"I am."

All four of them erupted, but she put her hand up. Mark was the only one who didn't heed it. "Absolutely not, Skye."

"Mark—"

"No, you cannot give her access to your magic."

"She won't hurt me."

His face reflected his disbelief.

"Look, I know you're trying to keep me safe—"

"It's my job as your commander and your husband, Skye."

The fierce determination in his eyes warmed her heart, but she would need to break it.

"If she were going to do something, she wouldn't have asked. You heard Derrant. He gave us the same warning and now he's armed her."

"Why?" Camin asked.

They turned to him.

"Why tell her now? Why not years ago?"

Noah shivered, "That's a terrifying thought."

"Exactly," Camin agreed. "He knows she's changed. Those two men in there, even that brutish looking one, have given her a foundation. They've grounded her so that she's no longer the same queen we once knew. She's ready now where she wasn't before. I'm hesitant to do so, but I agree with Skye."

"Really?" she asked, hearing the higher pitch of her voice.

"The Death God doesn't share information, and he certainly doesn't warn mortals of impending doom."

"He's arming her to fight alongside Skye," Mark said.

Camin nodded. "Yes, I believe so."

"Two daughters of the shadow goddess, but their abilities are so different," Trent observed. "Or maybe not so much."

He and Camin shared a look.

"What?" Skye asked, not certain she wanted to know what was going on their minds.

Trent went on to explain, "You bleed hues; she bleeds magic. Neither of you have power until you've bled either color or magic. Your abilities lie in the same sphere, the outcomes different."

She met Mark's eyes, seeing the worry in them. "Something's coming."

"And I can't protect you." The sadness in his voice broke her heart, but this wasn't the time nor the place to discuss it.

"What's your answer, Skye?" Noah asked.

She took Mark's hand. "Yes, I'm doing it."

His head lowered, and he squeezed her hand.

"Let's tell them, then. Before they start having sex on our meeting table," Camin added.

She scrunched her face in disgust. "Ew."

Mark lifted his head, a sly grin forming. He winked at her, and heat rose within her. They'd had their fair share of sex on that table, but neither was willing to share that tidbit.

She turned away, hiding her smile as she opened the doors. Expecting to find a scene, she was relieved to find Crimson seated on Bormick's lap, no body parts to be found. Pete stood in the corner, his arms crossed, and she couldn't help but notice the tightness in his pants. The definition, which was quite prominent, sent a quick comparison of size through her head. She scolded herself and looked away in time to see Bormick remove his hand from under Crimson's skirt and lick his fingers, the reason for

Pete's interest now as evident as the bulge in his pants. Skye bit the inside of her cheek to keep from saying anything.

Her cheeks flushed, eyes glossy, Crimson said, "You could have taken a few more minutes."

It irked Skye that she'd been fooling around with Bormick while they'd left the room.

"We're not here for your sexual pleasure, Crimson," Skye said, regretting the words as soon as they left her mouth.

"Oh, but you could be." Crimson kissed Bormick, a little too long, and Skye saw his hand grab her breast.

"That really doesn't bother you?" Mark asked Pete again.

Pete gave him a lopsided grin that was seriously cute on him. "Not one bit."

Mark shook his head, and Skye didn't blame him. She wasn't sure she'd ever understand the three of them.

"When do we start?" Crimson asked, wiping the corner of her mouth with her finger.

Skye scowled at her. "You don't know my answer."

"I know that you know Derrant well enough to understand this is serious and from the worry lining Mark's sexy features, I can tell you've agreed to it."

Mark made a feral sound she'd never heard from him before. The sound sent that warmth rushing through her again.

"You might want to make that sound in the bedroom, Mark. Judging from Skye's reaction, she's wet and you two likely need a few hours before we get started. I know you have the stamina of my men."

"I really don't fucking like you, Crimson," Mark growled.

"Get your head out of my arousal and back to the conversation, Crimson," Skye said, hearing the edge in her voice. There was so much pent-up aggression and sexual tension in the room that, for a moment, she contemplated ripping Mark's clothes off and taking him right there. She didn't care if they watched, she wanted him. Her thighs tightened at the thought. Maybe she did care if Bormick watched, but the thought of Pete watching increased the wetness she knew was there. She caught his eyes and the blue of them glinted as if he'd heard her thoughts. God, had he seen her check out his erection, too? She looked away, hoping the warmth in her cheeks wasn't a blush, as Bormick spoke.

"I think we need a few hours as well," he said, cupping his erection. "And, Skye, the idea of your arousal definitely didn't help that any, nor did it help Pete's." His laugh boomed through the room.

"I think I've had enough," Trent said. "Let me know if you need help later, Skye."

Camin gave a bow, a delighted smile on his face. "As fun as this has been, I think it's my time to leave. I have a certain human who sounds delectable after all this foreplay."

The two left, but Noah—the ever-present protector—stayed.

"It's fine, Noah. She's not in danger, at least any that I can't protect her from."

"I'll be outside."

The door closed, and the five of them stared at each other. Bormick rose and wrapped his hands around Crimson's waist, dropping his head in her neck to kiss it. She giggled as if she were a schoolgirl and Skye couldn't help but stare dumfounded at the sound. It was such a strange dichotomy to the sultry woman she was.

"Who's getting laid first, Mark, us or you?" Bormick asked.

"No one," Mark said, crossing his arms. "Skye agrees to Crimson's offer, but with terms."

"They're going down on each other and we get to watch?" Bormick said against her neck.

Crimson elbowed him. "He's talking about my magic, Bormick. Stop tormenting Mark. I know he's sexy when he's angry like that, but I promised Skye."

Skye was irritated that they were back to this banter and gave a stern, "Yes, you did."

"What are the conditions?" Pete asked Mark, sounding like the only rational one of the group. "You'll be present the entire time? As will we, not only to protect them from each other, but from anything unexpected?"

"Exactly."

"Good, then it's settled," Pete said.

"Take your man and please him, Skye," Bormick directed. "He's entirely too uptight."

God, how she wanted to do that right now, but she wouldn't admit it to Bormick and add fodder to his thoughts.

"Noah!" Mark barked, causing Noah to rush through the door. "Please take them to one of the servants and have them shown to a room."

"Do we really have time for this?" Pete asked.

"Get it out of your system now—the sexual comments, innuendos, and touching do not enter my training grounds."

Bormick didn't give Pete time to argue. "That sounds good to us. Shall we say when the sun reaches its mid-day peak?"

"Yes," Skye agreed, knowing she wouldn't be able to concentrate if she didn't have a piece of Mark first. She hoped her answer didn't sound too desperate.

Bormick and Crimson left to follow Noah, and Pete threw them an apologetic look on his way out.

The moment the door closed, Mark grabbed Skye, kissing her ferociously. She returned his kiss, wanting him with a fire that had been smoldering and was now ablaze. The burning within her only intensified with his kiss. She yanked at his shirt as he picked her up and placed her on the table, pushing her skirts up. His hand rushed below them to feel her arousal. He let out a groan when he reached it, tearing her lace underwear so hard she heard the material rip. She rarely wore them, but today had felt the urge. She was glad she did, knowing they were soaked after all the verbal foreplay that had occurred.

"I liked those," she mumbled between kisses.

Her hand worked his hardened length free, stroking it while Mark lowered the top of her dress and caressed her breasts.

"Too bad. I like you without them."

"No more panties it is," she said a bit too breathlessly.

"God, I want you," he said before his mouth met her breasts, his tongue licking around her nipple tauntingly.

She tipped her pelvis and guided him in, a pleasured sigh escaping with the feel of him when a thought occurred to her. She pushed him back gently, but he pulled her closer, penetrating deeper.

Trying to ignore the stimulation his movement had given her, she asked, "Are you this worked up because of the conversation with Crimson?" Her body was on fire with the fullness of him, but she had to know the answer.

He stopped his movement, drawing back to look at her. "Really, Skye?"

"It's not an unreasonable question, Mark. She's sexy, every-thing about her screams sex. She even had me wet. You know her, you've...had her. It's a valid question."

There was a flash of anger in his eyes. She'd moved past that time, accepted what he'd done, she'd been forced to do the same thing as he when she'd been with Derrant, but Mark had never forgiven himself.

"It doesn't bother me, Mark. If you want to go down to their room and join them, we can."

His anger turned to curiosity. "Is that what you want?"

"I'm not particularly keen on seeing another woman touch you, but if that's what you want, then yes."

He shook his head and gave her a small chuckle.

"God, I love you." For a moment, her heart ached because that was what he'd wanted, what was driving this sudden sexual intensity. "There's only one woman I want, Skye. That's you. Your body is the only one I want around my erection, which you're killing with this conversation, I might add."

And with those words, her heart was healed.

"Then what brought this on?"

He brought his lips to hers, running his tongue along her bottom lip, his hand encompassing her breast and bringing her nipple back out to play.

"Partly the conversation and, if you must know, the idea of the two of you was very hot."

She inhaled sharply, feeling his firmness twitch inside her. His pelvis pushed deeper as he resumed his motion.

"But that would involve me sharing—"

"I'm not touching another woman, Skye. Your body is the only one I want."

"But you'd happily let a woman touch me."

"The image of her tongue against your clit is a sure way to make me come, Skye," he said as he squeezed her hips to thrust harder.

"While you take her from behind?" she grumbled. "As I suck one of them off?"

"You know, when you talk dirty like that, it does nothing to make me last longer."

He kissed her with a heat that tore through her. Deciding to let it go, she brought her legs up, and squeezed him so that he went deeper. Freeing herself from his hold, she lay back, her hair cascading behind her. The position gave him further reach, which he happily took advantage of. He held the back of her thighs and thrust with such force and speed that there was no slow buildup.

Every part of her ached for release. Their foreplay had been the words spoken in that meeting. The desire had built for each other when they'd been forced to listen and imagine. Her climax hit fast, overtaking her so that she was lost in it when he joined her. Their moans united, their bodies succumbing until he thrust once more, the final effect of his orgasm ebbing.

She lay there on the table, staring at the ceiling, her body numb from the intensity. Kissing her leg, Mark let his fingers drift along her skin softy.

"Are you done fantasizing about me with another man?"

"Only if you're done fantasizing about me with another woman," she countered.

"I told you long ago, I'm up for that any time."

She sat up, dragging his lips to hers, and encircling his neck with her hand. "And I told you the same thing you told me. I don't play nice, and I don't like to share. That dick is mine and mine alone. Crimson had her chance at it just as the Death God had my body."

"You know, we technically both shared, just not the full experience."

"Damn."

He drew away from her and fixed his pants. As she pulled her dress back over her breasts and adjusted her skirts, he watched her. Seeing how his eyes were filled with love, she reached up and gave him one more sensual kiss.

Resting his head against hers, he said, "Let's take this to our room. Bormick was eye-fucking you too much that entire time and I feel that need to ravage you a few more times and claim that body with my mouth."

"Mmm, that sounds fun." She peeked at the sky. "We still have some time and since Crimson does nothing, but eye-fuck you, I think my mouth needs to do some claiming as well."

Giving her an impish grin, he grabbed her and drew her into his arms, picking her up in one swift move. "You walk too slow."

He carried her through the halls, and she distracted him with each step. As they approached their wing, he dropped her, shoving her into a shadowed corner and taking her against the wall. He left her breathless with the move, his aggression always stimulating her in ways that left her weak. When he was satisfied, he spread her legs and tortured her until she was convulsing against his hand, her own release echoing through the corridor.

They spent the next hour taking each other, depleting the arousal that had peaked in the meeting room, and releasing the hold the others had on them while they'd been together. They claimed their ownership of each other again as if the others had been a threat to their stability. Bormick was no threat. Though he did scare her. There was too much testosterone there, too much brute force. He was so opposite from Pete, who she wouldn't be opposed to experiencing if they ever did decide to share. There was something slightly tantalizing about his brooding presence, the way his eyes seemed to see straight into her. Then there was Crimson, always a shadow over them. Skye could never seem to be free of the shadow. Even after all these years, it hung heavy over her happiness.

BORMICK

ormick's eyes trailed down Crimson's body as it writhed under Pete's touch. She was maddening, and he tugged at his erection as he watched her lose it. He smiled, Pete entering her just as she screamed in pleasure, then pushing her to a second orgasm within minutes. He had to hand it to Pete, the man knew how to break a woman to a shell of desire. He had no jealousy as Pete spilled the remains of his orgasm into her, licking her nipple before meeting her lips. It was odd to admit, but there was no jealousy there. The bond was too tight.

"My turn again," Bormick said, looking at the window to check the time.

He shoved Pete aside and reached his hand between Crimson's legs, watching as she took Pete in her mouth, her tongue swabbing over their juices, then hovering on his head until he was fully erect again.

"Damn, I gave you a go alone with her. It's my turn," he said, shoving three fingers into her and watching her mouth fall from Pete's dick.

Pete glared at him, so Bormick pulled his fingers out and

deliberately licked them. The taste of Pete and Crimson's juices tingled on his tongue, sparking a current deep in his belly.

"You're quite tasty, Pete," he said, knowing it would irritate him.

He'd never fucked a man, but he knew that if Crimson asked, he'd bend Pete over and dominate him. He was raw sex—a walking god with those black markings on his arms and chest.

"Stop fucking me with your eyes, Bormick. You're making my hard-on shrivel."

"There's nothing about you that's shriveled, Pete," he responded, shoving his mouth over Crimson and tasting her. He reached up and grabbed Pete's dick, tugging it before he could react.

"See, nothing but hard cock there."

"You're a fucking ass, Bormick."

He let go with a smile, hearing Crimson laugh. "Mmm, I love you two."

"Yeah, you just like how we fuck you," Bormick said, flipping her over and pulling her further down on the bed. He caressed her ass, kissing it before taking his tongue and swiping it across her sprawled beauty. She moaned, accentuating his need for her.

Leaning over, he whispered, "Get on those sexy knees. I want you to suck Pete off while I fuck you, and I want you to come with us."

He drew back, his eyes meeting Pete's as Pete brought himself in front of her.

"I can oblige that request," she purred, pushing against his raging hardness. He was hoping he could last. Having watched the two of them had pushed his limits.

Pete tipped his head back with a groan. Crimson had wrapped her hand around his base and pulled him deep into her mouth. Bormick watched as Pete's dick moved in and out of her mouth, her tongue stopping to play along his tip.

"Jesus, Crimson," Pete said, breathlessly, his hand going to her head to push her back down.

Bormick had never known a woman who could take all of him down to the hilt, but Crimson did it with ease. He felt it each time and witnessed it when she took Pete.

His dick throbbed, and he spread her legs further. He wanted to be inside of her. Even if he knew he wouldn't last. Watching her on Pete wasn't helping.

"Damn," he muttered, Pete's eyes opening and meeting his.

"Stop getting off on my pleasure and make her come, Bormick," he commanded.

"I love it when you command me, *your highness.*"

Pete growled, but Bormick only laughed and worked his fingers into Crimson's warmth, finding her clit with his thumb and stimulating it. The little nub hardened under his touch and a quiver went through her. He slid his other hand across her ass, holding tight to her hips as he shoved his fingers into her again. She responded, her mouth moving faster against Pete.

"Shit," Pete muttered as she descended, then slowly rose back up.

Bormick wasn't going to make it. He needed release, *now.* Taking her hips in both hands, he tilted her pelvis, lining her up so that when he penetrated her, he slid right into her waiting warmth. He was so close, and she so wet that he came within minutes, filling her with a loud grunt as the waves of his climax overcame him. She moaned, her body quivering around him. She was about to break, and he'd missed it.

He gripped tight, moving through the remaining tide of his orgasm. Just as he was ready again, she fell apart, her mouth pulling from Pete with a cry. Her body was still trembling against Bormick as he continued to take her through it. His eyes were drawn to the slide of Pete's hand as it moved along his shaft until her mouth returned to him again.

Their rhythm continued, Bormick's need cresting again as he

watched Crimson's mouth move along Pete. He brought his eyes to meet Pete's desire crazed ones. The man nodded to him; the move flaming the building climax within. He pounded her, squeezing her ass with one hand, pushing her head down against Pete with the other. His eyes locked on Pete as he broke, Crimson's body shaking as her own pleasure peaked. The intensity threw him over the edge, his release drowning him.

Pete leaned back against the bed, Crimson's tongue coming out to lick the lingering drops from him before she collapsed. Bormick fell alongside her and pulled her against him.

"Shit, that was intense," Pete muttered, sliding down to lie on the other side of Crimson.

"Mhmm," she replied, leaning against Bormick's chest.

"How did I get so lucky to find you two?" she asked.

"It wasn't luck," Pete said, kissing her forehead. "It was—"

"Blood," she and Bormick said together.

Pete was obsessed with the notion that blood bound the three of them.

"So, what would happen if that blood ritual was ever reversed, Pete?" Crimson asked. Bormick let his hand drop to Crimson's breast and kissed her neck. "Would this be over?"

"No way. We're bonded now. I'm not going anywhere."

"Good." She reached up to pull Pete down for a kiss.

Bormick felt her reaction to the kiss, her nipple rising against his hand as Pete continued to make out with her. She was insatiable, and he loved that about her.

He brushed his finger across her nipple, hearing her purr. For fun, he reached down to feel Pete's rising erection, gripping it tight and tugging it to its full length.

"You're a dick, Bormick," Pete mumbled against Crimson's lips. "She may be stuck with me, but if that blood bond is ever broken, you're out of here."

"I don't feel you protesting, Pete. If anything, you're getting harder," he said, kissing Crimson's shoulder as his own length grew against her back.

Touching another man was a strange feeling, and one he'd never thought he'd enjoy. He gave himself over to the curiosity and continued to stroke until Pete grunted. He let go, moving to Crimson and gently playing with her, feeling her arousal increase. His other hand moved under her side, brushing Pete as they wrestled to take her breast.

Crimson's leg lifted to give him better access, and he slipped his fingers in. Sinking into her, he let her moisture coat them before he reached to Pete, spreading it over him. Pete cursed again. He was firm and a handful, his girth matching Bormick's. He didn't pull away, releasing a small groan as Crimson reached back and tugged at Bormick's length.

"Fuck her again, Pete," he whispered, tugging harder before letting go. Part of him wanted to continue, to feel Pete come apart in his hands, to know he'd controlled him, that he'd broken him, but he also wanted to take Crimson again. He wanted to slide into that firm ass of hers while Pete took her from the front, feeling Pete's length and movements against his.

The thought made him need it, but he needed her to take Pete first. Unable to resist, he gripped Pete once more, hearing his snarl as he tugged him, feeling the need there. Touching him stoked a fire deep in his belly, a reaction he'd never imagined having to another man, but one he couldn't deny. Crimson was soaked, his dick sliding along her folds to hit her clit. She was dripping still and very ready.

"Does that make you hot?" he asked against her ear, meeting Pete's eyes. They were a mix of anger and desire. Bormick licked his lips.

"Next time she's gone, you're gonna blow me while I jerk you off, then I'm going to bend you over just like I'm about to do to her."

The flash of need in Pete's eyes was quick before irritation replaced it. The look was fleeting, lasting only until Bormick rubbed the pre-cum from his head and the desire flared again.

Neither of them were interested in men, but something—likely that damned blood—drew them to each other and Bormick had a growing desire to see what it would do to their already intense sexual relationship. He released Pete and moved Crimson so that she straddled Pete. Then he pushed his fingers through her arousal, letting her soak them before wiping it on himself and up her ass. This wouldn't be their first time, and Crimson was quite adept at handling them both.

She was leaning over Pete, whose mouth was busy occupying her breasts. Bormick took Pete in his hands again before thrusting Crimson down around him. They both cried out at once.

He licked along her ass cheek as it rose and fell against Pete, his thumb working its way in to make sure she was relaxed and prepared to take him. The wetness he'd smeared on it from her arousal glistened, as did his dick, and hearing the two below him made it impossible to wait. He lifted her slightly, stilling their movement as Pete grabbed the back of her neck, pulling her down to kiss her.

Bormick wasn't a gentle lover, and she never expected him to be. He broke through the initial resistance and then shoved himself into her tightness, eliciting a cry from her. Slowly, he and Pete found their rhythm. The feeling of Pete's length against his through the thin barrier that separated them pushed him closer to release with each thrust.

"Don't even think about coming until I'm ready," she breathed out. The shake in her voice was enough to break Bormick, but he held on.

He leaned forward, his finger finding her clit. Pushing against Pete, he spread his fingers out to feel him each time he moved in her.

Pete snarled, but she said, "That's gonna do it for me so fast."

Bormick grinned at Pete. "I know what our girl likes."

He wrapped two fingers around Pete, his thumb still pressing against Crimson's swollen nub. Pete couldn't hide the reaction and went back to destroying her mouth, his fingers pinching and pulling at her nipples. The three climbed their peak together, but Crimson fell first, taking Pete with her, then Bormick as she tightened around them both. His climax flushed through him like a tidal wave of electric currents.

By the time they'd recovered, the sun had reached the time to meet the others. Crimson rose first and they both watched as she dressed, her walk a little wobbly. He smiled and elbowed Pete. "We did that to her."

Pete threw him dagger eyes, then rose over Bormick, hovering above him.

"You want me, Pete. It's that damned blood. If it's not with her, it'll be when she's with the Death God. It will happen, and I will dominate every inch of you."

"You could have warned me you were into men."

"I'm not, but you're like her. Now get the fuck off me. I'm the alpha in this relationship."

With a laugh, Pete rolled from him. Bormick met Crimson's eyes, which were twinkling with excitement.

"Oh, yeah, she wants it, too, Pete."

Crimson pressed against Pete and kissed him, her hands tracing his ink marks. "I wouldn't be opposed to it."

"I'm not letting his junk inside any of my orifices."

"You will one day, and I'll have you coming like she does when she's under me."

"I fucking hate you, Bormick."

"But you love me, too, *cousin*."

Crimson's fingers traced a particularly long inking on Pete's arm. "Should I leave you two to fight it out?" she asked.

Bormick rose, stretching. "We have more important things to deal with and from the looks of the sun position, I'd say we're late."

"Maybe later," she said with a with a sexy grin before making her way to him. Her arms came around his neck to lower his mouth to hers.

"Don't get him excited again, Crimson, or we'll be in here when the shit hits the fan."

Bormick stopped kissing her and peeked up at Pete. "You have strange expressions in your world. Why would shit be hitting anything but the ground?"

Pete sighed and proceeded to pull his pants up.

Crimson walked from his arms, gave Pete one more kiss, then headed out the door. A servant walking by couldn't avert her eyes as they landed on Bormick's length, her blush making him laugh.

"I'm not opposed to sharing," Crimson said playfully as the girl scurried by.

"Can we play with that hot Mage Queen?" he asked, grabbing his pants.

"I doubt she wants to play with you," Pete said.

"You never know. I could make her squirm against my mouth. I bet she tastes fantastic."

"Mark doesn't share Skye," Crimson said, peeking back, her eyes taking them both in hungrily as they pulled their shirts and shoes on.

"I'm gathering that. He's definitely the overprotective type."

"I would be, too, given what they've been through," Pete said in their defense as they walked down the hall.

Bormick shot Pete a questioning look. Pete was always the defender, never one to comment on the Mage Warrior. She was gorgeous and there was no way Pete hadn't noticed.

"Would you take her, Pete?"

"Crimson just addressed that—"

"No, she didn't. She stated a fact. Would you fuck her if Mark shared? There's no way you haven't checked that tight body out—the way her ass moves in those dresses she wears. Those eyes."

Crimson looked over at Pete, curiosity in her eyes. "Would you, Pete?"

"I have no desire to touch Skye."

"But you think she's sexy."

"Well, sure," Pete said tersely.

Crimson stopped and put her hand out to his chest to stop his progress down the hall. "What do you think is sexy about her?"

"Really? Why are you fixating on this?"

"Because you're too quiet about it."

"Bormick more than makes up for that with his big mouth."

"Damn, you want her bad. Do you hear that Crimson?"

She moved against Pete's chest, her eyes evaluating him. "Is it those eyes? She has bedroom eyes, doesn't she?"

"'Fuck me' eyes," Bormick added, thinking about the seduction that filled the navy in them.

"You two are sick. Mark and Skye are our friends—"

"Are they?" Bormick asked. "Because I guarantee Mark would slice me open in a heartbeat with that weapon of his if given the chance."

"And Mark is not my friend," Crimson added.

"Because you screwed him against his will."

"Not each time," she said, playfully.

"You two are insane. Yes, Skye is breathtaking and yes, I'd take her if we were all single and in a different life. And yes, she's probably on par with you in bed Crimson, you can tell because she has that look and Mark is too protective of her not to be. And yes, I've seen her ass in those dresses and those eyes that suck you in like she can see into your soul. However, I have no desire to act on those facts, and I can guarantee Crimson will never lay a finger on Mark."

His response left Bormick even more curious. "No desire? That tight body and all that power."

"You're unbelievable sometimes, you know that? Drop it, both of you."

Crimson dropped her hand and Pete stormed by. She met Bormick's eyes.

"He wants her," Bormick said.

Pete's irritation at the discussion wasn't normal, and it gave Bormick pause to wonder why. Pete clearly wanted Skye. Bormick couldn't blame him. Anyone who didn't would have to be out of his mind. And Bormick had seen the glances, the lingering looks. Which was why he found it so puzzling. He couldn't tell if Pete was defensive about it because he considered Skye a friend, or if there was something more to it.

"No question, although I'm not sure how I feel about that," Crimson said, echoing his thoughts.

"It's all right for me to want her, but not Pete?" he asked, throwing her an irritated look.

"As much as I play about it, I don't like the thought of either of you touching her."

"Hmm, I'll accept that answer." Bormick took her arm after grabbing a quick squeeze of her ass. "Come on, let's catch up with our broody Shadow Warrior. We don't want him too pouty when we meet the others."

"No, pouty is not a good look for him. Brooding, yes, but not pouty."

They caught up to Pete, changing the subject and turning his mood, or so Bormick hoped, as they made their way out of the castle and toward the training grounds. Crimson was right, brooding was a good look on Pete, but if ever pushed past it, Bormick had no doubt he would be terrifying.

PETE

Pete ran his hand over his face, falling behind as Bormick squeezed Crimson's ass. The man was going to drive him insane. He'd pushed his growing obsession with Pete, and Pete wasn't sure how he'd felt about it. Part of him felt depraved, the part that knew it had felt good, the part of him that was curious to a point.

Shit, he thought to himself, glad his sister had gone back to the other world to lead a normal life, not here to see his new life of sex, magic, and more sex.

His eyes lingered on Crimson's curves. Every inch of her drove him mad with desire. There was nothing like the sex he had with her. Ash had come close but that tie he had with Crimson made it deeper, spiritual almost. She was intoxicating, and he couldn't get enough of her, nor could Bormick.

His mind went back to that last position. He loved having her to himself, but Bormick brought an intensity to it. He was demanding, yet she listened. Pete clashed with him at times, but it only stoked the fire, driving the sex up a notch. When they took her together, she was so tight, so overwhelmed with pleasure, that he could barely hold it together.

Bormick hadn't helped, grabbing him like that, jerking him off, or at least attempting to. Pete bunched his fists at the thought, fighting against admitting it had felt good, damn good, especially with Crimson there.

He doubted he'd ever let Bormick touch him without her there, no matter what Bormick thought. But in the moment, it had felt good.

Pete shook his head, trying to get his thoughts from the act, knowing there was a bulge in his pants now. His mind went to the conversation in the hall. He didn't know what that had been about. Pressing him to think about Skye like that. He didn't want to think about her like that, no matter how gorgeous she was. She was Mark's and something about that made even thoughts of her off limits. He respected Mark and all the two had gone through.

But Bormick didn't, and he pushed at Mark's comfort level. Pete's, too. Pete had no explanation for why he felt defensive about Skye, protective of her, but the idea of Bormick thinking dirty thoughts about her bothered him. There was no particular reason to feel that way and he wasn't completely sure he understood why. But there was something he couldn't pinpoint, and it had nothing to do with the fact that what he'd told them was true—if he'd met her in the human world before she'd had Mark, he would have gladly taken that body and made it his. He'd felt the touch of her magic and could only imagine what she felt like when she was climaxing.

Good God, what had they done to him? He rubbed his face again, trying to clear her from his mind.

"Thinking about me, Pete?" Bormick teased, looking at the growth that remained in Pete's pants as they walked.

God, how he hated the man at times.

The midday sun distracted him as they walked closer to the training grounds. Skye and Mark were waiting. The Elite, Noah, standing with several other Elite close by. Guarding her.

"Close enough to defend their queen and take ours down," Bormick said under his breath, as if he'd heard Pete's thoughts.

"I don't think either of us will let that happen," he answered, falling in step with Bormick and flanking Crimson. All prior thoughts had now cleared from his head, keeping Crimson safe the only priority.

"About time you showed up," Mark complained.

"Judging from that flush on your wife's cheeks, I'd say you needed the time as much as we did," Bormick said. "Did you think about me when you—"

Pete moved swiftly, punching him in the side, halting his comments, his pent-up anger from earlier pushing him. Bormick grabbed him and had him in a headlock before he could react.

Drawing his mouth close to Pete's ear, he said, "You push it at times, Pete. I think I'll go rough on you next time."

Bormick liked to think of himself as the alpha. Pete let him believe it, but Pete's magic could kill him within seconds, which made him the true alpha.

He knocked Bormick back, elbowing him and slipping from his grip.

"Enough!" Crimson yelled. "Pull yourselves together, and Bormick, no more comments about Skye."

Pete rolled his neck, catching Mark's look of surprise at her words. Bormick's eyes flared a mix of annoyance and desire, and Pete threw him a look, trying to refrain from punching him again..

"Pull yourself together, Pete," Bormick said. "Wouldn't want to put a show on for everyone."

"I swear, I'm going to kill you one of these days," Pete growled.

Bormick grabbed the back of his neck, pulled him forward, and whispered, "Make sure it involves me with my head between Crimson's legs and—"

Pete jerked from his grip and growled again. "Don't even say it."

"Ah, you're so easy to fluster, Pete. You'd think you'd be thicker skinned by now."

Skye and Crimson were already talking, Mark looking on, all of them having moved beyond the episode between him and Bormick.

"So, what's so scary about Mage Warrior magic, anyway," Bormick asked as they moved closer.

"You've never seen a Mage Warrior in action?" Mark asked.

"No. Unlike you, I was not raised in a privileged castle."

"I wasn't raised in a castle," Mark snapped.

"But Elite usually are, Mark," Crimson said in Bormick's defense. "You and Skye are an exception."

"The only time we ever heard of them was in stories because they didn't leave their bloody castle until the mage wars killed them all. Can't be that strong if they all died."

Skye's head snapped and Pete could see the flash of power in her eyes. Feel it build in her.

"They died because Crimson's warriors betrayed them. My parents and Mark's were lost in that war, along with thousands of others."

"Including my parents," Bormick said with an edge to his voice. "While you were off hiding in another world, we were left to lick our wounds and move on."

"I'm sorry," Crimson said unexpectedly.

Pete was still trying to fathom what it must have been like for Bormick. He hadn't known, and clearly Crimson hadn't either.

"You certainly do leave a path of destruction in your wake, don't you, Crimson?" Mark commented.

Pete didn't know what to say in her defense. Mark was right. Crimson's decisions, her greed, her indifference to anything but herself, her power, and her kingdom, had impacted everyone here.

For a moment, she looked defeated. It was the first time he'd seen her that way and he wanted to protect her, defend her, and shield her from the words, but they were hers to bear. He glanced at Bormick, who was looking intently at Crimson, the woman he loved, despite the fact that she had taken everything from him. Pete was surprised he'd never said anything.

"She's not that person anymore," Bormick said.

Crimson looked up at Bormick, the sadness in her eyes tangible.

"She's changed. As have a few of us. The past is the past, Mark, and maybe that's where you should leave it like I have."

It was the first time he'd referred to Mark as anything but Elite. Mark studied Bormick, then gave him a brief nod.

"Skye, show him what a Mage Warrior can do. He's been craving your touch; let him have a taste," Mark said.

"He might like it," Crimson said, her voice still quiet.

"Knowing him, he likely will," Mark replied. "But don't get too excited, Bormick. She looks sweet and innocent, but she stings something fierce."

She looked anything but sweet and innocent, but Pete refrained from mentioning it.

"Are you flirting with me, Elite?" Bormick joked.

"Not on your life. You have those two for that."

Pete threw Mark a look. "I don't flirt with him." He was glad the mood was lightening, and he felt his shoulders relax some.

"Are you kidding?" Skye teased. "The sexual tension between the two of you makes me want to grab some popcorn and pull up a chair."

He gaped at her, but she only responded with a playful wink.

"What's popcorn?" Bormick asked. "Is it sex? Because if so, you can pull right up and watch while I assert my dominance."

Shaking his head, Mark said, "Jesus, you three are something. Skye, stay out of their play and show him what you can do."

"Please show me what you can do, Mage Warrior. I can't wait to feel you—"

"Bormick," Crimson warned.

"Skye, don't go easy on him," Pete said, knowing Bormick had no idea what was coming.

"This might hurt a little," she said.

"Good," Pete responded. "He likes it rough."

Skye's eyes twinkled, and he knew there was more to her in the bedroom. He couldn't help but wonder if she liked it rough, or if she was the dominating one. He had a feeling it was a mix of the two. She was too confident to be demure and reserved. He shoved the thought of it away, hoping Mark hadn't noticed his reaction to her, feeling the crooked grin he knew was on his face right now with the thought.

Crimson came to stand with Pete, and he wrapped his arms around her and kissed her head. Her very presence pushed the thoughts away.

She snuggled against him. "He has no idea what he's gotten into."

He pulled her closer, loving how she felt against him. She fit perfectly, like she was made for his body. She still felt small, vulnerable in that moment, as if the conversation had taken something from her, a part of that confidence he loved about her. But he also loved this soft side, the one only he and Bormick knew, or perhaps Skye did as well, and that's why she'd looked past the indiscretions, the scars that made her the enemy to so many people.

"I love you, no matter who you were," he whispered.

She reached up and kissed him as Bormick said, "That tingles, that all you got? It's turning me on."

Skye had summoned the black hue in Bormick's shirt, and it was weaving its way to her, leaving it a strange hue that wasn't quite gray.

"You sure you don't want to back away, Bormick?" Crimson asked.

"That's nothing," he returned confidently.

"Do you know why Mage Warriors were so valued in the kingdom?" Skye asked, a bit of seduction in her tone.

"To give the kings good blow jobs?"

Skye grimaced, but Pete caught Mark's chuckle until Bormick added, "I bet you give a good blow job, Mage Warrior, don't you? I can tell by Mark's face right now that you put Crimson to shame."

Mark's eyes narrowed, but Pete could tell from his reaction Bormick had guessed right. He couldn't imagine anyone giving head better than Crimson because she was amazing.

Crimson peeked up at him, then slid her hand back, brushing along the rise in his pants.

"Sorry," he whispered quickly, then yelled, "Bormick, get your head out of your pants and shut your mouth!"

"Why? She turning you on, too?" he teased.

"My wife's blow jobs are off the table for discussion and yes, she's enough to make you see stars. Now, Skye, tell him the answer."

Bormick laughed as Skye shot Mark a look. Pete felt Crimson giggle, her hand dropping from his pants even though he'd been enjoying her touch.

"It's because they have the power to bleed life from their targets. Only my line actually holds that power, the rest all stopping right on the edge of the essence."

The black hue danced across her skin, leading her to beckon for more hues. He'd seen her do it many times, but still found it mesmerizing. Her eyes sparkled, the blue dancing with her magic.

"Damn, that's hot," Bormick said. "You two must have some amazing sex."

His hand drifted through a stream of black that was coming from his shirt, the blue bleeding from his eyes.

"She's being gentle on you, Bormick. It's really a turn on when she bleeds the room as she's coming," Mark said, causing Pete's eyes to go wide.

His mind went to that image, and there was no taking it back.

A blush filled Skye's cheeks and she yelled, "Mark!"

"Oh, it really is," Crimson added.

Skye shot her a look. "This is taking too long, and you all are having way too much fun."

"Judging from Pete's hard-on, I'd say we're having just the right amount," Crimson teased.

"Crimson!" he whispered, but Skye's eyes were on him, her blush deepening.

Mark's eyes narrowed, and Pete gave him an innocent smile.

"Relax, Mark. I'll take care of it when we're through here," Crimson pressed.

Skye's eyes lingered on him, and he could have sworn there was a spark of something there before she looked away.

She increased her power until the streams grew faster. Pete saw the change in Bormick.

"What the fuck?" Bormick gasped as the color shifted from his skin, leaving it slowly paling.

"With each hue that flows to me, your life force flows with it, until nothing but an empty, soulless shell remains," Skye said.

Pete had never thought of it that way. He knew she could bleed a lifeforce, but a soul was sent to the Death God for judgement with her action. Her connection to the Death God was layered just as Crimson's was, and he wondered at that link and why it existed on so many levels.

Bormick's fists were clenched into balls, the tendons straining as he tried to remain upright, his eyes locked on Skye's. She released the hues, letting them slowly drift back to him, the tension escaping his form as his breathing returned to normal.

"I have the biggest hard-on right now," Bormick said.

Skye rolled her eyes, and Mark's mouth tightened. He was loosening up, but only to a degree.

"Think you can do that next time we fuck, Crimson? Pete, can you do that?"

"No, and no, I don't think having Crimson do that would be a good idea."

"Always so serious, Pete. So, you take color away and kill people, pretty neat trick, concise, no mess. Why is that something to worry about in Crimson? I mean, she's not going to kill you and she's had it before and didn't kill you, Elite."

"It's Mark," he grunted.

"I didn't know how to use it, other than what I knew from lower mage abilities," Crimson explained.

"Lower mage abilities?" Pete asked.

"Mage Warriors can do many of the things full mages do," Skye explained. "They just use color to enhance it."

Mark came to stand beside her. "The concern with Skye's magic is that she's the strongest of her kind. Her abilities are unprecedented. She can bleed color from everything all at once, bending the veil separating the realms. If she wanted, she could collapse the Shadow Realm and the Upper Realm into ours and, theoretically, every realm beyond those."

Pete was speechless. He had no idea she was that powerful, the power to truly release hell on earth was terrifying. He gaped at her, seeing her in an entirely different light.

"It happened—almost, when I was learning to use my magic."

"That was you?" Bormick asked.

"Yes. My powers are not timid."

Skye moved a hand, lifting the brown from the trodden ground below them, leaving it a shaded hue. Mark stepped back as the brown twisted around her. She brought her hand to the side, and it fled with a speed that sent a small building exploding. The pieces stopped midair, the color from them drawn before she directed them back to where they'd been, repairing the damaged stone until the building stood once again.

Wide-eyed, Crimson muttered, "I didn't know you could do that."

"There's a lot you don't know. My magic is very different

from Pete's. Plus, his powers are still growing. I can't imagine what he'll be capable of when he masters all aspects of it." She studied him as she said it, as if searching for something, her eyes serious.

"Now, do you see why we were so concerned about giving you access to Skye's power?" Mark asked.

"Teach me to wield it the right way," Crimson responded.

"Fine, but we need to change first. Dresses are not for training. And you might want to keep Bormick at bay because Mage Warrior training clothes leave a lot to be desired. I've made adjustments, but they're still skimpy as hell."

Pete remembered her training outfit and how much skin it showed. Seeing both of them dressed that way would be enough to break him, and he knew Bormick would be beyond turned on.

She pulled Crimson away, the three men left alone. Bormick and Mark stared each other down. Three alpha males left together, as if things weren't volatile enough.

"Make one comment about my wife's body and it won't be Pete you're fighting."

"Good, Pete's a pussy. I look forward to fighting a real warrior."

Pete stared at Bormick. "Did you seriously just call me a pussy?"

Mark raised a brow as they continued to stare each other down. "Are you two having sex with each other, too?"

"No, absolutely not," Pete protested.

"He wants to, though."

"I do not want to!"

"Admit it Pete, you've got a thing for my dick."

"I do not have a thing...it's in my face every two seconds. You can't help but see the damned thing."

"Yeah, you two might want to do something about that pent up tension," muttered Mark. "I'm sure Crimson will enjoy it."

"You're an asshole, Bormick."

The comment only earned Pete a wide grin. "I'm gonna be in your ass soon enough, Pete."

"Sometimes I think being back in the forest was less torment than a lifetime of you."

Bormick's laugh filled the air, and Pete wondered how either of them would make it together for the rest of their lives without killing each other.

MARK

Mark shook his head. Bormick grated on his nerves, but after finding out how his parents had died he'd softened his opinion of the man. He still didn't like him. Bormick's mind was always on sex, and the comments about Skye had irked him. But Mark was coming to realize that was Bormick's tactic, it was who he was. He used the persona to cover the person below. The gruff, over-masculine, misogynist warrior he wanted people to see. So, Mark had relaxed, adding to the banter, realizing like Pete, he was stuck with the man if they wanted to be prepared for whatever was coming.

Poor Pete. Bormick was surprising in his outward comments and the whispers. He would never have pictured Pete as the type to even consider a man, but the sexual tension between the two was distracting. Mark wondered if it was something with that blood pact that tied the three to each other. The two were still bickering when Skye emerged with Crimson.

She'd tweaked the training clothes some, but they were still tight, the pants hugging her ass and leaving a hint of camel toe. They sat low, leaving her belly exposed, hanging on the sexy curve of her hips. Hips he wanted to squeeze right now as he envisioned ripping the pants off her.

Her arms were mostly bare, the cut of the tight tunic still accentuating her breasts. The look caused his arousal to climb every time she wore it, and she knew it, giving her eyes a glance to where he was inadvertently pushing against the material of his pants.

"Damn," Bormick muttered, loud enough for all of them to hear.

Crimson walked beside her, but only Skye had drawn Mark's attention. He forced his eyes from her and took in Crimson's overtly sexual form. Her ample breasts were spilling over the top, her pants hugging the wider curves of her hips. She exuded sex with every step she took. She'd tied her red hair up, revealing a slender neck made for kissing, her green eyes seductive as she teased Bormick with a swipe of her tongue along her lips.

Jesus, she was something. Mark shook his head, focusing back on Skye, who was raising her brows at him. He shrugged, noticing her hair was piled atop her head as well, strands of it drifting along her neck, urging him to push them aside and kiss it.

Mark swallowed, gripping his weapon to keep from simply snatching her up and taking her a few more times.

"Focus, Bormick," Pete said, having trained with Skye before. The man looked rattled, though, seeing Crimson like that. Mark had noticed a few looks to Skye earlier, wondering at the intensity in his eyes. In that moment, Pete's eyes drifted from Crimson to Skye, lingering again as they'd done earlier, a shadowed flicker of desire in them before he covered it, his own brow furrowing before his eyes trailed back to Crimson.

He couldn't blame the guy, even if he didn't like it. Skye was stunning and irresistible. He'd often seen looks from his own men, and it was one of the reasons he kept her close, protecting her. She was the embodiment of a goddess and everything about her spoke of her power and beauty.

Mark's eyes fell to Crimson again, then looked away, knowing he didn't want to linger on her body, even though he knew what lie beneath the tight clothes, the way her body felt as it writhed in pleasure, the feel of that tongue against his skin. He cleared the thoughts from his mind. She was nothing compared to Skye, not her moves in bed, nor her looks, no matter how alluring she was.

Crimson smiled at Pete and looked like she wanted to go to them, but Skye grabbed her arm, stopping her. Mark caught the shift in both men's stances in reaction, Bormick's hand going to his weapon.

"No flirting. We train," Skye said firmly. "You can play later. You want to learn how to wield my power, then we need to work."

Crimson's lips formed a seductive pout. "You take all the fun out of it, Skye. Why wear this if we can't play?"

"Because it gives you movement. Trust me, it took me some time to get used to it."

"Not me," Mark said under his breath.

"I can see why," Pete said quietly to him.

Bormick stayed silent for a change, but the hunger in his eyes said enough. Unfortunately, his eyes were on both women and not just his.

"Fine," Crimson said. She brought her finger to her mouth and bit into it, drawing blood without a flinch.

"Ouch," Skye said, watching her activate her birthmark before sucking her finger.

"After a few visits to Derrant, you learn to tolerate the pain. You should know that, Skye."

The comment stung Mark, but he held back his reaction. The urge to see Skye slap Crimson was high and he flexed his hands as he imagined it. Skye restrained, however, disappointing him.

"Do what you need to do," Skye said.

Bormick hollered to them, "Is that an open invitation?"

"If you don't kill him first, Pete, I will."

"Again, I welcome the fight, Elite. I haven't had a fair one in quite some time. Pete's too easy."

A growl slipped from Pete, but Bormick responded first. "I do love it when you growl, Pete. It's like a feral mating call."

"Why you—" Pete punched Bormick, the move a solid one that landed square on his jaw.

Bormick spit blood from his mouth and rubbed his cheek.

"That was a pretty good hit, Pete."

"If I ever draw my power on you, Bormick, you won't live to respond."

"I know that, but you won't and that's what makes it fun. I'd say we're going to have some extremely rough make-up sex later."

Pete walked away, leaving Bormick with Mark.

"You pull that shit on purpose, don't you?"

Bormick gave him a big grin. "Definitely. He's strong, but he's not strong enough. Someone needs to break him, so he's indestructible."

"And that someone's you?"

"I'm the alpha for now. I'll take every advantage I can to remind him of it."

"What happens when he decides to show you he's the alpha?"

"Then I'll kneel for him. He is my king after all, and while I'm down there, I may even suck him off."

Mark wiped his hand down his face, trying to remove the image from his mind. "Had to turn it, didn't you?"

"Every time. Don't think Crimson's mouth won't be on mine while I'm down there."

"Good gods, you're unbelievable."

Bormick shrugged. "And he loves me for it, so does she."

"I think love might be a strong word."

"Not strong enough, Elite."

Mark bit back the desire to correct him and stood quietly as they watched the two women. Pete was standing across from them, his arms folded, while he studied their moves.

Crimson had Skye's magic now, but Skye still landed her with a not so graceful fall on her ass.

"Your mate is strong. I bet she's feisty in the bedroom."

"I'm not discussing my sex life with you, Bormick."

"Shame. Can Crimson handle her power?"

Mark turned away from watching Skye pull Crimson from the ground, surprised by his question.

"I don't know. I don't know enough about her abilities to judge."

"She hasn't mastered Pete's. She can hold it, but he says what she takes is a dimmer version of what he holds, leaving her weaker than him."

"Perhaps she's not meant to have what they have."

"Perhaps, or maybe she hasn't reached her full potential like Pete."

That was the second time Mark had heard Bormick say something like that. "How do you know Pete hasn't?"

"The same way I know the mage queen hasn't met hers yet."

Mark looked at him sharply. "Why would you say that?"

Skye had grown in power since the time she'd discovered her heritage. Mark's own strength had increased from their connection, as was the way with the Elite.

"Her aura's not complete."

He looked back at Skye, who was directing Crimson to pull hues. She looked the same as she always did.

"What does that mean?"

"Pete may have magic, but he's not the only one who inherited something from that blood ritual. I honestly never noticed it until the first time Crimson showed us that mark on her neck. I always thought Pete was just broody, that damned gray haze around him at times."

"You can see their magic on them?" Mark was stunned by the revelation.

"As sure as I can see that you're wearing a blue tunic. I don't always see it, but when their magic is drawn or something calls it, a mood change in Pete, your woman's desire for you, it shows. I've gotten so I don't pay much attention to it, but since Crimson's been playing with Pete's power, I've noticed her aura sits differently, as if it's incomplete. That's when I realized theirs looks that way, too. It skims their skin, but I don't think it's supposed to. There are points where it disappears like it's part of them and points where it doesn't. They don't have full use of it yet, none of them do."

"And that's why you said Pete was strong enough, but not strong enough?"

"Correct."

"What does that mean for them? For us?"

Bormick was quiet for a moment. "I don't know, but if the Death God is concerned enough to warn them of what's coming, and they haven't fully realized their power..."

Fear shot through Mark, his heart pounding at the thought of losing Skye to some unseen force.

"We'll lose them all," Bormick finished.

Mark was shocked, unable to respond, and Bormick didn't give him time to.

"Can you bend over for me like that again, Crimson? That ass is beckoning me," he shouted as he walked toward them. And just like that, the seriousness of the moment was gone, the deep, thoughtful man replaced by the horny brute.

Mark remained where he was, trying to see what Bormick saw, but to no avail. Skye had held her magic for over ten years, and they'd never noticed anything off about it. She'd spent ten years with Derrant and he'd never mentioned anything, nor had Eliana. So, what was it that Bormick saw? And what did it mean?

He made his way to Noah.

"I need to find Trent. Keep an eye on things here and if Bormick lays a hand on Skye, which I don't think Pete will allow... debilitate him."

An excited glow lit Noah's eyes. "With pleasure."

Mark made his way to the castle, hearing Skye's reaction as Crimson caught her off guard, a whip of red splashing against the foundation, shaking it slightly. His departure had distracted her, he was certain of it. She knew he wouldn't leave her side unless it was important, especially with Bormick and Crimson around. He didn't want to worry her. She needed to stay focused on training Crimson while he sought out answers.

Mark found Trent deep in the castle library, on the second floor, rummaging through books as he pulled them out, flipped through them, then put them back. He was on a ladder, hanging precariously over it as he reached for another.

Skye had insisted on a library, always the avid reader, and between her and Alex it had become a two-story room full of books Mark didn't think she'd ever have time to read, nor did he think she'd want to based on the size of the books Trent was picking out.

Mark climbed the spiral staircase to the second floor. Because, of course, Skye had to have one of those, too.

"You teeter any further to the right and I'll have to catch you, Trent."

"Ah, Markhem. This isn't usually your preferred place to visit," he said, coming down the ladder, much to Mark's relief.

Trent was a small man, scholarly, nerdy some might say, but Mark still didn't like the idea of catching him.

"Skye's currently occupied at the training grounds," he replied.

"With Crimson?"

"Yes," he sighed, "much to my dismay."

"I have the same reservations. But then, why are you in here rather than by her side?"

"Noah has her. I need to ask you about something Bormick just told me."

Trent cocked his brow. "That brute?"

"I'm finding he's more astute than he lets on."

"Really?"

Mark went on to explain what Bormick had told him, not sure if he understood it himself.

Trent was quiet for a moment, his fingers rubbing the scruff along his chin. "Fascinating. I've heard of mages who can sense that a person has magic, a sensation of sorts, but never anyone who could actually see it before a wielder has summoned it."

"Well, Bormick doesn't come from a magic line, only Pete's branch does. His ability is likely linked to whatever magic ran through the blood ritual and down through that line."

"Yes, the Shadow Magic is certainly unique and if Bormick comes from the same line, then any magic used in that ritual may very well be in his blood as well," Trent contemplated.

"I'm more concerned with what he observed. Could it be true that Skye's magic is incomplete?"

"I really don't know. The Mage Warriors were very secretive, never sharing with the other mage lines. And Skye is unique to others before her. We don't really know of what she's capable."

Mark ran his hand over his face.

"The warrior lair would likely have something," Trent suggested.

The warrior lair had been a hidden space where the Mage Warriors had once gathered. There had been lairs in each kingdom. Secret, hidden from the kings and queens and everyone else. Tunnels connected them, but the one in Kantenda had never been discovered, its entrance lost with the decimation of the kingdom by Theodore's line.

"I can't access that room and even if I could, we don't have an entrance here."

"Does Skye not know what you discovered?"

"No, she was training Crimson when he told me."

Trent was thoughtful for a moment. "You said Bormick mentioned Pete?"

"Yes, he said he saw the same on Pete and Crimson. Pete said Crimson's magic was a dimmer version of his when she took it."

"That very well may be. If she has only a copy of it, then it may be a distorted or weaker copy unless..."

"Unless what?"

"Unless it's that way until she fully reaches her abilities."

"Shit."

"I would venture to say you'll need to visit the mage lair, which entails a visit to Theodore's kingdom. Be sure to take the others with you."

"Oh, that's going to go over well."

"I don't think you have much of a choice. The five of you are bound in this, the three of them particularly. If they do not act as one, we stand no chance of defeating whatever storm is coming."

SKYE

A bsolutely not!" Skye raged. She stared at Mark, certain she must have misheard him..

He'd disappeared while she was working with Crimson, then reappeared noticeably more tense than he'd been, staying on edge the rest of the time. He'd waited until they'd returned to their room to clean up for a late dinner to tell her where he'd rushed off to.

"Skye, be reasonable."

"Reasonable? I'm the one who agreed to let Crimson use my magic to train her after convincing all of you. I've been very reasonable."

"Trent thinks there might be something there," he said adamantly.

"I'm not taking her there and I'm not going to Theodore for a favor."

They hadn't been back, leaving the mage lair behind, unable to access it from their kingdom. The entry point was now beyond their grasp. They'd left everything behind when she'd freed her people, including the book her mother had left her.

"Crimson is technically a Mage Warrior, Skye. Her birthmark is evidence."

Knowing he was right and not wanting to admit it, she sat on the bed in a huff. She didn't like the way Mark was on Crimson's side. The way he'd looked over Crimson earlier, had irked her. There had been a curiosity in his expression that had made her uncomfortable. Not until his eyes had fallen back upon her, had she felt better.

"What does Camin think about this?" she asked.

"I haven't talked to him yet. He went to Revina's kingdom when we decided to work with Crimson. Revina's already pissed that we gave Crimson back her throne and made peace with her. He went to warn her, to get her to look beyond her grievances."

"Crimson had her husband killed. I'd say she's allowed to have grievances."

"I know. Trust me, if it were you, Crimson would have died the moment she returned. It was hard enough not killing her for what she did to us."

Mark came over and stooped in front of her, taking her hands.

"You really believe what Bormick told you? That I haven't reached my potential yet?" she asked him.

She brushed her fingers through his thick brown waves, his hazel eyes warm and sincere.

"I do. I don't know what it means, but I wouldn't be a good commander or husband if I didn't find out."

Sighing, she caved, knowing he wouldn't ask if he didn't feel it was necessary.

"I don't like the idea of asking Theodore for any favor," he said, "but it's the only way to access the lair."

She thought about it, what she remembered from learning about the space. From wandering through it, into one of the corridors when they'd first arrived. "Is it?"

"What are you thinking?"

"Your uncle said there were connections, that each kingdom

had its own secret room and that they were all connected. And I saw that. The room grew, each lair merging into one large room when I was present."

A crease formed in Mark's forehead as he thought about it. "But we haven't located an entrance here in Kantenda."

"No, we haven't, and I'd venture to say the one in Pete's kingdom is lost as well, but not Crimson's."

"There's one hidden there," he mused. "I'll be damned. That would make sense."

"I suppose it's time to share the secrets of the Mage Warriors."

"I'd say it is, but not until the morning," he replied, standing. "You need to be fed. Your stomach is talking louder than me."

Laughing, she pulled the hand he extended so that she could bring him down for a kiss. Wrapping her hand through his hair, she parted her lips, allowing his tongue entry to explore her mouth as he pushed her further onto the bed, hovering above her.

"That was a dangerous move, my queen," he said, playfully nipping at her lip before letting his tongue run along it.

"I'm already playing with fire. What's a little more?"

He kissed her again, his hand moving her shirt up to feel the skin below, his touch as always driving her for more.

"I thought this was a quick clean up then dinner?" he asked, pushing his swollen growth against her body.

"I can guarantee it won't be quick and I think I want dessert before we eat."

"Skye, you are relentless."

"I know," she said, bringing her hand down to feel him.

His eyes filled with desire as she slipped below his belt and stroked his length.

"I want to taste you," she said.

His lips turned to a lopsided grin. "Any time you want, my dear."

She pushed him onto his back, straddling him, and meeting

his erection between her legs, the material suddenly too restricting between them.

Leaning over, she worked his shirt off, kissing his chest, her tongue licking each contour, the muscles below tensing each time. His hands pushed at her tunic, freeing her breasts before capturing them as she took her hair down, letting it topple around them. He threaded a hand through it, bringing her mouth to his and exploring it as his hands explored her breasts. She was on fire, each touch enticing, stimulating, and she felt the dampness seep from her.

Releasing his mouth, she moved from his hold, unbuttoning his pants, then sliding them off before standing over him and removing her own.

She loved looking at him. There wasn't any inch of him she didn't desire, the muscles that defined him, and the one that was fully erect, waiting for her to claim it again.

Sliding along his legs, she greeted it, her tongue draping up his shaft before pulling his head in and delicately letting her tongue caress it.

"God, I love you," he muttered as she dropped lower. He weaved his hand into her hair, tightening his grip the lower she went. He was large, but she was well-adept at taking him, working him far into her throat before gliding back up, her tongue adding an extra layer of seduction. She continued to break him with her mouth and her hands, feeling his release mounting, her own desire flaring with each groan he elicited. His muscles began to tighten until he lost control, spilling into her mouth in long streams. She swallowed, loving the taste of him, the feel of him losing control to her touch.

"Christ, Skye," Mark mumbled as she dropped her mouth down around him once more, making sure she didn't miss one drop.

Skye coaxed him back up again, knowing she still wanted to feel him inside of her. Her body rumbled with need. When he was firm again, she slid her body along his, currents of arousal whipping through her as their skin touched. Grabbing her, he smashed his lips to hers, his kiss needy. Breaking him with her mouth always worked him into a demanding frenzy, like he needed to assert his dominance after having lost control under her power.

His tongue was aggressive, but his fingers were gentle on her breasts, caressing and rubbing her nipples until she could hardly stand it. Skye moved to lower herself on him, but he stopped her and rolled her to her side. His one hand continued tormenting her breasts, the other sliding between her legs. He slipped his fingers into her, his moan at discovering her wetness driving her mad.

He pushed her leg up, bending it to let his fingers dip in again, gliding two deep into her. Heat scorched her, and a cry escaped. The pleasure Mark was giving her had her body enraptured and she tilted her head back, uncertain if she could take much more. His mouth took her breast, his tongue teasing like she'd done to him, and she slid her leg down, clenching tightly around his arm in reaction. One finger was taunting her sweet spot as the other two continued to plunge in and out of her until she could take no more, her body giving over to the current that swept her away, her climax soaring deep through her core, leaving her weak and breathless.

Mark's hand released its hold on her, and he brought it up to his mouth, licking each finger as if he needed every drop of her for sustenance. Pushing Skye to her back, he pulled her leg up around him and entered her, that demand returning. Each thrust called to the remnants of her orgasm until she was lost in the rising tidal wave. Clinging tightly to him, her legs wrapped around him, forcing Mark deeper as his hand dipped her pelvis to send him even further.

A lifetime seemed to pass where just the two of them existed. The outside world, the impending doom—everything disappeared until finally the arousal grew to a peak she could no longer surmount, and she fell, her body trembling with the force of the orgasm. Mark's body tensed as he fought to meet her climax, both of them tumbling to the abyss below.

He dropped his head to hers, and she felt one final small push from him, the last of it sent into her welcoming body. They stayed that way until he gave her a gentle kiss, saying, "I love you, Skye."

She put her hands on his cheeks to look into his breathtaking hazel eyes. "I love you, too, Mark, and everything you do to me."

Giving her a playful smile, he asked, "Not tired of me yet?"

"Are you tired of me?"

He brought his thumb to her mouth, smoothing it over her lips, letting it linger in the corner. "Tire of that mouth? I'd have to be insane."

"So, you only love me for my mouth?"

"Don't try that on me, but that mouth of yours definitely ups the keepability threshold," he replied with a grin before lifting himself from her.

Bringing herself to her elbows, she asked, "Keepability?"

His eyes perused her body. "That body ups it as well."

She stuck her tongue out at him.

"And that tongue, don't even get me started on that."

"I could say the same about your tongue."

"Go right ahead. Why don't you create us a bath so we can clean up and I can show you what this tongue can do?"

"Why, commander, don't we need to rush down to dinner?"

He pulled her legs over the edge of the bed, spreading them before dropping his head and sinking his tongue against her clit. The suddenness took her breath away. Rising, he crawled over her, pushing his growing erection against her. "Care to start that bath water now?"

SKYE LISTENED as Mark explained the need to find out more about what Bormick had seen. He'd pulled Bormick aside when they'd finally met the others, telling him he needed to share the information about the auras with Pete and Crimson.

Skye's mind wandered. They'd had sex again in the tub and when they were drying, Mark had dropped to his knees and made her climax again. Her release had been so intense, that she'd almost lost her balance and had to reach back to hold on to the tub. Even after so many years, her desire for him hadn't faded. They still did it like frisky teenagers, and she hoped it never changed.

"Skye?" he said, pulling her thoughts away.

"I'm sorry. My mind drifted. What was the question?"

He lifted his brow, his eyes twinkling, his lips turning up at the corner. He knew exactly where her mind had drifted, and she felt the heat in her cheeks.

"Must have been a good fuck to get that reaction," Bormick commented.

She hated how crass he was. Mark seemed to have adjusted to his dirty comments, letting them roll now, but she still hadn't.

"It was," Mark said, his smile a naughty one. "In fact, they all were."

Skye eyed him with irritation as Bormick burst out laughing.

"Well, it's nice to see you two are getting along," Pete commented.

"Surprisingly," Crimson remarked. "Skye, I had asked if you were okay with taking us into that space."

Skye almost did a double take. It surprised her that Crimson would care. "You did?"

"I did. That place sounds special to you, and as obedient as I made my Mage Warriors, they never once let it slip that the place existed."

Skye's mood darkened, and she couldn't help the bitter tone in her voice as she asked, "Was that before you had them slaughter all the other warriors and Elites, including my father?"

Crimson dropped her eyes. "I didn't do that, Skye," she murmured.

"Are you kidding me?"

"My father may have been on his death bed, but he continued to rule for many years after he fell sick. Yes, I corrupted them, manipulated them into turning against the others and framed Camin, but under my father's orders. No one said no to my father."

"You could have."

"And risk his wrath?"

"Anger versus unnecessary death? They murdered my father, Mark's parents, and, in some ways, my mother."

"I know and I am sorry, but...but you didn't know my father. Saying no to him—"

"What Crimson? Would have meant you lost a toy?"

Her eyes flared as she met Skye's eyes. "You don't know everything about me, Skye. You only know what I've cared to share and what rumors attribute to me. My father was an abusive asshole who sold me off to each of his brown-nosing loyalists for favors and support. Any time I went against him, it worsened. I put up with it, took claim over my actions, seduced his friends the way he wanted, but that didn't mean there weren't worse consequences. Have you ever been forced to fuck a group of dirty old men while your father watches and jerks himself off? Don't judge me for not turning against the prick who would have let half his council beat and rape me if I had said no."

She rose and walked from the room.

No one spoke. Skye didn't know what to say. She'd never known, never bothered to ask, always assuming the worst and judging Crimson by the acts she'd carried out. Had always been hard on her for what she'd done to them. Skye couldn't imagine going through what Crimson had gone through.

Finally, Mark put his fork down, breaking the silence. "Gives you a whole new perspective on her, doesn't it?"

"Yes, I feel terrible." She turned to Pete and Bormick. "Did you know?"

"No, I'd better go talk to her," Pete said, rising from his seat.

"Yeah, that's probably best," Bormick agreed.

Pete rose and followed Crimson's path.

"It would seem none of us came out unscathed," Bormick commented after Pete left. "All of us have our own histories. Well, except maybe Pete. Maybe that's why the five of us are now on this path together."

"There's actually a deep thinker under that dirty exterior of yours, isn't there?" Skye asked.

He winked and shoved a piece of meat into his mouth. "Don't tell Crimson; she likes my dirty side. I'd be happy to show you my soft side, but I have a feeling you like it dirty."

"And then it's gone again," Skye said, then looked to Mark. "You're not going to say anything in my defense?"

"I've grown used to it now. Besides, he's not wrong."

A laugh escaped Bormick. "I didn't think I was."

She huffed. "Some knight in shining armor you are." Looking back at Bormick, who was still laughing, she said, "Tomorrow morning we leave for Crimson's in search for the warrior room."

"Not tonight?" Bormick asked. "Shouldn't we be more concerned with our time? We don't know what's coming."

"You've spent plenty of time *coming*, as has Mark, so I'm sure we can spare a night of sleep."

"Oh, there won't be any sleep in my room," Bormick said.

"There will be in ours," she replied, rising quickly from her seat.

"Seriously, Skye? One joke I don't defend you on and you cut me off?"

"Guess you'll have to work for it tonight."

"I thought I already did that," he tried with a hint of seduction and a glint in his eye.

If he weren't so damn cute, it would be easier to stay angry at him, she thought.

"Well, you'll need to work harder, but not now. I need to talk to Trent for a few minutes and let him know where we'll be. Start thinking of ways to please me while you wait."

"Damn, she's a vixen," she heard Bormick say.

"You have no idea and do not imagine it."

She smiled at his response, knowing if Bormick went too far, her Elite husband would take him down without hesitation. But she'd still make him work for it later, after she found Trent.

She wished Camin were here to get his thoughts. She could have portaled herself to Revina's, but the woman was beyond pissed at Skye for forgiving Crimson. Her mind went back to Derrant's words to Crimson. Revina's kingdom would burn. The suggestion led her to believe Revina would be her own downfall. It would be a shame if she brought about the death of her people because of pride and a grudge she wouldn't move past. Whatever storm was coming would likely bring destruction, and Skye prayed that wouldn't be the case for Revina or her people.

CRIMSON

Crimson stood on the balcony that led from the end of the hall she'd run down, gripping the railing tightly. Her heart hammered, her mind screaming at her weakness. She was angry at herself for saying those things. She'd built a shell so thick that it never broke. Had taken the blame for the wars once Camin had returned and revealed the truth or what they thought had been the truth. She'd owned it, never admitting but never denying it. No one needed to know the truth and the lie only made her more of a threat.

Something had cracked under Skye's words. Whether it was the weight of the words that finally became too much or the idea of Skye thinking she'd been the one to kill her parents and Mark's, Crimson didn't know. It didn't matter what Skye thought. Or, it hadn't in the past but maybe it did now. She hated to admit it, but she liked Skye—had started to when Skye had visited her in the forest. It felt like friendship, but the idea was a foreign one to Crimson. She'd never had a female friend. Her mother had died when she was very young, the female servants always looked down on her for the things she did, the things her father had made her do and the things she'd continued to do after his death, not knowing any different. Not until her life had been transformed.

She felt Pete's presence before his arm wrapped around her waist, his face nuzzling her neck. She leaned into him. He was her island in the tumultuous storm of emotions, the rock she could grip to keep her grounded.

"Why didn't you tell me?" he asked softly.

"Because it wasn't necessary. It was my burden to bear; always has been. I'm the evil queen, Pete, the one who shoulders the blame and accepts her dented crown."

"But you're not evil, Crimson. You're not perfect. You've made some questionable choices, but I don't think you're evil."

She turned to face him, seeing the honesty in his eyes. She didn't know what she'd done to deserve this man. He made her want to be better, and that was not something she'd ever experienced.

He brushed a strand of hair from her face. "I'm sorry all of that happened to you."

"Don't be. It made me who I am today. It is what it is."

"No, it's not and no one should go through what you went through."

"Pete," she said, resting her hand on the strength of his chest, "you see me in a way no one ever has. You make me feel whole, clean...undamaged. But I am damaged, and nothing can change that. I took my pain, my humiliation, and I let it feed me. You know, the first time the Death God called me to his bed, I was fourteen. It was the act that made me a woman in my father's eyes. I was a whore to the Death God." She stared at his chest, remembering his words. "It hurt. I was already hurting, bruised, bloodied from an act that my body should not have experience. He was the one who had sold me to the Death God. None of it had been my choice, yet I was soiled in his eyes."

"Crimson—" She stopped his words with a finger.

"Shh. As traumatizing as all of it was, Derrant was gentle

compared to everything my father did to me. The second time Derrant called me, I was fifteen. My body had changed, as had my father, but I promised I would have my revenge. I asked him to teach me, to make me who I am today—a weapon. And he did. I learned what men wanted, what broke them, what sent them to their knees, and I took my power from it. I took those men places they'd never been and each time I did, I stared at my father, planning my revenge."

Her fists clenched at the thought.

"When he grew ill in my twentieth year, I was ready. I watched my father slowly fail, rejoicing in his pain, but by the end of the mage wars, I'd had enough. I eased his vile ass to sleep with a concoction the novice mages couldn't trace. He'd been sick for many years. Why would they question it? I climbed onto his body and watched him draw his last breath, saw the fear in his eyes when he realized it had been me, and I whispered that the Death God was waiting."

Drawing her eyes up, she met his, waiting for Pete's reaction, but he remained silent.

"It helps to have the Death God's favor and when he had my father's soul, he let me watch as his demons tore it to shreds, feasting on it until nothing remained. I returned that night and claimed my throne, bringing in each of the men who'd soiled me, taking them one by one and watching as Stavin slit their throats while they writhed in their orgasm below me. One by one, I killed them, sending them all to Derrant. They paid, they all paid, and my kingdom knew to fear me."

She'd expected him to step back, to run from her, but he didn't.

His mouth curved and he said, "You are a vengeful bitch, aren't you?" .

"That doesn't bother you?"

"Crimson, I knew you were flawed. I knew you weren't the good girl. You seduced me in the middle of the woods and gave me the best sex I'd ever had, multiple times. You were no innocent flower. I knew what you did to Skye and Mark, knew you were lover to a god. I never judged you for those things. What makes you think I'd judge you for these or love you any less?"

"Because I murdered my father and all those men."

"Men who forced a girl to have sex with them, a man who used his daughter instead of protecting her like he should have. I don't hate you for seeking revenge. They deserved what they got, and you probably saved other girls from a similar fate."

She'd never thought of that, never thought beyond her own hatred, and the need for revenge.

"I still love you and I guarantee you tell Bormick what you did, and he'll be coming in his pants."

Laughing, she snuggled into his chest, his arms encircling her.

"So, I have the Death God to thank for those amazing things you do with your mouth?"

"Yes, you do. After you've learned to take a god in your mouth, anyone else is easy."

He glanced down at her. "Is that a comment on my size?"

She replied with a giggle, "No, silly. You are very well endowed. Both of you are perfect."

"Good," he replied, kissing her head. "Now, what do you want to do the rest of the night?"

"I want you to make love to me."

His lips brushed her forehead. "That I can do."

He scooped her into his arms and carried her back to their room, indulging her request. Making love to her gently, bringing her to climax over and over. At some point, Bormick entered the room, but as if knowing this was what she needed, he only watched, leaving her to Pete's healing hand. His touches restored her, wiping away the sadness and doubt the evening had brought until they finally drifted off in each other's arms. Bormick crawled in and protectively situated himself behind her, holding her as

Pete was, the two of them shielding her from her past, from the hurt it had brought. Her protectors.

~

THE MORNING LIGHT forced Crimson's eyes open. Pete still held her, his eyes meeting hers, a lazy smile on his lips.

"Morning sleepy," he said, kissing her nose.

Bormick's morning firmness pushed against her. "About time you two woke up. After watching that last night, I am in serious need of a good fuck. You two are intense. Don't bring all that lovey stuff when I'm on top of you, Crimson."

She leaned back, tilting her head to see the lopsided grin on his chiseled face. "You love me, Bormick."

"I love this tight ass of yours and I'm going to love it when it's spread up in the air for me."

"And with just a few words, the remnants of what we had last night are wiped away," Pete said.

She leaned forward and kissed him. He'd given her what she needed and Bormick had let him, standing aside for her to heal. She felt his reaction with her kiss, but Bormick's hand came around to hold her breast and pull her back.

"My turn, Pete."

"That's fine. You won't last long, so I'll just lay here and wait for my turn."

"You might want to have your hand on yourself because I'm taking her more than once."

"I have no doubt."

True to his word, Bormick took her from behind to ease his morning need then dominated her, his massive form taking her as she lay under him. But his usual roughness was softer, his kisses lingering, less demanding, as if he wanted to protect her as well from the past she'd revealed.

As she matched his climax, her hands digging into his tight

shoulders, she said, "Fuck me this time. I want you rough, I need you to own me."

The deep rumble from his chest was his only reaction and with it, Pete broke, his climax spilling over his stomach.

"Good, because I'm going to make you scream once you clean Pete up, then I think we'll let him play with us. He doesn't have the patience I have."

"Fuck you, Bormick," Pete said.

Bormick reached over, gripped Pete, and pulled the remains of his release from him. The move was tantalizing and Crimson's body tingled in reaction.

He brought his fingers to her mouth, and she licked each one slowly. "Is that an invitation, Pete?"

Pete's stare could have killed a man, any man but her Bormick. She slipped from under him and licked the remnants of Pete's orgasm, delighting in the taste of him.

"You going to make me share already, Crimson?" Bormick asked, sliding himself against her ass.

"I think so." She lowered her mouth over Pete, feeling him grow and hearing his groan. Turning, she took Bormick in her mouth this time, tasting herself on him. He bent back on his knees, pushing himself further into her mouth as Pete's hand caressed her breasts.

"I want you two to play while you play with me," she purred.

She felt the reaction in Bormick, his dick jumping against her hand.

"Shit, Crimson," Pete said as a wicked laugh escaped Bormick.

Bending forward to stroke Pete's erection, Bormick said, "I'll go gentle, Pete."

"You suck."

"Not ready for that, but you're free to try if Crimson wants to share."

"I'm going to kill you."

"Not until you come in my hand," he said with an authoritative tone. Crimson watched as Bormick jerked his hand up quickly, Pete's eyes to rolling back in reaction.

There was something about the way the two went back and forth, the taunting, the touches Bormick had been slipping in, that was driving Crimson insane. The arousal the escalating sexual tension had caused left her drenched constantly. She drew Bormick in her mouth once more, and his hands lifted to thread through her hair. Then she released him, turning back to Pete, taking him in again as Bormick moved behind her. He yanked her hips back, penetrating her with the move and pulling her from Pete. The force sent a shock of currents rippling through her.

His hands squeezed her ass as he pounded into her. She loved how powerful Bormick was, and how that power came through in the aggressive way he took her. Pete slid under her, catching her breast in his mouth, his other hand holding her other breast tight, caressing her nipple until both were stiff. Her body was a cacophony of sensations that threatened to send her crumbling. Bormick yanked her back again, thrusting so deep that it nearly toppled her. Every part of her was alive with their movements, and she could barely hold herself together. Pete took his mouth away, his hands continuing their play as Bormick shoved her down on top of him, her ass still in the air.

Bormick's hand loosened from her waist and drifted below to Pete. The groan from Pete called to something far within her as Bormick's thrusts deepened. She felt Pete's reaction, the resistance against Bormick's move, then the acceptance of it. The more Bormick pushed, the more he relaxed. Crimson didn't think she could take much more. The position she was in left her head smashed against Pete's chest. She could feel his muscles clenching, the short breaths he was taking as his climax grew. His hands stilled on her breasts and she could feel that he was beginning to break. Crimson was so stimulated that she was one stroke away from release.

"Fuck," Bormick growled as Pete's grip on her breast tightened and his head went back. "Take him, Crimson, take him now."

Bormick let his hold on her go and pulled out of her. She knew he was close, but the curious part of him wanted to watch. His hand was stroking Pete's ready erection and as her mouth met the tip, Pete exploded, filling her mouth with the taste of him. His body tensed as Bormick jerked each stream from him. Pete's moan filled the room, and Crimson's climax hit, the act stoking a fire in her that she could no longer hold at bay. She cried out as Bormick released Pete and plunged back into her, his own orgasm hitting him within seconds.

As Bormick stilled, he grabbed her hips and moved her quivering body to the side, collapsing next to her, the three of them laying there in silence.

Finally, Pete said, "I can't believe you just jerked me off, you fucker."

Bormick let out a billowing laugh. "You can repay the favor next time."

"I don't think so."

"Fine, then I'll continue to dominate you and claim alpha."

"You're not alpha."

"I just made you come in my hands. I damn well own you, Pete."

"Technically, he came in my mouth," she teased, her breathing still strained. Her body was trembling from the intensity of her climax.

"Thank you, Crimson, that makes it so much better," Pete replied sarcastically as Bormick's laugh grew louder.

She crawled onto Pete's chest. "I liked it."

"Pete liked it, too."

"I'm not admitting that."

"And you're going to deny our girl next time my hand finds its way to your dick?"

"I'm not saying that either."

"Then you did like it."

"You're an asshole."

Bormick slapped Crimson's ass, then rose, stretching his enormous muscles. Crimson watched him walk across the room to grab his pants, taking him in. Everything about him was beautiful.

He caught her looking. "Are you trying to tell me you want another round, Crimson? Those eyes look hungry."

She kissed Pete before pushing herself away, leaving the bed and sauntering over to him. "I didn't say you could leave my bed."

He raised a brow, a devious smile taking shape. "Are you asserting your authority, dear?"

"Yes," she said in a whisper against his ear, her body pressing against his. "I want you to both take me."

"Hmmm, that can be arranged, but that ass is mine again." He squeezed her ass as if to emphasize his desire.

"Not yet. I want to ride Pete while you fill my mouth and then maybe my ass is yours."

"I have no argument against that," Pete said. "As long as he keeps his hands to himself."

"I can't guarantee that, Pete. Now that I've felt that thing come, I'm going to crave more."

"Shh," she said, kissing him before running back to the bed and jumping on Pete, who caught her and pulled her in for a kiss.

She knew what Pete needed. He needed to feel himself inside of her, reclaim the manhood he felt Bormick had stripped from him. He was wrestling with his feelings toward Bormick. Struggling with the fact that he'd enjoyed his touch. Crimson suspected it was their bond with her. Bormick was pushing to test the limits of it, his own fascination with Pete stirring it.

Pete flipped her, claiming his dominance. He was the true alpha. She knew it, as did Bormick. He was the strongest, the one who did things to her heart. Things that Bormick couldn't. She loved Bormick, but the love she had for Pete ran deeper, more on a spiritual level. One day he would claim the role of alpha, and Bormick's move had pushed him closer.

Pete held her arms down, and a thought occurred to her. Perhaps that was why Bormick pushed him. There was a motive behind the taunting and the playing. She let her eyes drift to Bormick. He gave her a knowing wink as he watched them.

She brought her eyes back, Pete's searching hers.

"Take me," she said. "I want your essence all over me. I want you to take me like Bormick takes me. I want to feel your magic, your power, as you show me who owns me."

There was a spark of fire in his eyes. He was her softer one, the one with the gentle touch. She'd never pushed that but now she had, and she wondered how he would respond.

Pete kissed her, his hand coming below her and tilting her pelvis before he thrust into her with a force that left her gasping. His magic flowed from him, wrapping around her and bringing a heat to her. The sensation was erotic, stimulating, and it fed that part of her connected to the Shadow Realm, to the Death God.

He took her as he never had before, demanding, forceful, hungry, bringing her to climax unwillingly. There was no resisting it. Her body was his as she unraveled for him. When Pete was done, he brought Crimson to her knees, taking her again, the force of him sending shockwaves through her as she broke again. He commanded Bormick to join, and she took Bormick as Pete continued his command, all three of them climaxing together. Crimson drowned in the pleasure of it as the waves took her again.

When Pete had finally tired, they lay there quietly. She looked at him with new eyes, worried she'd pushed him too far and lost the gentle lover she cherished. He drew a finger down her cheek, letting it linger on her chin, then dropped his head and kissed her soft and sensual before dropping his forehead to touch hers.

"Shit, Pete. I'm not ready to give it up," Bormick said. "You're gonna have to fight me for that alpha role."

Pete kissed Crimson's forehead. "It's all yours, Bormick. I don't think our girl needs us both to be rough and aggressive, although my alpha may come out to play a little more."

Crimson smiled, bringing her hand to his cheek. "I love you."

He kissed her hand. "I love you, Crimson."

"No love for me."

She laughed. "I love you, too, Bormick."

"I meant from Pete."

She rolled her eyes as Bormick kissed her shoulders.

"Not quite there yet, buddy. Maybe a few more hand jobs and I'll be willing to say it."

Bormick's laugh echoed around the room and Crimson realized just how complete these two men made her. For the first time in her life, she felt whole.

MARK

Skye's hair tumbled around Mark's chest, and he threaded his hand in it, bringing her mouth to his. He'd woken early to the dreamlike feel of her tongue on his morning firmness, something that never failed to start his day right. He loved the things she did with her mouth, the velvet feel of her tongue against his skin, the way she swallowed him like she'd hit the gooey inside of a candy, lapping every bit of him until nothing was left.

She was hungry this morning, and he was not about to deny her as she rode him, slowly building up his need again, her arousal evident in the ease with which he moved in and out of her. His tongue slipped into her mouth, finding hers and dominating it while his hands caressed her breasts, brushing her stone hard nipples before he gripped her hips. He lifted her from him and moved her body forward.

She protested, as did his throbbing length, but when he brought her to his mouth, her protests stopped. He sank his tongue into her, tasting the desire that radiated from her. She was soaked, and he licked her arousal, savoring the taste of her. His tongue rose to her clit and he teased it until her thighs were quivering. The sound of her moan filling the quiet morning space stoked the need him, bringing him closer to release.

He slid a finger into her, his tongue following as far as it could. In reaction, she pushed against his mouth. She was about to unravel. He could feel it in the way her muscles clenched, the shallow breaths she was taking, the taste of her. Removing his finger, he gripped her thighs; her engaged muscles threatening to take him over the edge. His tongue licked and sucked until, just as she was about to explode, he took her clit again, devouring it until she fell over the edge, her body convulsing around his tongue, the sweet taste of her orgasm filling his mouth.

He shifted her back down, her body still trembling, the quivers of her stomach muscles drawing his eyes. Kissing her stomach, he moved his fingers into her, wanting her to come again, but this time with him.

She cried his name, falling forward and clenching his shoulders, her wetness on his hand and chest where she rested. When he felt her climax rising again, he removed his fingers, letting her move her body down. Bringing his fingers to his mouth, he tasted her, stifling the groan as her mouth took them from his and she sensually swiped her tongue over them. She was hovering so that his tip sat in her warmth, and he gripped her hips to push her further, craving the feel of being deep within her. She resisted, dropping her mouth to his and kissing him before her tongue cleaned the remains of her arousal from his mouth and chin.

"Shit, Skye, let me in," he said.

Her tongue slid through his lips, her kiss greedy. Her muscles had relaxed and with them, his hands tightened, pushing her down. At the same time, he thrust upward, sinking into her and eliciting a cry from her against his lips.

She arched her back as he took her harder, desperate for her, for his release. Taking her nipple into his mouth, he sucked and bit until she was mewing with pleasure, but he wasn't going to make it. He was too close, the need to let go too great. His hands tightened on her hips as she brought herself up to watch him, her blue eyes heavy with desire, taking him beyond any hope of control.

Something in his periphery moved and as the tide took him, crashing through every nerve in his body, his head turned to find Crimson watching them.

"Crimson," he growled as the sensation overcame him, too lost in the release that was pummeling him to stop it. She only gave him a sly smile and no response, so he ignored her, throwing his head back and closing his eyes to the ecstasy still rushing through him.

Skye had stilled and when he could breathe again, he opened his eyes to meet hers, which were narrowed with irritation.

"Not the name I want to hear you call out when you're mid-orgasm," she grumbled.

He nodded his head toward the door, trying to calm himself, only then realizing she was still ready for her own release, but now her smoldering eyes along with her pursed lips distracted him from the quivering of her legs.

"Really, Crimson?"

"I like hearing my name from him as he comes. It's very sexy."

He thought he heard a growl from Skye, the sound turning him on again.

"Don't let me stop you. Mark's really cute when he climaxes, but you still need release Skye, and you are quite a scene to watch. If you want, I can take you over the edge." She swiped her tongue along her lips. If Mark hadn't been so annoyed at her presence, it would have been arousing.

"I'm fine."

But she wasn't. He knew the signs. Her muscles were clenched tight around him, her cheeks flushed, her breathing shallow. He wanted to see her come again and damn if Crimson hadn't ruined it.

"Make her climax, Mark. It's not like I haven't seen you both or been with you both. I'll just wait over here."

"The hell you will," Skye snapped.

"Fuck it," he said, grabbing her head and bringing her down to kiss him. His pelvis moved as his length grew again, the thought of an audience strangely erotic.

Let Crimson watch. There was nothing she could do to hurt them, to break their love, and he wanted to take Skye again.

"Mark," Skye complained.

"It's nothing she hasn't seen, Skye. Christ, she had my dick in her mouth more than you did back then."

Crimson let out a moan. "Mmm, that was tasty. I'd be happy to go down on you, Skye, and let Mark take me from behind."

The image of it was enticing.

"You're not touching my husband," Skye bit out, "and get that image out of your head, Mark."

"Then start moving those hips before you lose it. I want you to come." He brought his mouth to her ear. "Show her why I love you so much."

"You love me for my orgasms?"

"Definitely."

Skye laughed, relaxing, and he tangled his hand in her hair. Grabbing her neck, he pulled her mouth to his, devouring it, all thoughts of Crimson fleeing with the feel of her against him.

He could have done it with his hands or his mouth again, but that hadn't been his plan and he wasn't about to steer the course. He wanted to topple into the abyss with Skye.

Her kisses became more demanding with every stroke of his fingers across her nipples. She was tight, her body needy, the wetness surrounding his dick making him want more. He flipped her, bringing her legs around him, and letting her push him deeper. He was lost to her and everything she did to him. She was the aphrodisiac he needed in his life, the one he could never resist. She was everything to him and, as if she could sense his thoughts, she drew her lips from his, her eyes seeking his. He brought his hand up to hold hers as he watched the rise in her, the wave cresting like it was within him. His climax broke with the intensity of her stare and the shake of her body. The parted lips, and the moan that slipped from her at the same time his did, had not helped to keep it at bay. His release shattered him, sending every nerve within him convulsing. The feeling shook him to his core, and he dropped his head to hers, holding her as they clung to each other until the tide receded, the electricity calming.

He remained there until he had the energy to lift his head and he kissed her nose.

"I love you," he whispered.

Her finger traced the contours of his cheek softly. "I love you, Mark."

He kissed her lovingly, contemplating making love to her again when he heard, "I think I just came standing here. You two are... I don't even know the word. And, Mark, I'd forgotten what a fine ass you have."

He dropped his head, having forgotten she was there. Skye sighed, and he rolled from her warm body, pulling the bedding over himself and sitting up.

"I'm glad you enjoyed the show. Now, what do you want?"

Crimson walked over and sat on the bed, close to his legs. "So pouty, Mark."

Shooting her a look, he tightened his grip on the blanket.

"Did you think of me while you were fucking her, Mark? Imagining it was my ass up in the air while you pounded me?"

He narrowed his eyes. "No, in fact, I forgot you were there."

"What do you want, Crimson?" Skye asked, the irritation heavy in her voice.

"To see if it's me who turns him on."

"Are you serious?" he asked. "You have two men to taunt, and that's not enough? When will you realize that I love Skye, that she is the only woman I want, the only one I think about, the only one who turns me on? You're relentless, Crimson."

Skye sat up and leaned into him, kissing him. Her lips were soft, the kiss holding a delicateness that spoke of her love for him.

"Leave, Crimson," she said. "I think I want to make love to my husband again after those words."

"Really?" he said with a raise of his brow. "I'm game for that."

Skye giggled, a sound that made his heart leap. This time, Crimson sighed. "I came to apologize, although the show was quite a treat."

Skye sat back, leaning against him, then quickly pulled the bedding up further to cover her bare breasts, causing a wave of disappointment in Mark, as he'd been enjoying the view.

"You don't have to cover them, Skye. They're quite beautiful, full, and perky and those nipples were made for biting."

"I tell her that all the time," he said before he could stop himself. Skye shot him a look, her eyes narrowing, so he quickly added, "But only with *my* teeth."

A thought of Derrant with her breast in his mouth snuck in, taking the moment and shredding it. His dislike for Crimson came rushing back.

"Apologize for what?" he snarled. "For selling my wife off to another man, to the Death God no less, for ten years?"

"Yes," she said, "and for kidnapping you and forcing you to orgasm, to want me, tricking you into it. And I know you tricked me…" Her hand had rested on his leg and Skye abruptly picked it up and moved it. "But I know you broke at least that one time, and I forced it on you. It was the best sex I'd ever had until Pete and Bormick."

"That's not helping," Skye said, crossing her arms and moving from his chest. The mood was heavy with her jealousy and his guilt, the two things that continued to cycle through them. The things they could never seem to completely shed.

"No matter how good it was, he loves you, Skye. He always

has. I tried to break him of you, but he was too strong. He took more than any other man I'd seduced. His love for you only cracked when his faith in you did, and I drove that."

Skye looked at Mark, hurt still reflected in her eyes. He looked back down at his hands, thinking about all the times the Death God had pleasured her over the years and the guilt faded. He looked back at her with angry eyes, and he could see the realization there as they grew sad.

"See, I did this." Crimson gestured to the two of them. "I was jealous of you, Skye."

"Of me?"

"Yes, gods who wouldn't be, you're gorgeous, sexy, powerful, and you had Mark. He adored you, he still does. The way he looks at you like you are his entire world, hovering protectively, watching to ensure no one hurt you. I saw it the first time we met, and I wanted it. I'd never seen two people more in love. No man looked at me the way he looked at you. No man loved me."

She looked down at her lap, taking a deep breath.

"When I saw Derrant, and he was angry with you, complaining about how you'd tricked him, I leaped at the chance to take you out of the picture. It was a chance to have Mark to myself. I foolishly thought I could make you love me, Mark."

Her words had been sincere, and he had a sudden rush of pity for her. "No one can force love, Crimson," he said.

"I realize that now, but back then... That's why I spent so much time trying to please you with my mouth and body. I thought every time you came for me would bring you closer to loving me."

"How many times was that?" Skye asked Mark with an edge to her voice.

"I told you, Skye. I told you my dick has a mind of its own."

"He's right. No man can resist me, Skye. It's my power. But as many times as I brought you there, you still cursed me and proclaimed your love for Skye. He loves you, Skye, even when he did finally break, it was his love for you, the anger that you'd left him—that's what drove him to give in. I see now that it was the only time. The others were manipulations meant to bring me to trust him so he could make it back to you. It's always been you and I'm sorry for putting a rift in your relationship, for being who I was."

"Who you *are*," Mark said.

She looked at him, her green eyes hurt.

"You are a beautiful woman, Crimson, and yes, you are seriously sexy. Nothing will change that." He felt Skye stiffen and threw her a look. "But I already have a sexy wife, one who makes seriously sexy seem innocent."

Skye smiled, her shoulders relaxing.

"You are who you are, you've done the things you've done, and no amount of apologizing will take them away," Mark said. "This isn't you, the mopey, regretful person you're trying to have us see. Sure, you're damaged, more than the rest of us but it's who you are. Take your past, the deeds you've done and own them, then change them like you have been. I don't know if I will ever forgive you for what you did. It took Skye and me a very long time to get where we were when you came in and mucked it up. But you made amends, you removed her debt to Derrant, and that means more to us than apologies ever will. It's the actions that bring forgiveness, not apologies."

She looked between the two of them. "Are you sure we can't share just once? He says stuff like that and just like with Pete, I want to fuck him."

Mark threw his hand over his face, swiping it down in frustration.

"I'd let you have Bormick. The four of us would get along well. Pete would have to watch, though. He's made it clear that he has no interest in you, Skye."

"I'm so thankful," she muttered, staring at Crimson.

"Unlike Bormick, who undresses you every time he sees you," Mark commented.

"Oh, he wants Skye, likes her perky tits."

"Skye's breasts will be nowhere near Bormick's mouth." He grimaced at the thought.

"Can mine be in yours?"

Skye threw a pillow at Crimson, yelling, "That's it, out!"

"He said I should embrace who I am, Skye."

"A sexual deviant?" Mark asked.

"You have no idea. I went gentle on you," Crimson replied. She leaned over Skye, kissing her quickly before Skye pushed her back. "You still come the best out of any of them."

Crimson reached toward Mark on her way up, but he grabbed her wrist, stopping her.

"Oh, Mark, I can make it rough if that's the way you like it."

"Enough, Crimson," Skye growled.

Crimson snatched her hand away with a laugh.

"You two are too easy to have fun with. We'll be in the great hall waiting for you. My men were fed early today, but if you make them wait, you'll have to watch them take me before we go. They get hungry easily, especially Bormick."

She scurried from the room, leaving them to stare at the door long after it clicked closed.

Skye rested her head against the bed frame. "You know, part of me just wants to let her."

"Let her what?"

"Join us."

"Are you kidding me?"

"It's exhausting, Mark. She's clearly still infatuated with you."

"She does it on purpose, Skye. She knows it gets to us."

She moved to him, straddling him, waking the calmed part of him that rose to her like she had commanded it. "You wouldn't want to see that?"

He gave her a look of warning. "Skye."

"She's beautiful, Mark. Sexy, with a body to die for. You can't tell me you didn't picture it when she offered to go down on me and let you take her from behind."

He felt the further rise, his damned dick with a mind of its own. But he couldn't blame it all on his body. His mind filled in the image, the thought of picturing Skye like that, remembering for just a moment what it had felt like being inside of Crimson. He shut it away quickly, but he couldn't hide it from Skye.

"Should I call her back? Watch you take her like you did all those years ago?" There was a spark of anger behind the offer, and he felt slighted by it.

Crimson was like a stain they couldn't lift, neither able to move past those events from a decade before, the wounds too deep. He gripped her hips, seeing the hint of pain in her eyes.

"Is that what you want, Skye? Do you want me to fuck her? Or do you just want me to tell you how good it was? How it felt to be inside of her as I fucked her with an anger that I've never fucked you with? How she made me come, more than once and for that slip in time, I liked it. Is that what you want to hear? Then you can tell me all about Derrant. How he ate you out as you screamed in pleasure, how you tightened around him as he came in you. How his name slipped from your lips when he was throwing you into the abyss."

He'd flipped her, pinning her arms near her head roughly, knowing he was hurting her, and seeing the tears behind her eyes.

"Because if that's what you want, then we can do that. Bring her in and watch me fuck her and I'll let Bormick have you, or better yet, let's invite Derrant and you can show me how you climax for him."

His words were like daggers that cut, but they also cut him with the same force. They'd never moved on. Crimson's shadow cast far across them, with Derrant's on the other side. A nightmare neither had been able to escape.

"It won't help," she murmured, a tear slipping from her eye, further shredding his heart. "We're broken, Mark."

"No, we're not, Skye." He loosened his grip on her arms. "Damaged maybe, but not broken."

"It hurts still. Every time I look at her, I imagine you touching her like you touch me."

"Jesus, Skye, I never touched her like that. I... I..." He dropped his head, not having the words.

He felt the long breath she took and the quiver as she fought back tears.

"She broke me, Skye. I have no excuse but after weeks of seduction, I broke. It was rough and angry sex that I regretted the second I woke from my anger, and I realized what I'd done. She's good at seduction, her body was on me almost every day, forcing me, coercing the part of me I have no control over, and I fought as if my life depended on it, but she finally broke me and that one moment of weakness will forever haunt me, just like so many others."

Another tear slipped from her eye. They were reopening a wound that had never fully healed, Crimson's presence forcing it open.

"Please don't cry, sweetheart."

He kissed the corner of her eye and pulled her over with him so that she was in his arms. Part of him still wanted to remind her that she'd slept with the Death God many more times, that he knew she slipped from him to Derrant's seduction on occasion, but he didn't, his own guilt still too heavy after all these years.

"You're right," she said, her head against his chest. "There were times where I couldn't hold on to your image with Derrant. I lost that hold and...then that day I discovered you'd been with Crimson, that you'd willingly slept with her, I crashed and let him take me, forcing my pain away and doing exactly what you had done."

She drew back to look at him, and he couldn't hide the hurt.

"I'd forgotten or maybe I'd forced it into the recesses of my mind, but I was hurt, angry, and my resolve broke as well."

"Huh, so all these years I've carried that guilt and you did the same damn thing. I mean, I knew you had slipped from time to time, that connection you added going strangely quiet at times, but I never thought..."

He should have been pissed but instead he laughed, loud and full, the relief pouring through him that they'd both broken, both cheated.

"You're not angry?"

"Definitely am, but I'm also relieved. Do you have any idea how much guilt I've shouldered for the last ten years? And all this time, you were as guilty as I am."

"I don't know—"

"Ah, yes, you are. We both are. So now we're on an even playing field." He yanked her against him, his length hardening at the feel of her skin. "I'm going to take you now, Skye, and I want you to tell me everything Derrant did to you to make you fall apart and I'm going to tell you how it felt to have Crimson break me, to fuck her when she finally did, and we're going to make them wait while we get it all out of our systems."

"Do you really want to hear that?"

"Do you?"

She inhaled. "I don't know."

He smashed his mouth against hers and spread her legs, lifting the one to give him entry, and sliding into her warmth.

"I think it's time we lay it all out and I take you rough like I took her."

"Rougher," she said breathlessly, sending his heart racing.

"Rougher it is."

He kissed her again, not caring how late they were. This was what they needed to finally accept everything that had happened and take the first step to moving past it all.

SKYE

Skye shivered as Mark's finger traced a path down her back before tying her dress for her. He'd taken her like he never had before—rough, demanding, dominating—and she'd opened herself to it, welcoming it. The lovemaking had been amazing and cathartic. They'd talked dirty to each other, all the while describing their downfalls, the things Derrant had done, what Crimson had done, both climaxing multiple times through it. In the end, the experience had brought closure and opened her to a new side of him so that she craved him even more than she had.

Mark's hand brushed the bruise forming on her arm before kissing it. She had a feeling the bruise was one of many, and the scratch marks lining his back were the equivalent to what she had. He faced her, drawing her in. He was beautiful, his hazel eyes shining with satisfaction.

"You okay?" he asked sheepishly.

"Never better," she replied, and she meant it. He'd been amazing.

They'd needed closure and making love this way had brought it to them. For too long they'd carried that baggage of that time, never moving past it, the annual visit with Derrant bringing their pain back to the surface over and over again. This time they had owned the past, taking it for what it was, accepting it as they had brutally taken each other, their words driving the intensity until it was erotic. Until part of her wanted to see him with Crimson, to experience what he'd felt. Most of her, however, wanted him to herself. He was hers, no one else's. No matter that they'd both been taken by others, that they'd both held a past where they'd lain in another's arms, climaxed to their touch, even before Crimson had come into the picture.

Their relationship was layered. Why not welcome another layer? Another layer would make their bond stronger in the end.

"Are you?" Skye asked.

"Surprisingly, yes." Mark's eyes searched hers, his finger pushing a stray piece of hair back, then lingering on her cheek. Even after the number of times they'd had together this morning, she reacted to his touch, feeling the flush of warmth in her belly.

She gave him a seductive smile, which he returned with a curve of his lips.

"I think we should take our frustrations out like that more often," she said, pressing against him. "It really is quite exhilarating."

"Mmm, I can agree to that. I do love it when you talk dirty to me."

"Should I invite Crimson next time?" she asked, her hand resting on his chest. For the first time in years, he didn't flinch at the sound of her name.

"I don't think so. I don't want to share you with her," he teased with a laugh behind his words. His arms pulled her closer as he brought his head down and kissed her. "You're the only one I will ever want, Skye. There never has been another and there never will be."

She melted into him, his words like velvet against her lips. "And you are my everything, Mark. You always have been."

He drew away, giving her a deliberate kiss on her nose. "Ready to face the day?"

"Only if it means being back in your arms when it's over."

"Most definitely," he replied. "These arms are never letting go."

THEY MADE their way to the great hall, Mark's hand never leaving hers. A feeling of contentment filled Skye, her body satisfied, her mind at peace. All she really wanted to do was snuggle back under the covers and sleep while Mark held her.

Bormick had Crimson against the wall, his hands on her breasts, when they found the three. Pete stood on the other side of the hall, his arms crossed, one leg propped against the wall at an angle as he watched them.

Pete turned his gaze to them, raising a brow at their appearance. "All right, you two, it's time to leave."

"'Bout time you showed up," Bormick answered, Crimson's breast out and fully in his grasp. "I have a raging hard on, though." He sucked on Crimson's nipple, sending her head tipping back.

"You always have a raging hard on, Bormick, and you just relieved it. I think you'll survive," Pete said.

Crimson dropped her hand to Bormick's crotch. "I guess that means you'll have to wait."

"Don't tease me, or I'll take you right in front of them."

"That's tempting."

"You just took her in front of anyone who passed by. Let's go, Bormick."

Skye bit back her irritation that the two had gone at it in the open of the great hall. Saying nothing, she averted her eyes from the breasts that still hung free. If she hadn't just hashed it out with Mark, it would have bothered her, but it wasn't anything

Mark hadn't already seen or touched for that matter. Instead, she simply let out a sigh of annoyed resolve. This was who Crimson was, and nothing would change her. It was time, however, to put her in her place and keep her there.

Pushing Bormick back, Crimson walked toward them, slow to pull her dress back up until she'd ensured everyone in the room had seen her breasts. She wouldn't stop, and Skye knew she needed to take control of the constant come-ons, the teasing, the looks. It didn't bother her now, as it always had. She knew everything and, most importantly, she was secure enough in Mark's love to embrace it.

Skye walked over to Crimson, grabbed the back of her head, and kissed her. Surprise greeted her until Crimson parted her lips and Skye went for it, meeting her tongue in a forceful game, before pulling her mouth away and whispering against her ear. "I know everything. Every touch, every kiss, every climax. You no longer hold the power, Crimson."

She brought her hand down, lowering Crimson's sleeve to cup the same breast Bormick had before drawing it back.

"The game is over, Crimson," Skye said, walking away, taking in the speechless look on Bormick's face and Pete's amused smile. She met Mark's eyes, and he laughed.

"Oh, and Crimson." She stopped, turning back to her. "I am more than willing to have you do those same things to me, but Mark's not ready to share me yet."

"And are you ready to share him?" she dared.

"Frankly, I think you have your hands full, but I wouldn't be opposed to seeing him come as he dominates you. I do love watching him."

She turned back to Mark, who pulled her in for a hungry kiss.

"God, you're hot," he whispered. "Torment Bormick."

"Why, Mark? Still wound up?"

"More than you can imagine."

She strutted over to Bormick, closed his mouth, and pulled it to hers. He tasted musky, his large tongue forcing its way into her mouth. There was something brutish and aggressive about him, like he could hold your life in his hands and snap it in two easily.

"Holy shit," Pete said.

She drew back just as his hands reached her body and removed herself from his grasp.

"Neither of us is ready for you."

He licked his lips. "I bet you taste sweet."

"You'd be right," Mark said.

"Keep your eyes on Crimson because all you'll get from me is that taste."

"I'll have more."

"Don't count on it," Mark said.

"Pete, I hear I don't turn you on, so you're safe," she said, giving Pete a sexy grin. She wouldn't have minded kissing him and finding out what his lips felt like against hers. The thought was one that tantalized her for a reason she couldn't explain. But a part of her thought he might be a little too tempting to take the chance.

She was relieved when he said, "No offense, Skye, but Crimson's enough for me and the thought of you...it's like thinking of my sister that way."

There was something in his eyes, a shimmering that led her to believe the words weren't the truth, and a tingling in her belly that reaffirmed her disbelief in them.

"For once, a normal response," Mark said, drawing her eyes from Pete's and back to him.

"That's not normal," Bormick complained. "That's just strange. No man in his right mind would pass up a chance to fuck Skye."

"I know," Mark said, pulling her close. "And no man will fuck her but me."

"She just swapped tongues with me—"

"I know, I wanted to see how I'd feel about it," he replied.

"And?" Bormick asked.

"Hated it. For now, the three of you can continue whatever it is you do without us involved."

"I don't want to fuck you, Mark. I want your wife."

Mark laughed. "Not a chance, buddy. You're not her type."

"Let it go, Bormick. I see what she's doing. She's finally taken the upper hand," Crimson said. "I'd say you two spent that extra time wisely."

"You could say that," Skye answered.

"Nicely played and, Bormick, that's the only taste you get of Skye," Crimson replied.

"What?"

"She's off limits. The only one with any chance of touching her is me. You can watch when that happens."

"That's not fair."

She reached up and kissed him.

"Did it ever occur to you that maybe our girl doesn't want to see another woman touching you, Bormick?" Pete said, moving from the wall, his magic pooling around him.

"That didn't turn you on when she kissed me?" he asked Pete.

"I'm not sure how I felt about it."

"Huh."

"Let's go," Pete said, creating a portal before Skye had a chance to draw her own.

Bormick and Crimson walked through first. Pete remained, eyeing Skye and Mark.

"That was risky. Bormick's not one to tease like that. Crimson needed it, but Bormick's a different story. He could've taken control of that moment."

"And he would have had a fight," Mark said.

"I needed to see how I'd feel," she said.

"And?"

"Not something for me."

"Good, because you don't want him touching you, Skye. He's

brutal and rough. Crimson can take him, and she's softened him some, but he's not someone Mark or even I would want touching you."

An inadvertent shiver went through her.

"Is he a threat to her? It's clear he wants her," Mark said stepping closer to her.

"No, but if he ever gets an indication that you're inviting him, you'll regret it. Don't play with him any more than you just did. I know why you did it, and I know why you kissed Crimson. That worked, and she needed to be put in her place and shut down. Bormick...only Crimson and I can control him. Don't even contemplate anything with him."

"Point taken," she said, Mark's arm protectively encircling her waist.

"I will say, his expression, in both instances, was priceless. You likely have the upper hand for the moment as long as you go no further."

"We won't be. I'm not the sharing type when it comes to Skye."

"Keep telling yourself that, but the moment the two of them go at it, all three of us will be watching."

"That's disturbing, Pete, since you think of me like your sister."

"Ha, Skye, that means I won't touch you. It does not mean I don't find you immensely attractive."

"Is there anyone in this place who doesn't want to get into my pants?"

"Me. I'm happy just watching," Pete said with a roguish grin before walking through the portal.

Skye's eyes lingered on him for just a moment before she moved. Mark grabbed her arm, turning her so that she faced him. He threaded his fingers through her hair and brought her lips to meet his. She leaned into him, welcoming it. Thoughts of anything else fled her mind. No one kissed like Mark did. His kisses were enough to send her to her knees, weakening her every muscle.

"What was that for?"

"Because I find you unbelievably sexy. And I needed my kiss to be on your lips and in your mouth, not Bormick's."

She let out a chuckle, fingering his shirt.

"I don't like kissing other people, Mark. I think that was enough for me."

"Fine by me, but you may want to tell Crimson that. I think you left her a little wet."

"She deserves it for all the taunting she's put me through."

"Come on, let's get this over with so you can get back to training her while the three of us stand around and fantasize about you humping each other."

She elbowed him before stepping through.

Pete's magic had a different feel to it than hers. It was heavier, pulling at the depths of her core. His magic reminded her of the sensation she had when she pulled hues from the Shadow Realm. It was sensual and stirred something in her that she couldn't quite name.

The others were waiting for them, Bormick's eyes drifting across her body hungrily.

"Enough Bormick, she's not playing anymore. Consider that a consolation gift for trying so hard," Mark said.

"Shame, I bet she's a screamer."

"At times," he replied.

"She looks like a screamer. Does she tighten around your shaft when she comes?"

"Are we at the comfort level where I share that kind of information?" Mark asked.

"No, we are not," Skye said, walking past them both over to Crimson. "And for the record, I've been told I tighten so much that it's impossible not to lose yourself to the sensation."

Bormick let out a moan as Mark slapped him on the back.

"There you have it. Nobody climaxes like my wife."

"Shit, wanna take care of this, Crimson?" he said, cupping the bulge in his pants.

Skye looked away quickly.

"Later, Bormick. I promise I'll relieve you, but please stop asking questions about Skye's orgasms. It's making me wet."

"Jesus, you two are like children," Pete muttered, looking uncomfortable and running his hand through his hair. "What are we looking for, Skye?"

"The Mage Warrior wing. You have one, right, Crimson?"

"Yes, we did. Follow me."

They walked through the dark castle. Over a decade had passed since the last time Skye had been here. The dark, heavy, gothic feel had lightened a bit, she presumed from the prior prince, the cousin who had died, but she couldn't say for sure. Pete didn't seem the dark and gloomy type. Although he was what she considered broody in a sexy way. Maybe he'd had something to do with it.

Crimson finally stopped in front of a long wing, no sconces lighting the corridor, an eerie quiet falling upon them. "This is it."

"This? Where's the Elite wing?" Mark asked.

"We didn't have many Elite, and only two Mage Warriors. Theodore was greedy and didn't play fair when he shared with the other kingdoms. We had one wing to house them all."

"Damn, how do we find the entrance then?" Skye asked. She'd never seen another mage wing, never entered through any but the one in Theodore's kingdom. How were they supposed to find this one? There was a chance it couldn't be found, and they'd be forced to beg Theodore for entrance, something she loathed even the thought of doing.

Sighing, she pulled the hues from the sconces behind them, along with what color she could from the hall and aimed it down the corridor, lighting it.

Mark moved first, drawing his weapon, which glowed in the dim light.

"What do you think is down there, Elite?" Bormick mumbled.

"With as much as I know of this kingdom and its past, I'm not taking chances."

Mark's words gave Skye pause to wonder if there was more about the Kingdom of Apendia that she didn't know. Crimson's father sounded horrible. He was likely just as terrible to his Mage Warriors and to his people. Were the ghosts of vengeful mages and Elite lurking in the shadows?

Don't be ridiculous, Skye, she told herself, but she moved closer to Mark, a shiver against the hairs of her neck. Swallowing nervously, she followed him into the unknown.

PETE

Pete trailed behind the Crimson and Bormick, with Skye and Mark further ahead. He could sense Skye's fear, although he knew it wasn't warranted. There was nothing ominous ahead of them. He couldn't believe she'd kissed Crimson. The move had sent a surge of lust through him that had resulted in a very uncomfortable hard-on. His words had been truthful, to an extent. Although they'd sounded hollow when he'd said them. He had no desire for any woman but Crimson, but Skye was an alluring woman with a killer body. The idea of seeing Crimson bring her to release was tantalizing and he imagined it would be a sight to behold—those tight breasts quivering, hips pulsing against Crimson's mouth.

Stop it, Pete, he scolded himself, glad the darkness shielded the erection that had grown.

His eyes fell to her hips, and he had to admit he wouldn't turn them down positioned astride him if there ever came a time the sexual tension between them all came to a head.

"Stop thinking about the mage queen's ass in your hands," Bormick said, coming behind him and whispering in his ear. His hand grabbed Pete's erection, pulling at it.

"Get off of me, Bormick."

"You gonna come for me again, Pete?"

"Bormick, leave him be," Crimson said, thankfully averting his attention from Pete's pants. Bormick's hand curled around Crimson's waist and pulled her against him instead.

"Seems you're a bit hard, too," she said.

"Do you guys ever stop?" Mark muttered.

Pete rolled his neck. Bormick had worsened the pulsing erection in his pants, and Pete didn't want to think about the reason for that. He didn't know if he'd ever be comfortable with the way his body reacted to Bormick's touch, no matter how good it felt.

"No, it never stops, Mark," he replied as they reached the end of the hall.

Skye turned, her navy eyes glimmering in the magic lighting the hall. His heart skipped strangely in response. "This is it?" she asked as he shoved the sensation away.

"Yes, what did you expect?" Crimson asked.

"Something more."

They'd looked in each of the rooms to find nothing but cobwebs and dust covering discarded furniture, ghosts of a life past when Mage Warriors and Elite had once roamed the halls.

Crimson huffed. "Well, there's nothing more."

The magic of Mark's weapon shimmered in her eyes, making the green sparkle.

"That would have been nice to know," Mark said.

"You didn't give us a lot to go on. All you said was the Mage Warrior wing," Crimson complained.

"That's where it is in Theodore's castle."

"Well, as I said, Theodore had the majority of warriors and Elite. We got the scraps."

"It has to be here somewhere," Skye said under her breath.

"We don't know that," Mark told her. "We're only going by what we know of Theodore's."

"I saw the six rooms, Mark. The wings led to the other king-doms, the rooms combined to make one large space. It's here."

Pete wondered at what Skye had said. She sounded so certain. "How did you find the one in Theodore's?"

"My birthmark shimmers and the magic from it grants me access." She lifted her hair, exposing her long graceful neck, the birthmark sparkling below. A few strands drifted free, and he had the urge to brush them back and let his fingers drift along her skin.

"Like that?" Crimson asked, jarring him from his thoughts.

"It's shimmering, Skye." Mark grazed his finger along her birthmark. Pete saw the reaction, the flash of lust behind her eyes at Mark's touch.

Arousal stirred in him, his length growing again, and he cursed himself, wishing he could take Crimson into one of the rooms and test it on her birthmark, and get his mind from Skye's. Bormick and Mark were talking, so he pulled Crimson aside, pressing his excitement against her, her head dipping back as she felt it.

"I'm going to take you later and I want your magic active. I want to touch your birthmark like that and have you use it while I fill you." The thought tickled his mind that if she were holding Skye's magic, that it would be Skye's essence he'd feel against his body. The twitch of his pants in reaction caused him to tighten his hold on Crimson's waist.

He shoved the thought aside, feeling Crimson's body respond. She pushed harder against him, and he clenched his hand tight against her stomach, wishing he could sneak her away but knowing this wasn't the time. Her hand came around, brushing against the side of him, and he lowered his head to her neck, trying not to groan.

"Do we need to let you two have a room?" Skye asked. He looked up from Crimson's neck to see Skye's brow raised, an amused smile on her face that reached to her eyes.

"Only if you join us," Crimson purred.

The idea made Pete's length throb, and he dropped his eyes, hoping she and Mark hadn't noticed.

"I'm game for that," Bormick said. "Mark and I can watch."

Mark threw Bormick a dirty look. "No, I think we'll pass."

"Your loss," Pete said, knowing it was out of line for him, but he was entirely too aroused to stop himself.

"So now I see why you and Bormick get along so well," Mark replied with a laugh. "If you two don't keep the heat down, we're all going to need some time."

"I'm up for that, too," Bormick said.

"You had your turn, Bormick. The next one's mine." He let Crimson go, the painful need between his legs threatening to bend him over. "You're welcome to watch."

"Always gets me rock hard watching you, Pete," he teased with a wink.

Pete shot him a look and adjusted himself, catching Skye's eyes, watching the move. He gave her a sly smile.

"Sorry, Skye. Remember, it's all Crimson's." *Although maybe feeling that tight ass against me wouldn't be that bad,* Pete thought, knowing it was initially the thought that had started his dirty mind wandering. Her birthmark and reaction to Mark's touch had tipped him over the edge. That sisterly feeling had definitely dissipated with her kiss on Crimson.

Pete wasn't sure what to think of the slight sparkle to Skye's eye before she opened her mouth, ready to retort, the parting of her lips not helping his unexpected desire for her.

"If we could get through a conversation without sexual comments and innuendos, it would be a miracle," Mark said before she could respond.

"But it wouldn't be any fun," Crimson commented.

Pete knew he needed to focus, or the situation would get out of hand. "All right, what do we know?"

"Other than the fact that your dick is hard enough to see, not much. I can take care of that for you, Pete."

"Asshole," he shot at Bormick.

"I think we should give the room to you two," Mark commented. "You clearly need a good fuck to get this tension out of your systems."

"You're not helping, Mark," Pete replied, gritting his teeth.

"Just calling it like I see it."

"I'm okay with watching that," Skye said.

Pete's jaw dropped before Mark looked at Skye sharply.

"Oh, come on, the two of them naked and going at it, all that raw muscle and angst?"

Mark continued to stare at her as Crimson said, "I'll watch with you, Skye. We can leave Mark outside."

"I don't think so—"

"Hey, can we all stop imagining my dick in his ass for just a minute—"

"Wait, who says you get to dominate? You're taking it, Pete, and you'll like it when you do," Bormick said, his voice gruff.

Skye laughed, an adorable snort escaping. Crimson joined her while Mark continued to look curiously at her, his eyes creased.

"Mark, I think a few more times giving it to her rough like earlier is what she needs to bring her to the dark side with me," Crimson said.

"How do you—"

"That pretty flesh of yours doesn't usually have bruises on it, Skye. Trust me, I know what rough sex looks like."

Even through the dim light, Pete could see the flush of Skye's cheeks.

"That's enough, Crimson," Mark said, drawing closer to Skye. "I think that's enough in general. What is it with this place? It's like it's enhancing what's already a sexually charged situation, corrupting even Pete."

Bormick said something about Pete already being corrupted,

but he ignored it, thinking about Mark's words. "Corrupted," he said, looking around.

"We all are, Pete," Crimson said. "It's nothing to be ashamed about."

"No, he's right Crimson," Pete said, growing serious. "The magic, this entire wing, is corrupted. What did you do to the Mage Warriors who lived here?"

"She turned them, manipulated them," Mark said dryly. "Had them kill their own."

Crimson held her head high. Her pride was a dichotomy to the wounded woman he knew lay below. She'd been deadly, manipulative, destroying so many lives, yet he still loved the beautiful viper she was. Standing there, recognizing the corruption, he could sense the depths of the madness she'd lived in, a world built around pleasure and pain.

"How did you turn them?" he asked.

For a moment, the façade dropped, and he saw her vulnerability, not expecting that question from him. Then she covered it.

"I slept with them, stole their magic, used it against them as I toyed with them. It doesn't take long to break someone when they learn to need your body like they need air to breathe. At least, with one stubborn exception." She gave Mark a coy smile.

"Nice, Crimson," Mark muttered.

"And you did all that here?"

"Yes, years of it until...until they were ready to do anything I wanted, as long as they were rewarded when it was over."

"The magic turned as they turned," Skye said. "The more they went against the true intent of the magic, the more corrupt it became."

"Yes, I think so," Pete agreed, admiring how quickly she'd figured it out.

"Mage magic is protective, pure, a light in the darkness that Shadow Magic is," Bormick said.

Pete did a double take, surprised once again with his insight-fulness.

Skye nodded. "Yes, it comes from Eliana, and that's exactly what she is. A counter, a balance of sorts to the Death God."

"So, if it's changed, then it won't react to your magic, but it might to mine," Pete said. "Although…" He thought about the touch of Skye's magic. It wasn't all light and pure, there was an undertone to it that called to his.

"What?" Mark asked.

"Skye's magic…it's not only about those things, is it?"

"No," she said. "My magic comes directly from Eliana. Other Mage Warriors aren't born with the same degree of power because they aren't directly from her line. I am. It's a gift from her to her direct line. My blood runs with it, so it holds a connection to her home. That tie to her gives me the ability to walk the Shadow Realm."

Although that was an interesting bit of information, it still didn't seem like enough. "No, there's something else, isn't there? Something else that differentiates you, that makes you more powerful. I can feel it when you use your magic."

Skye's eyes seemed to shimmer and for a moment he was pulled into the power of them as Mark answered for her, "Skye can draw on the shadows and use her magic in the darkness."

"That's different," Crimson said.

"Why?" Pete asked, forcing his eyes from Skye and feeling the breath return to him.

"Because Mage Warriors are defenseless in pure darkness. It's their weakness. They need a sliver of light, something with color, to draw their magic from," Crimson said.

Pete looked back at Skye, braving that instinctive pull. "But you don't, do you?"

"No." Skye pulled the light hues from the hall, plunging them into darkness. Pete felt the warm velvety touch of her magic, the darkness lighting as streams of black, gray, even navy blue were drawn from it until the space was a dull white, ribbons of shadows swirling around her. They tempted his magic, he could feel the pull to it. Bormick and Crimson both looked stunned.

"I spent most of my life color blind, living in a world of shadows. These colors were all I saw until the spell was broken."

"That's...that's not possible," Crimson said.

"But it is in Skye," Mark answered.

Pete reached out with his magic, calling to the hues noticing how his magic reacted to them, the ribbons growing and answering to the call.

He let his power mingle with it, noticing the slight shimmer behind Skye. He commanded the magic so that it directed toward the wall, hunting the source of the shimmer and homing in on it with a force that shattered the wall. He directed the shadows to encase the resulting debris before it pelted them, halting it so that it collapsed to the ground before them. Releasing his hold on the hues, he recalled his magic and gave control back to Skye.

They were staring at him, and, for a moment, he dropped his eyes to look at his hands.

"Well, that's new," Bormick said, walking past them. Pete heard him say, "Untapped" to Mark as he walked by him and into the open space before them.

"The darker hues are Shadow Magic," Skye said.

"So, it would seem," Mark answered.

He looked at his wife, worry in his eyes, then glanced back at Pete. Pete recognized the look. Mark saw him as a threat now. Pete had stripped the hues from Skye, leaving her defenseless in that moment. Mark studied him.

"I won't hurt her, Mark."

Pete looked to Skye, whose brows were knitted, her mind thinking it through, piecing it together. Mark took her hand and led her through the doorway, sconces lighting around them as they entered. He stared at them, his eyes drawn to the sway of her hair, the way her hips rolled as she walked. For a moment he wondered if it was the magic that had Mark worried, or him. There had been something there, in the touch of his magic to Skye's. There always was, but this had been different. They responded to each other, as if they were meant to be joined, the ribbons of her magic answering to the call of his in a way that was seductive. No, he wouldn't hurt her, he'd only ever protect her.

He felt Crimson's hand on his arm, his thoughts drawn from Skye. He turned to Crimson. Her eyes were wide still, and she gave him a small smile.

"My shadow king," she said softly before kissing him gently. "Come." She took his hand and led him through the debris, into the room, the doorway sealing shut as he walked through. Leaving behind the strange feeling that there was more that connected his magic to Skye's than they suspected.

MARK

Mark held Skye's hand tight, keeping her close, playing the events in his head. Watching Pete so easily steal Skye's hues had been unexpected. The move had left her vulnerable. She'd only been defenseless a few times since gaining her powers. Even against the Death God, she'd held her own. Mark was left with a discomfort he couldn't name and with questions.

Pete and Crimson entered the room a few moments after they did, the door resealing behind them.

"Did you do that?" he asked Skye.

"No, I think it reacted to Pete."

Even more worrisome, he thought.

Bormick was walking around the room, studying everything.

"Untapped," Bormick had said to Mark as he'd walked past him.

Mark wondered what Pete's aura looked like now, curious if it was complete. If it was, he didn't know what that meant for Skye. Although he'd never seen Pete as a threat, after that last show of his abilities, Mark wasn't so certain anymore.

He pulled her a little closer, a nudge of fear seeping into him.

He wasn't certain the reaction was rational; Pete was on their side. He'd never given any indication that he wouldn't be. Just the same, he'd just shown that he was stronger than Skye. And Crimson had access to that power.

"You have more to worry about from me than you do Pete, Elite," Bormick said. "Relax, I can smell your tension over here."

Mark rolled his neck, trying to calm his nerves.

"So, because Crimson warped the magic of the Mage Warrior's by manipulating them and having them use it against their own kind, the room no longer answered to my magic?" Skye asked, waking him from his internal stupor.

Pete was thoughtful. "I thinks so. My magic has a distinct feel from yours, except what you did back there. If your magic was meant to balance the Shadow Magic like you said, then it stands to reason when Crimson corrupted it, she brought it closer to Shadow Magic. That warped the entry to this room so that normal Mage Warrior magic could no longer access it."

Mark grimaced. "As usual, there's yet another trail of your actions, Crimson."

"What can I say? I leave an impression. Now what are we looking for in here? That little magic move has me so wet I can barely stand. Let's get this over with so my men can relieve me the rest of the night."

Bormick's head jerked up at her words, a mischievous grin on his face.

Mark shook his head.

"When are you not wet, Crimson?" Skye asked, making him laugh.

"Not often when any of these men are around," she replied playfully.

Mark studied a small bookcase, saying, "Concentrate on your own two, please. I'm sure they'll be more than willing to help with that."

"But Skye said I could play now."

"She may have, but I didn't."

Pete moved behind Crimson, brushing her hair back, and kissing her neck. "I've got dibs on you anyway, Crimson, you'll be too exhausted to even please Bormick when I'm through with you."

"No wearing her out until I've had a piece, Pete."

"Fuck off, Bormick, you can have her in the morning or if I'm nice, I may let you suck my cock while I go down on her."

There was complete silence. Mark was trying his best not to laugh and Skye's face looked horrified but intrigued at the same time. He couldn't read Bormick until he burst out laughing.

"God, you two are something," Mark muttered.

Skye looked over at Mark, but all he could do was chuckle and shake his head.

Finally, Bormick stopped laughing.

"I told you, Pete, it's you who will do the sucking. It's right here when you're ready," he said, pointing to his crotch.

Skye moved closer to Mark. "What are they doing?"

"Well, I think they're bantering for dominance, but I'm not certain they're not about to have it out here and finally give it to each other."

She snickered, and they watched Pete walk over to Bormick, Crimson's hungry eyes trailing him. Pete leaned into Bormick, grabbed his crotch, and said to his ear, "I'm the alpha now. If you play nice, I may let you take the lead, but the game's mine now."

"You are sexy when you're assertive, Pete, but you're going to have to fight me for that title."

"Eagerly."

"Good God," Mark muttered to Skye, watching Pete's hand stroke Bormick's bulging erection.

"Yeah, tonight's going to be very interesting," Bormick said.

"Do we have to wait for tonight?" Crimson whined.

"I agree with Crimson," Skye said a little too loudly.

"Are you serious, Skye?" Mark responded, not sure what to

think of her in that moment. "You two stop playing with each other's dicks. The sooner we find something, the faster you two can go do what you need to do."

They continued to stare each other down. Pete removed his hand, but Bormick pushed it back against him. With his other hand, he grabbed Pete by the back of his neck and brought him closer, whispering something in his ear. Pete shoved him away. Bormick laughed as Pete shook his head.

"You're an ass, Bormick," Pete said with a laugh.

"Yeah, and you're gonna take me up yours tonight," Bormick replied.

"Yeah, no. I recall telling you that was where I draw the line."

Bormick laughed harder.

"Is it wrong that I really want to see how this plays out?" Skye whispered to Mark.

"I guess not, but that's a new one for you."

She shrugged. "So much testosterone and muscle, and manly tension."

"I'm not manly or muscle enough for you?" he whispered in her ear.

"I didn't say I needed to partake. Just watch."

Crimson had gone over to the others, who were all distracted, so Mark pulled Skye closer.

"Are you wet?" he whispered, his hand running along her thigh as he pulled her skirts up, slipping his finger along her ass, and thankful she'd foregone any underwear. He loved it when she did that. His fingers moved lower to feel the dampness that awaited him. The response between his own legs was immediate.

"Good God, you are and that was a mistake," he groaned against her ear.

Skye let out a sigh that called to his need for her. "Let's just do it here, let them do their own thing, and you take me?"

"While you watch two other men?" he asked, withdrawing his hand and regretting having touched her.

Mark brought his fingers to his lips, tasting her sweetness, wishing they could be alone. Her hand encased his length, feeling what he knew there was no hiding.

"You want to. I can feel it, Mark."

"You're relentless, woman. Let's get through this so I can take you back and take advantage of you."

She giggled.

"Wrap it up over there and let's focus," he said to the others without turning. He needed the bulge in his pants to recede before he could do so.

"You're a killjoy, Mark. I was just about to make Pete jerk me off while Crimson went down on him."

Mark glared at Bormick. "Save it for later. Take a minute to calm yourselves and look for anything that answers our questions."

"The only thing that will calm my raging hard on is Pete's mouth on it."

"Not mine?" Crimson purred.

"Damn, maybe both of you. Shit, that would do it."

A disgusted look overcame Pete's features. "My mouth is not going anywhere near your junk."

"Your hand was just on that junk and doing a good job," Bormick taunted.

Mark narrowed his eyes as Skye sighed and started looking around the room. She drew closer to the fireplace, stopping with a tilt to her head.

"Pete, help me open the connection. I don't know that it will respond to me here."

"Connection?"

"Damn, Skye, you're distracting him," Bormick complained.

"Good," she said, glancing down at the lumps in their pants. "I think you both need some distraction, and I'm not talking about Crimson."

Bormick's eyes glinted. "You?"

"Wow, you never stop, do you?" Skye asked.

"Not stopping until that tight body is riding me," he said, grabbing his crotch.

Mark had had about enough of this, especially now that Bormick's attention was turning to Skye. "Enough, Bormick, stop harassing my wife with your erection."

"You're no fun, Mark."

"I thought I'd have to stand in line behind Pete to punch you, but it looks like there's no longer a line. Shut your trap or my fist will."

"Again, I welcome that fight any day, Elite."

"Men," Skye complained. "Pete, come help me. I don't think this will work without you now, at least not in this section."

"Pete will *come* for you, Skye," Bormick said with a snicker.

"Shut up, Bormick," Pete said. "What do you need?"

"Do what you did before."

"You want him to grab me again?"

Crimson's elbow went to Bormick's rib before anyone could respond.

"You're gonna have to hit harder than that, babe, but I do like it when you're rough."

Crimson giggled, which was an odd sound to hear from her, and again he thought about how these two men were changing her. He wasn't so sure it was Bormick and doubted they'd be on friendly terms if Pete and even Skye weren't involved. Pete had changed Crimson, maybe had changed both her and Bormick. Skye had believed in her, looked past the indiscretions to see the woman below them.

He felt the touch of Skye's magic as the darker hues pulled from the room to encircle her before she gently sent them toward Pete. He captured them with his magic and Mark watched closer, seeing the ebony sparkle against the hues and noticing Skye's eyes were still a lush blue that shimmered with her power. Pete had only taken what he'd needed this time, learning from only that one time how to control it.

Mark glanced at Bormick, who met his eyes and gave a brief nod. As much as Bormick goaded him, he understood Pete's potential, and again, it surprised Mark that he willingly accepted that Pete was stronger. There seemed no jealousy, no rivalry, but more an appreciation. Perhaps it was the blood bond. That seemed the most likely explanation. The pact bonding them as cousins but more like brothers, Bormick older, wiser than he let on, and proud to watch his younger brother grow to be a formidable presence.

The room shifted as Pete sent his power to the wall, controlling it this time. The walls moved, the fireplace lengthening and rising, the space growing as the six layers merged to one, just as Skye had described to him.

"That was unexpected," Crimson said.

Pete looked around, his eyes large. "What just happened?"

"The rooms from each kingdom merged temporarily. The warriors and their closest Elites would meet here."

Crimson's face soured. "All of this was under my nose the entire time?"

"Not really. The space moves, I think. It's not really under any one kingdom but in its own space."

"That's insane," Pete commented.

"So why didn't your Mage Warriors kill the others here?" Bormick asked Crimson.

"That would have been too obvious. It needed to look like someone else did it. Camin was already attacking with his wizards. Why not make it look like he'd killed them? It took the heat off me, gave me your kingdom, and accomplished the task."

Mark gritted his teeth. "While you set Camin up, turned the Mage Warriors and Elite against him when he was fighting for them in the first place, and wiped even your own warriors out."

"I didn't know the magic was going to fade. Why did it fade anyway?"

"You don't know?" Skye asked.

"No, it just faded until, in time, the mages I still had were barely able to wield any spells."

Mark found it hard to believe she didn't know. "Theodore didn't tell you what happened?"

"No, did he know?"

"Huh, guess he was keeping his own secrets," Mark mused.

"It faded because of me," Skye said. "My mother did it to save me and our line. She cast a spell to send me away and bound the magic to the spell."

Crimson's mouth formed a perfect 'oh' before she asked, "So that's why it returned when you arrived?"

"Yes."

"Interesting."

"Interesting, she says about having killed both our families and countless others, then forcing the hand of the remaining Mage Warrior so that magic disappeared for decades," Mark muttered.

"In the past, Mark," Crimson said. "Remember, we've moved beyond that."

"I don't know that you ever move beyond seeing your father murdered in the battleground with friends you've known since you could talk. Nor having to be ripped from your mother's arms as she sends you to another world knowing you'll never see her again. It's not something you forget easily."

Skye took his hand. He'd never shared the specifics of the events that night with her. They were still engrained in his mind, as if the events had happened only yesterday.

"He's right, Crimson. We may forgive you, me especially, but there are scars, and watching your parents get murdered is one that takes a lot to heal," Bormick said unexpectedly. "Trust me, I spent a lifetime pillaging and murdering to numb that pain, thinking every time I hurt someone else, it would ease it. It never did."

"How does killing other people make that better?" Pete asked.

Bormick shrugged. "Eh, I was a little messed up with my thinking."

Pete glanced over at him. "A little?"

Crimson spoke in a soft voice as if she were hesitant after what Mark and Bormick had shared. "I was different then. I know you still don't believe me, but ten years in that forest gave me a lot of thinking time."

"Not Pete, who was busy fucking a tree nymph," Bormick interjected.

Pete shook his head as Bormick laughed.

"I don't think I want to know," Skye said.

Mark leaned in and whispered, "Sex demon," eliciting a snicker from her.

Pete's expression changed, and he grumbled, "No, you don't. Let's finish what we came here for so I can get away from him for a few minutes. It's bad enough I have to sleep with him every night. I need some space from him."

"You love me too much to be without me, Pete."

"Love, hate, buddy."

"He's right, we need to focus," Skye said, squeezing Mark's hand and beginning to search.

Crimson rubbed her arms as she came over to Mark, saying, "I am sorry." Before he could react, she kissed his cheek and walked away.

He furrowed his brows, catching Skye's eye, her own brow raised. He shrugged, then started helping her, ignoring the strange sensation of Crimson's touch.

～

THEY SEARCHED IN SILENCE, pulling books out, sifting through journals, but nothing they found explained Crimson's abilities. It was like no one had known she'd descended from the Mage Warrior line. Not even her own Mage Warriors had left any trace of their knowledge of her.

"This is fruitless," Pete complained.

"And boring," Bormick added.

"I have to agree with that," Pete continued. "The only interesting thing I could find was some writings on your gods and the rivalry between the Death God and the Upper God. Other than that, nothing."

Skye blew a piece of hair from her face, and Mark resisted the urge to reach over and kiss her. "You're right. I thought there would at least be something about your line, Pete, but I don't even see anything about the Digremile line. It's like they didn't know any of you existed. Which is strange since Elspeth and the wizards knew the history."

"We didn't know we existed. I doubt many did," Bormick said. "Our story is a myth. There's no credence to myths."

"Well, this was a wasted trip, aside from the mild entertainment earlier," Mark said.

"Maybe not," Skye said, standing and walking to the fireplace. "Pete, help me close this back up and all of you move back to the original room."

Mark moved back with the others while Pete helped her, the room shrinking strangely. The transformation created a disorienting feeling that left him slightly off kilter.

She drew the hues from the fireplace and began searching the wall.

"What are you searching for?" Pete asked her.

"This," she answered softly, lifting her hair to reveal her birthmark.

A matching violet moon shimmered on the wall, but Mark was too busy observing Pete's reaction to her neck to look at the wall. Skye dropped her hair, and Pete looked away. Mark caught the uncomfortable shift in his stature. It was brief, but it was there, leaving him wondering at it.

An opening appeared that led to a tunnel, and Skye walked through, Pete following close behind. Mark caught up, not sure why he felt unsettled by the sight of her walking with Pete or the way he'd looked at her neck.

"Where does this lead?" Pete asked Skye.

Mark brushed off the feeling, letting it go as Skye answered, "I think it leads to the other rooms."

"Skye, it's entirely too far to reach the other kingdoms," Mark argued.

"Maybe not. There's old magic at play here, Mark."

The tunnel forked in different directions, giving it the appearance of a star with six points.

Skye looked to each direction. "So, which one goes to our kingdom?"

"We don't even know if the one in our kingdom is even intact still. We haven't been able to find the source to it."

"It exists because it was part of the larger room. If it was gone, the room wouldn't have been able to complete." She was adamant and Mark knew there was no arguing with her when she was this determined.

"So, we're looking at a star, like a pentagram, but with six points?" Pete said.

"A what?" Crimson asked.

"Never mind. The star has six points based on the location of the kingdoms. See, the tunnels aren't perfectly separated, the space between each varies."

"So, Pete, if your kingdom is east of Crimson's, then that tunnel likely leads to yours," Mark said, pointing to the closest tunnel to the right.

"Yes," Pete answered.

"Then straight would be Revina's and left would be Theodore's," Skye conjectured.

"And the one between these two goes to yours."

"Only one way to find out," Mark said. "You two stay here so we know how to find our way back. Skye let's see if we're right. Pete, come with us in case we need your magic."

There were no complaints, so the three of them walked, reaching the tunnel's end within minutes.

Skye moved to it, the hues she'd brought with her floating around her like a torch. She'd separated a small amount to leave with Crimson and Bormick so they wouldn't be left in the dark, and Mark wasn't certain he wanted to see what they were doing when they finally returned.

"Do you need my help?" Pete asked.

"No, this one is pure." Skye placed her hand on the wall and pulled her hair back to reveal her birthmark, which began to shimmer in the dim light. Mark followed Pete's gaze, watching how it lingered as her hair fell gently back in place. His eyes dropped and Mark saw the crease of his brow as if he were just as unsettled about his reaction as Mark was.

The wall shifted, redirecting his attention, and he shrugged the feeling off again, thinking he'd ponder on it another time. The mage lair sat before them but not the one they'd just exited. This one was different, and he recognized the space from when all the rooms had been connected, the sconces lighting with Skye's first step in.

"Now what?" he asked.

"Now we see where it leads."

She moved across the room toward the door, which shimmered then disappeared, a flood of rubble and dirt toppling in at them.

Mark grabbed her waist and pulled her away.

"That's an issue," Pete said, surveying the mess.

"Glad we brought you. Can you help move while I dissolve? Maybe between the two of us, we can clear a path?"

"Dissolve?"

"Watch." She began drawing the hues from the rubble, bleeding them until finally they disintegrated.

"Holy shit! You can do that on everything?"

"I think so."

Pete shook his head. "And they call my magic frightening."

Mark smiled, a hint of pride surfacing. He watched as the two cleared a path until light shone through the opening. Mark grabbed his weapon and pushed past them, slowly climbing up the rocky slope until he emerged.

"Well, that's a problem," he said, looking around.

"Oh," he heard from Skye as she and Pete joined him.

Their castle in Kantenda stood to their right, the entrance to the room emptying to the training yard, which was filled with Elite who had lowered their weapons when he'd emerged.

"Mark? Skye? Pete?" Noah jabbered. "What? Where?" He looked from the hole to them, then back to the hole.

"I think this is going to take some work," Skye said.

"That's an understatement and something we don't have the time for," Mark said, noticing the position of the sun and how close to evening they were.

"Mind telling me what's going on?" Noah asked.

"Well, that's an interesting story. One I think we can tell you over food and beer."

"Ale, Mark. It's been years, get it right," Noah teased. "Where's the rest of your crew? Or do I not want to know?"

"I don't know if I want to imagine what they're doing back there," Skye said.

"Better not be. I have dibs," Pete said with a smirk.

"On that note, why don't you go back? Stay at Crimson's tonight and meet us in the morning for training. There's nothing we can do tonight, and I think you three need some time alone," Mark directed.

There was a glint in Pete's eye before he descended back through the opening.

"Do I want to know?"

"Food and *ale*, Noah," Mark said.

They needed to eat and contemplate everything they'd discovered and that which they hadn't. When they were through, he planned to spend the rest of the night making love to Skye and erasing the uncertainty that Pete's gazes had left in his mind.

BORMICK

We're alone," Bormick said, sliding his hand around Crimson's ass.

"In a gross tunnel of dirt," she said.

"I'll take you anywhere," he replied, kissing her neck.

"I thought Pete claimed me for tonight."

"Since when do I listen to Pete?"

"True, but that wall of dirt may have spiders on it."

He laughed. "You spend time with the Death God and you're afraid of spiders?"

She batted his arm, but he caught her wrist.

"Give me that sweet mouth of yours, then. I'm about to blow with all the tension today."

Pushing the sleeve of her dress down, he grabbed her breast, pulling at her nipple before bringing his mouth to it.

"Why don't you get on your knees and give me *your* sweet mouth?" she asked.

"Because you wouldn't be able to stand if my tongue was on you."

Her hand found him, and he groaned, wanting her so badly

that his dick ached. She undid his buttons, encasing him once she'd freed him, and gently stroked him.

"You want my mouth, do you?"

"Oh, yeah. I want you to take every inch of me and swallow what's dying for release."

Kissing him, Crimson let her tongue play with his, driving Bormick crazier when she slid it over his lips. Her tongue was a weapon of magic in its own right.

She dropped to her knees, her eyes still locked on his as she took him, her tongue licking his tip with a slow, tantalizing swipe before she plunged down his shaft. He moaned, spreading his legs to brace himself, his fingers kneading in her hair.

Her mouth felt fantastic around him, each move she made taking him closer to the edge. His dick pulsed in her mouth. He'd wanted her the entire time they'd been in this place. His thoughts of her mouth and her body had been relentless. Although it was rare that he didn't want her. He craved her constantly, needing her touch like he needed air to breathe. Her head bobbed to a rhythm that increased with his mounting need for release before she came back up, swirling her tongue around his head, delaying his satisfaction. Forcefully, he shoved her down so that she enveloped him again. The motion set him off. The orgasm ripped through him as she continued to take him until his body had calmed. Her mouth slowly lifted from him, her tongue taking a few more licks as he released a satisfied moan.

"Gods, woman, you are something," he said as she rose, her hand still wrapped around him.

"I want it," she said eagerly. "I need it."

Grunting, he pulled her to him, kissing her. He tried lifting her skirts to reach her but gave up, ripping her dress instead, her breasts falling free as a cry escaped her. Taking her breast in his mouth, he spread her legs with his knees as his length grew again.

Pushing her against the wall, Bormick's fingers slipped between her dampness, playing before moving to her clit. With his other hand, he massaged the breast his mouth wasn't devouring. Crimson squirmed as he drove two fingers deep inside of her. Her breathing grew ragged, a sound that left him throbbing again. With his thumb, he gently swept over her swollen nubs. With each lick, each touch, she grew closer, the quivers of her body against his threatening to take him over the edge. Her thighs tightened around his hand, her inner contractions squeezing around his fingers until he felt her crumble. Her climax rippled through her, the convulsions and her whimpers driving him mad.

When she stilled, her head fell back as she caught her breath. He gave her nipple one more lick, removing his drenched fingers from her warmth. The way she came was erotic in every way possible, and he loved it.

He brought his fingers up to taste her and she brought her mouth to his, licking his fingers with him, an act that sent him further into madness.

"You two couldn't wait, could you?" Pete said.

Bormick eyed him. "I've waited long enough."

"You're lucky I'm alone. I thought I said she was mine first."

"You did. We didn't fuck. Just had a little fun."

Pete didn't look convinced. "Is that why your pants are down?"

"His pants are down because my mouth had a little fun," Crimson said, the coy smile she was wearing stirring his need for more.

"You want your turn, Pete? You look like you need it. Too much time looking at the Mage Warrior's tight ass?" There was a distinct twitch in Pete's pants which gave away his arousal, even with the look he shot Bormick at his comment.

Bormick pulled his pants up. He was aching to be inside of Crimson but before he could button them, Pete had him against the wall.

"I got her ready for you, Pete. She's dripping. If you want to skip her and take me, go right ahead." He brought his finger up and licked it. "But she's soaked."

Pete reached his mouth out and took Bormick's finger in it, tasting what he'd tasted, the move making his erection pound. Something about Pete drove him as crazy as Crimson did. "Told you."

"If you two are going to do it, I'm definitely watching," Crimson cooed.

Pete's hand reached around his length, and a grunt escaped him. The warmth of his hand sent a barrage of sensations through him.

"How's it feel, Bormick? To have it turned on you? Does it feel good?"

Pete's mouth was close, and Bormick could feel his power, the seductive way it tingled on his skin.

"Shit, it feels good, Pete. finish me off."

Pete squeezed him, his hand moving the full length, then stroking him firmly back down. Bormick wrapped his hand around his neck and pulled him to his lips, forcing his tongue into his mouth where it wrestled for dominance with Pete's. Kissing Pete was a strange feeling, but not entirely unenjoyable. He dropped his other hand and grasped Pete's bulge through his pants.

Pete squeezed tighter, and Bormick let him go.

"Not unpleasant, but you don't kiss like Crimson."

"Gods, you two are killing me," Crimson whined.

He pulled his gaze from Pete's and looked at her. Her hand was between her legs, and she was squeezing them tight. Pete gave him one more hard jerk upward and let go, Bormick missing his touch.

"You'll finish me off later, I presume?" Bormick asked as Pete walked to Crimson, drew her in for a deep kiss, and picked her up over his shoulder. "Damn, I don't think I can walk," Bormick grumbled, holding his pants up and following them.

Pete made it out of the tunnel and out of the mage lair before he dropped Crimson in the dark hall and shoved her against the wall. Crimson let out a small gasp as Pete's hands ran the length of her naked body.

Bormick took a spot against the wall, cursing the need that had him pulsing and the annoying attraction he had for Pete. It confounded him and went against everything he was.

"I'm going to fuck you here," Pete said, Crimson catching her breath in response. "Then I'm going to take you into the closest room and fuck you again while Bormick joins us."

Even in the dark, Bormick could make out Crimson's expression. Pete's words had even turned him on, his length jerking in response. That aggressive side of Pete didn't come out often, but when it did, it sent Crimson into a frenzy. He absently wondered if it did have anything to do with Skye's presence. Pete wasn't usually the rough one. That was Bormick's role. There had to be more to that broody denial that he wasn't interested in her.

Crimson unhooked Pete's pants while he took off his shirt. Once he was free of it, he laced his hands under her ass and picked her up. Bormick heard her moan as Pete entered her. Her head fell back, and Pete's mouth dropped to suck her breasts, the sight causing a surge of need in Bormick.

They were going to make him come, and he didn't care. He let his pants go and brought his hand around himself, feeling the heat. Crimson's legs were wrapped around Pete, and he could see the man's leg muscles primed, his ass clenched tight with each thrust he made.

Gods, he thought, his hand quickening its pace with Crimson's cries.

There was something about the two of them together that was beyond what he and Crimson shared. She and Pete had an intensity that went further, one that spiked his arousal whenever he watched them.

His urge for release grew as Pete's rhythm became more frantic. Pete was close and judging from the quivers in Crimson's muscles, so was she. Her head tipped back again, the look on her face driving Bormick so that he climaxed as she did, his essence spilling to the floor. Pete's release followed, his body pounding her hard through it, his grip like steel on her skin. Bormick watched Pete's muscles relax as he caught his own breath, leaning his head on the wall to steady his shaking legs.

Pete walked with Crimson still wrapped around him and threw the closest door open with his magic. A white sheet covered the bed and Pete sent it sliding off, lowering her to the bed and moving over her. Moonlight seeped in through the window, illuminating them.

Bormick followed them and crawled onto the bed. "You're not leaving me out of this one."

He met both their mouths. Pete's mouth and his fighting to dominate her mouth. He felt Crimson smile against him, his tongue dancing with both of theirs until Pete backed away, moving from her and letting Bormick touch her. Crimson purred as his hand caressed her breast, and Pete sat back to watch him play. Bormick wanted to taste her, to taste their juices, but he wanted to be inside of her as well. Compromising, he made his way down her stomach, hearing her moan when his tongue met her skin.

Pete's remains were dripping from her and she was a sweet mix of both their juices. He let his tongue roll around the moisture before spreading her open with his fingers and sucking the rest of it with a groan. Lifting his head to look at her, he said, "You two taste good. Suck on Pete for a few minutes, Crimson, while I lap this goodness up. Wanna taste, Pete?"

He licked his lips in exaggeration. Desire flashed behind Pete's eyes; something in him had moved him past his hesitancy. Whether it was the power he still had pouring from his aura or something else, Bormick wasn't sure. Pete moved to him, pulling his mouth to his and licking his lips before sinking his tongue into his mouth.

Crimson groaned. The kiss didn't last long. Pete drew away and dropped his head to lick Crimson, his eyes never leaving Bormick's. There was no explanation for what they were heading toward, nothing but the blood that linked them. Bormick's dick was pounding in anticipation for it.

Pete lifted his head and sat back, his length protruding, still glistening with their sex. The sight was inviting and a part of him longed to lick Pete clean and see what it felt like to have him in his mouth, the other wanting Pete to be the one to bend, to experience his mouth around his cock. It wasn't something he'd ever imagined, but with Pete he could.

"Just take it, Bormick, or get your tongue back on me," Crimson said.

"Just for that, I'm going to make you come twice. Suck him while I play, Crimson."

Pete gave him a lopsided grin then positioned himself near Crimson's mouth, which took him in like she'd been craving him. Bormick watched, his groin tightening. He dipped back down, pushing his tongue along Crimson before plunging into her. Bringing his thumb up to rub her hard clit, he kept his other hand gripped snuggly around her leg.

With each lick, she quivered more, Pete's moans urging his own dick to beg for release. Her muscles clenched as he brought her to climax, her moisture filling his mouth while she continued to squirm below his touch. Rising, Bormick scooped her ass up and penetrated her with a force that jerked her against Pete's dick. Crimson's teeth slid down Pete in reaction as she gripped his hilt. Her mouth released him, and Bormick could tell Pete wasn't far from losing it.

"Time to join me, Pete," Bormick growled, sinking deeper into Crimson and smashing his mouth over hers. He reached his hand out, gripping Pete, who pushed against him, sliding in and out of his hand at the same rhythm as Bormick's own length moved in Crimson.

Crimson's hand latched onto Pete's hair, her body quivering, close to another climax. His hardness was hot in Bormick's hands and Bormick's own need crested as Pete broke first, spilling over his hand before he pushed forward and streamed over Crimson's breasts.

When he tried to move away, Bormick held on, jerking through the remains of his orgasm as Crimson fell apart below him, her body so clenched around him that he was forced to release Pete and dig his hands into the bed as his own climax crashed over him, the waves reverberating through him until he collapsed onto Crimson. Pete's essence squished against their chests.

Crimson's chest heaved below his, her legs squeezing as another climax hit her.

"Shit," he said, kissing her neck and holding her through it.

Pete had fallen back, his hand across his face, his own chest rising and falling, a few drops of his sex on the tip of his head. Bormick licked his lips at the temptation. He had the sudden urge to taste Pete, knowing if he did, there was no turning back from what that step meant and what it would do to their relationship.

Bormick raised himself and took Crimson's breast in his mouth, a groan escaping her. He sucked it, taking in Pete's essence as he licked her clean, watching Pete, who's softening stopped, his manhood jerking slightly in reaction. Bormick rose above Crimson's head, letting her lick his chest clean and grunting as she took his nipple with her teeth.

When she was done, he moved from her and, throwing caution to the wind, ran his tongue over Pete, wiping away the stray drops. A current of arousal flushed through him, as he tried to comprehend why his body was reacting this way. His dick rose with Pete's moan, and he couldn't stop his own groan from rumbling through his chest. He started to draw away, a mix of confusion jumbling with the pleasurable sensations halting his move, but Pete pushed him down, forcing his mouth to take him further.

"Christ," Pete mumbled. "What the hell, Bormick?"

But his hand remained on Bormick's head, and Bormick lowered his mouth as far as he could, wondering just how Crimson did it. Pete's hand pushed him further, asserting his dominance, making Bormick his beta. The thrill of it had his length pulsing. Pete removed his hand and Bormick rose, slowly licking him like he would Crimson's breast.

"Gods, you two are driving me insane," Crimson said.

Pete wrapped his hand in Bormick's hair and smashed his lips against his again, kissing him as if he his life depended on it. Waves of need flooded him before Pete pushed him back aggressively, his body hovering over Bormick's while his tongue continued its assault on Bormick's mouth. He was a good kisser—strong, assertive, commanding, and every part of Bormick yearned for more.

Pete drew back, then lowered himself, taking Bormick's length into his own mouth. Crimson lost it, her cries meeting Bormick's groan as she climaxed again. Bormick took his hand and pushed Pete further just as Pete had done to him. Their dominance was now equal. Pete had surrendered his with Bormick's move, bringing them both back as alphas.

Bormick released Pete's head. "Fuck him, Crimson. I want you to ride him while both of you pleasure me."

Pete rose and moved back to the bed frame, sitting up before wiping his mouth with the back of his hand. He gestured for Crimson and she spread her legs around him and enveloped him, Bormick moving closer to watch them.

"I want to see your magic," Pete said, bringing her finger to his mouth and biting her hard enough to break the skin.

She inhaled sharply, and Bormick pulled her hair back so that she could reach her birthmark. The mark sparkled, turning a rich crimson. She leaned over to kiss Pete, pulling his magic out to play, then taking her own copy as her body rose and fell on him. Her aura shifted, the room suddenly tingling with magic as he and Crimson both let it go.

The magic was sensual, dancing across Bormick's skin. Crimson's hand pulled Bormick to her mouth, the velvety feeling of her tongue against his shaft sending shivers through him. Pete was in a mood, his aggressiveness unusual, and it excited Bormick when he was like this.

He switched between her mouth and Pete's hand until he finally came, her mouth catching his release as Pete held her steady. Pete flipped her when Bormick's climax calmed, taking her from behind as the magic grew heavier. He pounded against her and Bormick came under her to play with her, his fingers finding her clit. His other fingers wrapped around Pete's shaft as he slid in and out of her.

"Fuck," Pete muttered. Bormick knew she felt good. Crimson was soaked and close to another orgasm, but Pete broke first, thrusting into her until he finally went still and Bormick pushed him away.

"I'll finish her," he said.

"You finished her last time," Pete said, still breathing hard.

Bormick grabbed Pete's dick and tasted her on him. It was an erotic sensation, and he meant it to be quick, but the taste and the feel was too much. He licked Pete clean, sucking on his head until Pete cried out. Pete's fingers were pulling his hair, pushing him down until Crimson said, "I'm waiting. Let Pete finish me off."

Bormick went to rise, but Pete shoved him back down.

"Keep doing that while I take care of her."

"Asshole," he muttered as Crimson climbed over Pete and clung to the headboard. Pete's other hand grasped her hip, his tongue rising to pleasure her.

Bormick listened as she cried out, her cries rising with her ecstasy. With each cry, Pete's erection grew firmer in Bormick's mouth. When he heard her scream, Pete's hand moved from holding Bormick's head in order to steady her convulsing hips. Bormick rose and sat back, watching Crimson as Pete held her steady, his tongue torturing her until she finally pulled away, collapsing next to Bormick.

Sweat dripped between her breasts and Pete moved to lick it away, the magic slowly fading from the room. He kissed Crimson again, then moved his head down to trail her stomach before kissing her between her legs. Bormick saw her legs clench in response, the sight an enticing one. Pete released his magic again so that his entire aura was shadowed in gray, the seductiveness of it feeling like fingers along Bormick's skin.

Pete took Bormick in his mouth again, going further before rising back up, returning the dominance back to Bormick in that single move.

"Shit," Bormick said, pulling him in for another kiss, Pete's magic urging him on, the need pulsing through him.

Pete drew back and situated himself between Bormick and Crimson, scooting them both to make room. The move didn't go unnoticed; it had been deliberate. A statement of where he was in the relationship.

"Dick," Bormick said.

"Yes, I am," Pete answered.

"Do you two fantasize about other men?" Crimson asked. "I mean, I'll gladly bring a few more in—"

"No," they both said.

"Then what is this? Trust me, it's a turn on, but what is it?"

"I don't know," Bormick said, "but I am not touching another man."

The thought was revolting. He liked his women...his woman, now that Crimson had tamed him.

"Nor am I." Pete made a grimace that matched what Bormick was feeling.

Crimson looked between the two. "Blood ritual?"

"Gotta be," Pete said.

"Agreed. I have never craved another man's dick. Sure, in rough times, I've had a hand or two do the job for me. It gets desperate out there."

"Stavin?" she asked.

"Yeah, but that's all, and that's because I trusted him. I did not return the favor, though. He just liked experimenting and so I let him."

"Experimenting?" Pete said with an eyebrow raise.

"Just the hand, Pete. You're the first man to lay a mouth on this puppy."

"I feel so privileged."

"You should. Wait until I come in that pretty mouth of yours, then you'll really feel privileged."

"As long as I'm coming in yours at the same time," he returned.

The laugh came from deep below, Pete joining him.

"Should I be worried that you two are going to run off and leave me for each other?" Crimson asked, her voice sleepy.

"Not a chance, babe. Without you, there is no us," he said, leaning across Pete to kiss her forehead.

"Good," she replied, running a hand down his face, her finger lingering on his lips. "Because I think I would die without you both."

Her sleepy eyes closed, her head tipping against Pete. He scooted her down with Pete's help, Pete moving down beside her and pulling her in against him.

Bormick lowered himself over Pete.

"Guess this means you're my plaything, Pete," he said.

"I don't think so. We're on equal footing, Bormick, only because I let you there."

Pete's eyes were dangerous, their blue mesmerizing, the same shade Bormick knew his own were.

"Now, if you're done drooling over me, we should get some rest before you suck my cock in the morning," Pete continued.

"Ha! I love it when you talk dirty to me, Pete."

Pete rolled over, brushing Bormick's reforming erection with his leg.

"Does that thing ever go down?"

"Not around the two of you. Why do you get to snuggle with her while you sleep?"

"Because I'm the alpha."

Bormick grumbled before pressing up against Pete's back out of spite, his length situated on his ass.

"Seriously?"

"You put me here." He reached his hand around Pete, making sure to hold on to the length that was still present.

"You're a real shithead," Pete said, but Bormick heard the humor in his voice. Whatever this was, they'd crossed the line and accepted it with no way to turn back.

BORMICK

Bormick woke well before dawn. His body was still relaxed from the previous night's endeavors, but his mind was wide awake. Pete was sprawled out next to him, his hand over Bormick's morning growth. Crimson was leaning against Pete, his other arm around her. He thought of waking Pete and harassing him for his hand position, maybe forcing Pete to jerk him off, but he didn't. Pete was moody before morning sex. No need to wake the beast.

Bormick slipped out from under him, Pete turning and moving Crimson's body into his arms. They often slept like that. It was part of the connection they had that went further than what Bormick had with Crimson. It didn't bother him. He still loved Crimson, and she loved him. The thought occurred to him that the feeling might have spread to Pete, but admitting love for the man took what they were doing to a different level, and he wasn't ready for that. He craved Pete like he craved Crimson, but he would admit no more. He didn't know if he could admit that he'd lay his life down for either of them, either of his lovers. It was a thought that was foreign to him.

He dressed, glancing at them once more before making his

way through the dark hallway. The darkness didn't frighten him, not much did, save for the thought of losing Crimson and maybe even Pete.

As Bormick made his way through the castle, he stopped and listened. Everything was quiet, but he couldn't shake the feeling he needed to be aware of something. He should have returned to his quarters and cleaned up—he could smell Crimson on him, taste her and Pete on his lips—but instead, he left the castle, walking out to the grounds.

The moon was lowering in the pre-dawn sky, making way for the sun. Barely any light shone from it. He paused again, that feeling calling to him, like an instinctual drive. The air felt thick and heavy with something he couldn't define. The feeling reminded him of the auras around Pete and the others. There, but not quite whole. Bormick closed his eyes and let himself relax to the sounds of night, but there were none. No chirps from birds, no insects humming. Nothing. Something was coming. He'd felt it since the day Crimson had returned from Derrant, but had never been able to pinpoint the sensation. All he knew was that he had a nudging that there was something he needed to be concerned about. It was stronger now, a fact that he didn't like.

Moving back to the castle with haste, he made his way to the room where he'd left Crimson and Pete, a strong relief filling him that they were all right.

"Wake up, you two," he said abruptly.

Crimson made a sound similar to a grunt, and Pete threw a pillow at him.

"Come on, we need to get back to Skye and Mark."

Crimson sat up, her breasts bouncing with the movement. "You're dressed?"

"It's not even daylight. Go back to sleep, both of you," Pete complained.

"Pete, he's dressed."

Pete rolled over, his erection proud and blatant.

"I see you missed me," Bormick joked.

Pete ignored him. "Why are you dressed? You never skip relief from your morning hard-on."

"We need to go."

"They're not even up," Crimson said, crawling over Pete to him, then tugging at his pants.

"Why is it so urgent we go now?" Pete asked as Crimson's foot played with his length, her hands finding Bormick's.

The feel of her hand around him, threatened to distract him. "Dammit, Crimson, you make it hard to focus."

"I know," she said, taking him in her mouth.

Bormick grunted but persisted with his need to get the two to stop playing around. "There's something wrong, like something in the air. I don't know what it is, but I can sense it."

Pete narrowed his eyes, and Crimson lifted her head, sitting back on her knees.

Bormick's dick leaned toward her, seeking more.

"Like what?" Pete asked.

"I don't know. It's just a feeling I've been having, and it's strong today."

Pete glanced out the window. "We can't very well storm in there and say you feel funny. They're all asleep."

"Yeah, I'm sure it's nothing that can't wait until you relieve that need and take me," Crimson said.

He looked to Pete who was the more level-headed of the two.

"She's right, it can wait until dawn, then we'll discuss it with Skye and Mark. For now, one of you needs to take care of my raging hard on."

"You two are deviants."

"Says the man who can't go five minutes without sex."

Giving up, Bormick removed his shirt and pants, then joined them, taking Crimson from behind while she went down on Pete. His eyes stayed locked on Pete as they both relieved their need. It was well into morning when they were all sated, the urgent instinct to leave submerged below the insatiable craving for his mates.

THE MORNING WAS UNEVENTFUL. None of them mentioned Bormick's earlier suspicions that something was on the wind, thinking it best to have some hint of what it was first. Bormick stood aside as Skye taught Crimson more about her magic, and the subtle ways to use it. They were both dressed in those tight outfits again, but he was distracted, that feeling intensifying as the morning faded. He stared to the east where a haze had formed. It sat in the sky like a layer of fog, indistinct to anyone but him.

Bormick wiped his eyes, wishing the haze would fade, but his attempt didn't help.

"What's wrong?" Mark asked.

He hadn't noticed the man approach and cursed himself for not being on guard. "Why do you ask, Elite?"

Even teasing Mark with the nickname he'd given him didn't have the same pleasure it normally did.

"For one, you've been staring off toward the Fettered Forest all morning. And I don't think you've ever gone so long without making a sexual reference about either of the scantily clad women training before you."

His eyes flicked to Crimson and Skye, taking in their curves, the breasts that seemed to spill over, especially on Crimson.

"Do you want me to?"

"Not particularly. Something's bothering you. I've trained enough Elite—been trained long enough myself to know when someone's on guard. What is it?"

"A feeling I've had all morning. That's all, though, just an unsettled feeling. A shift in the air."

Mark studied him. His mind was sharp, his own warrior instinct always on guard like Bormick's. "What kind of shift?"

"Well, that's the crux, I don't know. All I know is something's coming."

"Why didn't you tell us this earlier?"

Bormick shrugged. "I had planned to, but then it didn't seem like it was necessary. I mean, what do you do about a feeling?"

"You heed it. What do you see to the east?"

"A subtle aura, sitting on the horizon," he said, looking in that direction.

"You've been a fighter long enough to listen to your intuition, Bormick."

He turned his eyes back to Mark. "And what would you have done if I'd told you? The aura to the east only just appeared. I was contemplating it when you approached. It was only a feeling, now it's a presence."

Mark glanced to where Bormick had been staring.

"What will you do with the information, Elite? Do you send your men on a hunt for something you can't describe? Or do you wait for it to present itself and pray it's not death?"

Mark was quiet as he continued to look. Bormick could see his mind strategizing. A true commander, much like himself.

"Now, do you see my conundrum?"

"Yes. The wizard village lies to the east, deep in the Fettered Forest."

"What's your call, commander?"

"Now you use my title?"

Bormick let out a laugh. "Don't get used to it."

He glanced at Crimson and Skye. Pete was making his way over to where they stood, likely knowing Bormick was telling Mark what he'd experienced earlier. He hadn't talked to Pete about the growing sensation.

"We've got a Shadow Mage and two Mage Warriors. I'd say our odds are high for facing whatever it is on the horizon," Mark finally said.

"What are you two up to? You've never been this civil for so long," Pete said. His blue eyes were inquisitive, still holding a satisfied look within them.

The morning for the three of them had been another interesting one. He and Pete had pushed their new comfort with each other, Crimson only adding to the thrill of it. That strange attraction he had to Pete was growing, the bond between the three of them strengthening. Bormick had the urge to pull Pete to his lips and kiss him but shook it off, listening as Mark suggested they take a trip to the Fettered Forest.

"Wizards?" Pete asked.

"Wizards," Bormick answered.

"Isn't a mage the same as a wizard?"

"No, wizards are...closer to you. Shadow Magic layers their magic, but their power is also a mix of what full mages have. The kingdoms once saw them as mages who'd turned bad, gone rogue, and embraced the darker parts of magic," Mark explained.

"Interesting. This world is still taking some getting used to. All these different mages and now wizards."

"Ranks, the mages are different ranks," Bormick corrected. "Like in an army."

Pete scowled. "I was never a soldier, Bormick, you know that."

"Oh, I do. You're a soft, pretty boy."

"Really? Don't make me hurt you."

"I invite it," he said, laughing at Pete's attempted bravado.

"While you do whatever it is you two do, I'm grabbing some Elite, just in case." Mark walked off, shaking his head.

"It's really worsened?" Pete asked.

"Yeah. I can't shake it. There's something off."

"Maybe we should have told them earlier like you wanted instead of sleeping in."

"That was sleeping?"

"You know what I mean."

"What would we have said? Only now do I see the aura. I had nothing more." He moved closer to Pete, pulling his head in so that his mouth brushed his ear. "Besides, I enjoyed your mouth on my cock this morning. One of these days, I'm going to come in it and watch as you swallow me whole."

"Who says it will be me swallowing? You presume I'm going to give first."

"You will. You already have."

Bormick moved quick, bringing his mouth to Pete's. Pete matched the kiss hungrily before pulling back and wiping his mouth on the back of his hand.

"Not outside the bedroom, Bormick."

"Are we going to be a dirty little secret?"

"Ha, you're dirty all right, but you're not little."

Bormick laughed, then caught Skye and Crimson watching them. Skye's mouth had dropped and there was a distinct flush to her face. Crimson's eyes were shimmering with lust, leaving her looking like a hungry predator.

"Secret's out, Pete, and I think the Mage Queen likes it."

"Dickhead," Pete mumbled.

"That's not what that bulge in your pants says."

"I hate to break it to you, but you've got the same bulge."

"Wanna go play with it?"

Pete rolled his eyes.

"Hey, you two," Crimson yelled. "You're turning Skye on. Now either give us a show or stop being clit teases."

"Gods, I love our dirty girl," Bormick groaned. "You know, I really want to jerk you off right now."

"I thought you did enough of that this morning."

"Doesn't mean I'm not still tempted."

"Not gonna happen. Now shut it down and be serious. Here comes Mark with his men." Pete stood straighter, his demeanor turning serious.

"You're no fun."

"You want to get it on in front of a bunch of Elite?" Pete replied with a raise of his brow.

"Not particularly. You're the only man I want seeing or touching my dick."

"Nice."

They'd drawn nearer to Skye and Crimson. Skye's eyes were looking between them.

"You guys..." she started, and Bormick could see the desire behind her eyes. There was something in the way she looked at Pete each time that gave him pause. It was the same way Pete looked at her, then dropped his eyes, as if he'd had an improper thought.

"Let's just say our relationship is developing," Pete muttered hesitantly.

"It's sexy, Skye. I can come just watching them," Crimson said.

Skye gave Crimson a look that Bormick couldn't read, not knowing whether it was disgust or envy.

"I had no idea you were bi, Pete," she said, turning back to them with a slight blush to her cheeks.

"Now what a minute. I do not like guys, Skye. I'm straight all the way."

"It's not something to be ashamed of."

"I'm not bi and neither is Bormick."

Mark had come up to them by this point.

"I missed something, didn't I?" he asked.

"What's bi?" Bormick asked.

Crimson shrugged, clearly as lost as he was.

"Wait, did you two... Finally! Jesus, the sexual tension was almost too much to bear." Mark's relief made Bormick chuckle, but he was still confused as to what Skye and Pete meant.

"We're not into guys, Skye," Pete said defensively. "And no, we didn't, Mark."

"Nope," Bormick agreed, understanding now. "I need a nice pair of breasts and three holes for this guy." He grabbed his crotch and gestured.

"Three?" Skye asked, her eyes wide.

"Mark, you haven't—"

"Enough, Bormick. We do not need to be dragged into this."

Crimson whispered to Skye, and her cheeks flushed again, causing Bormick to laugh.

"You might want to try that with her sometime, Mark. I'd be happy to loosen her up for you."

"I think you've got enough to play with," he gritted.

Skye's eyes were still on Bormick, her flush fading as she studied him. It unnerved Bormick that she was having trouble looking at Pete, her eyes lingering briefly before they focused back on him. There was definitely something subtle to the way she and Pete were acting around each other lately. Something that hadn't surfaced enough for them to understand, nor for the others to notice.

"If you two don't like men, then why?" Skye asked, bringing his focus back.

"We think it's our blood," Crimson said. "They want each other as much as they want me."

Pete rubbed his face like he wanted the conversation to end, but Bormick was enjoying his discomfort.

"That's different," Mark said.

Bormick couldn't help saying, "Want to watch, Elite? I might take him in the ass later."

"Like hell you will," Pete groused.

"Oh, that's right, you need to swallow me first."

He could see Pete's anger building, his aura shifting, layering in places. Pete's fist met Bormick's eye before he could avoid it.

"Damn, Pete, that's gonna leave a mark."

Mark threw his hands up in the air. "And then they're back to this again."

"You know I like it rough. Why don't you bring that temper the next time you're sucking my cock?" Bormick teased Pete, rubbing his sore eye.

Pete grabbed Bormick's shirt. "Why don't you the next time you're sucking mine, asshole?"

"Gods, you're hot when you're angry," Bormick taunted.

"If you two don't stop, Skye and I are going to orgasm right here. She's got to be as wet as I am," Crimson whined.

Mark looked at Skye sharply.

"I-I... I'm fine."

"Why don't you check her, Mark?"

"Why don't you stop antagonizing Pete, leave my wife's wet panties out of the subject, and focus?"

"I don't think she wears panties, Mark," Bormick said, knowing it was the truth. The tight pants she wore left nothing to the imagination.

Mark glared at him.

"I'm not wet, Mark," Skye argued.

"Like hell you aren't, and I will gladly take care of that later. A few times."

She gave him a sexy smile, her eyes lighting. There was no way those two would ever consider sharing each other. She and Mark were too close, their bond visible to Bormick in the slight aura that floated between them as though their souls were connected. They took love to an entirely different level.

Bormick noticed Pete's aura flicker for just a moment at Mark's words. So, Bormick wasn't the only one who found the Mage Warrior enticing, no matter how much Pete denied it. He looked back at Skye, noticing a shimmer in her aura that leaned away from Mark and in the direction of Pete's before it dissipated. Bormick blinked his eyes, unable to contemplate what either of their aura shifts meant and choosing to let it go. They had other things to worry about.

"You're a mood killer, Mark," Bormick said instead, removing Pete's hands from him. He grasped Pete's neck and pulled his ear close, whispering, "You gonna have your mind on Skye's curves while you're fucking Crimson tonight? Maybe imagine it's her mouth on you?"

"Fuck you, Bormick."

Pete tried pushing him away, but Bormick held tight. "I invite it, and I want you to play rough like that tonight when you're fucking us." He let go and walked to the others. "Let's go."

He caught Skye's eyes flick to the bulge in his pants.

"It's there if you want to touch, Skye. I'd say I might break such a delicate flower like you, but I have a feeling Mark's dick is just as big."

"Jesus, you are something," Mark muttered, using one of those strange expressions like Pete used. "And for the record, I am just as big, if not bigger. Now, let's go."

Bormick couldn't help laughing. Mark was growing on him. They were alike in many ways, and Bormick respected the man.

"How do you concentrate, Crimson?" Skye asked.

"I don't."

Crimson met Bormick's eyes and licked her lips.

Yeah, this evening was going to be their best yet, and he was planning to take her until she passed out. After, he'd play with Pete until they had sufficiently satisfied themselves. Maybe then he'd sleep.

SKYE

Skye hated to admit how sexy she found Pete and Bormick together. And that kiss. Mark was right, she was definitely wet, and the first chance she had to drag him into a private space, she was going to use him to her full ability.

They'd risen early, and she'd woken him, taking that waiting length into her before his eyes even opened and then riding him until he was fully awake. She'd climaxed twice before he'd flipped her to her back and made her melt like he always did. She couldn't imagine having two of him. He filled her in so many ways, brought her crumbling to her knees and lifted her right back up, just as he'd done with his mouth earlier.

"Are you blushing, Skye?" Mark whispered. "Since when do you blush?"

She turned into him and whispered back, "Just thinking about everything I'm going to do to you later."

"Shit," he muttered.

"Do we need to take a break before we go investigate?" Bormick asked.

Mark looked over his shoulder at Noah and the two other Elite, then sighed, saying, "No."

"Investigate what?" she asked, resting her head against his shoulder.

"Bormick thinks something is coming."

"And it's not Crimson," Bormick joked.

Crimson elbowed him.

"Like what? Whatever Derrant was hinting at?" Skye asked, ignoring the two of them.

"I have no idea, but Mark thinks we shouldn't take a chance, that we should check it out and I agree."

He was so different when he wasn't being a sex-obsessed brute. His presence was commanding, warrior-like. He was a leader like Mark. She wondered what else lie below the surface.

"With you, Pete, and Crimson, since she still has your magic in her, whatever it is should be easy to defeat."

"Sounds a bit confident," Pete said.

"She did trick the Death God," Mark said.

"But I didn't defeat him."

He kissed her forehead. "It'll be fine."

"All right. Let's go test these new abilities out," Crimson said. "Where are we going?"

"The Fettered Forest."

"No one goes there," Crimson said, her eyes wide in surprise.

"We do," Skye said. "The wizards are our friends and our allies. If anyone knows what's going on, they will. Is that where you sensed it, Bormick?"

"Not sure. It's to the east. A strange aura, like a haze in the air."

"Well, then, let's not keep it waiting. I want to return so I can take my fantasies out on Mark," she said with a flirtatious purr to her voice.

Mark groaned, a sound that only managed to leave her even more soaked.

"Ha! I knew there was a siren under there, Skye. There would have to be to keep a man like Mark satisfied," Bormick said, a huge grin on his face.

Skye caught Pete's eye, the quick flash of something that looked like desire there before she pulled her eyes away, unsure why she liked that it was there.

"He's never satisfied," she said, looking into Mark's hazel eyes and forgetting the others were there.

"Yes, I am," he said, pulling her close and kissing her.

"We'd better go before they do it right here," Pete said, eliciting a laugh from Crimson.

"I wouldn't object to seeing that," Bormick said.

"Crimson already had a view, the rest of you don't need one."

Bormick's mouth dropped open. "You watched them fuck?"

"Good gods did I. Don't put that image back in my head or none of us will go anywhere."

"When did this happen?" Pete asked, crossing his arms. Skye detected a hint of irritation in his voice.

"She let herself in the morning she came to talk to us," Mark said.

"Really, Crimson?" Pete asked.

"Well, I didn't know they were like us."

"You tormented my husband for how long and you didn't notice his sex drive?" Skye couldn't help the snarky tone.

Crimson gave her a devious grin. "Do you really want the truth about that?"

"No, forget I asked."

"Okay, I'm ready to move past my sex drive now," Mark grumbled.

"I'm up for that," Pete said.

Bormick's hand went to Pete's crotch before he could react.

"Not enough, you aren't," he joked as Pete pushed him away.

Skye couldn't help noticing the slight rise where Bormick's hand had been, wondering absently at the size that pushed against his pants.

Gesturing to Bormick, Mark said, "You are a saint, Pete, for putting up with that every day."

"What's a saint? A pervert who likes to fuck, 'cause if so, that's what he is."

"All right then," Skye said, not sure what to say. Pete was glaring at Bormick. "Let's see if there's something going on in the Fettered Forest, shall we?"

"That would be best," Mark agreed, gesturing for Noah and the others to join them.

Noah looked irritated at having been made to wait, and Skye didn't blame him.

"Whenever you're ready, dear," Mark said.

Since Pete didn't know the way, Skye would have to form the portal. She pulled the hues around them and summoned the portal, directing its location. As she went to step through, Mark stopped her.

"I think it would be best if I go first," he said, drawing his weapon.

She put her hand on his to stop him. "You go in like that, and Bridget will have a fit."

"I don't care. If there is something wrong, then I'm going in prepared."

"Mark, they would have alerted us."

He glanced back at Bormick. "I'm not taking a chance."

He stepped through, disappearing before she could argue more.

Skye started to follow, but Noah stopped her. "Someone should go in with you."

"I'll go with Skye," Bormick said.

She looked quickly to him, having not expected Bormick to be the one to offer.

"As second in command, I go with her," Noah argued.

Bormick only threw him a look and shoved him out of the

way. "I'm bigger and stronger. I'll go in with Skye. Pete, go through with Crimson. You three Elite go last."

"The Elite stay with their warrior."

"Then consider me a temporary Elite. I'm going through with her."

"I don't need an escort," Skye argued.

"Well, you're getting one," he said, drawing his weapon and directing Noah to move behind Pete and Crimson. Noah looked like he wanted to fight Bormick, but he stormed away. Hopefully, Mark wouldn't punish him for heeding Bormick's command.

"A Mage Warrior is only weak without her Elite, Bormick," she tried once more.

"You really believe that shit?"

"You're not going to persuade him, Skye," Pete said, his voice reassuring. "Just go with him. I've got your back if something happens to you."

"I really don't need an escort," she said, meeting Pete's eyes, that strange tingle going through her before she dragged them away.

"Too bad. Now come on before I push you through that portal," Bormick grumbled.

She huffed and stepped through with him, straight into a world of chaos.

"Shit!" Bormick yelled, but something hit him, sending him slamming into her, the two of them tumbling together.

When they landed, she saw his weapon in the ground inches from her face. He jumped up, yanking it from the ground and shoving her behind him. They were too late to stop the others who were stepping through.

Skye drew her hues, trying to find Mark and figure out what they had stepped into.

"Close the portal!" Mark yelled from across the field of disarray.

Noah and the two Elite were through, weapons warding off

an attack. She aimed her magic at the portal, sending it fragmenting and the hues scattering like diamonds.

"Start fighting, Skye," Bormick commanded, his weapon cutting down a man in a white and gold uniform.

Mark was fighting two of them, his face tense and determined. Pete stood in front of Crimson, his shadows leaping from him with deadly intent. Crimson pulled hues and dropped a figure in robes.

Two wizards were across the field, their magic filling the air, along with bright flickers of magic that came from more robed figures. Not many wizards remained, a fact that was both heartbreaking and terrifying, but Skye didn't have time to think about it. She yanked the hues from a soldier's uniform, strangling him with them before he could reach Bormick, who was positioned in front of her.

"Good girl," he said, raising his two weapons to fight a sudden rush of guards.

He forced them away from her and she began drawing what she could, downing a soldier about to attack Mark from behind. He caught her eye before stopping a blade.

Bormick had moved further from her, and it was only then that she noticed everyone had been separated from her.

"Mark!" she yelled, and he looked over again, his weapon tearing through the man he was fighting. She had to hold back the bile the scene induced.

Mark's eyes widened and her heart thumped at the fear his expression caused her.

"Skye!" He started running to her, a look of desperation and terror in his eyes, but a bolt of golden magic hit him, sending him toward more soldiers.

"Mage Warrior," she heard from behind her.

"Skye!" Bormick yelled, his voice filled with the fear the voice had invoked in her.

She swiveled to find a man with piercing blue and gold eyes standing behind her.

She pulled the gold from his cape, but a splitting pain ripped through her head, a scream escaping her as magic pinned her arms and legs in place. Her eyes burned with an intensity that heightened the scream.

She heard Mark yell, followed by Bormick, then nothing but silence surrounded her as the world went black.

MARK

When Mark stepped through the portal, the scene before him sent his heart racing. An unseen force grabbed him as he tried to warn the others, sending him across the battlefield. He pushed himself from the ground to find two men in white and gold running toward him with their weapons drawn. Having no time to do anything but defend himself, he could barely take in the sight of the bodies of people he'd known for years. Bodies were sprawled across the ground, only a handful still fighting.

He struck one of the fighters, seeing Skye emerge from the portal with Bormick at her side. He thanked the gods the man had come through with her. They needed to close the portal before the others came through, until he knew what was going on, or they might all be dead.

"Close the portal!" Mark yelled. He went to add that she should flee, but one of the fighters nicked him, slicing through his sleeve.

Mark struck with a blow that downed the man, leaving him to fight only the second man who was matching his blows with the force of ten men. With Skye's presence, his weapon hummed with power. From the corner of his eye, he saw a bolt of magic hit Bormick and send them both toppling. His gut clenched, as Bormick's sword spiraled close to Skye's head, but Bormick deftly angled it away, so they landed with no injuries.

Two more fighters set their sights on Mark, and he had to draw his eyes from Skye against every need to get to her and protect her. He caught sight of Pete and Crimson as he turned. Pete's magic was already attacking as Noah and the other two Elite emerged.

They needed more. This was an army versus their few, but there was no way to call more Elite at this point. Mark cut down another fighter, seeing the portal shatter and thanking Skye silently. It was too late for them to do anything but fight and they didn't need any chance of this army slipping into the rest of the kingdom. He heard a roar and saw a Noctum snap the neck of a fighter before a streak of magic took it down.

He couldn't get a good view of who they were fighting. Some were in robes, others with swords as if they were another version of Mage Warrior and Elite. Magic bounded around him, Pete's shadows casting an angry fog over them. Crimson was holding her own with Skye's magic, Pete still keeping her as close to him as possible.

Mark heard Skye call his name and he sliced through a final fighter, turning to see her. He needed to get to her. Bormick was protecting her, allowing her the ability to use her magic, but Bormick had been pushed away, five soldiers engaging him.

"Skye!" Mark called running toward her, fear striking him as a robed figure approached behind her. His worst nightmare was taking form. He was separated from Skye, his Mage Warrior was without her Elite, just as in the mage wars. Fear clawed through him with a force that had him running, taking down anyone who stood in his way until a strike of magic hit him and he was thrown. He landed on his feet in time to see two more soldiers running toward him with deadly intent. They were purposely keeping him from Skye as if they knew she needed her Elite. He spotted Noah, who had also been forced further from her with the other Elite.

They knew that a Mage Warrior was only vulnerable when her Elite were not by her side. The fear grew as he heard Bormick yell Skye's name.

Skye turned to the figure. The first soldier brought her sword down to meet Mark's. The feel of the two weapons as they met reverberated through his arms.

He cut the woman down, using his other weapon to hold the second soldier at bay. Skye's scream broke through the battle noise, sending his heart pounding. His fury at her pain was so strong he decapitated the solder and ran, seeing Bormick's weapon explode through three soldiers, hitting one then slicing through the other two.

Bormick turned as Skye fell before the figure. Mark ran, cutting down anyone who stopped him, but he was too far from her. He screamed Skye's name, seeing Pete's shadows engage the figure. Skye's body lifted, a blinding light appearing behind the figure, snuffing out the shadows. Magic entangled Mark. He pushed against it, never taking his eyes from the figure who disappeared through the light.

A portal formed in the space where the light had been, and Skye's body started moving to it. Two more robed figures stood next to her, and Pete's magic struck again with lethal force, killing one of them. But his effort wasn't enough to save her. Another robed figure appeared through the portal and struck back, engaging him one on one, forcing his attention to the fight and away from Skye.

Bormick met Mark's eyes then ran, tackling Skye's body. The two of them disappeared into the portal. A flash of light filled the area and Mark screamed Skye's name. The portal faded, leaving them alone, the soldiers, the other robed figures gone as portals closed around the battlefield. Mark and the others had been too focused on saving Skye to realize the enemy had created them.

His heart fractured, fear encapsulating it, but all he could do was stare at the space where she'd been, his weapons falling to the ground. The world seemed to stop. She was gone. Even when she'd been taken by Derrant, it hadn't been this painful. He'd known where she was, how to find her, he'd had a chance of saving her. But now. He was lost. He didn't know what had happened, who these people were, where they'd taken her.

He didn't know how long he stood there before he heard Noah's voice.

"Mark, we need help."

Mark forced his eyes from the empty space to Noah's. His friend looked worn, his own pain clear on his face. His queen was gone, his only job to protect his Mage Warrior, and he'd failed. They'd all lost her.

Mark looked to Pete. He was holding Crimson in his arms, his expression one of devastation. They'd lost Bormick, along with Skye. He'd followed to protect her, just as he'd tried to protect her during the fight when Mark couldn't reach her.

"Mark, we need healers," Noah finally said.

Mark wiped his face with his hands and took in the scene before him. There was no way to describe it as anything but a bloody battleground. Only a handful of wizards remained, their wounds obvious.

He nodded, then bent to retrieve his fallen weapons. He was commander of the Elite, King of Kantenda, and he needed to put aside his pain and get help for his people.

"Assess how many are injured, then find the children, make sure they're safe. Send one of the men to alert the novice mages. Pete can create a portal back for them."

Noah nodded, putting his hand on Mark's arm.

"We'll get her back. Bormick's with her. He'll keep her safe."

"Will he? I couldn't. Can anyone against that power?"

Noah dropped his eyes, walking away, the other Elite following. His silence providing his answer.

"Where did they go, Mark? Who the hell were those people?" Pete asked as he approached.

"I don't know." His voice sounded foreign to him, a numbness cascading over the pain in his heart, removing any emotion from it.

Crimson drew from Pete's arms, and he saw her quickly wipe her eyes before turning to him. The tears remained damned behind the dim green of them.

Her voice quivered when she asked, "How do we get them back?"

A part of Mark wanted to ask her how it felt to have someone she loved ripped from her like she'd done to them years before, but he didn't have the energy. She lowered her eyes as if she sensed his thought.

"I don't know. I don't even know who those people are. We'll figure it out but, Pete, I need you to open a portal so we can get healers and care for the wounded."

"Sure," Pete said. Streams of black fled his body to form a portal within seconds of Mark's request.

One of the Elite approached, ready to go, but the man looked as defeated as Mark felt. An Elite who couldn't protect his Mage Warrior was one who questioned his purpose.

"We'll leave it open for your return. Bring as much help as you can."

"Yes, commander," he replied before he disappeared.

"We need to help here then...then maybe we can figure out what the hell just happened."

"What did they do to her?" Crimson asked. "I felt it...through the connection I had with her magic."

"What did you feel, Crimson?"

"It was like a strange feeling that went through me, like all the colors faded for just a moment, then they were back."

He creased his brow, not entirely certain how to interpret what she'd felt.

"They'll let Bormick live, right?" she muttered.

He didn't answer right away, taking time to think about the question. He wasn't certain they would let Bormick live.

"It was Skye they wanted, Crimson," Pete said, a slight shake in his voice. "There's a chance..." He didn't finish the thought, bringing her against him.

Mark sighed, unsure what direction to go—the emptiness in his heart, the fear that encapsulated it making all else impossible. He prayed Skye was safe, Bormick as well, but they were faced with a thousand unknowns. Unknowns that held nothing but pain and death.

BORMICK

S kye." Bormick gently shook Skye, trying to wake her like he had been since they'd been dropped into what looked like a prison.

She moaned, her head rolling a bit.

"Skye, wake up. You need to get us out of here with your magic."

He'd tried to find a way out, tugging at the bars, digging where he could into the stone that surrounded them on most sides. The light in the cell made it easy to detect its features. It was the brightest dungeon he'd seen.

Skye's eyes fluttered open, and he took a step back. Gone was the rich blue they carried, a dull gray now in its place.

"What in the gods' name did they do to you?" he asked, stooping back down to help her sit up.

"Bormick?" she said, her hand moving to her head.

"Yeah."

"Where are we?"

"I don't know."

"Why is it so dark in here?"

He looked around the space, then back at her. "Dark? It's bright as day in here."

"You must have hit your head. There's no light. You look like a figure in pitch black."

"Skye, it's light in here." He scrunched his brows in worry, his nerves even higher now.

Fear passed over her features and she brought her fingers to her eyes, where they lingered until she brought them up to touch his face.

"You're just an outline of black against a darker black." Her voice caught, and she drew her hand back. He couldn't help but note how it shook. "I'm color blind," she said in a whisper. "Completely this time. They didn't leave any shades."

Bormick didn't know what to say. If they'd severed her connection to her hues, he had to think that rendered her power useless. "What does that mean for our ability to escape?"

He knew the answer from the way her face fell further. "It means we have no escape. Without my hues, I have no magic."

He sat, collapsing next to her, and leaned his head against the wall. "Fuck, that's not what I wanted to hear."

"Who are they, Bormick? And what do they want with me?"

"I don't know, but I'll be damned if they're going to hurt you with me here."

She sniffed. "Mark—"

"Is fine. I'm sure he and the others are searching for us now."

He closed his eyes, thinking of Crimson and Pete. He'd taken enough prisoners, stolen enough, kidnapped enough to know you hold on to the prize. Any stragglers were disposable. Skye was the prize here, and he was disposable.

Skye leaned into him. "I'm scared, Bormick. Even with Derrant and his demons, I was never this scared."

He wrapped his arm around her and brought her against him. She seemed so fragile in that moment, broken even, and his heart ached at her vulnerability. She was strong like Crimson and seeing her this way brought out a side in him that he didn't often let others see, only Crimson. He held Skye close, rubbing her arm and feeling the fear-filled tremors in her body as that protective part of him vowed to keep her safe as long as he could.

"I won't let them hurt you."

"You won't have a choice," a voice said.

Bormick stood, pulling Skye up with him and shoving her behind him. A man in white and gold stood on the other side of the bars. What was it with those colors? They were just waiting for blood to stain them.

"You're not touching her," Bormick bit out, his hand reaching for his weapon but finding nothing.

"Looking for this?" the man said, pulling Bormick's weapon from below his cape.

"Interesting device, tainted with Shadow Magic, just as you all are."

The cell door disappeared, and Bormick went to rush the man, but two soldiers stopped his path. He punched the one as another slammed him back into the cell.

He heard Skye scream as he fought. Two more soldiers had entered. He could take three, but four might be difficult with no weapons.

"You see," the man said as Bormick continued to fight. "You are tainted, all of you. And we are here to cleanse you."

Something gripped Bormick, leaving his hands unable to move or even block his attackers. He rammed them with his head and body, but as the punches continued, he weakened, falling finally to his knees.

"Stop it!" Skye screamed. "Leave him alone!"

Another force tore through him, an angry howl escaping through his gritted teeth.

"Please stop!" Skye was still screaming, and he could hear the tears in her voice.

He'd suffered worse. It was the blasted magic he couldn't

fight. His insides were burning, an internal fire scorching them. The man grabbed Skye's arm, and she fought back, scratching and kicking at him until he slapped her hard enough that the sound echoed through Bormick's ears.

He roared, an intense need to protect her overwhelming him, overriding his pain. He fought to break free, but the four soldiers had him. Even though he'd dragged them closer to Skye, they were still too strong, and his adrenaline was fading.

An unseen power dragged Skye from the cell.

"Bring him, let him witness what we do to their kind."

Bormick struggled as they pulled him, stopping when he realized he'd still be with Skye if they took him. In that one look he'd given to Mark before throwing himself onto Skye, he'd promised to protect her. Somehow he knew if roles had been reversed and it was Crimson, even given their past, Mark would have done the same. The five of them were connected. Not on the same level he was to Crimson and Pete, but it was there. Whatever this was, the five of them were on this trajectory together.

They entered a large room. Three ornate golden chairs that reminded him of thrones sat at the end of the room. Gold banners hung from the wooden ceiling, white and gold marking the wall, white marble lining the floor.

"What is it with you people and white?" he grumbled, earning him a rough punch to the jaw, his cheek splitting in his mouth with the impact.

"Damn," he groused, spitting the blood as they dropped him. One soldier pinned him to the floor by stepping on his calves, while another stepped on his back. It hurt like a demon, but he gritted his teeth against the pain.

A tall man and two women, all in white robes with gold embroidering upon them, walked into the room and sat in the chairs. The man clasped his hands, eyes surveying Skye.

"So, this is the Mage Warrior."

"Yes, King Japeer," the one holding Skye answered.

He threw her so that she landed at Japeer's feet. He bent down, ripping her hair back to look at her face. Bormick heard her cry of pain and struggled again. Japeer stopped, his hands still wrapped in Skye's hair, and looked at Bormick, tilting his head as he studied him.

"This is not the Elite."

"No, your excellency."

He stood, pulling Skye upright by the hair. She reached up, crying, her hands digging to free herself, but he took no notice.

"You fucking hurt her anymore and I will rip those hands off and feed them to you," Bormick growled.

"Lift him up," Japeer ordered before pulling Skye up further, her scream hurting Bormick on a level that would have buckled him if he'd been standing.

They jerked his upper body so that he was upright, his knees grinding into the marble floor.

"Why do you care? This is not your mate. Oh, I know your mate and I know you, Bormick of Digremile. In trouble since the enemy slaughtered your parents in front of you, leaving a trail of destruction in your wake. Your anger and need for vengeance feeding an insatiable appetite for blood. You traveled the realms, wreaking havoc until you finally stole a kingdom. Now you're mated with the red haired one, her own past as colorful as yours. I have yet to decide what to do with her."

"Don't you touch her," he growled.

Japeer's laugh was terse. "Oh, I have no desire to touch her tainted body. Impure, all of you, undeserving of the gifts you have. Undeserving of anything but the death that awaits you."

He yanked Skye closer and Bormick could see the tears that streamed her face, blood slowly climbing down her roots where some of her hair had been ripped from her scalp. He gritted his teeth as Japeer shoved her close to him. Her face was directly in front of Bormick, her now gray eyes filled with fear as they pleaded with him.

"Will you fuck her for us? Just like you do your whore? Just like you did every woman you forced yourself on through your years of conquest? Show us what a strong man you are? Or better yet." He dropped Skye, not letting her go, no matter how she struggled. He shoved her toward Bormick's pants. "Maybe she can suck you off for us. I hear she likes that sort of thing, and I know you do."

"I take it back. I'm going to rip your limbs off as you plead for me to stop, then slit your throat and let you slowly bleed out as I make these assholes come on your dying body."

The punch to Bormick's face was fast, breaking his nose, blood spurting out on Skye, who screamed before they yanked her back up. He didn't care, he'd take the pain. No one talked about Skye that way, no one treated her this way. In all of his joking, his taunting, the respect for her was still there. This man had no respect for her, and anger surged through Bormick at the thought.

Japeer lowered himself to Bormick's level.

"You will watch as we destroy her, your whore, and your shadow brother. Then I will bleed you out over their corpses for days."

Bormick sucked in the blood and spat it back out into his face. He didn't flinch, standing instead and wiping his face with his sleeve. "Oh, look at that. I've gotten your pretty white cloak dirty."

Japeer pulled Skye close, tipping her neck, her birthmark revealed.

"Do you know what this is?"

Bormick remained silent, staring him down.

"This is a mark of the Death God. Evil." He threw Skye on the floor and walked away. She looked up at Bormick, her eyes swollen with tears.

"We tolerated you Mage Warriors and the other mage ranks, watching, observing. At first, you appeared to be no threat. Then your kingdom fell, and the conquerors divided your mages among the other kingdoms. The threat became less, and so we let you be. In time, the magic faded from your kingdoms, the Mage Warriors wiped from our world like a scourge.

"Still, we watched to ensure there were no other threats. For fifty years, it was silent. Until you returned, Skye, daughter of Lyra. We had watched your mother closely. There was potential for her to become a threat but not enough to be a concern."

He sat on his throne. "You, on the other hand, are a serious threat. You nearly collapsed the veil between realms, you consorted with the Death God, not just the lowly shadow gods but the Death God himself. And bedded him. We've watched you and your Elite. Watched your power grow, your connection to the shadows enhancing, all the while continuing to please the Death God. You are a threat, favored with your mark, with your power. Your body belonging to death itself."

"I do not belong to the Death God."

"No? He shares you with your Elite, does he not? How pleasant. Ten years we watched, waiting for a sign that it was time to strike, to cleanse your kingdoms. The final move, a Shadow Mage, drawing power from the Death God himself. Walks your lands, freely. Entwined with you and the Death God's other whore. His touch is everywhere on her."

"Hey!" Bormick yelled. "You call either of them a whore again—"

"And you'll do what? Defend them with pitiful words? Your lover is the Death God's whore as much as this one is, and she will die along with the Shadow Mage."

Bormick struggled, throwing the soldiers from him, and leaping over Skye, directing his anger toward Japeer. A move of his hand pinned Bormick to the ground where he could only struggle to breathe.

"Stop!" Skye called, and he heard her crawl over to him, feeling her hand on his arm.

"You are as tainted by the shadows as your brother. Where he manifests it through his magic, you do so through your ferocity. Both of you are too far gone to cleanse, as is your whore. He is the bigger threat, as is this one, their fates entangled, their magic too close to the Death God and his mistress to tolerate any longer. To risk what they would become. You will all die now, and we will cleanse the future of their shadows."

Bormick fought again but couldn't move. The words should have concerned him, but there were pressing matters at hand—Skye's life for one.

"Bring her. Let him watch as we create our weapon and destroy them all."

A soldier grabbed Skye, dragging her by the arms. She fought to free herself, and Bormick tried to get to her, but the magic kept him pinned. Someone grabbed his hair, stretching his neck to force him to watch as they tied Skye's hands to two columns that rose from the ground.

"Don't you hurt her!" he screamed as she struggled against the binds.

Japeer grabbed her face. "If you continue to struggle, I will shave that pretty head to reach that birthmark."

Bormick heard her spit, and the man smacked her again.

"Too much time in the Shadow Realm may have cursed you. Your fate—though already determined—can be changed. Let's see if we can sway it some. Get her hair."

A guard pulled her hair roughly, exposing her birthmark, the two women coming forward. They stood side to side with Japeer.

"It's time to strip the Death God's touch from you. You will fight for us and you will bring me the heads of the Death God's whore and his shadow son, and your infected Elite. Then you will rein terror on his subjects."

"No!" she cried, but it was cut short as all three released a fury of golden magic at her neck. Her scream echoed through the hall.

Bormick watched in horror as sparkles of color streamed from the birthmark, whipping around the room in a frenzy before fading, her hair slowly streaking with thick strands of white. Her screams continued until he could take it no more and dropped his head, fighting the pain they caused in him, the helplessness.

In time, the screams faded, and he dared to lift his head. Her hair had turned the white of a shimmering star, streaked with strands of navy blue, the same blue that matched her eyes, eyes that now opened. Bormick inadvertently tried to scoot away. No more were her eyes the blue of an endless night. Instead, they shone an unnatural golden hue and stared back at him with complete malice.

CRIMSON

rimson stared at the table, her body pressed against Pete's. She'd never been so devastated, never felt so helpless as she did now. There was an ache in her chest that threatened to crush her and no matter how she tried, it wouldn't stop.

Bormick was gone. Skye with him. He'd gone to protect her. She knew it. The part of him that was loyal and good had made him selflessly jump to an unseen future. She loved him for it, but also hated him for it because now he was gone, and her heart ached.

Mark paced the room with angry steps. The mages had taken over the battlefield, one strewn with bodies, all killed at the hands of an unknown group, the same people who had her Bormick.

Noah entered the room, his face lined with worry. "Trent has gone to warn Theodore, Elspeth to Revina, and to collect Camin."

Mark stopped his pacing, his hands clenched in tight fists.

A woman stepped from behind Noah. She had a healing wound on her forehead and her hair hung at a strange angle as if it had been chopped. Crimson looked closer, realizing that was it, the ends of what had once been a braid were still attached to her scalp.

"Bridget," Mark said, pulling the woman into a tight embrace.

He drew back and looked at her head.

"It's nothing compared to the rest of my people."

Crimson could tell she was trying her best to be strong. A portal appeared, Camin stepping through with Elspeth. He took one look at Bridget and ran to her, holding her tight.

"Your father fought bravely," she said so low that Crimson barely heard her.

Mark looked down at the floor, and Crimson looked away. These people were all friends, a group of which she'd never been part. Pete pulled her closer and kissed the top of her head.

"Revina?" Mark asked.

Camin pulled away, struggling to compose himself, Elspeth shaking her head.

"No," Camin said. "She will not assist. She is determined that her walls will hold, that they are safer on their own."

Mark put a hand on his shoulder. "Thank you. If you need to go—"

"No, Skye is missing. I stay. She's more important than my grief. I can grieve later."

"We all can," Bridget added.

Another portal appeared, Trent stepping through with Theodore.

"Elspeth, please go to Alex; let him know what's happened."

She nodded, squeezing Bridget's hand on her way out of the room.

Mark greeted Theodore with a terse, "Theodore."

"Markhem." Theodore replied in the same tone. He glanced around the room, meeting Crimson's eyes before looking her up and down.

"Crimson, I see even the Death God didn't want you."

"I don't remember you complaining when your dick was in my mouth, so why would he be complaining?"

Pete tensed next to her, and Theodore's eyes moved to him.

"She's all yours—"

"I never doubted she was," Pete replied, his power seeping from him.

"So, it's true. A Shadow Mage. I thought they were a myth."

"They're not," Mark replied.

"Someone strong enough to incapacitate your queen and best a Shadow Mage walks our lands?"

"It would seem."

Theodore sat, looking shaken. The others might not have noticed, but she knew him well enough to detect it. Crimson was aware Mark and Skye had formed a truce with him, that they'd settled their differences. Theodore had even changed his ways, finding a wife. He seemed different to her. She just hoped he didn't seize this as an opportunity.

"What can I do?" he asked.

Mark sighed. "I don't know, but if they're a threat to us, if they can wipe out the wizards, your kingdom is vulnerable. As is Revina's, even if she's too stubborn to admit it."

"Revina won't bend. She blames Crimson for her husband's death—"

"With good reason," Mark said.

"I remember you being part of that scheme, Theodore," she countered.

"You are correct, Crimson, but I didn't order the blade to be brought to his neck."

"We were both different people then."

"Perhaps, but you will always be that person to Revina and because of your actions, she distrusts everyone. She will not leave her kingdom."

"Then she will burn." They all turned to Crimson. "Derrant's words in his warning to me," she explained. "There is nothing we can do about her. She's on her own. We focus on finding Skye and Bormick and defeating whatever this scourge is."

"Bormick? The thief? The one who stole your kingdom and threatened mine?"

The weight of Theodore's stare was heavy.

She tried not to let it bother her. "Yes, and you can thank me for pulling his troops from your land."

"Bormick is an ally now," Mark said.

Theodore looked to Pete, then back to Crimson. "Two lovers, Crimson? You are something. And taming a rebel like Bormick? I'm impressed."

"Now that we've caught up on Crimson's sex life, Bridget, tell us what happened. And do you have any idea who these people are?" Mark asked, taking control and looking at the woman with the marred hair.

"No, they came from nowhere. Through a portal like the ones our mages make but all of them came through at once. They attacked without hesitation, even our women and children, our elders. There were fighters and magic wielders. The fighters...they were like our Elite in their moves, their weapons, but their magic was different—"

"I noticed that, too," Mark said. "Did any of them say anything?"

"No, they simply killed—silently, swiftly."

"Gods," Theodore said, sitting back against his chair.

"Their magic felt like when Skye draws the brighter colors—the yellows or whites. There were no...shadows to it, no darker hues like she prefers or like mine," Pete said.

"I noticed that as well," Mark agreed.

Theodore looked pensive for a moment before saying, "Like the original Mage Warriors? Their magic was always light driven, none able to wield in the shadows."

"No," Crimson said. "Pete's right. It was different, but it

wasn't like the Mage Warrior magic. Their magic acted distinct to these wielders."

"And you would know," Theodore said with a raise of his eyes.

"I would. I've held mage magic enough to know the difference."

Mark shot her a look before shaking his head. If the situation hadn't left her devastated, she'd have flirted with him, those hazel eyes sexy even with the sadness and worry they held.

"Trent, have you ever heard of anyone with other magic?"

"No, no one in the kingdoms differs, save for Skye and Pete."

"What about beyond these kingdoms?" Pete asked.

"There's nothing beyond the kingdoms," Crimson said. She was trying to stay focused, but her birthmark had started tingling. She brought her hand up to itch it.

"Wait, this is the entire world?"

"We don't know," Mark said. "This world doesn't sail, the oceans are deadly, no one ventures into them, so no one has ever explored beyond them, and no travelers have ever come from them. If they have, the sea dragons devoured them before they arrived."

Pete's mouth fell open. "Sea dragons?"

"Nasty things," Theodore said. "They make our land dragons look like innocent children."

"You have dragons here? How did I not know that?" There was an excited tone to Pete's voice that made her smile, even with the heaviness of their current situation.

"Are you not from here?" Theodore said.

Mark shook his head, answering for Pete. "He's from the world where Skye and I were raised. It's a long story."

"But you've claimed the throne of Digremile?"

"Like he said, a long story, but yes, it's my heritage as well as Bormick's."

Theodore raised a brow, but Crimson's eyes blurred, her birthmark burning. She pushed her hair away, digging at it.

"Crimson?" Pete asked, as it grew worse.

She tried standing, the seat rearing back as an excruciating mix of heat and pain gripped her. She collapsed to the floor, a scream not quite her own escaping. The world becoming nothing but fire and agony.

PETE

Pete tried to catch Crimson as she fell. Her body arched severely, and she let out a scream that cut through his heart like a thousand daggers. But the scream wasn't quite her own. It was Skye's, something that worsened the wound. Mark rushed to her other side as the scream continued, her body convulsing. A golden glow poured from her birthmark.

"She's still connected to Skye's magic," Mark said, his voice breaking.

White streaks appeared in her hair, another scream tearing from her mouth, this time her own. Pete held her in his lap, his ears pounding from the sound. Mark was back on his heals, his face a distorted mix of anguish and pain.

"What are they doing to her?" he whispered with a shake in his voice as Crimson grew quiet. The streaks receded, her body stilling, her breathing calming.

"Crimson?" Pete said, brushing her hair back. Her birthmark had returned to the violet shade of Skye's, only darker, nearly as black as when she held his magic.

His eyes met Mark's and the desperation he saw there nearly broke him. They both knew. Crimson still held the copy of Skye's magic in her, not letting it go in case they needed it, especially with Skye gone. Whatever had just happened to Crimson had been funneling from that connection. Worried thoughts bombarded Pete. He didn't know what they'd done to Skye to have caused this much pain to pass through to Crimson. There was a chance she hadn't survived. That Bormick hadn't either.

Crimson's eyes fluttered open, a kaleidoscope of different dark hues until they settled to her usual green, only now richer. He brushed her hair back, noticing it too was darker, a deeper shade of red.

"They're hurting her. The burning was like flames eating at my insides. It burned her, changing the magic." Her voice was weak, her body trembling slightly against his.

"Is she alive?" Mark's voice was desperate.

"Yes, but..." She put her hand on Mark's. "They did something to her magic, Mark. It touched what I have of hers. Stripping, that's what it felt like—stripping it."

"Of what?"

Pete picked her hair up, draping it forward. "Her hues, the darker ones." He could sense the change in Crimson's magic. Her power called to him like Skye's did. "Your connection pulled the light ones from you. Whatever they did pushed the dark ones from her, and the connection sent those hues to you."

"How do you know that?" Trent asked.

Pete looked up at him. "I can feel the dark hues on her, her magic is changed. Her magic is shadowed, more similar to mine."

Camin drew in a breath. "Look at your weapon, Mark."

Mark looked down and pulled his weapon out. The usual bright blue was a dull navy now.

"Mark, my connection to her is gone," Noah said. "I can't feel it through my weapon."

Mark gripped his weapon. "Nor can I."

"The Elite are only a threat when their Mage Warrior magic

runs through them," Theodore said. "Looks like we're not the only kingdom vulnerable."

Mark stood, staring at Theodore, the commander within him present again. Even without Skye's magic, Pete had no doubt Mark and his men were formidable and Theodore was playing with fire. He hadn't needed introductions to know who this man was. Crimson's comments and the looks he'd given her had said enough. Given all he knew of the king, he wasn't impressed, nor did he find him trustworthy.

"Can you stand?" Pete asked Crimson.

She nodded. Her dark eyes held fear, something he'd never seen in her.

"They're going to be all right, Crimson."

"We don't know that, Pete," she whispered.

"We have to believe it," Mark said. "There's no other option. Now, we need someone who knows what the hell is going on and who these people are."

"Derrant," she said. "We need to confront the Death God."

Theodore grew pale. "No one confronts the Death God."

"I do," she replied, standing taller.

Pete noted the shake in her hands. "You're not in any state to do that, Crimson."

"If we delay, we risk—" Mark started.

"If we push her, she loses her magic or worse, she's down for longer and we risk more time. She needs to rest. Whatever just happened weakened her more than she'll admit."

"I'm fine, Pete." But her knees buckled, and he caught her, scooping her up.

"She rests, then calls him. We lost someone we love, too, Mark. Trust me, I want to find them both, but I won't risk her to do that."

Mark wiped his hand down his face, and Pete could see the frustration that lined his features. "Fine, we'll deliberate while she rests, but as soon as she's up to it, she calls Derrant. She's right, he's the only one with answers."

Pete took her from the room back to their quarters, laying her gently on the bed. She looked weak and exhausted, but she pulled at him.

"Hold me, Pete," she said.

He crawled in next to her, drawing her against him, her body curving into his. She directed his head down, her lips meeting his, the kiss laden with emotion. There was a desperation to it, like she needed his touch, his strength.

"I miss him, Pete," she said against his mouth.

"As do I."

And he did—more than he ever thought he would. The thought of Bormick hurt or killed was devastating. It was like a part of him was lost and there was a hollow emptiness in that part of his heart he hadn't realized he'd given to Bormick.

"Fill me, make love to me," she pleaded.

"It won't bring him back, Crimson."

A tear slipped down her cheek, and he brushed it away with his thumb.

"Something needs to take away this pain. It hurts."

Hating to see her so broken, he dropped his forehead to hers and her mouth found his. He relaxed into her, pulling her closer in an effort to numb the wound in his own chest. They made love, clinging to each other, his mind on Bormick just as he knew hers was. The feel of her skin against his alleviated the pain to a dull ache. His body moved with hers fluidly in harmony, ebbing and flowing until release found him. They clung to each other until desire and emotion swept through them again and they started over, still searching to numb the pain to no avail.

As her body quivered against his, his own climax flowing through him, he met her eyes, seeing the love and the sadness, the tears that stained her cheeks. Pushing the last of his orgasm into her, he stilled, kissing her forehead.

"You were right," she said, her breathing still labored. "It didn't take away the pain."

He laughed and kissed her neck. "I warned you. It felt good, though."

"Always does."

He moved from atop her and pulled her into him, his mind wishing they were all here.

"You know, if he were here, I'd make him clean me up and you," he joked.

"He'd enjoy that too much."

"Yeah, he would, wouldn't he? God, I miss that asshole."

She scooted down and licked him, slowly, her tongue making erotic circles around his tip.

"Mmm. Yeah, you do it best," he said, closing his eyes and imagining it was Bormick for just that moment until it became too much, and he brought her up.

"Rest. We need to see the Death God and Mark will grow impatient if we don't go soon."

"I'm up to it now. I just needed you, Pete."

He looked at her with doubt.

"Sex rejuvenates me."

"Well, damn, if I'd known that..."

She let out a giggle, laying her head against his chest.

"Ready to see the Death God?" she asked.

"Now?"

"Yes, Mark needs to stay here. He's too broken without Skye, and he'll say or do something foolish. I know Derrant well enough to get answers from him."

She was right. Mark wasn't levelheaded. He was lost without Skye. Pete had only had Bormick in his life for a brief time, same with Crimson. He was a part of them, but Mark and Skye had been together for a decade, loved each other for longer. What they had went deeper and as painful as it was to lose Bormick, he couldn't fathom what Mark was experiencing.

Thinking about Skye brought a different feeling of loss. One that wasn't nearly to the depth he felt for Bormick's absence, but one that was there. Worry mixed with a strange emptiness. Had he grown that close to Skye and Mark? He supposed he had, and the magic that Skye held was seductive to him, his own magic feeling the missing touch of hers. Perhaps that was it. He considered her a friend, a sexy friend, but a friend nonetheless, and her absence was noticeable.

They cleaned up, Crimson changing into a long green gown that flowed loosely down her legs. She stood before him, her dark green eyes drawing him in.

Resting her hand on his chest, she said, "Derrant does not give easily. There may be a price if he helps us. Are you willing to pay it?"

"More days where he takes you from us?"

"I think you and Bormick can entertain each other and there's always your tree nymph," she replied with a wicked grin.

"She's not you, although she does provide a pleasurable release, and Bormick's hands are rough."

She kissed him softly. "If he takes me in front of you?"

He grimaced, his teeth clenching.

"He may ask, or he may simply take, his claim on my soul trumps our blood bond."

"I know, but I don't want to watch another man touch you."

"Bormick touches me."

"That's different. Damn." He ran his hand through his hair. "Yes, if that's what it takes to get them back, I'm willing."

She took a long breath, then turned from him. "I don't know that this will work when my birthmark is already active, but here goes."

She bit her finger, drew the blood, then placed it on her birthmark, her hand reaching out.

"Death God to whom my soul belongs, take your claimed and bring me home."

The words were strong and confident, reinforcing his awareness of the claim the Death God had on her, forcing him and Bormick to share her.

Nothing happened. She took his hand while they waited.

Still, nothing happened.

"Derrant. Let me through, please. I need you. I need your help," she tried again.

Again, nothing.

"Dammit, Derrant. I know you hear me. Bring me into the Shadow Realm now!"

"It's not working, Crimson, or he's not listening."

"He's not listening. You stubborn ass, I command you to bring me to you now! That ought to piss him off. Hang on tight."

There was a stillness in the air before an ugly black portal opened, dragging them both through. Pete landed, toppling across a hard marble floor with her.

"You dare command me!"

The voice shook the room. Hesitantly, Pete helped Crimson stand and faced the terrifying creature he remembered from the forest. The mere sight of him was enough to bring even the strongest of men to his knees and Pete prayed the god would transform into the beautiful version who had taken Crimson from the forest. This version was horrifying, like looking at the devil himself.

"No one commands me!"

There were about twenty ugly demons, some part man, part demon, some flickering like their bodies couldn't decide if they were man or beast. They all stood around stairs that led to a black gnarled throne of bones upon which the Death God sat.

"You wouldn't hear me any other way," Crimson said.

He roared, the room shaking again as he stood, descending the steps two at a time with his long misshapen legs.

"You have been back in my favor, Crimson, but that status is on tenuous ground."

"We need your help, Derrant."

Something ripped her from Pete's hands and brought her before the Death God.

"Leave us!" His voice boomed and the demons scattered.

Pete was ready to run to her, but the god's eyes turned on him.

"You were bold to accompany her. My Eliana has a particular distaste for your line since it was created in vengeance against her acts with Crimson's line."

"So, the son has come home," an enchanting voice said.

Pete turned toward Eliana. For a moment, he thought Skye was before him, until he noticed the glow of power in her blue eyes. She walked to him, her hips swaying seductively, eyes lush with desire. He couldn't help but take her in, having forgotten how gorgeous the goddess was. She exuded power just like Skye did.

"Don't get any ideas, Eliana. I won't risk you slaughtering him in his sleep."

She turned to the Death God. "You mistake me for your demons, dear. You touch and taste his lover. Why can I not have the same privilege?"

He shifted to his mortal form, and Pete relaxed.

"What do you want, Crimson, and why do you try my patience?"

Eliana's fingers grazed Pete's chest, and he swallowed uncomfortably, not sure what to do. She was beautiful, and he had no doubt she would be amazing to experience, but something about the fact that she looked so much like Skye made the thought uncomfortable—like he'd be having sex with Skye. Her eyes, navy and endless like Skye's, studied him, shimmering as if she knew his thoughts. Bormick was never shy about his lust for Skye, so Pete didn't know why it bothered him so much when the thoughts entered his head. Bormick. That's where his mind needed to be, not on Skye's body or the goddess before him. Saving Bormick and Skye was his concern, not to mention his loyalty belonged to Crimson. But how did he tell a goddess that?

"You don't," she whispered. "And I am amazing in bed, as is Skye. My daughters receive their talents from me, especially her."

Shit, he thought, fighting the rise in his pants at the thought.

"Bormick and Skye have been taken. The wizards slaughtered," Crimson said quickly.

Eliana's head whipped to her. "It has begun," she said.

Derrant scowled. "You should not have come." There was anger in his voice, but something else Pete couldn't quite put his finger on.

"We need to know what we're facing."

"And we must remain impartial. This is not our war," Eliana said.

"Not your war? I remember him coming to take Crimson back on the terms that there were too many bodies for you to ferry. How many bodies await you today?" Pete said.

She closed her eyes, her expression changing after a few moments. Sadness had overtaken her eyes when she reopened them. "Too many."

"Please, you know what's happening. We need to find them."

The goddess tilted her head, eyes studying him. "You love him."

"Yes," he answered without hesitation, never having considered it before, but knowing it was the truth.

"Three lovers, bound by blood."

"I could break that blood bond," Derrant said.

"No!" he and Crimson replied together.

"It would ease the pain, lessen the desire."

"No," they both said again.

"Now, please tell us how to find them and what we're up against," Pete said.

"We cannot," Eliana said, and Pete noted the sadness in her voice.

"They are hurting Skye," Crimson said. "I can feel it. The pain was excruciating."

Eliana's eyes grew anguished. "They hurt them both, torturing my daughter, turning her from me."

"Eliana," Derrant said sharply.

She brought her hand to Pete's chest. "He suffers to protect her, but he cannot. No one can."

A tear slipped from her eye as his heart crashed. They were both being hurt, Bormick putting his life at stake for Skye, like the true man he and Crimson knew him to be.

"Eliana." Derrant pushed past Crimson and grabbed Eliana's arms to turn her to him, his blue eyes livid with power. Blue eyes that matched Pete's and Bormick's.

"Stop, we cannot risk a war with our brother. Not now."

Pete caught the reference to the other god and wondered what this situation had to do with him. As the two argued, he slipped to Crimson, pulling her to him.

His mind went back to a conversation they'd had, about the kingdoms and what lay beyond. Nothing was beyond the lands they knew. Only an ocean that was insurmountable. It had seemed odd at the time for a world to be so small.

"This world is bigger than they know, isn't it?" Crimson looked at him, her eyes growing wide at the suggestion. "That's why no one recognized those people or their magic. They've naively thought they were the only ones who existed. But they're not. What does the Upper God have to do with it?"

"He's sharp like you, Derrant," Eliana said.

"Yes, he is." Derrant turned his eyes to Pete. "And what would you give me for confirmation of that statement?"

"Me," Crimson said.

"No," Pete said, the heat rising in him at the thought. He gripped his hands to keep the jealousy at bay.

"Yes, we cannot live without Bormick, and Mark cannot live without Skye."

Pete couldn't believe she'd agree to such a thing. "So, you'd make us live without you?"

"I have to put up with her in my brother's bed two extra days. I do not want her here anymore," Eliana snapped, a distasteful look upon her face.

Pete's stomach turned at the term brother, knowing it meant something else to them, that they weren't actually related, but the thought was still nauseating.

Derrant returned to stand before them, taking Crimson from his arms and bringing her against him. She didn't resist. She was comfortable there, but Pete didn't like it. His jaw twitched as he watched. "And what if I want her now? Will you stand aside and watch as she pleases me? Would you trade that?"

"Yes," Crimson said rather breathlessly, too breathlessly for Pete's taste.

"I wasn't asking you. I was asking my son."

The term seemed strange coming from a god, but no stranger than being asked if that god could have sex with Crimson while Pete watched. He knew he'd have to agree, but he didn't want to.

"He won't watch because he'll be pleasing me," Eliana said.

Pete raised a brow, unsure of what to say, his eyes meeting Crimson's, whose green eyes flashed to jealousy briefly before she said with a sigh, "You remind him too much of Skye and he won't act on that. He's too afraid to." He furrowed his brow as she gave him a knowing smile. "It's not hard to see Pete. And I'm fine with it if it brings Bormick back. Take us both."

"I don't know that I like being traded," he said. He chose not to respond to the comment about Skye, not sure how he felt about it or why the thought had turned him on for that brief moment.

Eliana's fingers slid across his back, her mouth dipping to his neck, then grazing his ear. *You'll know what she feels like in time,* her voice whispered through his head.

He jumped from her. Her voice in his head and the assuredness with which she'd made the remark left him shaken.

Before he could think more on it, Derrant spoke. "Eliana, you dislike my sons, the fruit of my vengeful acts against your infidelity."

"Yet you have no qualms about taking both my daughters repeatedly. Both the fruit of that infidelity."

Holy shit. What the hell is going on here? Pete thought, still shaken by Eliana's words.

"Tell us what and who is on the other side of that ocean," he demanded.

Derrant pulled Crimson to his mouth, kissing her. She didn't resist, and Pete looked away, meeting Eliana's blazing eyes. Eliana moved against Pete, reaching up and kissing him before he could react. Power radiated from her, seductively weaving around him like a drug. She tasted like an autumn day, crisp, sweet, desirable and for a moment, he did forget it was her, his mind replacing her with Skye. He knew now why Derrant had taken her in Eliana's place, stolen her from Mark. The two were so alike that he wondered if Skye tasted this way, wondered what the rest of her would taste like.

"Enough, Eliana. You've made your point."

Her lips drew away, and reality returned. Pete realized his hands had gone to her waist, drawing her close against him. He cursed himself for falling under her spell, for thinking of Skye.

A mischievous grin was on her face.

"Oh, he tastes good, Derrant. I like your deal."

Pete looked over at Crimson.

"For Bormick," she mouthed.

He knew after that kiss, he wouldn't hesitate, even if he wanted to. A goddess couldn't be denied. And he didn't want to hesitate, wanted to explore the feeling that had swept through him. He wiped his face, not understanding what was wrong with him.

"Are you jealous, Derrant? You don't have to watch."

Derrant growled and grabbed her from Pete. "I have to share you with our brother—"

"And I've had to share you with Skye, and now with Crimson. Do not lecture me when you bring her into our bed, even when I have returned," she spat.

This was frustrating. They needed answers, and time was being wasted on a lover's quarrel.

"Either take us or answer our question," Crimson said. "We don't have time for your games."

"Time works differently in my reality, Crimson. You know that."

"Yes, but we have very little."

Relenting, Derrant sighed, saying to Pete, "You are correct. There is land beyond the kingdoms."

"So, these people are mages from another kingdom?"

"Not mages."

"Then what?"

Derrant looked at Eliana. "We cannot tell you. We must remain impartial as our brother must."

"Because...this is somehow connected to all of you," Pete said.

Derrant raised a brow as Pete thought through it. His power came from the Death God. Crimson linked to him, Bormick as well. Crimson and Skye tied to Eliana. All of them, even Mark and his Elite tied through their connection to Skye.

The mages all to Eliana because of the Mage Warrior who had started with her. He remembered Skye's brief history lesson, as much as he had soaked in while trying not to look at her subtle curves or the swell of her breasts, the blue eyes that seemed to pull him in. All of it was coming back to him, as well as the images that had raced through his mind every time Skye had been present when he'd first come to this world...and every time since.

What had Eliana done to him? It was like a floodgate of attraction had been opened, spurred by her words, by her moves.

"Pete?" Crimson asked, crinkling her brows.

"All of us are tied to you two, to the Shadow Realm," he continued, focusing again.

A slight smile holding something like pride formed on Derrant's face. Eliana's eyes glinted with humor, like she knew Pete's thoughts, knew why they were now there. He didn't know if she'd done something to him or if that kiss had freed some desire that he'd been forcing away.

Let it go, Pete.

"If you must remain impartial as he must, then the other kingdom is tied to him. Their magic comes from the Upper God."

"Well done," Derrant said.

"Light against dark? Good versus...shit, evil? We're the evil ones?"

Derrant laughed. "We are not evil. I'm not the nicest, but my brother in the next realm is distinctly more deviant than I."

Eliana shuddered.

The devil. Shit, he's referring to the devil.

"I don't follow," Crimson said. "We are all children of you two, the five of us—"

"No, all of you," Eliana said. "When we created this world, our brother was not happy with us. There are very few women gods created, and those who do exist are coveted. But I chose Derrant. He was my true mate. In his annoyance, my brother cast us to rule this realm, to rule the dead of the world, to shepherd them through to their final destination."

"We were given claim to your kingdoms, the people of those kingdoms created by us, just as our brother created the other lands, on the compromise that we would do our jobs, and leave each other's lands alone," Derrant continued.

"So, all the prayers we send to the Upper God, to his radiant gods, are going to you?" Crimson asked, her eyes wide with disbelief.

"No," Eliana said. "We give our people free will and some choose to worship only our brother, some all three of us. Our brother's realm is still the favored resting place and just as we take souls of his lands, so he, too, accepts those of ours. It is a mutual agreement."

"But only you are their true creators," Pete said.

"Correct."

"What does any of this have to do with Bormick and Skye?" Crimson asked.

"Just as Eliana and I have explored the flesh of our people, so too has our brother. Only our brother is not so reserved about it as we have been. My shadow gods are not allowed to play with mortals. They feast only on the pleasure of the demons. My brother lets his radiant gods free. They have a particular penchant for mortal women. I told him when we first created this world that making other gods was not a good idea. We could control the three of us, but sharing our power so strongly among lesser gods would not bode well to that control. He chose not to listen, creating his radiant gods, gods in his own image with like powers to help him rule his realm."

"But you have the shadow gods," Crimson said.

"Yes, it was a necessity to balance out what he had done. They do come in handy. This realm is a beast to rule, and they help keep it in check. But they require control, discipline, obedience, something my brother lacks. He lets his cavort with the flesh of the mortals and he himself partakes. Eliana and I have each other, and even when we were angry with each other, we each only strayed the one time, creating your lines."

"But they have no goddess," Crimson said.

"And so have created more lines than us because there is no goddess to satisfy my brother."

"Lines that have discovered our part of the world and if I were the son of the Upper God or any of his radiant gods, raised to believe the Shadow Realm and the magic from it is inherently corrupt, I would want it purged," Pete said as the pieces fell into place.

"Correct."

Pete felt the blood drain from him. How were they to win a war against a powerful group of magical zealots? "We can't win this fight. Their numbers are greater. They just plowed through an entire village of wizards like they were fighting children."

Crimson sat on the steps, her legs clearly too weak to hold her. "How do the five of us...three of us fight that?"

A wave of nausea pounded Pete at the thought of the impending loss of everything he held dear in this world. There was no way they could beat this. If Skye, who was trained and the most powerful Mage Warrior this world had seen, had been taken out so easily, how could the rest of them even fathom victory?

CRIMSON

rimson had no choice but to sit. The revelation was too much and had left her legs shaking uncontrollably. She'd always known she belonged to the Shadow Realm, to Derrant, but she hadn't been the only one. The entire kingdom...all the kingdoms were the product of the Shadow Realm. It was a terrifying discovery, especially to know that there were enemies in another land who hated them because of it, hated them enough to kill. She stood to lose everything because someone had judged them all.

"I'm bad. I can accept a fate handed to me because of my past deeds, because of who I am. Bormick is the same. Neither of us are good people. But Skye, Mark, Pete, they're not evil, they're good. Those wizards were good people, as are the people of our kingdoms. I won't let them die because someone judged them for what they think of their heritage. I will fight. I will die before I let them."

Eliana smiled. "You are my daughter, Crimson. I have not always wanted to accept you. You have a past that haunts you, but under it all, you are mine and there is good in you. Peter makes you better, Skye makes you better, Bormick, and even Mark. You have a family now, a dysfunctional one, but the five of you are on this journey, bound by blood, bound by me and Derrant. It is up to all of you. And you do have the power to stop it."

"Five against an army?"

"Four against an enemy you do not know and a weapon you do. There was a reason Derrant was sent to rule this realm, separate from our brother, and it wasn't just because of me."

"My brother is a jealous bastard."

"And weaker."

Crimson's head was turning in a million different directions.

"Your power is stronger than the Upper God's?" Pete asked.

"Combined with his radiant gods, no. But I easily best my brother on his own and he knows that. He knows his realm could easily have been mine. I simply prefer my shadows and my demons."

"Then—"

"You have more power than you know, son, you and Bormick. You simply haven't tapped it, but you will. And Crimson is a vessel that has not yet been filled."

Pete stared at Crimson, his eyes showing how he was thinking it through. She touched her birthmark, her mind still on Derrant's prior words.

"You said four of us, not five." She felt the tingle of the magic below the birthmark, then noticed again how it felt different, darker. "What did they do to Skye?"

"You already know," Eliana said.

"That is all we can tell you. I don't wish a war with my brother any more than I wish one between our children. I am beyond that point now." Derrant stood, his eyes darkening. "It is time for you to leave."

"And my payment?" Pete said.

"As much as I'd like to torment Derrant with a night of pleasure with your body, your payment is to win. Bring my daughter back to me, make her whole again."

Derrant created a portal, black and ugly.

"No payment for you, Death God?" Pete asked.

"Eliana's happiness is my payment. Save Skye or all is lost. I ask no more at this time."

Pete put a hand out for Crimson and she took it, rising to his side.

"Remember, they have not noticed all of our children. There are some who have stayed hidden as I was hidden from Derrant."

Crimson inhaled sharply.

"This war will take every weapon you have, and it will cost all of us greatly if it is not stopped. This is only the beginning and the tests you face will redefine the five of you."

"Thank you both," Pete said. His hands were shaking slightly, and Crimson knew Derrant's words had unsettled him.

She tried to shrug off the tension in her shoulders, the worry at the unknown that was barreling toward them.

As they stepped through the portal, Derrant's voice followed them. "Don't forget, the shadows are not always the enemy. Those in the light can be just as deadly."

The portal closed behind them, and Crimson felt her knees weaken again. This was greater than anything she'd faced, even during the mage wars.

"What do we do?" she asked, her mind hurting from all the information Derrant and Eliana had divulged. Information she didn't even know how to begin processing.

"We talk to Mark, tell him what we learned. Crimson, what is it you know?"

She looked at him questioningly.

"She said you already knew. What?"

She touched her birthmark again. "They changed Skye's magic. All the connection to the light hues are gone for me and that to the dark hues is greater than it was. They stripped her of the darkness just like you thought. And when they did, they warped what she now holds."

"But you only have a copy of her magic. How could you know that?"

"I think it remains connected. When she fell, I felt her pain—felt something trying to clamp down on my magic, a flash of darkness in my eyes."

"Why didn't you say anything?"

"I don't know. I didn't think it meant anything and then I didn't know what it meant."

"If the Death God deals in shadows like my magic, then the Upper God must deal with light. Those people all wore white, and gold and the color of their magic was gold."

"She's the weapon, Pete. Eliana said four and one weapon. They've changed her magic to their own."

"Fuck, she's strong now, if they manipulated her magic, and her—"

"Then she would be an unstoppable force. One we will have no ability to defeat."

BORMICK

Pain clawed through Bormick, Skye's magic tearing like razers over his skin. It was excruciating each time she sent her power at him. The stream of golden energy stopped, and he remained on the floor, trying to catch his breath.

She was killing him, just like they'd instructed her to. His insides ached, his head throbbed along with every inch of him, but he forced his hands to the floor and lifted his head to look at her.

"Skye, stop. Don't listen to them. Think of Mark. Please don't do this, Skye. It's not you."

If she killed him, they were all dead. He had no doubt that if she did, Crimson and Pete would turn against her. Even if Mark somehow saved her, returned her to her former self, they would not hesitate to kill her in revenge.

Her cold, soulless eyes stared back at him, golden flickers of light cascading through them. There was no sign of recognition there. Whatever these freaks had done to her, they'd stripped the Skye he knew. This was only a shell of her.

"Kill him this time," Japeer said.

"Skye," Bormick tried again. Her hands drew her magic, no

longer pulling it from hues of the world but some internal source that seemed never-ending.

He closed his eyes, thinking of Crimson and Pete, praying they would be okay, that they would survive this madness. Her magic surged against him, searing his skin, and he held his hands tight against the pain.

"Stop," one of the women ordered her. The flow of magic stopped at her command.

He peeked an eye open.

"What are you doing?" Japeer asked with a sneer as the woman stepped over to Bormick.

"You know, I bet you're as cold in bed as you are here—no fun to fuck whatsoever," Bormick joked, his voice laced with pain. She kicked him hard in the side and he felt something break, his body in too much pain to determine the source.

"Why do you waste my time? Kill him already."

She shook her head. "No. He is a sign."

"A what?" Japeer's face was scrunched in confusion.

"Send him back, let him be a warning that there is no escape, that we are coming to take their shadows, their corrupt ways, and leave a trail of devastation in our wake," she said to the others before she lowered herself to Bormick's eye level. "Tell them that we have their weapon and their gods will watch as you all burn in her fury."

"Do you think that wise?" the other woman asked. "They don't know what is coming. Why warn them?"

She stood and turned to them.

"Because I want to see what they bring without their Mage Warrior. Without her, all they have is darkness and shadows. Only the light survive. Let them bring their shadows and we will show them our merciless retribution."

"Gods, you're a bitch. Maybe you are a good fuck, after all," Bormick said, his jaw clenched.

She swiveled, her magic slamming into him as something sucked him away, dropping him with a hard crash to the ground.

He tried to recover the breath that had been knocked form him. Lifting his head, he saw a man running toward him, magic drawn, a woman with a lopsided hairstyle rushing to his side.

"Gods, Bormick?"

He let out a sigh of relief when he recognized Camin, having met him on prior visits to Skye and Mark.

"Mark, I need to see Mark now."

"You need healers before you do anything," he said.

"No, take me to Mark. We have no time. She's coming."

"Who?"

"Skye."

Camin's face fell, and he rushed to Bormick's side, the woman to the other. Together, they helped him up.

"Can you stand?" she asked.

He tried, but his legs gave out, too weak from the repeated beatings and attacks.

"I'll go with you. We were heading back anyway," the woman said.

Camin created a portal and together they lifted him through.

He heard Crimson's cry but met Mark's eyes first. "She's alive," Bormick told him. "But they've changed her and she's coming to kill us all."

His strength gave, and he collapsed against Camin, Pete grabbing him, someone moving a seat behind him. Pete took his face in his hands. "You look like shit, buddy."

"I feel like shit. Skye's a vindictive bitch when someone else is controlling her."

"She did this?" Mark asked, his composure breaking to reveal the shock.

Crimson had pushed in next to Pete and was kissing him. "Yes, but it's not her. They changed her magic. She's lost, Mark. That woman, she's not Skye."

"She hurt you?" Crimson asked with a hiss to her voice.

"Eh, not all of it was her. The bruises are from the assholes I'm going to kill when I get the strength."

Several novice mages bustled in and moved the others, working on his wounds.

"You need to go to the infirmary," one said.

"Not until I talk to them."

Mark looked torn.

"I'm fine," Bormick said.

"All right. Tell us what happened."

He started from the time they were taken to the moment he was dropped back in the wizard village, Mark's face reflecting the myriad of his emotions.

"Gods," Crimson said.

"She would have killed me if they hadn't changed their mind."

He shooed the mages away, having had enough of their poking and prodding. The room was quiet, no one knowing what to say.

Finally, Noah asked, "How many were there?"

"A lot, but there were three main ones, a man they called Japeer. I think he was their king. Two women were with him. They took us to a room that was filled with the ones that look like soldiers, like the Elite."

"We think they're just like our Elite," Mark said. He was leaning over the table, his expression grim.

"How is that?"

"We paid the Death God a visit," Crimson said.

The muscles in Mark's arms bulged. Through clenched teeth, he said, "Without my authorization."

"Last time I checked, I was queen of my own kingdom, Pete the king of his. We don't need permission from you Mark," she snapped.

He brought his hands down hard on the table. "When it has to do with my wife, you do!"

"Mark, it was best that we went, trust me. We would have walked away in debt if your emotional ass had gone with us," Pete explained. "I'm still not completely certain we aren't in debt. The Death God was in no mood for our visit. He would have been worse if you'd gone in there demanding answers."

Mark sat back in his chair, running his hand over his face. It was the first time Bormick had seen the commander look defeated. Pete was right, someone levelheaded had needed to travel to the Shadow Realm, and Mark was far from that.

"What did you find out?" he asked.

"That we're screwed," Pete said.

"That's reassuring."

"We're all the product of the Death God and Death's Mistress —our people, our kingdoms created from their magic. The Upper God created his own kingdom. Like the five of us, there are lines descended directly from the Upper God, as well as his radiant gods, from their own affairs with mortals."

"Fuck, so we're fighting our equals?"

"Maybe," Mark said, "but considering Skye only discovered her magic ten years ago and Pete months ago, Crimson only now understanding hers, I'd say we're not on equal footing."

"No, we're not," Bormick agreed, his mind thinking through all the possible scenarios. "We're screwed."

Camin leaned forward in his seat. "Not necessarily."

"Yes, we are, especially my kingdom," a man sitting at the table said. "We have no mages, no Elite. We'll be the first to fall."

"Who are you?" Bormick asked, noting his stately appearance.

"That's Theodore," Pete answered for the man.

"Ah, that explains it."

"Explains what?" Theodore asked.

Bormick was about to make a smartass comment, but then he thought about Theodore's words and what the captors had said.

"It doesn't matter. I don't think you will fall first. If anything, you'll be the least of their concerns. Their biggest threat is our kingdoms. We're the ones they see as the most cursed. They want the magic wielders first, the tie that's strongest to the Shadow Realm. They think they're the pure, the blessed ones, and we all need to be purged. They were very specific about that."

"Christ," Pete mumbled. "They think we're all the Death God's minions, under the devil's spell and that they're holy, doing the Upper God's work. It's not just any war, this is a holy war."

"And zealots are the worst enemy," Mark said. "Nothing will sway them from their cause."

"Nothing but death," Bormick added.

"We need everyone ready to fight. Elspeth, call every mage from full to novice."

"And us? We're just left to slaughter, Mark? At least spare us some Elite for protection."

Mark's face dropped. "There are no Elite that can protect you, Theodore." He pulled his weapon out and tossed it on the table. It lay there, dull and lifeless, its gem void of any color. "When they twisted her magic and stripped her connection to the darker hues, they severed our connection to it as well. We're no stronger than any other army now."

There was a deafening silence. Everyone, even Bormick, knew the power of that connection, Mage Warrior to Elite. He'd once met an old Elite who had told him that the day the Mage Warrior's fell and their tie was severed, it had felt like a limb had been cut from him.

Bormick glanced at Mark, searching for the aura he'd always seen, the one that linked him to Skye, the one that had appeared unbreakable. It was gone, no trace of it. Mark had known she was gone, would have felt that connection fracture the same way he would have in his power, yet he hadn't broken. He still led, still carried the brave posture of the commander even though he was no longer whole. Bormick's opinion of the man grew, and he had no doubt he would follow him into whatever battle they were facing.

"Theodore, go home, prepare your people, your army, hide your women and children, your wife, your heir, and pray your kingdom is overlooked. Trent, please take him home then work with Elspeth. I want every mage, even those at the school. I don't care how green, they are now fighters. Noah, I want a message sent to Revina. She won't heed it, but at least we'll have tried. Crimson..." He paused. "What will you do? Your kingdom lies defenseless with you here. As does Pete's. What will the three of you do?"

Bormick turned to her. He knew why Mark had asked. She owed no allegiance to him, to Skye. They had a past that was rife with scars, misdeeds, deception.

"I will stay and fight with you, Mark. Skye, despite our differences, is my friend, my only friend and you...well, you're stuck with me."

"With all of us," Pete said.

Mark glanced at Bormick. "You don't even have to ask. I just had the shit beat out of me and have yet to even get a feel of that tight ass of hers. Ungrateful woman."

Mark laughed, his tension easing a bit.

"It's the four of you," Camin said, "just like Eliana told you. You can have all the mage power in this world but it's the four of you who hold the key to stopping this, to saving her."

"I pray that's true," Theodore said, rising. "Gods be with you, although at this point I'm not sure which gods those are."

Trent took him through the portal, Camin leaving to send the message to Revina.

"Bormick, go to the infirmary. You're no good to us if you're not one hundred percent healed," Mark ordered.

"I'm fine."

"Maybe, but until they clear you, I want you in their hands."

"I'll take his stubborn ass," Pete said.

"I can go, too," Crimson said.

"Can you stay? I'd like to go through the conversation with the Death God again," Mark said.

"Okay," she replied, but Bormick heard the disappointment in her voice.

He pulled her close and kissed her. "You'll have plenty of time when this is over to lick my wounds and ride me like I've been fantasizing for the past day."

She giggled and kissed him deeply.

"Yup, he's back," Pete said, dragging him from her.

"Take him before they lose control and he hurts himself more," Mark said.

"Sex is medicine, Mark," Bormick replied.

He rolled his eyes, but Bormick caught the hint of his smirk.

"Come on, lover boy." Pete gripped his neck and forced him out of the room, not letting go until they were down the hall where he pressed him against the wall and grabbed his face.

"You asshole! I thought I'd lost you. We both did. What the hell were you thinking?"

He kissed him and Bormick pulled him in tighter, the pounding of his heart echoing through his soul.

"Fuck, Pete, you're making my dick hurt."

"Good," he said, his hand sliding down his chest. "You ever pull something like that again and you'll never have that mouth on me again."

Bormick pushed him away and shoved him against the opposite wall. "You wouldn't have done the same thing? We're all too close now to let one of us go, even Mark and Crimson. Whatever the three of us are, Mark and Skye are connected somehow. I wasn't letting them take her, just like you wouldn't have."

He had Pete pinned with his body, feeling his matching erection. He smashed his lips against Pete, hungrily kissing him. "And I will have my mouth on you. I'll taste you, just like you'll taste me as I come in your mouth. We're well past experimenting, Pete.

Whatever this is, you and Crimson were all I thought about, all I wanted. All I want."

He kissed him again, Pete's hand threading through his hair, pulling him further into the kiss. He was lost to the man in ways he never imagined, wanting him with every fiber of his being on the same level he wanted Crimson, with a desire that was never waning.

"Fuck," he said, drawing back, breathless. "There's no way I can go to the infirmary with this hard-on."

Pete dropped his head to Bormick's. "You're wounded, you need to go."

"I know what I need."

Pete looked up, meeting his eyes. It was a dangerous thought, but one they both had. "The world is falling down around us, and you want to fuck me?"

"I can't have Crimson, so I'll take you."

"I'm your sloppy seconds?"

"No," he said, sliding his lips over Pete's and letting his tongue linger.

"It's dangerous, Bormick."

"Avoiding the infirmary?"

"That too, but...us. This thing we have. If we go further—"

"There's no turning back. I know. When you're close to dying, you think about things, Pete. I thought about Crimson and how I hadn't told her that I loved her more, that she'd stolen my heart, that she'd turned me, and I thought about you. How I hadn't pushed us past this, how I'd never experienced you, how a part of me aches for you as much as it does for her."

Pete pushed him away. "Let's go."

It wasn't the response he'd been expecting, which pissed him off until he realized Pete was heading in the opposite direction of the infirmary. His dick throbbed and something in his chest ached. He wasn't healed, but he didn't care. As they neared their guest quarters, he grabbed Pete's wrist, turning him around.

Pete's expression was serious, his blue eyes intense, causing Bormick's heart to race. He ripped his wrist away, saying, "Do you have any idea what it was like not knowing if you were dead or alive? Not knowing what was happening to you? To see you return"—he brought his hand up to touch the black eye Bormick knew was there, and felt each cut and bruise that lined his face—"like this?"

"I do believe the black eye was your doing."

Pete laughed before kissing him again. "I fucking hate you, but I also love you and need you with the same desire I have for Crimson. I can't undo it, can't ignore it. I need you."

"Shit," he said, pulling away, his heart racing. "We're gonna do this."

"Yes."

They kissed again; the intensity increasing until they reached the door, Pete throwing it open with his power, pulling at Bormick's shirt before stopping to stare at the marks, bruises and cuts where Skye's magic had torn into him, slowly healing from the healing magic that still tingled under his skin.

"You've seen me naked hundreds of times, Pete," he joked. Pete's fingers traced each wound, his lips kissing them, sending shivers through him. His breathing tightened, and he ignored the pain it caused. Pete's mouth rose to kiss him, his lips parting. Bormick's tongue slid in to explore, his own hand lifting Pete's shirt then skimming the muscles below before finding his hardened length, freeing it, and stroking it.

Pete groaned, which only intensified his need.

Bormick pushed him to the bed, his own pants falling with the move. Pete's hand gripped him, caressing him so that he could barely move. A million sensations were assailing him, accompanied by a flood of emotion that was spurring him on. He forced Pete back, drawing his lips away. The next move was in his hands, and he took it, knowing they had no other direction to go but forward with this.

He kissed his way down Pete's chest with no hesitation until he met his firmness, taking him into his mouth, tasting Crimson on him.

He lifted his head, looking up at Pete. "You fucked Crimson while I was gone? And recently, I can still taste her on you."

"She needed consoling, and I needed release again this morning."

Bormick let out a throaty laugh before plunging his mouth over Pete's hot erection, forcing himself down as far as he could manage, Pete's loud groan encouraging him. He imagined Pete taking Crimson, their bodies together as they came, and his own length pulsed with need.

Pete's hand was in his hair, pressing him as his pelvis rose. Gods, how did Crimson take them so deep? The thought only worsened his own need for release. Pulling his mouth back, he slid his tongue over the tip then down the length of Pete, Crimson's scent eliciting his own groan. He gripped Pete's shaft then took him, knowing he was close, having tasted his pre-cum, and feeling him thicken. With a cry, Pete's body tensed, the warm, thick juices spilling into Bormick's mouth, coursing down his throat as Pete shook below him.

Every part of him was on fire with the thrill of it.

"Holy fuck," Pete muttered, his body calming.

Bormick licked his way back up him, circling his tip once more, getting the last tiny bit seeping out before collapsing next to Pete.

"Shit, you taste even better fresh. If you don't suck me off soon, I'm gonna come all over myself after that."

And it was the truth. He was so turned on that he was aching. Never in his wildest dreams had he imagined going down on another man or enjoying it, but he had. Pete was different, and he'd accepted that. He was the exception, just as Bormick knew he was Pete's exception.

With a laugh, Pete rose, hovering over Bormick. "Time to give you back the alpha title?" he asked, letting his tongue slide over Bormick's lower lip before biting it and kissing him. The man could kiss as well as Crimson. The experience was different when he kissed Pete—one that reached to the lower depths of his arousal and gripped it.

"I never gave it up," he returned, grabbing Pete's neck and pulling him in for another kiss.

Pete's mouth kissed every bruise, every cut, sucking on his nipple until Bormick pushed him back. "Damn, you make me feel like Crimson doing that. Use that mouth on my dick, Pete," he commanded.

His head fell back as Pete's mouth enveloped him, his tongue pressing against him. Pete's mouth rose, then sucked gently on his head, his hand taking Bormick's shaft tightly and pulling before his mouth dropped to meet it. He'd thought about it for so long that it felt amazing. Everything fell away—every ache, every bruise, all of it, leaving only Pete and his mouth. Too quickly, the arousal that had been rising since their first kiss in the hall met its limit and crashed through him. His grunt filled the room, his hands pushing Pete down as his hips thrust deeper into him. His body convulsed with the wave of his orgasm until it finally settled, and he released Pete's head, his arms falling to his sides, his breathing labored.

Pete licked him once more and he let out another groan before lying next to him. "No returning from that, huh?"

"No, would you want to?"

"Never."

Bormick smiled before rising to kiss Pete, his arms shaking slightly as he brought himself over him, hovering above him like Pete had done. Kissing Pete, he tasted himself on his mouth.

He drew back and searched Pete's eyes. "I hate that I love you, too, but I do."

Pete gave him a goofy grin. "It is what it is."

"Damn blood," Bormick mumbled.

"If any other man thinks this is an invitation, I'll kill him," Pete said.

"I'll kill him first for even thinking of touching you."

Pete pulled him in for another kiss.

"Are you shitting me?" He heard Crimson's voice, one filled with irritation and annoyance.

"Uh-oh, I think we're in trouble," Bormick joked before rolling off Pete.

"I go to the infirmary to find you, only to be told you never went, and this is what I find?" She gestured to them before putting her hands on her hips.

"Are you angry with him for not going to the infirmary, me for encouraging him, or both of us for not letting you watch?" Pete asked.

"All three! He's injured."

"I'm fine. My dick was aching for release and now I feel fine."

"Did you two fuck? What did you do?"

"Let's just say I know why you go down on him all the time, but I have no clue how you take the entire length of either of us in that pretty little mouth of yours," he said.

Her eyes lit up. "You did that to each other? All the way? Damn, I missed all the fun."

"Are you wet?" Bormick asked, his firmness returning at the thought.

"You have no idea."

"Well, come on over. Pete had you a few times while I was gone. It's only fair that I get a piece."

"You are injured," she said, and he couldn't help but laugh at how she was trying to stay serious.

"I just went down on Pete, then came quite intensely in his mouth. I think I can handle you riding me for a few hours."

"Well, we don't have a few hours." She looked like she wanted to pout, so he rose and went to her, moving her hands from her hips to his now full erection. Gods, what even her presence did to him.

Her eyes glinted as her hand stroked him.

"You can spare a few minutes," he said. "I haven't touched you in forever." He kissed her neck, and caressed her breast, feeling her nipple rise below the material of her dress.

"Mmm, but we need—" He stopped her with a kiss ,and she fell against him.

"Let him do it, Crimson. I'll go and help the others."

"No," Bormick said. "I want you both. You stay. Mark has an entire group of people helping—"

"But he's waiting for us. We need to go to—"

He stopped her with another kiss, undoing the bindings of her dress and letting it fall.

"How wet are you?" he asked, his hand sliding between her legs, a sigh that called to his need for her escaping. "Not wet enough."

He scooped Crimson up, ignoring another stab of pain, and laid her on the bed. Spreading her legs, he let his fingers explore her as Pete dropped to kiss her. Pete's hand slipped to her breasts, his thumb drawing her nipple further out. Bormick's thumb rubbed her clit as he watched them, feeling her respond, her body leaning into him as he stimulated it. Her legs tightened, her head falling back, and he pushed her legs apart again, dropping to taste her.

Mark was waiting, but Bormick wanted Crimson. He'd nearly lost his life, the two of them the only thing keeping him fighting. His tongue sank into her while Pete encouraged her rising orgasm by continuing to tantalize her breasts. Her body was pressing for release, the quiver of her legs increasing with each lick until she lost the fight, crumbling against Bormick's mouth.

He resisted the urge to lick up the flood of moisture that met his mouth, knowing they would need it.

"Now she's ready."

He rose, kissing Pete, hearing her sharply inhale as Pete licked her juices from his face. Gripping her ass, Bormick plunged into her, her legs automatically drawing around him.

"Gods, your soaking," he said, kissing her and turning her, so they were on their side.

He pulled out, letting his wet length slide against her, teasing her and encouraging her desire.

"Take me," she said, grabbing at him.

"We will. Feel her, Pete, she's soaked."

Pete laid against her back, his hand moving against her and encasing him.

"Shit, I said her, not me."

"I want to see you two fuck," Crimson cooed.

"No time for that," Pete whispered against her ear. His hand still gripped on Bormick, he tilted himself and pushed into her. Her groan made Bormick throb, and Pete gave him a knowing smile, squeezing him firmer.

"Dick," he muttered to Pete.

"I think she's ready," Pete said, letting go of Bormick and pulling free of her.

Bormick grunted at the loss of his touch. Pete's fingers dug into Crimson's moisture, then ran along her ass. She bucked against him, and Bormick knew Pete's finger was testing her. Bormick had always been the one to take her ass but this time he was giving the dominance to Pete who was embracing it.

Bormick picked her leg up and slid back into her, Pete working into her slowly as Bormick kept Crimson still. Her arms clung to him, her kisses growing more demanding. She bit at his lip, and he felt Pete fill her. The sensation was almost enough to send him over the edge. Crimson moaned, deep and ragged, sending his arousal to a dangerous peak. Crimson's own mounting need threatened the hold he had on his. He met Pete's eyes, seeing the lust there. He wanted more, as did Bormick, both from Crimson and each other. The muscles in

Pete's arms were accentuated as he gripped Crimson's side, increasing Bormick's high with the tension that could be seen with each thrust until Crimson cried out, her body shaking intensely. Bormick kissed her through it, his eyes never leaving Pete's, his moves never ceasing as they remained in rhythm with Pete's.

"Shit, I'm gonna come," Pete said, his breath ragged.

Bormick pounded deeper, increasing his movement with Pete's, the intensity between them pulling him under and washing over him as he grasped tightly to Crimson. His climax drowned him with waves that wouldn't quit. Pete's groan and release amplified Bormick's release, and Crimson's body quaked as another orgasm washed through her.

As their bodies calmed, Bormick kissed her shoulder, Pete brushing her hair back and kissing her neck. A residual tremor shook her body, causing him to smile.

"Now, what was so urgent that we needed to see Mark?" Bormick asked, kissing her forehead and releasing his grip on her. Resting his head against Crimson's back, Pete drew out of her.

"Aside from the fact that Skye's gone and is now some kind of possessed killing machine," she said sarcastically. "While you two gave each other blowjobs."

"I believe you partook in some of that pleasure," Pete said.

"Next time I get to watch."

"Next time I take him from behind while he fucks you," Bormick said, her response a sensual chill.

"I said no orifices—"

"And I just claimed your mouth."

"You are not touching my ass."

He reached around and squeezed Pete's ass.

"Shithead."

"You two, stop flirting. We need to clean up and get back," she said, maneuvering from their hold.

"Did they find something?" Pete asked.

"No, but I remembered something, and Mark knew what it meant."

Bormick rose, watching Crimson dress while he grabbed his own clothes. Pete drew water in their tub, a trick that still awed Bormick, and rinsed himself. Bormick washed up next to him, eyeing Pete's length. Pete threw him a look, his eyes dark. Continuing to talk as if nothing was happening between the two of them, Crimson's words shut the rising desire in him down quickly.

"Eliana said something about all their children not being noticed. She and Derrant have their own direct line."

He turned to her, ignoring a stabbing pain in his side.

"The dragons," she said.

His mouth fell open. "What?"

"Dragons? This world really has dragons?" Pete asked, his eyes wide.

"Yes, they were hiding with Eliana and now fly over Eltander and Kantenda from what I've been told."

"Hiding? Wait, that myth of her running from Derrant is true?" Bormick asked, a feeling of wonder taking over him.

"How do you think our lines were created? Eliana fell in love with a mortal, and Derrant got angry and slept with the queen of your line."

"And the dragons?"

"According to Mark, Derrant dragged her back and raped her before the Upper God agreed to hide her in the Dranth mountains."

"Where she gave birth to dragons?" Pete asked.

"Apparently."

"Jesus, that's some messed up mythology."

"You think that's messed up? They're children of Derrant and Eliana, like our lines are," Bormick said.

"So, we're distant cousins with the dragons?" Pete asked, knitting his brows.

"It would seem that way," Crimson said.

"That is one insane family tree," Bormick commented as he dressed.

Rubbing his face, Pete asked, "Why haven't we ever seen them?"

"Mark said they tend to stay close to the mountains now. While I was gone, they roamed the skies above Kantenda and Eltander, but after a few years, they returned to the mountains. I've never seen one myself."

"Dragons," Pete said again, sounding very unsure of himself, which was not typical of him.

Pain stabbed Bormick's side, and he grabbed onto the bedpost.

The uncertainty on Pete's face was quickly replaced with concern. "Are you okay?"

"Fine."

"You don't look fine," Crimson said.

"What does the dragon thing have to do with anything?" he asked, avoiding her comment.

"We're going to recruit the dragons."

This time, they both stared at her. He didn't know how to respond. The idea was unfathomable.

"That's why Mark is waiting for us."

Another pain tore through him, and he doubled over at the force.

"That's it, you're going to the healers. Dammit, why did I let you sway me?" Pete muttered, grabbing his arm and moving under it to support him.

"I can walk, Pete, and it was you who kissed me first. I didn't sway you to do anything."

Crimson's face reflected her annoyance. "I'll go with Mark. You take him to the healers."

"No way you're seeing dragons without me."

"And there's no way I'll convince Mark to wait any longer. Skye is out there somewhere, and we need to rescue her."

"Dammit, buy me some time, Crimson," Bormick said, pulling from Pete and walking to the door, ignoring the pain.

"Stubborn ass," Pete muttered, following him down the hall.

Pete grabbed his arm again, but he was too proud to take his help. He yanked it away and trudged to the infirmary, his mind wandering back to the situation with Pete and what it meant for their relationship.

"Slow down, Bormick, you're going to hurt yourself more," Pete complained.

"I'm not missing those dragons, Pete. Now shut up before I make you blow me again."

"Really?"

He peeked over at him, knowing Pete had enjoyed every second of it, just like he had. "Really. You know you want it again. And damn if I can't wait to fuck that broody mouth of yours again."

Pete shot him a look, but he knew it wasn't serious. "Fuck off, Bormick, or I'll leave you in the infirmary and see the dragons without you."

"Now, that was just low," he replied as they came to the door of the infirmary.

He stopped in front of it.

"Go on," Pete urged.

He hated this. Injuries made him look weak, and he hated looking weak.

"Bormick?"

"I'm feeling better—"

"You're afraid of novice mages?" He could hear the laugh in Pete's voice.

"Don't make me hurt you, Pete."

"Damn, you are."

"No, I'm not. I just don't like being injured." He looked away, not wanting Pete to see the vulnerability he knew was in his eyes.

Pete grabbed his face and forced him to look at him. "You can't be serious. You just went down on me, which is probably the most vulnerable you could be, and you're afraid to tell me you don't like being injured because it makes you look weak?"

"I never said that."

"I know you well enough to know that's the reason. Now get your ass in that infirmary so we can go rescue Skye."

With his words, reality returned. "Skye."

"Yes, Skye. We need to find her and save her. Derrant and Eliana said it's up to us." There was a subtle shift in Pete's eyes.

"What else did they say, Pete? Something you didn't tell Mark —what is it?"

Pete looked flustered for just a moment, then moved away to open the door. Bormick jerked Pete's hand back and pushed him against the wall. "You know me well enough to sense my vulnerability; I know you well enough to sense yours. What did they say to you about Skye?"

"Nothing," he said, trying to free himself from Bormick's grasp, his magic escaping slightly.

Bormick put his body flush against Pete's and kissed him, feeling the nervousness there. They'd told him something, something maybe even Crimson didn't know, something he wanted kept quiet.

"Tell me, Pete."

Pete's jaw tensed. "It's nothing."

Bormick thrust him harder against the wall, ignoring the stab of pain it caused. He stared Pete down, knowing he'd break. Knowing whatever he was hiding was about Skye and had to do with that strange habit of diffusing any talk of his attraction to her.

"I'm not going into that room until you tell me."

"Dammit, you're an asshole."

"I know, and if you don't tell me, I'll bend you over right here and take you in yours."

The jerk of Pete's erection let Bormick know it wouldn't be an unwelcome act—one he'd be trying once they were out of this mess.

"Fine, Eliana whispered something to me before she kissed me."

"The goddess kissed you?" A surge of jealousy went through him.

"Yes."

"And you liked it," he teased, hiding his envy.

"Yes."

"What did she whisper?"

Pete remained silent, his jaw tight.

"What did she whisper, Pete?"

"That I'll know what Skye feels like in time," he mumbled, looking away as he said it.

Bormick forced Pete's eyes back and stared at him. His words had been unexpected, taking Bormick by surprise. "What the fuck does that mean?"

"I have no idea."

But he did, and Bormick saw it clear as day. He did want Skye. He simply hid it from them all, just as he and Crimson suspected. And the goddess had confirmed that he'd have her one day. That was the shocking part. His mind tried to grapple with how that would even be a possibility.

Pete pushed him away. "Let it go, Bormick, and don't tell Crimson. I don't know what it means and there's no sense in having anyone else know."

He walked through the infirmary doors, leaving Bormick speechless. The words could only mean one thing. There was something more to Pete and Skye than any of them had imagined. He wiped his hand down his face, his mind suddenly concerned that the storm Derrant had warned them of was one with many layers and that this was only the beginning of it.

MARK

Mark couldn't think. He'd gone back to their quarters to try to rest, but just as it had the prior night, the room reminded him too much of Skye. Everything reminded him of her. It had been two days, yet it felt like a lifetime.

He'd always hated his time away from her when she was with Derrant, but this was worse by tenfold. At least then he knew she was safe, that she was under Derrant's protection. Now? She'd been hurt, Bormick's description matching what had happened to Crimson. The thought of it was maddening. He was her protector, her husband, her Elite, and he'd been unable to save her.

He stared out the window. Having nowhere else to go, he'd come back to the meeting room. Training had been an option, but his heart wasn't in it. Losing Skye had impacted everyone in the castle, especially the Elite. He'd felt the snap in his connection to her, the wrenching of her magic from him as Crimson had continued screaming, echoing the pain Skye was experiencing. It had broken him, and he didn't know how to pick up the pieces.

He wanted her back, but he didn't know if she was even there to bring back. The thought that he may have already lost her, sent his heard crashing.

He heard the door open and turned, hoping it was Crimson and the others. He'd sent everyone else away to find answers, solutions he knew weren't there.

"Hey," Alex said, coming in slowly.

"Alex." He hadn't seen Alex since before Skye had been taken. Had avoided him, unsure what to say, or how to tell him he'd failed his job. That he hadn't protected his mother, that he'd lost her again.

Alex looked so much like Skye that it was painful to see him. He said nothing, only walking to Mark and embracing him tightly.

"You'll find her," he said.

Mark hugged him back, relief settling in for the first time, if only briefly. Mark put his hand around Alex's head, leaning his forehead against his. "I will. I'll bring her home, no matter what it takes."

"You always do."

"I'm sorry I didn't—" Mark started.

"I know. You weren't ready and you've been locked in here trying to find a way to save her."

"Something like that."

"When was the last time you slept or ate?" Alex asked.

"I have no idea, but it doesn't matter."

"It does. How can you help Mom if you're hungry and exhausted?"

"I can't sleep, Alex."

"Maybe not, but you can eat. Come on," he said, walking toward the door.

"I'm waiting for Crimson, Pete, and Bormick."

"And from what I've heard about them, you might be waiting a while. Come grab some food with me. We'll raid the kitchens."

He walked out, leaving Mark no choice but to follow. Which he silently did.

"Here," Alex said, pulling out bread and leftover meat from the cabinets once they made it to the kitchens. The staff had turned in for the night, leaving them alone. "Eat."

"Since when are you the parent?"

"Since you lost all sense of who you are."

It stung, but he knew Alex wasn't far off. He was lost without Skye.

"Mom's strong. Whatever this is, whoever has her, she'll survive it. Look at everything else she's been through and survived."

"This is different Alex—"

"Why?"

"Because this is unknown. We have no idea about these people or how their magic works."

"Which is why you're recruiting the dragons?"

"Word gets out fast around here," he grumbled.

"Grandmom Elspeth told me."

"We need everything we can. We have no Mage Warriors, aside from what power Crimson has from your mother and she barley knows what she's doing. And we have Pete. I'm not sure that's enough."

"Well, the mages have gathered, Clover and I included."

"That's great. Now I have to worry about you out there as well."

"I'm trained now."

"You're still my nephew—"

Alex raised a brow.

"Always will be, Alex, and with Skye out of commission, it's up to me to keep you safe."

Alex laughed. "I'm thirty years old. I'm old enough to manage myself."

"You're still a babe in this world."

"All right, old man."

They both chuckled before the heaviness returned to Mark's chest.

"I don't know if I can save her this time. She's lost to me." He pulled his weapon out and laid it on the table. Alex's reaction said everything. "Her magic has been morphed, severed from all of us. Bormick confirmed it. That part of her that we love is gone. How do I save her when she's coming to kill us all?"

Alex was quiet for a few minutes.

"I know my mother; you know her even better. If they've corrupted her, she's in there somewhere fighting to hold on. She loves us too much to let go."

Mark stared down at his wedding ring, twisting the band in his fingers.

"You're right. I suppose I'm just...scared. Scared I won't reach her this time. Scared I won't be able to save her."

"Well, there are four of you fighting for her this time. Maybe it's all of you or maybe one of them who will be the savior this time. Does it really matter if it's not you?"

He gave Alex a smile. "You know, you're pretty smart for a kid."

"Yeah, well, you're pretty stubborn for an old man."

They continued talking until Alex began yawning and Mark forced him to bed.

"Are you seriously going to the dragons tonight?" Alex asked as they made their way down the hall.

"Yes, as soon as the others get their asses moving."

"You know they don't care for visitors at night."

"Great, it's your mother they favor, not me, so I've already got one strike against me."

"They don't dislike you."

"They're terrifying."

"They're dragons. They should be." He gave Mark another hug. "See you on the battleground, old man."

Mark watched him walk through the great hall toward his wing. When Alex was no longer in sight, Mark made his way back to the meeting room. Crimson was sitting with her head on the table, and she lifted it quickly when he entered. Her hair fell softly against her cheek and for a moment her features were delicate, fragile almost. Her dark green eyes were heavy with drowsiness and something that looked like satisfaction. It was a sexy look. But then again, most looks she carried were sexy. He shook his head and let that thought go.

"Where are Pete and Bormick?"

"Pete is taking Bormick to the novice mages."

"Taking? I thought he was there already or...that isn't where you came from, is it?" Now the satisfied eyes made sense.

"They didn't make it there."

"Do I want to know?"

"Eh, my boys were bonding, and I joined them."

"Christ, he's injured, and he can't keep it in his pants long enough to get healed?"

"I'm not sure it was all Bormick this time. Pete was a tad more aggressive than he usually is." There was a glint in her eyes when she said it.

He stared at her. He had never understood their dynamic, now he certainly didn't. "So they're..." Not sure how to say it delicately, he paused.

"Fucking each other?" she finished for him. From her mouth, that word sent a strange sensation through him. The same as when Skye said it.

"Uh, yeah," he said, ignoring the feeling.

"I don't think they're there yet, but they're most definitely tasting each other. Pete's flavor was all over Bormick's mouth. Well, until mine was."

"Shit," he muttered.

"You never tasted me, Mark. That's a shame. I hear I'm quite addictive."

He wasn't certain how to respond, the thought of it flickering in his mind before he brushed it away. "I've got my own to taste, Crimson. She's all I need."

She leaned on her elbows. "And what if you can't get her back, Mark?"

His heart cracked at the thought, just as it did each time he thought about it.

"What if she's gone for good? What will you do?"

"I don't know. What would you do?" He turned the question back on her, not wanting to answer it.

"So, if Bormick and Pete went rogue on me? Forgot me and started killing innocent people? Would I kill them?"

"Yes." The thought of Skye doing that left him shaking.

She rose, coming around to him, her hips swaying, her hair moving with them. "You assume I'm like you, Mark. That I am the hero, that I sacrifice for my people. I'm not a hero. I'm selfish and I would take them and burn this world down with them before I ever turned on one."

"And that's why you're not allowed to make those decisions," Pete said, entering with Bormick. "Bormick, if I'm ever taken by those fools and I start killing, just pull the trigger."

"What's a trigger?"

"Seriously?"

"No guns here, Pete, remember?" Mark said.

"Whatever it is, you assume I'm not like Crimson. I am. My ass is keeping you just like hers will," Bormick said.

"Great, let's hope I'm never the enemy."

Mark couldn't help but think of Skye. He didn't know what he'd do if he couldn't reach her, or if she began killing innocents. If there was only one way to stop her, would he be able to do it? Could he kill the love of his life to save the world?

"You couldn't, Mark," Crimson answered his thought. "You love her too much."

"But if I have to—"

"You'd kill the two of you because you can't live without her."

Her words hit him square, and he knew what she'd said was true. He couldn't live without Skye.

"Why are you back so soon?" Crimson asked Bormick, drawing Mark's attention from his thoughts. "You didn't distract him again, did you, Pete?"

"I wish," Bormick said.

"No, he threatened to kill the entire infirmary if they didn't mend him faster."

Mark clenched his fists. "You can't threaten my mages."

"I can and I did. It worked. They did their job. The magic is still tingling in there."

Pete threw Bormick an irritated look. "Although they did tell him to rest."

"Then why aren't you resting?" Mark asked.

"I'm not missing dragons. I'll heal, but dragons I'm not missing."

"Stubborn ass," Crimson muttered.

"Fine," Mark said, grabbing the cloak he'd brought down with him earlier. "Is that how you're all going?"

The three gave him an odd look before Bormick said, "Yeah. What's with the heavy cloak?"

"Mountains. Snowy and cold?" he replied with a smirk.

"Shit," Bormick said.

Pete moved his hand and brought a black stream of magic before them. From it, three cloaks appeared. Two black, one red with fur lining it.

"Ohhh, I love it," Crimson said, grabbing it then kissing Pete a little too long.

Bormick grabbed his cloak, looking at it while they kissed. "I don't do cloaks."

"Then freeze," Mark said.

Bormick shot him a look as Crimson unlatched her lips from Pete's.

"Keep that up, Crimson, and he won't be able to walk," Bormick teased.

Ignoring him, Mark studied the cloaks, amazed again at Pete's growing abilities. "Your magic is so unique to the other mages. Skye has to pull colors to create things. You just create things. Even the full mages can't do that."

"Perk of having the Death God's blood in my veins, I guess."

"I suppose there should be some perk from that heritage."

"How do we get to the dragons?" Bormick asked.

"Pete can take us."

"No, I've never been there. I have no idea how to find them with a portal."

Mark hadn't thought of that.

"I can try," Crimson said. "Skye created portals, so I should be able to. She showed me a few times. If her magic knows how to find them, then the imprint should be within mine now, right?"

He wasn't certain that was how it worked, but it was worth a try. There was risk to it and his jaw tightened as he pondered if it was worth taking that chance. Crimson was untrained, even with the few days she'd had with Skye. Her magic was unstable, only a copy of Skye's and now she had access to only some of the hues.

"I know what you're thinking," Pete said to him, "but let her try."

He acquiesced, and Crimson called her magic, pulling only the hues that would respond to her, the darker shades that Skye had always embraced.

"Don't bleed them," he said to her.

"I know that, Mark," she hissed, still concentrating.

Eventually, a portal formed, blues and grays funneling around it, reminding him of Skye. Skye had always preferred the darker shades. That's where her strength lay, her tie to the Death God, his mark on her birthmark.

"Do you think they know about it?" Bormick asked, as if he'd been thinking the same thing. "About her tie to the Death God, the difference in her birthmark?"

"I don't honestly know. Why?"

"Well, they targeted her birthmark when they changed her magic. I wonder if it changed the marking or if the true marking is still under the surface of what they did to her."

Mark felt a bit of tension flee his muscles as hope simmered in him.

"Like a cloak concealing her true self?" Pete said, picking up the corner of his cloak as a reference.

"Yeah, if they only touched the mark of the Death God and didn't tap into the true birthmark, the one that matches Crimson's—"

"Maybe she's still in there and we can pull her out," Mark said.

"I have no doubt," Crimson said. "She loves you too much to let go. So don't you let go or her grip will slip."

"Well said," he told her.

"Someone needs to remind you of who you are before you wallow away in your grief."

"I don't wallow," he defended himself, following her through the portal.

She pulled her cloak tight around her. "Yes, you do. Gods, it's cold out here!"

Bormick gave a visible shiver, rubbing his arms. "I'm going to freeze my balls off out here."

"I'll warm them up for you when we get back," Crimson said.

"Let Pete while you warm up my dick with those beautiful lips of yours."

"Pete's mouth not good enough for you anymore?" Mark quipped, looking around to see where they were on the mountain, surprised Crimson's theory had worked.

Bormick let out a massive laugh while Pete shot Mark a look.

"What? I'm sticking up for you, Pete," he responded.

Bormick slapped Mark's back. "Oh, I like you more and more each day, Elite."

"I'm not touching your dick, or your balls, so don't get any ideas," Mark said quickly.

Bormick laughed again.

"Crimson and I have those covered," Pete said with a smirk. "Now that the conversation about my mouth is over—"

"It is?" Bormick said, grabbing his face and kissing him.

"Does this ever stop?" Mark asked Crimson.

"No, it just keeps getting more interesting."

Pete pushed Bormick away. "Ass. What's that down there?"

Bormick went to grab himself, but Pete quickly clarified, saying, "Over there."

They were like a couple of kids or two brothers who couldn't stop going at each other. Couldn't stop touching each other, either.

"That's the Kingdom of Eltander."

Crimson had landed them midway up the mountain and Revina's kingdom—with its enormous wall—could be seen in the distance.

"It's a walled-up kingdom?" Pete asked.

"The royal family built it ages ago to keep out invaders. They're very sheltered, living a false sense of security that nothing will harm them," Mark explained. He didn't bother covering the annoyance in his voice. Revina was a fool to think her kingdom was safe. No one was safe, wall or no wall.

Pete stretched his neck, taking in the sight. It was impressive and Mark knew Pete had never seen the likes of it before. "Has it worked?" Pete asked.

"So far. That is, until Crimson lured their king out and had him murdered."

"Not letting that go, are you, Mark?" she asked.

"Nope. That's going to stick with you, especially when I'm forced to let the other things go."

She gave him a startled look and parted her lips to say something when a brilliant flash of light filled the sky, followed by a massive rumble.

"What the hell?" he muttered, his eyes turning back to Eltander.

The light eclipsed the kingdom, hiding the wall and as it faded, he drew in a breath. Crimson let out a cry, her hand going to her mouth. The wall was gone, turned to rubble, only a cloud of dust in its wake. Flashes of light flickered through the smoke, followed by screams that were faint but discernible.

"Skye," Mark said, rushing forward. Bormick grabbed his arm. "Let me go, Bormick. She's down there. I need to get to her."

"No, that wall was her doing. You go down there, you're dead."

He jerked his arm free. "Pete, take me there. We can get her." Bormick moved in front of him. "There are people dying down there. We need to help them."

"How? We can't defeat them, and we definitely can't defeat her. We go down there and we're all dead. The best course of action is to stay on our path, to go up this mountain—"

"And let them all die?" Mark asked, staring at Bormick in disbelief.

"They're already dead," Pete said. "He's right. Even if we go down there, we can't fight that. She took that wall down in seconds, Mark."

"That's my wife—"

"That's not Skye," Bormick said. "Listen to those screams, even if she's not the one doing the killing"—there was another flash of brilliant light and the castle crumbled—"she's standing by and she's letting them die. Would your Skye do that?"

He looked past, staring at the kingdom, watching and listening. Bormick was right. Skye would never harm another unless it was to protect her own.

"What have they done to her?" He heard the crack in his voice, felt the shake in his knees as he faced reality.

"Pete, can you get us further up the mountain?" Bormick asked, and Mark was thankful Bormick had taken the lead. He didn't think he had it in him to do so.

"I think, but I can't guarantee we'll land on solid ground."

"That's reassuring," Crimson mumbled.

"It's a chance we'll have to take. We need to move before they notice us over here."

"We're miles away."

"I don't trust them, and we don't know their powers. Now get us up there, Pete."

Mark stared at the scene while Pete called the portal. His heart thundered in his chest. She was down there. So close, within his grasp, but he had no way to get her, no way to break through to her, no way to even fight her. Even if he did reach her, he wasn't certain she wouldn't kill him. There was a chance she was so lost that even he would be foreign to her, that she wouldn't recognize him or even remember that she loved him.

The thought threatened to drop him to his knees. As the screams continued, he turned away, knowing he'd have to leave her, to turn his back on the voices of the dying or all would be lost.

SKYE

Through the darkness, screams of terror echoed. Skye drew her hues closer, shaking, praying for it to stop. She saw nothing, only the empty black of her prison, but the screams reached her and each one cut her deeper.

She'd fought to escape, remembering the searing pain that had ripped her apart. It had shredded her bit by bit, stripping her away until, finally, all that remained was a tiny piece of her, blinding light shoving her further and further back until the ebony of the prison had enclosed around her.

She remembered the faint echo of Bormick pleading for her. She didn't remember if she'd killed him or not. Tightening her hues closer, she fought the tremor of fear that slinked through her at the thought and at the terror the screams held. She didn't know where she was or what was happening. Nor did she know whose voices they were. She prayed Mark wasn't among them. A silent sob escaped, for she had no voice here, only her thoughts.

And Alex. There was a chance he was out there as well. Her heart pounded in fear. God no, they couldn't be out there suffering whatever wrath she was bringing down upon them. She had to stop this, to get back to them. To reach Mark. How she longed for him to hold her, to let her know it was all right, that it was over. To feel his strength. Even that connection she'd had through her magic was gone. She'd felt it sever, torn from her as the rest of her identity was. She had no idea what they'd done to her or what they were forcing her to do. Whatever it was, it sounded devastating, and that hurt her even more.

As the screams continued, she thought of Mark, taking strength from the image she held of him. She clung to that image and opened her eyes, looking out into the emptiness of her prison, and she began to fight back.

CRIMSON

Her feet slipped, but Pete's hands grabbed Crimson, pulling her to the ledge beside him. Pete did the same for Bormick and then Mark.

"Shit, Pete, could you make this any more precarious?" Bormick said, looking down.

"Precarious. That's a big word for you," Pete teased. "I warned you. You're lucky we landed on a ledge."

"I don't like heights, unless they're sexual," Crimson said, clinging to the rock behind her.

Bormick ignored Pete's jab, saying, "That would have been good to know before we set out to climb a mountain."

Mark was silent, his eyes locked far below, even though they were too far up to see, and clouds blocked their sight.

She was worried about him. Touching his shoulder, she said, "Mark?"

He continued to stare. She'd never seen him so devastated. Even when she'd held him prisoner and Derrant had Skye, he'd still been full of fight. Ever since Bormick told him what they'd done to Skye, he'd been wavering between a state of hopelessness and overzealousness. Part of him was broken. Whether it was the disruption to his connection to Skye's magic or the loss of her to whatever force held her, he was not the man he'd been.

"Mark?" she tried again, gently touching his arm.

He turned to her, his hazel eyes fractured with pain. Her breath caught at the look of sheer agony she saw there before he blinked it away. She'd never realized how deeply he and Skye loved each other until that moment, and her heart ached for him.

"How far are we from the dragons?" she asked.

He seemed to wake, his eyes shifting, coming back to life. He looked up.

"Not far, but we'll need to walk from here."

She tightened her cloak around her, snuggling into the fur lining Pete had given her. Bormick grumbled about the mountain and started climbing the small path. As they climbed, she felt Pete behind her, his presence solid and supportive. She really didn't like heights. To take her mind from it, she thought about Pete and Bormick. She hadn't been surprised when she'd found them together. The intensity between the two had been building so she had anticipated it at some point. The thought of them stirred her blood, that blood she knew bound them all. Now the three of them were completely bound, all three mated to each other, not just them to her.

She was still irritated that they'd done it without her present. Sure, they'd played other times recently, Bormick jerking Pete off, something that stoked the fire within her, but they hadn't made the final steps. Now they had, and she knew there was no returning from here, they would continue to explore their new level and she would watch and participate.

A smile curved on her lips at the thought but then faltered when they came to the mountain peak. It sloped downward, a white wonderland beyond it. A valley where several dragons stood in the moonlight, ready to strike. They were beautiful. There were dragons of different colors—blues, grays, whites, and even a few black ones—their scales shimmered in the moonlight. Although their appearance left her jaw dropping, she also felt the increase in her heartrate and the tightness of her breaths, her body knowing the danger that these creatures posed.

For once, Bormick was speechless.

"Welcome to the Dranth mountains," Mark said with a confidence Crimson was finding hard to understand.

"What do we do now?" Pete said, and she could hear the awe in his voice. She glanced over at him, seeing the wonder in his eyes. In that moment, he looked boyish and innocent. Her heart beat a little more rapidly as her love for him deepened.

"We talk to them," Mark said, bringing her back to the terrifying beasts that sat before them.

"Dragons talk?"

They continued going back and forth but Crimson tuned them out, drawn to a dragon emerging from the snow, a gray and black one that eyed her. Its blue eyes were as startling as Pete and Bormick's.

Bormick grabbed her wrist, but she pulled it away, walking closer to the dragon.

"Crimson, they seem agitated. I wouldn't—" Mark started, but the dragon roared.

Crimson cringed at the sound and stopped, her heart racing. There weren't many things that frightened her. She'd slept with the Death God, had played with his demons and his shadow gods since she was a child, but these creatures terrified her.

It took a step forward, and she noticed the red markings on its hide, like the ink that lined Pete's body.

"Now would be a good time to start talking," Pete said, and she heard the nervousness in his voice.

"No, it's evaluating her."

"Why? To determine if she'd make a good snack?" Bormick asked.

The dragon stood over Crimson, eclipsing her with its size.

She held her breath as it dropped its head and sniffed her, its slanted blue eyes set on her. It nudged her with its nose.

"What does it want me to do?"

A million thoughts went through her mind until she remembered that these were Eliana's children. Bringing her hand up, she rested it on its face, right between its eyes, feeling the leathery hide, tough and indestructible.

"I am Eliana's heir," she said. "Distant cousin to Skye. We need your help."

Yes, we know of you, Crimson, a deep male voice said as the dragon lifted its head. *I am Keliamar, and we have awaited your arrival.*

The shaking of her hands betrayed the calm Crimson wanted to exhibit, the dragon's words only enhancing their trembling.

A war has begun. The fate of our world rests on the children of the gods.

The dragon moved past her, its enormous body brushing against her, then stopping in front of Pete and Bormick. She watched the dragon raise its wings, their span shadowing the width of the mountain.

Shadow Mage, what will you do?

"It's talking," Bormick said under his breath.

"No shit, idiot," Pete replied.

The dragon tipped its head to Bormick, bumping him with its snout.

"I think you offended it," Pete muttered. He was staring with wide eyes at Keliamar, but Crimson knew her eyes mirrored his.

Keliamar snorted, saying, *Son of the Death God. His shadows do not own you as they do your brother, but his strength does. Will you fight to protect the kingdoms of the Shadow Realm?*

"You know?" Mark asked.

Keliamar turned his head to Mark.

Our mother's heir wreaks vengeance against the kingdoms. Her power has been corrupted, her spirit imprisoned.

"She's still in there?" Mark asked, hope in his voice.

Barely. What will you do, guardian? And you, warrior? And you, Shadow King? And you..." He turned his long neck to Crimson. *"The vessel. The conduit. A queen of untapped potential waiting to fall into her sister's footsteps, to follow our mother, to embrace the gift our father has given you and your sister. Queen of shades to her sister's hues. What will you all do?*

"Fight," she said, not flinching from his icy glare. "I will fight, as will you and your brothers and sisters."

Will we?

"They threaten all of Eliana's children," Mark said.

No, they threaten the kingdoms of the Shadow Realm. The Death God's lands. They fear what they do not know. They fear what threatens them and you, fiery daughter, are as much a threat as your sister. They just don't know this.

"Me?"

He dropped to his front legs and circled her, his long tail draping around her.

You, the dragon said, and fear gripped her for the first time, her body succumbing to the shaking of her nerves. *The prison will be her undoing unless you understand your place and accept it, unleash it upon those who would doubt it. Else, she will be the undoing of you all.*

"I'm not a hero," Crimson whispered, fear still weighing her down. She looked at Mark. "I'm not Mark, I'm not Skye."

Keliamar stopped and brought his face to hers. His blue eyes had darkened and were now so close to the color of Skye's that she caught her breath..

"I'm not. I'm the bad girl who wreaks havoc. I'm the one who hurts people, who destroys...that should be me down there, not her." Her hands were shaking, the beast continuing to stare her down. "It's not me."

Pity, then you will lose everything, and we are all doomed.

Keliamar drew away, walking back to where his brothers and

sisters waited. She swallowed the rising bile, looking to Bormick as he crossed his arms and narrowed that knowing gaze on her.

"We're not the good guys. They are, Pete is, but not us."

"Who says?" Pete asked.

"Everyone. History. I can't—"

"Can't what?" Mark asked.

She turned her eyes to his, the hazel in them dark, his mouth pursed. "I can't be what they need. I can't be the savior."

"No, you can't. Not if you fail to leave who you were in the past." He stepped closer to her, reaching his hand out and tipping her chin up, forcing the eyes she'd dropped at his words, up again. "You've been hiding behind the façade you wanted the world to see, playing the part you thought was yours, thought Derrant had marked you with. That's what Skye saw when she began visiting you, when she befriended you against her instinct, against my objections. She saw what no one else had bothered to look for. What they see." He gestured to Pete and Bormick. "What those dragons see."

"And what do you see?" she asked.

"Someone I wish had never hidden. Someone strong, determined, loyal. Someone who was broken for too long and finally has her footing, someone who can bring Skye home because she is the kind of queen who knows no limit, who will show those fools what a daughter of Eliana is. Someone with a past that has scars, that holds mistakes, but those things make her who she is—a badass bitch who will bring those bastards to their knees."

She stared at Mark, unable to speak.

"Skye fought for you, Crimson. Will you fight for her?"

Her breath caught. "Are you calling me a bitch?" she asked, teasing him.

"Damn right I am."

She forced back the pressure behind her eyes and lifted her head, standing taller. "Good, because I am."

She gave him a coy smile, then turned to the dragons, raising her hand and calling the black hues from Keliamar's hide, dimming it to a dusty gray. The red hues followed, swirling around her as she moved forward, pulling colors from the other dragons and letting the hues strengthen her.

"Will you fight with us?" she asked.

Keliamar glared at her. *Will you fight?*

"With every ounce of power I have. No one threatens my kingdom or my family."

He launched forward into the air, followed by a brilliant blue dragon. The two roared, a wave of blue flame filling the sky. As if answering their call, more dragons appeared until many stood around them, the two dropping before her. Slowly, she let the hues return.

Keliamar tipped his head, studying her before dropping to kneel before her, the others following suit. Her fear fled, her heart strong and proud, filling with a sense of awe at the sheer magnitude of what they were doing.

We will fight, he said, raising his head, *and we will watch you bring the cowards to their knees and avenge your sister.*

"No, I won't avenge her. I will free her and together, we will rip them to shreds."

I like you, Shade Queen.

"Good, because you don't want to be my enemy."

Bormick laughed, then said to Pete. "She's so fucking sexy when she's like this."

She shot him a look, noticing Pete's lopsided grin.

"Gods you three," Mark said. "All right, Crimson, what's the next move?"

"Me?"

"Yeah."

She sucked on her lip, thinking. There was an army below. She wasn't sure the four of them were ready, but they had their own weapon with the dragons. She didn't know what to do. This wasn't a game of manipulation. This was war, something for which she'd never been at the frontline. She was an undercurrent in wars, the unseen enemy, the instigator, not the defender.

"Might I suggest we fortify the other realms? If they haven't decimated this one yet, they will, then they'll strike their next target," Bormick said, to her relief.

"Kantenda," Mark said.

"My thought, too. This was another precursor to the bigger battle. Your kingdom is the prize. The seat of power in these realms, and the last remaining seat of magic. After yours, the other kingdoms are easy. Send three dragons to each, four to Kantenda to stand guard. These two come with us to confront what remains in Revina's kingdom."

"Are you ready for a fight, Crimson?" Pete asked, drawing his magic, his blue eyes lined with excitement.

"Ready as I'll ever be."

Then those are your orders? Keliamar asked her.

"Yes, just as he said."

The beast let out another roar, and she flinched at the ferocity of it. The dragons lifted, rising into the air and taking off to their destinations.

"That ought to give Theodore a fright," Mark said with a small chuckle.

"Are you ready for this, Mark?" Crimson asked while Pete created a portal.

"Yes, she's still fighting. There's a way to save her, to bring her back." His hazel eyes were light again and filled with hope.

"We will," she said before moving to him and hugging him. It was the first time she'd touched him since that last day in their past. She felt the hesitation, the confusion, the tension in his muscles, but he didn't push her away. "Thank you."

She reached up and kissed his cheek before drawing back.

"For what?" he asked.

"For seeing me," she replied before walking toward the waiting portal.

"Does this mean we need to make room for him in our bed now?" Bormick asked.

"No," she said before Mark could respond. "He's Skye's, and he's off limits to the two of you."

"But not you?" Bormick asked.

She glanced back at Mark, giving him a playful wink. "Definitely to me."

Mark shook his head as Bormick said, "Good, because Pete and I don't like to share."

"There is so much that's warped about that comment," Mark said as they all walked through the portal.

"Too much," Pete muttered.

PETE

Pete's heart swelled with pride. He'd always seen the true woman beneath Crimson's checkered past. Sure, she and Bormick had histories that would make most shudder. With Crimson, there had been a sensual brutality. But he saw the truth behind it, the fragile delicacy of the woman below, the woman he loved. He'd recognized it the first time he'd seen her. And within the fragile woman lay a dichotomy. One of strength and power. She was no weak flower. She could hold her own, fight her own battles and win them.

She'd simply never seen those sides of her. But others had taken notice—Bormick, Skye, and now even Mark.

The question remained—would she embrace it, own it, and continue to own it? Would she leave the broken vengeful woman behind and become who the gods wanted her to be, who Skye, Mark, and the kingdoms needed her to be? It looked that way, but he knew bravery was a delicate tightrope, one that could wobble when confronted with doubt.

He moved through the portal, his magic drawn on edge at the unknown that faced them. He'd tried to concentrate it on the front gates and prayed it had worked.

"Holy shit," he said, stepping through.

He'd never seen the Kingdom of Eltander, but what was left of it was rubble and ash.

"Gods, even I never left a trail this bad," Bormick said.

Smoke and the smell of death lingered, the army gone and with it, Skye. Mark walked forward, his eyes taking it in, surveying the destruction, a dragon flanking him, its stance guarded.

"Did Skye do all of this?" he asked, bending next to the body of a woman, her face bloodied.

"No," Crimson said. "I think they did this. They used her to break through, to decimate the city, but they did the slaughtering. This was a test run for your kingdom."

"Agreed," Bormick said. "They'll have a harder fight against a kingdom of mages. That's where they'll let her loose, that's when the blood will be on her hands if we don't stop it."

"Then we need to stop her. We need to be ready," Pete said, the thought of Skye as a killer not sitting well with him.

He didn't know what that meant in terms of the four of them. They all played a part, all of them with Crimson as the center. The vessel they kept calling her. But that word didn't help him understand what she was meant to do. He needed to get Bormick alone and pick his brain. He was the only other one who knew her like Pete did. But the last time they'd been alone, there had been no talking. He stared out at the devastation, trying not to think about that time. It wasn't the right place or moment.

"We need to get back. I need to talk to Camin, Elspeth, and Trent. We need to prepare for war," Mark said, after they'd searched for survivors, any sign of life, and finding none.

"Can I talk to them?" Crimson asked, surprising them all. "I want to understand magic better, to learn what I can. There's something more I'm supposed to do and maybe talking with them will help me figure that out."

"I think that would be wise," Bormick said. "And I agree, we're missing something."

So he had picked up on that, too. Good, this would give Pete a chance to talk to Bormick, to get his thoughts. They portaled back, sending the dragons to fortify the outskirts of Kantenda, the first line of defense.

~

"THEY WON'T ATTACK from the outside," Bormick said, leaning against the wall of the great hall. Pete was looking out of a window that overlooked the castle grounds. Mark and Crimson had left to talk with the mages.

"Why do you say that?"

He turned, Bormick's blue eyes meeting his. His heart sped, a reaction that still irritated him, but it was one he couldn't stop. It was too late. They'd taken the next step, sealed their attraction to each other. There was no denying it at this point.

"Because they'll strike hard and fast. They know this will be a challenge if they don't. They know I warned you. They know the magic that lies in this realm is far greater than Eltander, and they know we're prepared. The dragons can only help if they strike on the outer edge of the kingdom, otherwise they risk killing innocents while trying to protect them."

"Shit." Pete ran his hand through his hair. "How do we beat that?"

"We don't. Crimson does. I think this is her fight."

"She can't defeat Skye like she is. She's lethal and Crimson—"

"Crimson is a weapon we haven't figured out how to use."

Bormick acted like a brute, but he was sharp, something he hid from most others. Pete had come to realize it quickly.

"You think we're missing something, too?"

Bormick pushed off from the wall and moved closer, looking out the window.

"I do, and it's bothering me. They keep calling her a vessel like it means something. And then there's that term conduit. I can't figure out what they mean."

"She copies our magic."

"Yes, but that seems too simple."

Bormick winced and stared at the grounds. His injuries were still bothering him, but that was something Pete knew he'd never admit. "You notice how the magic she copied from Skye hasn't faded? Even when the lighter control was stripped?" Pete asked.

"I did. It's like the two are still connected, like a funnel between them, a flow of power. What they wanted, they took from both, what escaped from Skye..." He stopped and looked at Pete, his eyes serious. "It fled her. I watched it, the room filled with darker hues, long tendrils like they were flowing from her."

"Crimson said she felt it. Her hair darkened and her eyes."

"I noticed that," Bormick said.

"So, did they end up in Crimson?"

"You think the dark hues found her? But that doesn't make sense, does it?"

The word vessel continued to repeat in his head and he couldn't get past it. From Bormick's expression, the word bothered him as well. His brows were knitted, his jaw tight.

"What are you thinking?" Pete asked.

"Maybe we've been looking at this all wrong. Maybe she's not a vessel to hold someone's magic and use it."

"Then what?"

"The power over the darker hues. It stayed in Crimson because the light connection drew to Skye. Something in her held on to the rest. Otherwise, why would it not have dissipated by now or been drawn out like it was in Skye. If the magic is connected to the host still, it should have gone," Bormick explained.

"But it didn't because she didn't give it up. And all that remained were the darker hues."

"What if that vessel is still incomplete? She's still waiting for more, something else. Something more she's meant for."

"But what?" he asked, not certain he was following Bormick's thinking.

"Power. She just hasn't found it, not all of it."

"And so, we're back to where we were, which is nowhere."

"You know, for someone so good in bed, you're not that keen," Bormick said.

Pete scowled at him.

"We're closer. She held onto the darker part of Skye's magic. The same magic Mark says drove Skye, the same those bastards stripped from Skye."

"They're magic is similar or it should be, both stronger in the magic of the Death God."

"The same magic you have, the magic of the Shadow Realm."

"But they stripped it from Skye—"

Bormick grabbed his hair and pulled his head forward so their foreheads touched.

"It's her tie to the Shadow Realm they took away, but if she's still in there and she's still tied to Crimson through the magic Crimson holds in her—"

"Then she can be pulled out with that same magic."

"Exactly. Fuck, you're sexy when you think."

"I could say the same to you." Pete saw the flash of desire and shook his head. "You don't stop, do you?" He pulled Bormick forward, kissing him, his tongue penetrating his mouth, an aggressive battle ensuing, the two fighting for dominance through the kiss.

Bormick pulled back. "I'd stop before I take you here, Pete."

"You wouldn't dare."

"No? I'd bend you over and fuck you so hard, you'll be screaming like Crimson by the time I spill into your ass."

He shivered, not entirely sure he wanted to experience that, even though his dick had grown massively hard at the thought.

"Let's set that thought aside."

Bormick engulfed his length with his hand and moved against him, Pete's breath catching. "I don't think that's what you really want, Pete."

Damn him for pushing it. "What I want is for you to get your mind out of your pants or my pants, for that matter, and concentrate on Crimson and Skye."

"Damn, you had to get serious, didn't you?"

He dropped his hand, Pete missing the touch, something he would never admit.

"If we don't, we'll all lose. If we get this right and we survive this, you can bend me over all you want as long as Crimson distracts me with her very much alive body."

"Deal. Now, let's find her so we can end this thing and I can get some release."

"Release? We just had sex a few hours ago and you're hungry again?"

"I'm always hungry, Pete. You should know that by now."

Pete rolled his eyes, walking away, Bormick following. They were halfway through the room when the windows shattered inward. Pete's power fled from him in response, shielding them both without him even realizing he'd done it.

They turned to the window, running toward it. They were one floor up, looking down on the open portal. Skye was below, staring ahead blankly as an army poured out behind her.

"Time to find Crimson now," Bormick commanded, drawing his sword and running.

Pete grabbed him and opened a portal to where he knew she would be. The mages and Elite had converged in preparation for the battle that now stood at their gates. Bormick had been right, they'd come directly to the heart of the kingdom and with force.

Pete couldn't clear the image of Skye from his mind. She'd been lifeless, her eyes gold, hair streaked with white and blue, an aura of light around her. She was terrifyingly beautiful. But it hadn't been her. The softness was gone, the part of her that held her true beauty stripped from her.

They burst through the portal into a frenzy of commotion. Mages and Elite were filing out to defend the castle and the kingdom. Running to their death.

And there in the midst of it stood Crimson, looking lost and vulnerable, Mark likely having ordered her to stay to keep her safe. He and Bormick would have done the same, and it was the same Bormick had done for Skye. Keep them safe, protect the two. Pete stopped, tugging Bormick back.

"What are you doing?" Bormick asked, ripping his hand away.

Pete saw it now, the two, the connection, all five of them tied by their creators, Eliana and Derrant. The two protectors, the three wielders. Shade Queen, the dragon had called Crimson, and he was the Shadow Warrior. Skye the same, a Mage Warrior but one who lived in the shadows just as he did. The shadows were their home, their tie to the realm of their ancestors. That was why Skye had always favored them. That was why she'd never gone blind, only colorblind. The spell they'd told him about had stripped all but what was innately part of her, what was in her blood—the shadows. He thought of the way his magic responded to hers, the sensation that went through him when their magic touched, the connection that was there. Conduit Mage Crimson had called herself. She wasn't only a vessel, but she was a conduit.

"I know how to save her. Grab Crimson. I need to find Mark."

He ignored Bormick's yell, dashing away, fighting through the movement.

Just do it, Bormick, and bring her outside, he thought. Another tremor shook the ground and the outer wing of the castle collapsed, a blinding golden light flaring with it.

He had to find Mark in the chaos. If he didn't, all would be lost. And he only had a matter of minutes before complete chaos began.

MARK

Mark had been in the barracks, Crimson and Elspeth training while he and Trent discussed strategy regarding the mages. The Elite were on the practice field, Noah giving out orders.

He looked over at Crimson. She had scrunched her face as she tried to follow Elspeth's directions and he couldn't help but laugh at her struggle. Elspeth was a lot on any given day for a full mage, but for someone with no magic experience, she was overwhelming. It was hard to imagine how they'd come to this point. The woman he'd hated for years, who he'd cursed on a daily basis, envisioned killing hundreds of ways, and now she was the key to saving Skye, the same person she'd tried to kill years before.

Her red hair slipped to her cheek, and she brushed it back. The movement was an innocent unconscious move, but even it had been laced with seduction, as if it were a part of her being. He supposed it was a power she'd developed over the years, one that had become a part of who she was.

She glanced at him, her green eyes distinctly darker than they always had been, more sage, yet still beautiful. They eyed him questioningly, but he continued to look, noticing only now the subtle similarities to Skye. The upward turn of her full lips, the slight wave to her thick hair, the power behind her eyes.

Power she now shared with Skye, just as she did her blood.

"Mark?" Trent asked, but Mark ignored him, stepping over to Crimson. He knew Elspeth was watching him, but he disregarded her stare, and picked up Crimson's chin.

"Mark?" she asked.

He continued to stare into her eyes, watching the power that flickered behind them. The magic danced in the darker shade of her eyes.

"You know, I wouldn't object to you kissing me, but I think Skye would and Bormick and Pete are quite protective."

"Shut up, Crimson, I have no intention of kissing you."

"Well, you don't have to be rude about it."

"The shadow shades stayed in your control. Why?"

"I don't know."

"They've grown, too."

"I think so."

"Why? Why would you get the hues that were stripped from Skye? Why would they flock to you? Unless...your blood connects you to Eliana, but you're both marked by Derrant."

He pushed her hair back. Her birthmark—sparkling violet—had morphed to the same shape as Skye's, the crescent moon surrounded by the web of night. The Death God's mark.

"Dammit, Derrant marked her and you, but hid yours until you were ready. The shadows connect you both."

Her eyes grew wide, and she opened her mouth to speak, but the ground shook beneath them, a crash above cutting through the space.

"They're here!" Noah screamed.

"Stay here. Don't move and do not leave the barracks," Mark instructed Crimson.

"But, Mark."

"No, you stay safe. Do not move. Elspeth, Trent, ready your mages!"

He ran, screaming for the Elite to arm themselves, all those still in the barracks running toward the entrance. This was it. The enemy was here, Skye was here, and they weren't prepared. Chaos ensued as people ran in every direction. Voices filled the air as he and Noah readied their troops, and Elspeth and Trent sent the first wave of mages into battle. He spied Alex far in the back with Clover, who clung to his hand. Elspeth had purposely put them in the back. They'd be the last wave out. Mark prayed they could end this battle before that point, before Alex had to witness his mother or even face her as the deadly weapon they'd made her.

The first wave of Elite flanked the outgoing mages when he heard the crumble of stone, one wing collapsing to Skye's magic. The second wave was sent, and he was readying Noah and Donakin to take over command when he heard Pete scream his name.

"I don't have time, Pete. Crimson's safe, she's—"

"I know. We need to get to Skye. I think I know how to stop her."

Mark let out a relieved breath until he heard the fighting and felt magic filling the air.

Bormick and Crimson came running in their direction, and Mark asked Pete, "How do we stop her?"

"This is our fight, not anyone else's," Pete said.

"Tell me what you need. Now," Mark demanded.

Pete pulled Crimson to him. "Do you trust me?"

"Of course."

"I need you to take my power, copy it, and merge it with yours."

Mark was having trouble understanding how this would save Skye, and as Pete still had not answered his question, he shifted his feet, his heart beginning to race. He needed answers.

Crimson was looking at Pete with a confused expression. "But I have Skye's power still."

Mark's mind pieced it together then, as he realized what he'd seen, and why her birthmark had changed. "No, it's not Skye's anymore, is it?"

"No. Her body owns it now, all of it, and now you need mine to make Skye whole again. Skye holds only light but needs the hues that connect her to Derrant, to the Shadow Realm. Copy my power. Just like you did to Skye's. Only then can you fight her and save her."

"Fight her?" Mark said quickly, the suggestion turning his stomach and not easing his tension about any of this.

"Yes, she has to fight her to get to her."

"She won't get close," Bormick said. "That army—"

"Will be preoccupied by the three of us. We will fight their mages while she saves Skye."

"How?" Mark asked, not following.

"Trust me, please. Your people are dying out there, they don't stand a chance." Mark looked over as another wave went to battle, inching closer to Alex's wave. If anything happened to Alex or Clover, he'd never forgive himself.

"All right."

"Crimson, take my power now."

He felt the strange presence of her magic as it lifted Pete's magic to copy it, her eyes growing a darker green, the aura around her shadowing her. "Now accept it like you did Skye's. It's yours to hold. You are a vessel, waiting to be filled, but you are also the conduit."

"I don't understand. What's the difference?" she asked, letting the shadows run through her fingers.

"The auras," Bormick said. "That's why they never looked settled, because the Shadow Magic connects the three of you. She's a vessel for mage magic but a conduit for—"

"My magic. She can't give back what was taken from Skye because she owns it now."

"But she can give Skye your Shadow Magic, a conduit to funnel it to her," Mark said, not certain he liked the idea.

"Yes, only the hues of my magic can free her and Crimson is the only one who can carry it to her and balance them both again."

"Take out the light and fill the space with darkness," Crimson said.

"But what does that do to Skye?"

"If her power accepts my shadows?" Mark nodded, still unsettled by the thought. "I don't know, but it saves her."

"I don't know that I like this plan, Pete."

"Do you want your wife alive or dead?" Bormick asked. "She's already changed, her magic has been morphed and even if there were another way to bring her power over the dark hues back, her magic won't be the same."

Mark wiped his hand over his face, the battle continuing as they talked. He wanted Skye back, no matter what it took.

"Derrant was specific in his use of the word conduit, Mark. He's right. Pete, what do I do now?" Crimson asked.

"You find Skye and save her with my shadows. Balance the light they've corrupted her with."

"How do I do that?"

"You'll figure it out," Pete said as another blast shook the building.

"Go, Crimson." He kissed her, Bormick taking her from him and doing the same before Pete dragged him from her.

The roar of a dragon split the air, the ground shaking with the landing impact.

"You two come with me," Pete said to Mark and Bormick.

Crimson created a portal, the colors of it distinctly dark and moving like snakes around it. She stepped through, the portal closing behind her.

"What are we doing?" Mark asked, no longer feeling in charge of anything and completely lost on how to think about the connection Crimson and Pete held to Skye.

"We're taking out the firepower and their mages, one by one."

"And you don't think one of those portals will be an obvious sign of our entrance?" Bormick asked.

"Who says I need a portal?" he replied, smiling.

He grabbed both their shoulders, then drew his magic. It seeped from him in long wisps of gray and ebony, surrounding the three of them and moving them, dropping them in the middle of the battle.

Mark shrugged the sticky feel of it away, drawing his weapon and killing a soldier who had been startled by their appearance. A bloody battle was ensuing, his mages putting up a fight but losing.

"Ready?" Pete said, grabbing them again.

He didn't have time to reply or even question how Pete had moved them, as the world disappeared, and they were now in a new spot. A surprised mage drew his magic. Pete snaked his power out, grabbing him. Without even thinking, Mark charged the mage, sliding dancelike to him, his weapon drawing across his neck while the mage's attention was focused on Pete. The mage collapsed, his hands dropping to the blood that seeped over his white cape.

"And that's how it's done," Pete said.

They moved with precision through the fighters, Bormick and Mark taking turns landing the fatal blow while Pete engaged each one.

"That one is mine," Bormick pointed to a woman across the field.

Something hurtled through the battle, knocking into the fray, bodies flying at the impact.

"What was that?"

"Skye," Mark replied, watching her pull herself from the ground. It was the first time he'd seen her. Her auburn hair was white with streaks of midnight blue throughout it, her eyes—those beautiful navy eyes he would lose himself to—had become a frightening gold, lifeless and hard. Bormick had been right, this was not his Skye. Her magic struck a mage coming toward her, her head not even turning to him as his body crumbled.

"Mark!" Pete yelled.

Mark started to run, Skye now his only objective. "I need to get to her!"

Pete's magic wrapped around him, pulling him back.

"Let me go, Pete!"

"She isn't yours to save this time, Mark. This is Crimson's fight. Trust her and help us."

"That would be nice!" Bormick yelled. He was pulling his sword from the body of a soldier.

Mark looked back at Skye. Crimson opened a portal behind her, black shades like tendrils rushing from her, the hues of the burned ground below meeting them, all encasing Skye and throwing her behind Crimson.

"You're right, this is their fight."

He felt Pete's hand on his shoulder and the scene disappeared. Pete dropped them before the female mage, who scowled at Bormick.

"Miss me?" Bormick asked, clenching his sword.

"I told my sister to kill you," the mage growled.

"Good thing she didn't listen. Now I get to kill you."

"I think you have something of ours," Pete said. A stream of his shadows snaked into the mage's robe before she could react and tossed Bormick's dagger to him.

Bormick dropped his sword and bounced the dagger in his hands. "I'm going to have fun destroying you with this, bitch."

She snarled and raised her hand to attack, but Pete's magic pounded into her, catching her off guard, nearly knocking her over. Mark spotted the soldier sneaking toward Pete, and ran, sliding gracefully below him as he leapt for the kill. His weapon sliced the artery precisely, blood splattering everywhere as Mark landed. He drove his weapon into the man's back just in time for Mark to see Bormick's dagger explode in the mage, her body collapsing.

"No!" a female voice bellowed. The flash of magic from her knocked the three of them over.

She was storming toward them, all three trying to rise, when a massive wave of shadow and light swept over the field. Everything seemed to stop in that moment, all eyes on Crimson and Skye. Magic encircled them, the world blanketed in gray and gold. The shades emanated from their bodies, the two caught in some kind of final battle for dominance. From the corner of his eye, Mark saw the female mage soar through the air, a stream of Pete's magic battering her.

His eyes stayed on the two women in his life, the love of his life and the woman he'd once taken in the heat of his anger, who had brought him to his weakest point. The woman who now held the survival of their kingdoms and the woman he loved in her hands.

The magic intensified, everything across the battlefield seeming to slow as Crimson took a step closer to Skye. He could see the strain in her muscles as the color bled completely from the ground.

"Be careful Crimson," he heard Pete say.

Skye's eyes glowed a magnificent gold, to which the sun paled in comparison. Her face was clenched in the effort to hold Crimson back. But then, he felt it, a small spark, a small bit of magic, his connection to Skye waking.

Whatever Crimson was doing was working. The thought of it warmed his soul, and he clung to it. She was alive in there. Now, if Crimson could just keep her alive and free her the rest of the way, they could survive this battle.

CRIMSON

S kye was pissing Crimson off. Crimson bit the inside of her cheek, tempted to stomp her feet and scream at Skye who refused to stay down. Every strike she sent at Crimson stung her skin with that foul magic.

"Damn, you're a bitch sometimes, Skye," she said, flinging her across the battlefield.

When she'd first found Skye, she'd been stunned. Gone was the beautiful, serene woman she'd known. Her gorgeous blue eyes bled of their hue, which now shaded her hair. Replaced by those horrifying gold eyes that looked out of place against the beauty of her face, beauty now marred by the scowl she wore.

Crimson had portaled to her, attacking her from behind. She caught a glimpse of Pete, Bormick, and Mark before Skye had fought back. Skye's magic met hers, forcing all of Crimson's strength to hold it. They were equally armed, the magic having no place to go but to sweep around them in a black and gold haze.

Crimson struggled against the torrent of white and gold magic pouring from Skye. It seemed hopeless. If they were equally matched, then there wouldn't be a way to defeat her. The dragon's words came back to her. Skye was trapped inside.

But if she were trapped, imprisoned, where would she go to hide?

Where she felt safe. In the shadows. That's where Crimson would go, that's where she would feel safest. Crimson pulled more hue from the ground, knowing she was bleeding the color but that she needed it. The hue encircled her, strengthening her before she sent a tendril of magic out, a whisper on it.

Skye, the magic called as it rushed to her mind, seeking the shadows as Crimson had commanded it.

Skye fought Crimson's attempt, her hold on her magic increasing. Crimson struggled to fight back, sending another tendril out, calling Skye's name again, this time making the magic find its sister shadows within.

Skye...

She felt the recognition through the tendril. Skye was there, weak and overpowered, but there.

Damn, she thought to herself, unsure of what to do next.

The dragon had called them sisters, Mark saying Derrant had marked them both, connecting them. That's why she'd always been obsessed with Skye, with Mark. There had been a tie between them—one that ran deep on a magical level, the magic of the gods. She'd never understood her fascination with Skye, seeing it as jealousy and hurting her for it. She'd always wanted Mark, but perhaps it had only been her bond to Skye that had fueled it.

If Skye and Mark had been so powerfully drawn to one another, then it stood that her connection to Skye allowed that to bleed through, only her blood bond with Pete and Bormick over-shadowed it. They were sisters bound through a powerful magic both claimed by the Death God and by their mother Eliana. Two sides of the Shadow Realm. Eliana a bit of light in the realm of darkness.

Light and shadow joined through the two of them. Pete had instructed her to give Skye his shadows to balance her again, but Crimson wasn't convinced that was possible. There was only one way to test it. Maybe their connection to both gods would allow a merging of Pete's shadows to Skye's magic. Although at this moment, they were distinctly polar. Skye now light, Pete and Crimson both dark. But Crimson wasn't completely bound to the darker shades. She could still sense the tie to the lighter colors, she just couldn't wield them now that Skye's magic had been morphed. Pete's magic was temporarily filling the space where her own balancing connection of light hues should be, still a vessel waiting for completion.

Skye had drawn all hues prior to this, only favoring the shadowed hues. Crimson had been able to do the same when she'd copied the magic. There was a chance she could balance them both again. She didn't really know how but Pete was convinced his shadows were the key. Somehow she needed to unlock the shadows in Skye again and steal some of her light, balancing them both again like Pete said.

She stumbled when a blast of Skye's golden magic hit her, her attention temporarily distracted by her thoughts. She summoned Pete's magic, feeling it run through her differently than the magic she had garnered from Skye. Flexing her fingers, she thought about that difference. Maybe it wasn't about unlocking but feeding. Pete's Shadow Magic was a pure connection to the Shadow Realm, and it was tied to Skye's. They'd all witnessed how it had danced with Skye's in the mage lair. Pete himself was drawn to her, even if he refused to admit it.

That was it, the key that she hadn't seen. Pete had told her to copy his shadows to funnel them to Skye because they had been hers to claim, not Crimson's. They were for Skye. Meant to purge the overwhelming light from her and call back her own shadow hues. They were the balance to save Skye and Crimson needed to feed them to her.

She sent her hues out around the onslaught of magic the two were putting out in their battle against each other. Then she stepped closer, using all her strength. She needed to wake Skye up.

Here goes nothing, she thought.

She laced the tendrils with her seduction, grabbed Skye and kissed her. Skye fought back, but Crimson snaked the shadows she'd taken from Pete through her kiss.

Skye, she called to her, *reach for me.*

The golden magic burned against her skin, the Shadow Magic fighting it as she reached for darker shades. Something in her flipped, the two sources of power igniting, soaring through her, replenishing her as she kept Skye pressed to her mouth.

The struggle between the light and Shadow Magic grew frantic, and her shadows pulled even harder at the light, drawing it out, allowing the darkness room to move forth, the shadows taking their place in Skye. Skye's mouth opened with a gasp, Crimson smashing her lips harder against her. Reaching in to seal the kiss with her tongue, she felt Skye respond, her body relaxing, mouth compelled and reacting.

Power danced around them, flowing between them, light meeting the dark as the two continued their bond. Skye's arms drew Crimson closer, her chest pressing against her as the kiss deepened, the magic fueled seduction overcoming them both until Crimson could feel the distinct change. Gone were the shadows she'd taken from Pete, replaced with the light feel of the hues she knew were distinctly Skye's. Pete's had bled from her own, funneling to Skye, restoring her connection to her own Shadow Magic, the darker hues she favored.

Skye drew her lips back, her eyes opening. Midnight blue awash with sparkles of gold looked back at Crimson.

"You kissed me?" she said.

"And it felt fantastic," Crimson replied.

"Yeah, it did."

Crimson glanced up at the colors that surrounded them—colors of the night, of the Shadow Realm, with a ribbon of gold flowing through them. Unable to resist, Crimson pressed her lips against Skye's again, tasting the power that flickered between them as their tongues fought for control.

"Damn," Skye said, biting at Crimson's bottom lip.

"Guess we're going to need to change the sleeping arrangements," Crimson said with a grin. "Time to share—"

Skye brought her finger to Crimson's lips. "I'm not sharing Mark and I guarantee he won't share me, but that doesn't mean they can't watch."

Crimson laughed. "I think we have a war to stop before we cross that bridge and begin that feud."

Skye's face dropped. The barrier of magic still surrounded them, and they couldn't see beyond it.

"We need to stop the fighting before we lose them," Crimson said.

"No, I need to."

A rush of power swept by Crimson as Skye pulled the encircling magic into her, her eyes laden with power, her expression one of vengeance. Her hair, which had returned to her natural color, was quickly filled with streaks of blue and gold, the gold flickers in her eyes increasing their frenzy.

Crimson took a step back. Skye was terrifyingly beautiful and in that moment, Crimson knew she had never felt the fear that those eyes now induced.

SKYE

The small amount of darkness Skye had found contained her, calming her, but trapping her. She'd tried many times to break free, to cross into the blinding world outside her small corner, but each time it had burned, the pain she'd felt whenever she'd tried escaping, coming back to her.

She was aware of the power flaring, of being hit by something, each hit making the light flicker, the touch of it a moment of strength that faded too quickly.

Skye, she heard, and she peeked out into the brightness to see a wisp of black. It called to her, calming her, but it faded too fast.

Skye, it came again, seductive, feminine. Crimson.

This time she reached to touch the strand, feeling a connection—a mix of touches, the warmth of Pete's magic, then the seduction of Crimson's, and the faint strength of her Elite bond with Mark. But the light reacted, snuffing out the tendril and so she yanked her arm back into her safety. Crimson was out there. Skye couldn't tell if the others were with her, but the magic had Pete's imprint on it. Her feeling of Mark had been too faint, but the other two had been strong. It didn't make sense why Crimson or even Pete was trying to save her and not Mark.

Magic. Mark had none, only what he had through his connection to her, and that had been shattered. She felt a jolt, tendrils of black mist seeping in. This was her chance. She needed to escape, to get back to Mark, to Alex. She leapt, grabbing the stream of shadows, stretching the blackness in her space out to reach it, an internal battle beginning as she took what they'd given her and clung to it. As she touched it, she realized it wasn't Pete, it was only Crimson. The seduction encased the hue, leaving only her imprint on it, but below she could feel the Shadow Magic, that strange feeling that stirred in her each time Pete's magic touched her. This was Crimson. He'd given her a copy of his magic, just as Skye had before this had begun. The two were now within Crimson.

There was a give and a take as Skye met the strand of shadows. Crimson pulled at the light magic, the brightness around Skye's cloak of darkness, draining it until Skye surfaced. She embraced the shadows, letting them strengthen her, letting the darkness of them coat the remains of the bright hues within her. With a gasp, she became aware again, aware of lips against hers, soft and feminine but demanding, a tongue entangled with hers. It wasn't Mark but the seduction of the magic, the strange mix of Pete's power with Crimson's seduction, left her wanting more. Magic soared through her, power twofold from what she'd had before, shadow yet light.

She pulled Crimson closer, knowing it was her body and not caring. Her own body was flush with desire as it came alive again. The magic cascaded over them until she felt whole again.

She drew back, confronting Crimson about the kiss and receiving an unapologetic answer before Crimson kissed her again, her own body responding because she wanted this, too. It felt right. It felt good. And she needed more, remembering how Crimson had touched her when she'd been with Derrant. At the time, Skye had been lost in the pleasure she'd brought as it mingled with Derrant's spell. But then, it wasn't completely

Crimson that she was reacting to this time. The touch of Shadow Magic still lingered, the touch of Pete's magic. That hint of Pete stirred something below the physical response of the kiss, something she recognized had been there, but she had never claimed. Something she couldn't claim, so she'd pushed the sensation to the recesses of her mind, accepting it but ignoring it. She preferred to think it was Crimson who had caused the feeling but wasn't entirely certain it hadn't been the presence that was tangled with Pete's essence.

Shit, that's going to be hard to explain to Mark, she thought, as she and Crimson decided they would explore this heightened magical connection after they stopped the war. And knowing she'd leave out the undercurrent of that connection, the one she knew came from Pete's magic. The touch of it that left her craving more, and had driven the deeper kiss because she'd enjoyed the sensation. Skye could still feel the touch of his magic as it played within her, merging with her own as her body slowly accepted it.

She needed to stop the madness ensuing in the background. She'd contemplate whatever this was with Crimson and whatever that other spark had been later. The war was Skye's to stop, and as she stepped from Crimson's arms, she took in the chaos around her. Soldiers and mages, Elite, and full mages scattered across the castle grounds, all waking up as if from under a spell. Crimson's spell, a sensual one she could feel in the air.

The fighting began again, and she looked around wildly for Alex and Mark. Her eyes fell on Alex, who was fighting. Clover was by his side and Elspeth with them. Elspeth would keep him safe, but Skye knew she needed to end this fast to ensure that happened. She spotted Mark, her eyes meeting his, her heart fluttering in response. From the periphery she saw the magic pummeling toward him, and she whipped hues from his uniform out to stop it, sending it to a flicker of dust.

You want her? Crimson's voice stirred in her mind.

Why can I hear you?

Not sure, but do you want the screaming idiot, or should I stop her from killing our boys?

She's mine.

Skye blasted the mage with a flick of the green before she returned it to Mark, then she glared at the woman who was now facing her. She stormed toward Skye, who stood still, feeling Crimson's magic protect her from behind and seeing Pete help Bormick and Mark slay a soldier.

"You will not attack me!"

The woman raised her hand to draw her power, Skye narrowing her eyes.

"You can't hurt me, you uncouth spawn of the Death God."

"I beg to differ," Skye said, commanding a shadow of black she took from the shades billowing around Crimson. Sensing the hues as if she could see them, she wrapped it around the drawn magic of the mage, snuffing it out.

"Parlor tricks. You can't hurt any of us because we wear the color of the true god," she said too confidently.

"I think you underestimate the Death God's power, as well as Death's Mistress."

Without lifting a finger, the brown from the sodden ground rose, morphing to a sword shape. She commanded it silently, listening as the brown swords of her magic ran every soldier and remaining mage through, leaving only her own people standing.

She heard the surprised reactions; the woman taking a step back with large eyes.

"I think you greatly underestimated my family and me and my people. We are the people of the Shadow Realm, and I am their queen. I have traversed the Shadow Realm, lain with the Death God, and am favored by his lover, claimed by his magic and hers. I am not someone you want to fuck with."

The sky grew dark as she pulled the lighter hues of it away, bleeding the white from the clouds and enhancing the red tones of the sun, the world now dark with a blood red sun.

The woman's breathing became strained, her fear slipping through the façade.

"I gave your friend his freedom," she said, the shake of her voice clear.

"Did you? After you and your friends beat the shit out of him and had me torture him? After you tore my colors from me and tried to shatter my connection to the Shadow Realm? How kind of you. I'll ensure your death is swift."

"Your magic can't kill me." She gestured to her cape. Skye moved her eyes to the now black sky.

"Interesting thing about my magic. When you bled it, you morphed it. The light colors...well, they look darker to me now." She turned her fingers slightly, the robe turning gray. "That's better. Wouldn't want to stain your nice white robe with your blood."

The woman raised her hand to call her magic again. Skye grabbed it as it flowed from her hand, encasing it in black, then sending it back into the woman. She stumbled back, holding her hand as veins of black appeared.

"What have you done?" she asked with a terrified expression.

"It's called vengeance and what's that other word? Oh, that's right, punishment for the lives you took."

Her nose began to bleed.

"Hmm, doesn't look like you're as strong as me after all. You hit me with what? Three sources of your magic and I survived? I suppose I should be kind and end your suffering."

The woman tried to talk but only blood escaped her mouth; the shadows were tearing the light within her apart.

"Hurts, doesn't it?"

Skye yanked the hues back, then flung them back at her so that they collapsed on her body, her screams echoing from within. She ripped her hues away, bleeding every inch of the woman until the colorless cape drifted to the ground, the ashes of the woman scattering upon it.

No one spoke, no one moved.

"What? Was that too much?" she asked, looking around.

Mark's mouth was agape, but he still looked hot. Pete stood next to him with wide eyes but a bit of a proud smirk, looking just as hot.

That may have been above even my standards, Crimson said, drawing her attention back.

I aim to please. Oh, and I think Bormick just came in his pants, you may want to clean that up after you help clean this mess up.

"Skye!" she said out loud, but Skye had made her way to Mark, her eyes glancing over at Pete, who shook his head as if shaking a dirty thought from his mind. She gave him a wink then rushed into Mark's arms. Her lips found his, and he returned the kiss.

"Come on," she heard Pete say to Bormick.

"Gods, she's even sexier now, Mark. We need a taste of that. Shit, she and Crimson just made out. I think that means it's all of us now," Bormick said.

Mark drew back, his eyes shining, a hungry look in them.

"No, I don't think so."

"Take me," she whispered.

"Gladly. You guys have clean up duty."

"Crimson already knows."

"I do not!" Crimson yelled.

Skye called upon the hues around them, letting the streams move them to their quarters, not questioning how she had this new ability. Mark's lips never left hers. He pushed her against the dressing table as her hands removed his shirt.

"God, I missed you," he said, his lips soft against hers.

She magically removed the rest of their clothes, and he laughed through the kisses, lifting her onto the table and spreading her legs with his thigh before penetrating her. Heat rose within her and she threw her head back, the feel of him erasing the nightmares of the past few days.

Bringing her legs around him, she pushed him deeper. The corresponding groan he emitted touched a part of her deep in her core that almost sent her spiraling. His mouth edged it on, his tongue finding its way over her neck, then down to her breast. One hand held her ass tight as the other caressed the breast his mouth wasn't currently devouring. She dipped her head back, arching her back, filling his mouth with her breast, his teeth sliding delicately over her nipple until she could take it no more.

She dragged his face up so that her lips met his, forcing herself further against him, the warmth and solidness of his body cascading her into oblivion with him. They continued to tear at each other through it, her wave rising a second time, sending her crashing against him. She remained hungry, a need in her that couldn't be sated until he took her repeatedly, each climax replenishing the terror of the last days and pushing the undercurrent of desire that still skittered through the shadows that she'd claimed.

SKYE WOKE LATER THAT NIGHT, only knowing it was night by the dark room. She felt no fear. Darkness was her friend and Mark's arms held her tight. He kissed her head, and she looked up at him.

"Didn't you sleep?" she asked.

"No," he replied, turning, so they were face to face. "I went to assess the situation on the battlefield where I should have been when you lured me here."

"I didn't lure you here."

"No, you took me," he replied playfully.

She gave him a smile before quickly saying, "Alex—"

"Is fine as is Clover. Not a scratch on them, and from what I hear, your son is quite the mage. Takes after his mother on the battlefield."

Her tension fled as relief swept away the worry. "I should have—"

"No, they all understood. You were captured, used, twisted to be something you aren't. You needed the time. We needed it."

"I love you, Mark."

Kissing her nose, he replied, "I love you, too, but"—he brought his finger to the corner of her eye—"that's going to take some getting used to."

"What is?"

"Your eyes. They have gold flecks now."

"Oh." She pursed her lips. "Is that bad?"

"No, it only makes you more alluring." His fingers drifted through her hair. "I thought I'd lost you this time, Skye."

"You almost did. Are you getting tired of saving me?"

Caressing her cheek, his fingers drifted over the curve of her mouth. "Never, but I didn't save you this time."

"No, you couldn't."

He studied her, a sadness to his eyes. He hated that he hadn't been the one to save her, and she knew that. "It had to be Crimson this time," she said. "My power would have destroyed you."

She left out the fact that, although Crimson had been the instigator, it had been Pete's magic that had really saved her.

"I know, it still irks me. Though I have to admit, seeing you make out with Crimson was pretty hot."

She laughed, feeling the color rise in her cheeks.

"Are you embarrassed? You who never ceases to amaze me at your sexual prowess?"

"Sexual prowess?"

His hand drifted across her curves, lingering on her breast, then continuing until it tightened around her, drawing her against his arousal.

"I don't know how I feel about it," she admitted. "How do you feel?"

"Quite turned on, as was every man in that field and possibly the women. I swear Bormick came in his pants."

She threw her head back and laughed. "I think he did."

"I'm not sure I like the idea of anyone touching you, but I may be tempted to allow that."

"Allow that?" she asked with a raise of her brow.

He squeezed her waist, pulling her flush against him, her desire soaring. "Yes. This body is mine. I claimed it, I own it. I've shared it too long and now I want to be selfish."

"As you should."

"Mmm." His head dropped, his lips softly kissing the curve of her neck as his length continued to press against her.

Lifting her leg, she maneuvered him so that he rested flush between her dampness, teasing her. From the groan that escaped, it was teasing him as well.

"Do you want to see her fuck me?" she asked, and she felt the reaction, his length pulsing below. "To watch her lick me out as I come undone against her mouth."

His breathing shortened, the reaction tangible.

"Jesus, Skye," he muttered. "What do you want me to say? That the idea of your two naked bodies writhing against each other gets me hard? As it would any man? You ask Pete or Bormick that question and they will have the same reaction."

"Would you play?" she asked, curious about how far he'd envisioned it.

He stilled, the history that lie between the three of them still under the surface. She was the woman who'd stolen him, broken him for just that moment, but long enough that the act had lingered a long time.

She watched his hazel eyes work through it, a little too long, and she swatted his arm. "Stop fantasizing about fucking Crimson," she growled.

His eyes narrowed, and he took her wrists, flipping her.

"I wasn't," he growled back, rising over her. "I was thinking about you. I don't want to touch another woman, Skye. If you demanded it, I would do it, but there is no one who comes close to you, no one who turns me on the way you do. There never has been and you know that."

"Crimson doesn't turn you on? She's gorgeous."

"You're really pushing this, aren't you?"

He was right. She was pushing it, and although she wasn't completely certain why, she had a suspicion it was her own conflicted feelings about what she'd felt in the shadows that had brought her back. The draw to them, to Pete's touch. A way to justify the sensation, to feel better about it.

"I don't know. She's the only woman you've ever cheated on me with." His face dropped, the guilt still there. "Shh," she said. "It's been a long time, Mark, and we both were put in situations that were hard to resist. It's behind us, we worked through it, remember? But there's still a part of me that has always wondered what it was about her that turned you on, that broke you, that brought you to climax like you do with me."

"No one has ever made me climax the way you do, Skye, and no one ever will."

She lost herself in those hazel eyes, her mind still working through it as she always had, wondering how he'd looked, how Crimson had felt to him, if he'd looked into her eyes as she'd taken him over the edge, just like he did with her. It wasn't right. She knew that, but the thoughts were there. Even after all they'd shared about that time.

"You want to see me fuck her, don't you?"

She furrowed her brow.

"Christ, Skye. Are you serious?"

"I don't know, Mark. I just…a part of me wants to know what it was about her that drove you to it. To know what you look like when you're taking her, to see what it was she did to bring you to that point."

He moved from her, dropping back to the bed, his hand

combing through his hair. "I'll do whatever you want, Skye. But it won't bring you answers. Put me in a bed with the two of you and yeah, I'll fuck you both, but there's a lot that comes with that. A lot of risk that whatever vision you have in your head does come to life, that I do enjoy it like I did that time, and you don't like it like you thought you would.

"There was a reason I made you break that link to me when you went to Derrant. At first, curiosity wanted it, just like what you're saying now. I wanted to know if you came differently with him. Part of me even wanted to watch, to see your body respond to him, to tell myself it didn't react the same. But once that connection was there, I knew it had been the wrong choice. Sure, I knew you were thinking of me, but it was still his hands, his mouth, his dick bringing you to ecstasy and the intensity of it stung."

He paused before continuing. "I had opened Pandora's box and couldn't get it closed. And that's exactly what you're trying to do. I can take her, I can look into your eyes the entire time I'm inside of her, but it will still be her body that makes me climax, Skye, and that will never ease your thoughts, trust me."

She snuggled against his chest. "Leave it behind us where it was, Skye, just like I left Derrant the day you were freed. You're the only woman I want, the only woman who I crave, the only woman who brings me to the cliffs of ecstasy and with whom I want to jump." He kissed her head, his hand lazily brushing over her nipple, which instantly reacted.

He gazed down at her, an impish smile on his face. "Besides, if you bring Crimson into our bed, I have to bring Bormick because there's no way he's not making a trade and the idea of that man or any man touching you sends me over the edge."

She thought about the way Pete had looked at her, that flash in his eyes. "Might have to bring them both into our bed at this point," she said.

"Damn, have you turned even Pete?"

The thought was a strange one, and she wasn't sure how she felt about it, thinking of the sense of his magic against her skin, the way she'd felt as his magic had pulled her free from the light. It had been Crimson's doing, but she had no doubt it had been his shadows that had flooded her body and that she'd claimed, their touch lingering still deep within her.

"Nah, probably just Bormick," she said, hearing the doubt in her voice.

He pulled her on top of him and she leaned into his strength; the thoughts falling away.

"No one's touching this body ever again," he said, his hand sliding over her back and cupping her ass.

"Does it make you jealous? Thinking of another man inside of me?"

"You're playing with fire, Skye."

She liked it when he got angry. There was a fierceness he brought to their lovemaking that pushed it to another level. But then she remembered how it had been anger that had fueled his moment with Crimson.

"What was that?" he asked.

"What was what?"

"That drop in your face."

"Maybe you're right. Maybe I don't want to know."

"Why the sudden change of heart?"

"Because I like it when you get rough, when you're heated, and that's what you were with her."

"Christ, Skye, stop thinking about Crimson. Nothing I do with you even compares to that."

This time, she rolled from him.

He looked over at her, moving to his side. "I tell you what. Go get Crimson, have her call Derrant and we'll fuck them both in front of each other. Then make him come and I'll watch him eat you out, and you watch me pound Crimson until she's screaming for me to stop. Or better yet, grab Bormick and let's get it out of his system, too."

She swatted at him.

"Then we'll get it over with, end of story, end of it hanging over our heads. Maybe we'll even make it a regular thing." He waited for her reply, but all she gave him was a sour look. "I'm serious, Skye."

"Take me like you took her, Mark."

"I can't."

She seethed, gritting her teeth. All that talk that she didn't compare.

"I can't because I don't love her and didn't care if I hurt her. There was no emotion between us but raw anger. When I'm angry with you, it's still layered with the love I have for you. That's what I'm trying to tell you. I have never loved anyone the way I love you and I hated Crimson fiercely. Those are two completely different emotions. I could never replicate what I did with her that day and everything after was exactly what you were doing with Derrant—emotionless, robotic, a means to getting to you. No matter how much you want to experience the way it was, for whatever sick reason, you never will, because I only love you."

She felt the tears behind her eyes, finally understanding what he'd been trying to tell her for years.

"Damn. I was looking forward to a little fire, but now you look like you're going to cry."

She laughed, pushing away the tears and he drew her to him, brushing her hair back.

"Now, no more talk of bringing anyone into our bed?"

"No more talk of it. I want you all to myself."

His hand slid down her backside, then pushed her legs apart, his fingers slipping into her and sending butterflies through her.

"Good. Now I'm going to remind you that your body is mine." His thumb brushed her clit, his fingers climbing, and she lurched against him. "Then you're going to claim me again with that mouth of yours before I make love to you for the next few hours."

She let out a breath, his kiss catching it before his mouth traveled the length of her body, claiming it again just as he said he would and bringing her to an ecstasy that reminded her that he belonged to her and always would.

CRIMSON

Crimson yawned as she walked through the halls. Several days had passed since the battle, busy relentless days of burying the dead, fortifying the castle with Pete and Skye, and talks. Talks and talks and more talks. The castle repair could have easily been done by the full mages, but Crimson had suggested they do it just to get out of the discussions. All the talk of the kingdoms, allegiances between the remaining four, what to do about the Kingdom of Eltander had her bored to tears.

It had taken Skye a few days to get over the loss of Eltander. She blamed herself, but it hadn't been her doing. The white capes had done the killing. They still didn't know who they were, so the nickname 'white capes' had taken hold.

The dragons had claimed Revina's fallen kingdom, saying it would honor the nature side of the fallen people and provide room for them to spread out.

She sighed, thinking she should have heeded Pete's touches and gone to bed with them, but something in Bormick's eyes had told her they needed time alone, that he wanted to play in a different way tonight. Shaking her head, she smiled. Their days had been filled with work, but their nights with pleasure. The new bond between the boys took their sex to an entirely new level, and it stirred her blood. Just this morn she'd woken Pete, riding him as they shared Bormick. Pete finishing her work for her as her climax soared through her.

He'd taken her again, his usual softness gone as he'd thrust behind her with the ferocity she typically only experienced from Bormick. It was like he needed the roughness, the dominance back after giving into his desire for Bormick. And she let him have it, taking them both until they finally had to face the day.

Crimson stopped at the door, raising her hand to knock, then lowering it and walking in unannounced instead.

Mark rested in a chair near the fire, his chest bare but the rest of him covered by pants. An unfortunate thing since she'd been hoping for a glimpse of all of him. It didn't matter that they'd all moved on. She still desired him. There was something about him that still aroused her, and she would take him if the chance ever came, and Skye ever gave him up. Maybe it was that connection she had to Skye, the bond Skye shared with Mark coming through somehow. Or maybe it was simply the fact that he was amazing in bed and very satisfying to look at.

Skye was seated on the floor, her head leaning between his legs, hair splayed across his knee, his fingers gently combing it. She wore a white tunic Crimson assumed was Mark's; the sleeve having fallen to expose the top of her breast. It wasn't a sexual scene, but an intimate one that spoke volumes about their relationship and its sensuality.

"Still not knocking, Crimson?" Mark asked, his hazel eyes flickering with the light of the fire.

"I was hoping for some action, a little glimpse of your ass or more, Mark," she teased.

He didn't grimace or glare at her, his eyes set with humor. It had been that way, as if everything they'd gone through had been resolved that day of the battle.

"I guess you'll have to settle for his chest then," Skye said, tilting her head to look at Mark as Crimson took a seat across from them.

He leaned over and kissed her, grazing the top of her breast with his fingers as he pulled her sleeve up. There was no hesitation with Crimson's presence, no shyness at her seeing it. She'd watched them already, and she'd sit and do it again if they wanted. That comfort that had settled over the five of them allowed it.

They were like a family now, fate, blood, time having tied them all and the thought of leaving to return to her kingdom saddened her.

"Why that look, Crimson?" Skye asked, her hand drawing delicately down Mark's face as he lifted it from hers. "You have two men. Do they not kiss you like that?"

She gave Skye a sly smile. "Oh, they kiss me in all different ways and places."

"I bet they do," Mark said, sitting back, the fire defining his strength.

"I need a few minutes to talk with Skye."

He raised a brow. "You want me to leave my wife alone with you so you can feast on her mouth again?"

"Oh, I'd feast on more than her mouth, Mark."

She saw the flush of Skye's cheeks and the flash of hunger in Mark's eyes.

"But if I were going to do that, I'd have you watch, then I'd watch as you pounded her until she was begging for more."

He shook his head. "I think you've spent too much time with Bormick."

"I've always been like this, Mark, or don't you remember?"

"Did you like fucking my husband that much? Is that why you won't let that go?" Skye asked, looking down at her nails.

Crimson gaped at Skye, her eyes wide. The question had been unexpected, and she didn't know how to react or what to say.

"What did you like most about him, Crimson?"

Her eyes looked directly at Crimson, calculating and deep

with color, the gold flecks sparkling in them. Mark's head dropped against the chair, his eyes to the ceiling, hand still stroking her hair.

She thought about it. He'd been good, raging with that anger, taking her over the abyss but she had that with Pete and Bormick, she'd had it with Derrant. All four of them were intense.

"He was a good fuck, Skye, as good as Derrant, as Pete and Bormick. But that's not what I wanted from him. That's not the only thing I craved about him."

"And what did you crave from my husband?"

"That look he had, that he has when he looks at you."

Mark picked his head up and studied her, his brows furrowed. She gave him a smile.

"You love her like I had never been loved. I wanted that. I wanted to see that look of sheer adoration, feel what it was like to have a man who would die for me, who would kill for me, not because I gave him pleasure, but because he loved me undyingly. That's what I liked most about your husband, Skye. You two loved each other, and I'd never seen anything so intense. It was palpable, and I yearned for it, not understanding that it can't be forced. No matter how much pleasure I provided, it wouldn't replace what he had with you, wouldn't change it to me."

"And now?"

"And now I have two men who look at me that way. Both would die for me. Bormick almost did, and...and I would die for them. I can't say I don't want you anymore, Mark. You're too sexy to say that, but I don't need you, not like I thought I did."

"That's reassuring," Skye said.

Crimson laughed. "Don't worry. He's all yours. There's no way I'm coming between what you two have again. It's overwhelming. Which brings me to why I'm here."

"Still need me to go?" Mark asked.

"Nah, not after that conversation."

Skye gave her a smile that warmed her heart, and Crimson sat back in her chair.

"That kiss...those kisses were amazing and when you were with Derrant that time, gods, that was memorable—"

"Get on with it, Crimson," Mark said through gritted teeth.

"Wait, she's calm now about what happened with me, but you're still holding grudges about Derrant?"

"It's not a grudge—"

"It sure sounds like you're still angry."

"I'm not angry anymore. I just don't need a visual or to know how good it was."

"You are something, Mark."

"I know I am," he replied, his eyes sparkling with humor.

She shook her head, moving her eyes back to Skye.

"What are you trying to say, Crimson?"

"That I don't think it's good to explore that any further."

Skye looked surprised. "Go on."

"Mark's clearly very possessive and as much as Bormick fantasizes about it—"

"He fantasizes about my wife?"

"This is Bormick we're talking about, Mark."

Mark grunted but calmed.

"Pete is like you, Mark, and is very possessive of me. I'm pretty sure Bormick is as well, but he may not admit it when it comes to sharing me with Skye. I think he's too tantalized by the idea to say it."

"So you're quitting me?" Skye asked playfully.

"Yes, it's not a good idea. We need our men to play nice and if Mark and Pete are too on edge with sharing us with each other, it won't end well."

Mark evaluated her, his strategic eyes boring into her. "I don't think that's the entire reason, although that is the reason Skye and I decided it's not a good idea."

"Really?" Crimson said, relieved.

"Really. Now what's the real reason?"

Crimson's mouth fell open as she searched for words. Damn Mark and his calculating mind. She wasn't good with things like this. She was the bad girl.

"Crimson," Skye urged.

"Oh, all right," she said, throwing her hands in the air. "We're too close now and I don't want to risk it. You're my only friends and Skye you're like my sister in many ways...and well..." She drifted off, not finding the words.

Skye's smile sat perfectly on her beautiful face, her eyes lighting. "I love you, too, Crimson, past and all—"

"I don't, for the record," Mark said. "That's all her."

"Good," Crimson replied with a laugh, still flustered by the words and the feelings. "Because the guys would kill you if that were the case. I prefer this witty banter we have, anyway. You know, where I comment on your hard length, and you say some defensive words back while you glare at me."

"Yeah, I prefer that as well," he replied with a smile.

"Okay, well now that that's over, why don't you two take your clothes off and have some fun while I watch?"

"That's where you go after that rather decent confession?" Mark asked.

"Of course it is. You know me well enough, Mark, and gods, you two are a massive turn on when you're fucking."

"Go. Play with your men and get yourself off that way," he said.

"I'm giving them some alone time. I think Bormick is in the mood to explore. I just hope he's gentle on Pete."

Mark's expression was horrified for a quick moment before he covered it.

"Are they..." Skye started, her eyes sparkling with curiosity.

"I think so. Bormick seemed quite aggressive when we finished up with Revina's kingdom today. In fact, he had Pete half stripped before I even left the room."

"Shit," Mark muttered, looking uncomfortable.

"And you don't want to watch that?" Skye said softly. There was a hint of desire in her blue eyes. Crimson didn't blame her. They were sexy when they went at it.

"Not their first time. Trust me, I watch when they use their mouths, gods is that stimulating, but I don't think I need to watch this until they're...well, Pete's more comfortable."

"Poor Pete," Mark said, running his hand through his hair.

"Oh, he'll enjoy it. Trust me on that one."

Skye's cheeks filled a lush pink, and Mark shook his head. They sat there in comfortable silence for a few minutes before Crimson finally said, "I don't want to go home."

They both stared at her this time.

"Why would you not want to go home?" Skye asked.

"I want to see my kingdom and I do miss my castle, but...gods, how do I say this without ruining my reputation?"

"You just saved the kingdoms. I think your bad girl reputation has already been tarnished," Mark replied.

"Great," she grumbled, then hesitantly said, "I don't want to leave you two. There, I said it. You've grown on me, on all of us, as annoying as it is."

Skye's smile lit the room. "You're like a weed that keeps coming back, no matter how many times you pull it."

"What's a weed?" she asked.

"Try ivy, you know the thing that likes to climb on your castle," Mark said.

"Oh...wait, that's not nice, Skye."

"You assume I'm nice, Crimson. We're related, remember? That same bitchiness runs through me."

"Funny, Skye. So, I'm an annoying vine."

"One we've grown to adore," Skye said, "even though it made our life hell in the beginning."

"I don't adore you, Crimson. I tolerate you."

"Feeling's mutual, Mark, but I'm never against another rage fuck if you feel the need."

She felt the tear of the dark hues flowing from her dress before she saw them, Skye's eyes darkening. "Just playing, Skye. Banter, remember?"

The hues flowed back. "Just reminding you not to cross the line, Crimson."

Crimson stood, stretching. "I only dip my toe over it, Skye. There's no harm in that."

"You can stay here any time you want, Crimson," Mark said. "But my ass is never stepping foot in your castle again."

"Aww, you do like me, Mark. Perhaps I'll convince Pete to build a castle in his kingdom close to my border. It may be time to move forward. That castle holds many more bad memories than just yours."

"That sounds like an excellent idea," Skye said. "We'll provide mage help if you want it."

"I was thinking you could provide your magic. With the three of us, it would be easy."

"Easy she says," Mark scoffed. "Why would Skye need to help build?"

"So we can all have a tantalizing orgy when we're finished," she joked.

Mark pointed to the door and gave a commanding, "Out."

"You're no fun, Mark," Crimson replied as she walked to the door.

Skye rose, Mark's unhappy sigh letting Crimson know the move was unwanted. She leaned down and kissed him. "Don't worry, I have a more comfortable position in mind," she said seductively.

Gods, they were a turn on. Mark's hand tangled in her hair and Crimson saw the peek of flesh as his other hand scooped below the tunic to feel Skye's breast. Skye drew away, leaving him groaning, the bulge in his pants causing Crimson's brow to raise. He caught her eying it and she gave him an appraising look.

"Eyes off, Crimson. It's mine and only mine," Skye said, moving to her.

"You know, you can see straight through that shirt, Skye."

"I know. Mark likes it that way."

"Yes, I do."

Skye kissed her cheek, whispering in her mind, *We have a past that defines us but a future that lies unmarred.* She pulled Crimson's head down so that their foreheads touched. *Stand with me and you have my loyalty forever. Just keep your hands off what's mine.*

Crimson looked up, catching the glint in her eyes, the gold specks glittering. "I suppose I love you, too, sister."

"The Death God claimed us both for a reason, Crimson, never forget that."

"How could I with your voice in my head? Now go fuck your husband and let me hear your screams."

"Jesus," Mark muttered.

The corner of Skye's mouth rose, a hint of seduction in her smile.

Only if you reciprocate, her mind whispered.

Done.

She pulled away and watched as Skye climbed atop Mark, her hand sliding up his chest, both forgetting her presence as passion overtook them. Mark's hand pushed Skye's sleeve down, her breast freeing as his mouth devoured hers.

Leave, Crimson, Skye called.

I think that would be wise, before I change my mind and join you.

Skye hissed in her mind as she left their room, the hiss turning to a moan.

Crimson made her way down the hall, the mental connection

to Skye still open, a wave of pleasure rippling through her mind so hard that she had to grip the wall to not fall.

Gods, Skye, she whispered, another ripple rocking her core. She needed to get back to Pete and Bormick. She should have closed the mental link, but it was too exciting, too tempting to feel it from Skye's perspective. After a second wave of climax, she was finally able to make it to the room.

She hesitated, unsure what she would find, before she opened the door to see Pete gripping the sheets, his body sprawled out. Bormick hovered over him, droplets of his orgasm glistening on the end of his still very enlarged erection.

"Did you hurt my Petey?" she asked with a coo.

"I went gentle for his first time," Bormick said, smiling as he sat back.

"That was not gentle," Pete complained into the bed.

"Must not have been too bad," she said, eyeing the damp spot on the bed.

"I had to make sure he was enjoying himself while I was."

"Ass," Pete muttered, turning his head to look at her. His eyes were a haze of sensual pain, a wounded look to their vibrant blue.

"The idiot swallowed me first. I warned him it would make me last longer this time."

"You just taste too good to resist, Bormick," she said, removing her dress. "Go wash up and let me make Pete our alpha again."

Pete turned, wincing slightly, his eyes perusing her body hungrily.

"I don't think I need to wash up if I'm just going to take your ass, Crimson."

"Hush," she said, crawling into Pete's arms and kissing him. "Pete needs it rough, and I'm ready for some rough."

Another powerful sensation coursed through her, and she lurched into Pete.

"What was that?" he asked, nipping at her neck, his hand

squeezing her breast. She could sense he needed to take her rough and hard, to reclaim his dominance. He did each time he and Bormick played, and this had been the end game.

"Skye and I are still mentally connected. She and Mark are having quite the time."

Pete gave her a look she couldn't quite read. It was a mix of curiosity and something else.

"You can feel it every time she comes?" he asked.

"Through every part of me."

"Does it work both ways?" Bormick asked.

"I think so. This is the first time we've tried."

Pete's eyes glinted, his hand sliding between her legs. "You are dripping."

"That's not the first time she's climaxed since I left her room."

His brows rose, and she caught the slight moan that slipped from him at the thought. As much as he tried to hide it, she knew he found Skye attractive. All his talk of not wanting to touch her leaned too far to not have it be a lie.

"Looks like we've got some catching up to do," Bormick said.

"Looks like I do," Pete said, thrusting into her. She cried out, feeling it hit Skye, whose reaction was enough to take Crimson to the edge. "Not we. You're benched until I take my fill."

"Benched?"

"Just sit the hell down and watch. I'm about to take Crimson to new heights and give Mark a run for his money," he said, crushing her mouth with his and forcing his tongue in.

Yes, this is going to be aggressive, she thought, moaning as his hand tightened around her waist.

"I guess that means you'll be taking Skye to new heights, too?" Bormick joked.

Crimson felt the reaction as he jerked within her, his pulse quickening, confirming her suspicions that there was a desire there, one he kept quiet, unlike Bormick. The thought fled as his moves increased her arousal, her orgasm mounting before his, plummeting through her with his own. She felt Skye's reaction on the other end, the moan that whispered through her mind. Pete didn't stop, taking her from behind as Bormick watched until Pete had filled her a second time. Between the two of them and Skye's own responses to Mark and to Crimson's pleasure, her body was on fire until finally, she shut Skye out, letting her men overwhelm her senses, taking her into oblivion over and over.

PETE
TWO MONTHS LATER

Pete left Bormick leaning against the shower wall, trying to recover. The shower had been an idea he'd fought for when building the new castle in Digremile and with Skye's help, they had figured out how to make one work here. Magic was an amazing thing. He ran the towel over his head, hearing Bormick curse him as Pete walked away.

They'd taken turns with Crimson until she'd been too worn to do anything and had gone back to sleep. They, however, hadn't had their fill, Bormick taking him in the shower unexpectedly after he'd jerked Pete off. Bormick's new obsession was taking either of them in the shower, and he'd taken Pete hard. Pete had gotten even, lathering him up, then dropping to his knees and bringing him over the edge before he'd relentlessly done it again, Bormick's knees shaking from the back-to-back climaxes.

Pete climbed onto the bed and nuzzled Crimson with his nose before giving her a sensual kiss.

"Mmm, you taste like Bormick, Pete," she said, licking his bottom lip and biting it. "Did you go easy on him?"

"No, he's still recovering."

"You leave that ass in the air like that, Pete, I'm coming for it," Bormick said, emerging from the tub-room.

"I'm surprised there's anything left in their Bor," he replied. "Hasn't it gone dry yet?"

Bormick grabbed his dick and jerked it toward them. "This baby never runs dry."

Pete shook his head.

"That's enough of that, you two," Crimson said. "It's dawn, and we told them we'd meet them at dawn."

Pete nipped her lower lip. "Too bad. I was ready to sink myself into you one more time."

He always liked taking Crimson after Bormick claimed him. It had become less of a need as he'd grown accustomed to it, but it helped him feel in control again. Bormick was demanding and rough, flaunting his dominance. Pete let him have it, knowing it was his domain, his one place where he could take that alpha role. Pete's power was always greater. Pete was the alpha in this relationship, but he stepped back because he knew Bormick well enough now to know if he didn't have that role, it would crush the man he was, the man Pete loved in him, and he wasn't willing to give that up no matter how it made Pete look.

He knew the difference, as did Bormick, and he suspected, Crimson.

They dressed, his eyes dropping to Bormick's still enlarged lump in his pants.

"You want it again, don't you, Pete?" he asked, grabbing it.

"I always want it, jackass, but right now, all I want is to get this over with so I can fuck the shit out of Crimson for a while longer."

"Mmm, I love it when you talk like that," she purred.

He pulled her against him, letting his magic flow around her as hers drifted out to meet it. The feeling was alluring.

"Cut it out, you two, before I tie you both down and make you fuck me."

"I don't think tying would be necessary, but it could be fun," she said, Bormick's eyes lighting with the suggestion.

"Gods, I love you."

"I know." She sauntered to him and pulled him down for a kiss, one Bormick reciprocated roughly.

Pete created a portal, forcing them to stop. "Come on, or we'll never get out of here."

"You're a prick, Pete."

"And you're a deviant, Bormick, but you still love me."

"That's questionable when you're not on our knees," he said as they walked through the portal. "Or bending over."

Mark eyed them from where he stood with Skye pressed into his side. She had a violet dress on that brought the blue in her eyes out; the gold flecks flittering around them were entrancing.

For a brief time, she and Crimson had shared their connection while they were having sex, Crimson's reaction intensifying the act, but it had grown too dangerous on both sides. Pete was glad they'd stopped. The effect was strange, calling to a part of him he preferred not to acknowledge, that draw to Skye. He preferred to think of her as a sister, an extremely sexy sister, but one he'd never fathom touching, even though the thought was there at times. That thought had been more persistent recently, that kiss from Eliana having started it. The touch of his magic as she'd claimed it the day of the battle had continued it.

There was something there now, deep below everything else that the shadows had awoken, or perhaps had simply coaxed forth. He shouldn't have felt her claim his magic that day, but he had, and he still couldn't figure out why. So, he ignored that stir, that slow growing hunger that he kept submerged below, the one he hid under the pretense that she reminded him of his sister. Otherwise, he didn't think he could control his reaction to her. The idea of her on the other side of the orgasm he was giving Crimson, that she was responding to his touches in some way, had been too much for him to take. Too tempting to imagine.

"Took you three long enough," Mark grouched.

Pete forced his eyes from Skye, not realizing they were still locked with hers until that moment. She looked away uncomfortably at the same time. He tried to shake it off, the need to hold on to that sisterly excuse growing more desperate. There was something there, a sensation he didn't want to acknowledge, one he had a feeling she recognized as well. Something about her stirred a part of him Crimson hadn't touched. He set the thought aside, turning back to Mark, who hadn't noticed their interaction.

Pete had gotten to know him enough to read his moods, and his gripe wasn't a serious one.

"I needed to dominate Pete a few times before we left," Bormick said, slapping Pete's ass hard.

"Fuck you, Bormick," he replied, still not comfortable announcing the depths of their relationship.

"No, that's my job, Pete. You do the bending."

He gritted his teeth.

"I hear your mouth does a bit of bending, Bormick," Skye said, surprising him, her eyes twinkling, the gold in them flickering. That gold that had never faded, giving her eyes an enticing look that was hard to turn from. The sight of them called to a part deep within him that wanted to correct it, to bring the full navy back, to fix the stain that had remained from the white capes.

"Why yes it does," Bormick replied with a laugh. "And he tastes as good as he looks, doesn't he, Crimson?"

"Mmm, yes, he does."

"If we're all done discussing the taste of my dick, can we get on with this?"

"Well, unless you'd like to demonstrate for us," Mark said, a curve to his lips.

"I might enjoy that," Skye said, taking him aback again.

"Wow, even you're turning on me, Skye?" he said, his eyes flicking to her but drawing away quickly to avoid the earlier reaction to her.

"Come on," Mark said, kissing her head. "Let's give Pete a break. I think it's time for us to go assert our power."

"I think that sounds like a great idea," Pete agreed, glad to move the conversation forward.

"Do you remember how to get there?" Bormick asked.

"I remember the signature," she said confidently as Bormick drew his weapons, Mark drawing his.

Crimson's power tingled against his skin, her sage eyes turning to him. His heart flipped, all thoughts of Skye fleeing. She was every bit his queen, something Bormick also knew. Pete had claimed her first. Their power made them the perfect mates and when he made love to her, truly made love to her, it was like nothing else he experienced with her. Their bond went deep. Bormick was her warrior, his bond to Pete and Crimson equal now. The Shadow Warrior, guardian to the Shadow King and his queen.

Skye drew her hues, golden colors from the sun but rich, a second source of power then meeting it from within her. Her power was no longer distinctly Mage Warrior but a strange mix of whatever they had done to her blending with the shadows she'd claimed from him. The feel of her magic brushed against his skin, distracting him from Crimson with its call, beckoning to his shadows and he narrowed his eyes at the feel. He didn't know what it was, whether it had to do with the change in her magic, or the link she'd shared with Crimson. Or a lingering connection to the magic he'd given her through Crimson. Whatever it was, it was hard to ignore.

The gold in her eyes sparkled in her hues as the portal glowed brightly. Pete turned his eyes from her and stepped through first, drawing his shadows, feeling how they lingered behind him where Skye still stood. Bormick stepped through by his side, ready to kill. Crimson following behind with Mark and Skye in the rear. Skye drew her portal closed as she came through.

The room they emerged in was bright white, no color save

gold, to be found. It was cold and impersonal, hurting his eyes.

"This brings back unpleasant memories," Bormick mumbled.

Pete glanced at Skye, who was rubbing her arms, and he wondered what her thoughts of the place were.

"There's no one here," Crimson said, stating the obvious.

He shot her a look.

"What?" she mouthed, gesturing with her shoulders and hands. He shook his head.

"All right, we need to find their leader," Bormick said, storming through the room.

He threw open a large set of gold doors, and several guards turned, startled.

Pete sent his magic out, Crimson drawing her shades of color as Bormick grabbed a guard by the neck, punching him square in the face and breaking his nose. The others had fallen easily. Skye's magic skimmed past him, adding to the power that surged through the air with his and Crimson's.

"Take us to your king. Now," Bormick commanded, weapon to the guard's neck.

The guard argued, but Bormick punched him again. Bormick was all brute strength and fighter. Nothing about him was soft, and it aroused Pete the same way he knew Crimson was aroused.

"This is what we've come to?" Mark said.

"Yes," Bormick answered, following the soldier. "This is how you overthrow a kingdom."

"We're not overthrowing a kingdom, we're negotiating," Mark argued.

"With force."

A mage positioned herself before them, but Skye had bled the gold from her cloak before she could react, suffocating her with it until she dropped to the floor. Skye called the gold back, and it encircled her body like a shroud before finding a home in her hair, making long golden streaks.

"That's new," Mark commented, voicing Pete's thoughts.

"It is, isn't it? Every day I find something fun."

"It's sexy, too," Bormick said, voicing another of Pete's thoughts.

"Keep your focus on the mission, Bormick, and off of Skye," Pete said.

"It's hard to, Pete. She gets hotter by the day and don't tell me your mind isn't picturing her—"

"Bormick," Pete scolded, knowing his mind was picturing that magic wrapped around her naked body as it moved below his.

He cleared the thoughts away in frustration. They weren't new thoughts, but they were persistent and dirtier than they typically were. Bormick was right. It was always hard not to look at her, not to imagine what that body would do to him.

Shit, focus Pete.

He needed to stop and to get his mind from Skye. He tore his eyes from her, and focused back on Crimson, who threw open the doors to the room behind the mage. A group of mages and soldiers were gathered before a man on a throne who lifted his head to the distraction. His gold eyes narrowed as the guards attacked, and the mages summoned their magic.

The gold from Skye's hair bled out in long golden tendrils, merging with the gold she'd pulled from the uniforms before them. Her magic distracted Pete momentarily, his eyes drawn to the beauty of the way the hues flowed from her, but he quickly refocused. Mark and Bormick had drawn their weapons, ready to attack.

Pete sent his magic out, wrapping it around Skye's golden tendrils, fortifying it, finding her intent, then watching as it ensnared each mage, pinning them to the ground, their hands immobilized. If they hadn't been fighting, he would have taken more time to think about the erotic feel of it. The way their powers perfectly fit, wrapping around each other like they were one. Instead, he watched the mages struggle to access their magic.

Unlike Pete and Skye, with her heightened abilities, their magic required their hands to wield.

Thank you Derrant, he thought.

Crimson ensnared the other soldiers with a band of color, throwing them against the wall where their heads splattered with the force. The wall shook, bits of stone falling.

"Oops," she said, as Bormick and Mark killed their opponents.

"Gentle, Crimson," he whispered.

"Still getting the hang of this," she said with a shrug.

"I find it sexy. Bring that force to the bedroom tonight, Crimson," Bormick said.

They turned to face the king, or Pete assumed he was the king. He rose slowly from his seat. His white hair made his tanned skin seem to stand out when paired with the white clothing he wore. This was a man who enjoyed life, spending his days in the sun. He reminded Pete a little of a surfer until he opened his mouth.

"So, this is the trash the Death God favors."

"Trash? Did he just call us trash?" Bormick asked.

"Ah, the uncouth, untrained warrior. So you've returned, still alive." Bormick's muscles were bulging, and Pete could tell he was holding back. There was no question this was their king, Japeer, the one who had ordered the distortion of Skye's magic while he'd had Bormick nearly beaten to death. Japeer's eyes glanced to Crimson. "And you've brought the Death God's whore."

Crimson bristled. "You did not just call me a whore."

"I did. You are marked by a monster, and you are bedded by him, claimed by him, owned by him. I believe that, and your many other transgressions, make you a whore."

He'd moved closer. Bormick looked ready to attack, but Pete stepped in front of Crimson, staring the man down.

"And the lost king. You we did not expect but given your Shadow Magic and the company you keep, I suspect there isn't much more to say."

"You have no idea who I am—"

"No, but I know them—all of them—enough to judge you by the company you keep. Even these two."

Mark stepped out, taking a protective stance before Skye.

"You two seem worthy, but you stink of his touch, especially her. We tried to bleed her of that touch, but alas, the Death God's stank is hard to remove."

Mark let out a sound that reminded Pete of a growl. How had this turned around on them? This was their big moment, declaring their victory and offering negotiation. Now they were being belittled, and they were letting him. Like a spell sat over them.

Pete slid his foot over and kicked Skye, who glanced at him while the man laid into Mark.

He tried not to become enamored by the way the gold flitted in her eyes when they met his. "Wake up," he mouthed.

Her eyes grew wide, and she nodded. She slapped Mark's ass and moved beside him.

"Skye?" he grumbled, looking at her.

"You needed to wake up, too." She stepped closer to the king. "You really think you can enchant us with some spell and have us stand here while you insult us?"

"It was working quite well. You were much more amenable to my instructions when you were under the control of our power. The only power that deserves—"

"I've had enough of your bullshit. Now, your army is dead, your mages gone. All destroyed by us. You cannot erase us, and you certainly can't wipe out our kingdoms because you don't like our heritage."

"Your heritage?" he asked, laughing before he spat at her feet. Mark tensed, Pete doing the same. Even Bormick reacted, gripping his weapon tighter. "You come from the Death God. You are spawns of evil."

She narrowed her eyes at him, the four of them following her lead, waiting for her move. As much as Pete was the alpha with Bormick and Crimson, Skye was the alpha for the five of them. She was the connection that tied them all, holding them together, bringing them to this point where they were now all bonded, a family.

"That's what you spout, but that's not really the reason you want to eradicate us. It wasn't the Upper God who spawned your kind, it was his gods. Your power isn't direct from him, your power is diluted. You are the spawn of the radiant gods, not the Upper God." She took a step closer. "I am a daughter of Death's Mistress. Her lover, the Death God, has marked me as his. Crimson, my sister in that heritage and his claim. Pete is the son of the Death God, as is Bormick. Even Mark's line is marked by Death's Mistress, his power connected to mine through her. All of us direct descendants. Have you ever met Death's brother?"

Japeer drew his power and Pete drew his, sending his shadows to envelop the light that glimmered in the man's hand.

"I have," Skye continued. "And I have walked the Shadow Realm, slept in Death's bed, and sat beside his mistress. I have walked realms beyond ours and hold the power to bring them all crashing upon each other. I am chaos unleashed and you would be wise to fear me." Her words were like a fire in Pete's chest, summoning the shadows within, the essence of his connection to the Death God. "There was a reason you chose me to manipulate, and the fear in your eyes tells me I'm right."

As she spoke, the white of the room bled, replaced by darkness, one that seeped over his white clothes.

"You can't do that," the king whispered.

"I like my shadow hues and you unleashed them, transformed them. Now I am no longer Eliana's daughter but Derrant's, too. Bow to me."

Pete glanced at Mark, unfamiliar with this side of Skye, knowing her magic had changed but not understanding how until now. He could see that she had claimed his Shadow Magic, that it had become part of her magic, and that's why her power was so different now. So distinctly dark. There was a seductiveness to it that he couldn't quite place. Mark shrugged, and Pete noted the proud look to his eyes.

"My kind do not bow to yours. We are the holy sect, favored by the Upper God, our magic pure. We will never stand with the likes of you. A vagabond group of depraved people and whores."

On his last word, his eyes grew wide, a sharp exhale exiting his body. He looked down, Bormick's dagger in his chest.

He drew his magic again, hand raised at Bormick, who stood unfaltering as the weapon unleashed, the back of the king's body exploding out before he collapsed.

The white fled back to the room as Sky turned, her eyes flaring so that she looked lethal in a way that stirred Pete's blood.

"I had that handled," she hissed.

"What the hell, Bormick?" Pete said as Mark complained with him.

"That was taking too long. He wouldn't shut up, and I told myself if he called Crimson or Skye a whore one more time, I'd kill him. He did, so I did."

"Aww," Crimson said, leaning into Bormick.

Pete glared at them both.

"Guess who's getting that sweet mouth first tonight, Pete?"

"Bormick, you just murdered their king," Mark said.

Bormick walked over, pulled his weapon free, and wiped the blood on his pants.

"So, isn't that what they tried to do to us? Take out our reigning lines? They already annihilated one race. I think killing their king is fair game."

He had a point.

"Now what do we do?" Crimson asked.

As if on cue, the wall she'd nearly destroyed earlier disintegrated into a pile of rubble. They moved close as the dust settled.

Before them lay a sprawling kingdom, a thriving metropolis, unlike what they had expected.

"Fuck me," Bormick muttered.

"Next time, don't kill the king of a land we know nothing about, one we don't even know the location of," Mark groused.

"So, what do we do now?" Skye asked, repeating Crimson's question.

"Bormick doesn't have a kingdom. Let's give it to him and let him clean up his mess while the rest of us go home," Mark replied.

Pete and Crimson shot him a look.

"Just joking, wouldn't want to tear you three apart, and the thought of Bormick ruling a kingdom is frightening."

"I'm not a ruler; I'm a fighter. I keep telling people that, but no one listens."

"Oh, we listen, and we see," Pete joked.

"Well," Skye said. "I guess it's time to find a new ruler for... what's the name of this place?"

"Hell, if I know."

"We don't even know the name of the place, yet we just toppled its monarchy," Pete muttered.

"Seems on par with the way things go for us," Mark said as he looked out across the kingdom.

"Yeah, it does," he agreed.

He stood with the strange little family that he now called his own, staring out at the next adventure that awaited them and wondering how he'd ever survived such a mundane life before he'd been hurled into a life of magic, war, and sex. He shook his head as the doors crashed opened, an army of shocked and pissed off soldiers taking in the scene of their dead king before raising their weapons higher.

Pete summoned his magic as the others drew theirs, Bormick and Mark moving forward with their weapons. There was no going back to the simple life he'd had before, but he wouldn't trade what he had now for the world. He glanced at Bormick, his muscles taut and ready for a fight. Crimson beside him, coils of color running around her.

"Let's get this over with so we can go home and shower," he said, throwing a coy grin at Bormick.

"It's gonna be a good night!" Bormick said. Pete's magic snaked out to block the first bolt of magic aimed at them.

"Yes, it is," he agreed.

"Do you think they have showers here?" Bormick asked. "If we're conquering the place, we might as well do it right." He slashed the first guard down.

"Really, you two?" Mark asked as he fought.

"I claim the king's quarters," Skye called.

"I do believe we've corrupted her, Mark," Bormick yelled through the fighting.

"King's quarters are mine, Skye!" Crimson said.

"I had dibs first."

"Sounds like we'll just have to share it," Pete said before he caught himself.

Bormick's laugh permeated the air, joining the noise of the fight.

"I suppose we might," Mark said, causing Bormick to laugh louder.

"Gods, I love this dysfunctional family," Crimson said, her magic strangling a mage whose eyes bulged from his head.

"Me, too," Pete said, knowing it was true. Knowing that they were entirely dysfunctional, and one sexually charged comment to tipping to insanity but bound now so tightly that they needed each other, their connections running as a series of strands that could never be broken. Their lives, their destinies, their loves now all interconnected like abnormal puzzle pieces that fit beautifully together.

As he fought further through the fray, he prayed they would remain that way, for the alternative would be devastating for them and for their world.

About the Author

J. L. Jackola discovered her passion for writing in grade school when she wrote a short story that earned her a spot in a local writing workshop. She has been creating fantasy worlds ever since. When she's not weaving tales, she can be found logging miles in her running shoes, watching movies with her family, or curled up with a book. She resides in Delaware with her husband and three children.

To learn more, visit her website at
www.jljackola.com